VIVIENNE...
ON GUERNSEY BLUE

Yvonne Ozanne

Vivienne

...on Guernsey Blue

by
Yvonne Ozanne

ELSP

Published in 2010 by
ELSP
16A New St John's Road
St Helier
Jersey   JE2 3LD

Origination by Seaflower Books, Jersey
www.exlibrisbooks.co.uk

Printed by JF Print, Sparkford, Somerset

ISBN 978-1-906641-24-5

**All enquiries and correspondence
regarding this book should be
sent to the author at**

**4 Les Fontenelles Mews
Mount Hermon
St Peter Port
Guernsey   GY1 1JD**

For my mother Mary Brehaut with love

'Verbum caro factum est' : The word made flesh

John 1:14

ACKNOWLEDGEMENTS

Vivienne's journey would not have been possible without the contributions of Christopher Finch, California, Lara Cooke, Roger Jones, Kate Green, Amy McKee, South Carolina, Nikki Travis, Robert Brehaut, Justine Gilman and Stephen Ainsworth. Love and thanks to my husband Tony, Alison and Michael Ozanne, Emily and Penny Dawes who all supported me and gave me valuable advice.

Prologue

London 1964

She could hear herself crying out, but couldn't stop. The iron pole of the stretcher's side hurt her hand as she clenched it. The baby moved down with each contraction. Sweat, unchecked, blurred her eyes. Her wet cotton dress clung to her body. The glass doors of Accident and Emergency automatically swung open as they wheeled her through an antiseptic corridor. Into the labour room and a nurse hooked a red plastic bag near Vivienne's head. A white circle of light on the ceiling exposed her. Breath came in great gasps that she couldn't control. Her arm felt the wasp-sting of injection. Out of sight at first, another woman came into focus. A groaning, severing pain then she pushed as the slither of a newborn child left her womb.

It cried, just once, with little more than a sigh.

'Female. A girl,' said the woman doctor, stone-faced as she briefly examined the baby. 'Twenty one, could be twenty two week gestation,' she said to the nurse who was taking notes, then pulled off her Vinyl gloves slowly, one at a time. A tall woman with a high waist, dry, permed hair and round glasses, she stared at Vivienne. Vivienne, who neither understood the word 'gestation' nor the significance of 'twenty one or two weeks', flinched. She drew her legs together trying to shrink away. The afterbirth slid out in a warm flood. The doctor leant over her so closely Vivienne felt her breath misting her cheek.

'Why did you leave it so long? You must have known she could have survived. At this stage? How could you? I practise medicine, my girl, not butchery.' She gestured for the nurse to leave them. In the London hospital, alone in the room with Vivienne, she carried out the cruel act that Vivienne knew would stay with her forever.

Afterward, in the silence of the sterile ward, the baby no longer murmured. As the doctor strode out, the nurse returned, this time shaking her head not looking at Vivienne. She switched off stainless steel machines. With her back to Vivienne, so she couldn't see, the nurse placed the tiny form in a kidney dish, covered it with a white cloth and bore it out of her sight.

Vivienne twisted a corner of the sheet, screwing it into a ball and stuffed it into her mouth, making her gag and choke. Maybe she should just do that, suffocate and die. 'Guy, help me.' She thought of home, of Guernsey, her island. London was frightening: a huge city. Yet, come to London. It seemed the only way out. Hadn't known what else to do. See Jocelyn. Jocelyn in London, training to be a nurse...

She should have told Guy. Things might have been worked out. No, that would have made it all much worse. Guy had married Amanda. It seemed a long time now, since their times after school. His parents out. His bedroom. His bed. Guy had taught her what to do. He needed her. Once, on her blue skirt she found a splash of red, although it wasn't her time of the month. He was her first. She had him first, long before Amanda. Guy was hers.

Now, he had this brand new wife who hadn't let him near her until they wed. Amanda didn't believe in sex before marriage, so Guy said. Vivienne had seen them marry, heard the vows, saw the white dress, the white veil, white flowers, the whole works. She had gone to the wedding with her parents. No, she could neither tell Guy nor her Mum (always so ill) nor her Dad, who would have killed her. Couldn't tell Granmarie either. She would be so ashamed. Vivienne longed to feel Guy's arms around her like in their stolen times close together, tumbling into the sea at midnight, her neither knowing the time nor caring.

Jocelyn, her usually confident face drawn and sad, came to collect her. Vivienne rubbed away tears from her sore and reddened eyes. 'You look awful. Poor love. They wouldn't let me come in.'

'No,' said Vivienne, glad that at least Jocelyn hadn't seen the worst of it. She must hide that wound. Jocelyn helped her into the fresh floral dress she had brought with her and put Vivienne's sandals on her feet. She began to brush Vivienne's hair for her, darkened with the dampness of sweat and the stifling hospital. Curls lay heavily on her neck.

'You know, that doctor, that woman,' said Jocelyn quietly, her hand starting to tremble as she wielded the brush in short, rough strokes, making Vivienne call out to her to stop. 'Sorry. She read the riot act to me. What did she say to you? You'd think she would try to understand.' Jocelyn stopped brushing. 'It's not illegal in some countries.'

'Not legal in Guernsey,' Vivienne whispered.

'No, not in Guernsey. Bloody men, leaving us to clear up their mess.'

Vivienne took Jocelyn's hand into hers. Jocelyn looked just as pale as she felt. 'Two free spirits' people called them. Vivienne rubbed Jocelyn's fingers gently, remembering when Jocelyn had her miscarriage. It had been very early. The pregnancy a mistake. Still. Jocelyn would be thinking about it.

'I don't know what I'd have done without you. I'm so sorry about all this.' Cramps seized her again. Above the cotton dress Vivienne pressed her hands over her swollen stomach.

'Yeh, well I thought I knew what to do. This is all bloody horrible.' Jocelyn grabbed a tissue from Vivienne's box and dabbed at her eyes. She ran her fingers through her hair. 'It...was supposed to be a solution, an answer.'

Vivienne nodded, her head heavy with images of the baby, the labour bed, the woman doctor, her face twitching with accusation. Vivienne flinched again, throwing her head sideways.

'I could lose my job if she reports me,' said Jocelyn.

Vivienne choked tears to the back of her throat. She swallowed, 'she treated me like a murderer. The baby was alive, Jocelyn.'

'What, what? Alive? Viable? Oh my God,' Jocelyn seized Vivienne by the shoulders, 'you must have been way over four months! I thought...'

'I didn't know what I was. They took her away.' Vivienne could say no more.

A nurse in crisp white uniform rustled past them, looked curiously but said nothing.

'For heaven's sake let's get out of here,' said Jocelyn, 'get back to the flat. What time's your flight to Guernsey on Saturday?'

'Forgotten. I'll check.'

Vivienne's legs took her out of the building, into the noisy streets of London. She looked up at the window of the hospital room where she had lain, for one last time. The glass panes stared back, with an empty gaze.

Her drained face expectant, Vivienne watched for a second longer. There was no sign of loss, no evidence. Only then, aching, standing on the granite road the word 'daughter' came to Vivienne. She had just given birth to her daughter.

Jocelyn caught her as she collapsed, retrieved her bag from the pavement and got them a taxi. The taxi driver ignored them, grappling with unyielding London traffic. In the back seat Vivienne hunched down into Jocelyn's coat. Part of herself had come away, unprotected and exposed. Not only that, although Jocelyn had had a miscarriage, lost a baby – that was part of nature: not to be. Vivienne's loss was an intended destruction.

Closing her eyes, Vivienne pressed her muffled face against Jocelyn's shoulder, 'What's viable mean?'

'We'll talk about it later,' said Jocelyn.

'If I ever go mad, Jocelyn, if I never have another night's peace, it will be because of this.'

Jocelyn had cleaned up the mess in the flat. Days passed. The bleeding lessened. Without help, without intervention, Vivienne's body adjusted. From their rooms, Vivienne could hear cars parked near the pavement have their engines started up and then be driven away into the distance. People walked past, talking loudly, laughing, like it was just any, ordinary day in London. Jocelyn made them comfort food: hot toast, warmed pots of tea.

Vivienne took a hesitant walk to the corner shop for bread and milk and a copy of *Nova* magazine.

'If they have one – but not,' said Jocelyn, *Woman's Own* on any account. I want to read about this American writer – Betty Friedan:

The Feminine Mystique.' There was a new movement, Jocelyn told Vivienne, starting up in America. Something called 'Feminism'.

Walking sore-muscled, stiff and aching, Vivienne counted out English cash in her purse. It was the same currency as Guernsey money – sterling – but looked so different. And the London streets were all so wide and grey, identical to the ones she had seen in London with Guy – so unlike the lanes where she lived – where she knew every field, practically every blade of grass, each pebble on the beach.

She wasn't far from Jocelyn's lodgings, yet, walking as quickly as she could, Vivienne mentally noted colours of gates, house numbers and road signs as she went along. She hurried to get the shopping done.

The plate glass door of the cluttered shop opened with the ding of a coiled bell. The door glass reflected a round-faced girl with wind-blown fair curly hair: the type that would frizz like a million corkscrews given the slightest opportunity. Around her neck Vivienne had wound a woollen turquoise scarf that Polly from work had knitted for her birthday, saying she had chosen blue to 'match your eyes, kiddo'. The scarf fell to her feet. Here Vivienne stood, forever on some diet, on her short Guernsey legs with the kind of ankles that just could not take flat shoes. She leant her head closer to the mirroring glass door. Above the small white OPEN sign, stuck on the glass with a grey suction pad, Vivienne saw herself: wide eyed and sleepless.

The shopkeeper fetched some bread and milk in a bottle. Even that seemed unfamiliar. Not so long ago, Vivienne's Granmarie, her grandmother, had milk delivered in a jug. Their milkman owned his own herd of cows.

The man lifted a copy of *Nova* from the shelf behind him. Not looking up, he busied himself with putting her things into a brown paper bag. Without a word he returned the paper Guernsey pound note Vivienne had, after all, inadvertently given him and waited patiently as she fumbled, all thumbs, in her purse to find the correct money.

A shameful blush instantly rushed from her neck to her cheeks. But the silver-haired shopkeeper slammed the money into the till, turned and had already begun serving someone else.

Later, Jocelyn decided they'd do some real shopping. 'We're two pretty women! We are young, we are free, for goodness sake!' She ignored Vivienne's weak protests.

'I don't think I'm pretty,' said Vivienne.

'Don't be so daft, course you are! You always say that. Anyway, we must get you some decent gear. Guernsey is so behind the times. I'll treat. We could both do with cheering up.'

They went to Kensington and Biba and bought identical paisley smocks, yellow and pink with puffed sleeves and three pearl buttons. The dresses barely reached their knees. In Oxford Street, Vivienne cautiously dabbed on fashionable make-up with a trademark black and white daisy packaging, whilst the shop girl – with eyes made up as if for some trendy nightclub – held up a round, plastic-framed mirror, sighing with exaggerated boredom.

They drank in the Eight Bells pub in Cheyne Walk, near Chelsea Art College. They sipped frothy coffee and shopped on the Kings Road.

Vivienne dragged Jocelyn to the National Art Gallery – mostly so that she should see Titian's 'Bacchus and Ariadne'. A year ago now, Guy and Vivienne had seen Titian together. He'd shown her the Chelsea College of Art. 'Dad, I want to go to Art college. I want to go to Art college!' Vivienne had nagged her father, not adding 'With Guy', naturally. But it hadn't made any difference. Her father simply would not hear of it.

How Vivienne's parents Edward and Jean had worried and fussed about it. Art College? That would mean her leaving Guernsey to live in England, The Mainland! Like it was outer Siberia. No, that was an idea they would not, could not even begin to contemplate. No, because her brother, Oscar, only four, had drowned. They did not want to lose, 'could not lose', another child. As a clincher, in his bereavement, Edward had fervently turned to 'His Bible'. Her mother Jean, bereft, drifted between sanity and a world where little Oscar still existed.

No. Her parents distrusted uncontrollable, unknowable London, where bad things happened. Where people vanished without trace.

'Ariadne...' Vivienne told Jocelyn in the Gallery, '...was abandoned by her lover, Theseus.' Thoughts of Guy and herself flooded back again: beautiful, deadly luscious Guy. 'But Bacchus rescues her. See Jocelyn? Bacchus rescues Ariadne in the end!'

'Oh, Viv! You and your gorgeous naked boys! You know you are such a romantic!' said Jocelyn, impatient. 'You'll have to read my *Nova*. Come on, up to Oxford Street, now!' Jocelyn's black hair, cut like a curtain to her chin, swung freely. 'I've seen some pink-laced boots I want. Live a little, kid!'

On the plane, flying back to Guernsey, Vivienne strapped the safety belt over her waist. She clipped the metal buckle, pausing momentarily as her hand brushed over the top of her skirt. She had fastened the buttoned waistband, this time, with no effort at all.

PART ONE

CHAPTER ONE

Guernsey 1963

Vivienne pushed the typewriter away from her, wishing for rescue. Did prisoners think about it all the time, about release, about being far away. Otherwise how to survive? For a human, no cage should be borne. She's here, fettered to a metal desk at Hughes, in an office in a timber yard. Outside she could see the yard, where sunshine bleached the sheds so white it pained her eyes to look at them. Dazzled, she felt herself flying, right out of the office window to Guy, gliding in the blue air, waiting for her. As she took his hand they flew, fleeing from the office, over the grey roofs. Then, in a free fall, straight into the sun-warm sea with Guy telling her the things that no-one else ever did.

Instead, Vivienne made herself turn back into the dark office and stab at the keyboard. Never mind. Soon they'd be in London – in secret, without his girlfriend, without anyone knowing. Even if Guy was – kind of – engaged to Amanda, they'd be away, just the two of them. Vivienne and Guy. Together.

Guy was only sort of spoken for. He hadn't given Amanda a ring. So, it wasn't sinful. Guy was still a little bit free.

Through the window, dirty with wood-dust, Vivienne saw, not the busy yard stacked full with freshly-cut timber, smelling like matchsticks with growling machines lifting wood with yellow claws, but Guy's fabulous face. When Vivienne showed Polly Guy's photograph, Polly erupted with a snort, claiming Guy looked just those Greek gods Vivienne kept doodling on her notepad. Vivienne smiled at that. Guy had only just told her about the Aeolian harp, played by the wind, named after the Greek god, Aeolus. Yes, only the other day Guy beguiled Vivienne with his stories of classical myths. Perhaps they might go to Greece one day? To Athens. To the birthplace of mythology! Guy said so. Bliss. Although of course, she would have, somehow to get round her parents. Not easy. For her sixteenth birthday she wanted Gala nail varnish (Heart Red), Evening in Paris scent and maybe Elvis Presley's *Heartbreak Hotel*? Her father said over his dead body so she got a Fair Isle sweater Aunty Mary knitted for her and a fountain pen.1963, but might as well be the Dark Ages, for all her parents knew, so locked into that guarded way of life they had. Going anywhere at all, just being any place with her Guy was difficult enough.

Vivienne's father didn't like people having imaginings and ideas about anything, let alone art and Greek mythology. Those were dangerous. Creativity was God's realm, not mankind's, especially not pagan mankind: 'thou shalt not make any likeness of anything'. Thou shalt not practically everything – according to Vivienne's father.

'You are such a romancer, Nin,' her father would say, pursing his thin, disappointed mouth as he did so. 'Such an arty-crafty sort of girl. Always so full... up to here,' making a saluting hand, he would tap his forehead high on his hairline, '...so full of darned fancies.'

Vivienne opened the window, letting the warm air blow inside, scattering wood dust all over the papers on her desk. Guy asked why her parents called her 'Nin'. 'Vivienne is such a pretty name.' Vivienne told him it was a childhood thing. She hadn't been able to manage the full 'Vivienne' but something like 'Nin'. So it stuck.

Sawdust wafted in, micro slivers of harmful splinters. So she'd let the beautiful Guy go for now. Let him drift silently, safely, back into her heart. Again, her father came to Vivienne's mind; Edward with his watchful air, sleeves rolled up, ready for work. Edward, with his dark and vigilant face, bore the look of his French Huguenot ancestors. He could look quite sepulchral. Especially when hungry or when he lectured Vivienne. And Edward always harped on about Vivienne's friends. They were peculiar, he said, forever on about art, filling her mind up with dreamy stuff when she was bad enough already. And he didn't care for Guy.

'Not one of those ruddy bohemians is he? That Guy Beaufort?'

Vivienne told Edward he was a complete philistine.

'Don't talk posh to me, my girl,' Edward replied.

Stifled in the sunny office, Vivienne fetched paper from the stationery cupboard, wondering how her father would actually like working here. Edward insisted she must come down to earth, down to reality, like he had been made to and work at the perfectly good job he had gone to such trouble to find her: at Hughes. And, what's more, he'd got her the position through 'Dear Edna', through old Ma Jones. Whenever Edward spoke about 'Dear Edna' he always cleared his throat and would inevitably follow it with 'a fine woman.' The job offer was excellent, so Edward said, with paid holidays, Christmas bonus and pension scheme. Whatever more could Vivienne possibly desire?

'Oh, Dad.' So Vivienne had left school, before Sixth Form, before any more Dangerous Learning. After all, Hughes awaited. As for her mother, as for Jean, Vivienne knew she was never really well. Her mind rambled, anywhere, without warning. Her poor Mum. Jean hadn't been right since she lost her dear little boy, little Oscar. Found drowned, only four. Poor woman. Vivienne tried hard to imagine her mother's loss, but you would have to lose a child yourself, wouldn't you, to know how that really felt?

Vivienne tapped at the unforgiving keys, her fingertips cold at the touch of hard steel. She had had to tell so many lies. Didn't want to worry her mother. Jean always muddled up times and dates and reasons for doing anything anyway.

Going with Guy on this holiday to see the Chelsea School of Art needed planning. Guy just raved about the place. You couldn't blame him. Hadn't he been accepted at the school? Guy would show Vivienne The National Art Gallery, especially to see Titian, and the Italian High Renaissance paintings he admired, saying she would to. Guy insisted: Vivienne is bound to fall in love with Titian.

Even with all its green lushness and hidden sandy bays for meeting Guy, Guernsey still felt so remote, so hopelessly far away from Guy's future in civilized London. Time went by so slowly. Vivienne rocked so far back in her chair it nearly tipped over. One day Guy would be a really great artist. Think of it – what with all his originality and talent and clever talk. Guy was exceptional, probably a genius. Anyone could see that. Surely her father could see that too?

Slowly, Edward and then Guy's image morphed into Amanda's, the girlfriend, the kind of fiancée who wasn't going to London. Vivienne recalled Guy talking about her: 'Amanda's knitting me a new jumper,' like it was something he was proud of. 'She's not into art and cultural stuff. Amanda's a real home bird, a homemaker. She doesn't mind me having – my own interests, though.'

Amanda liked Maltesers, Guy told Vivienne. And she cut her nails every Friday evening and didn't believe in sex before marriage. Amanda sounded like a proper little Sandra Dee to Vivienne. Yet, all her friends agreed, Amanda Le Croix might not be, well, sexy, exactly, but she was pretty. She had a pretty face. One of those quiet, naturally nice faces. Soft, with no vanity.

Been to the same school as Vivienne, yes, Amanda was nice. You couldn't help noticing her, what with all that calmness and niceness and being Guy's girlfriend. Out of school uniform, Amanda wore plain, pastel clothes, perfectly ironed white blouses, skirts and cardigans in pale pinks and yellows. Vivienne saw her on a pebbly beach once changing into her swimming costume. Amanda's bra was brilliant white against her slim, smoothly tanned shoulders. In spite of the Maltesers, Amanda never once put on one single ounce of weight. Not one.

It might seem ridiculous, but Vivienne half-felt a kind of admiration for Amanda. She wished she could be half as together and, damn it, even as decent as Amanda always seemed. In fact, Vivienne wondered if, perhaps, she should start knitting? But, so far, her attempts hadn't been in the least bit wearable. Polly said her efforts were, 'Actually, kiddo, laughable.'

Polly held up the pea-green pullover Vivienne finally finished, waving the knitted garment about like a woolly flag. They both laughed outright at a quite unrecognizable shape. So, of course, Vivienne didn't give it to Guy after all but gave the damn thing to her grandmother, to Granmarie. A hot water bottle cover.

The symbols on her notepad stared back at her, undecipherable shorthand. Outside men stacked wood from the sheds onto lorries.

'Wakey, wakey!' called Polly cheerfully, coming in with a tray. 'Coffee up kiddo.' Polly started at Hughes as a school-leaver, then a filing clerk and worked up to senior receptionist. 'General dogsbody, really,' Polly said, smiling. A couple of years older than Vivienne, Polly knew every trick of the trade. Polly took no prisoners. A wily, peroxide blonde, Polly dyed her hair herself, never getting it quite even.

With her large, seemingly permanently surprised, pale blue eyes and slightly protruding teeth, Vivienne loved her.

'Oh, thanks Polly. Lifesaver.' Sighing, Vivienne took the coffee.

'What's up with you today? You're miles away, kiddo.' Polly waited for an answer.

Vivienne typed up a page, painted mistakes with white corrector fluid – Tipp-Ex – but, in her haste, tore the page as she yanked it out of the typewriter. 'Aw heck, have to do it again.'

'Don't fret our kiddo, ' said Polly. Polly was ace in getting time off for Vivienne from old Ma Jones. They called the widow Mrs Jones, although she probably wasn't more than forty-something with ample bosom and searching eyes.

Polly reckoned Ma Jones had eyes like ruddy radar. Vivienne thought old Ma Jones – childless – had a real soft spot for Polly.

Vivienne rattled the black typewriter, 'Can't read my notes, Polly.'

'Calm down, kiddo,' said Polly. 'Old Jones'll notice. Oh, give it 'ere. Won't take a sec.'

Vivienne handed over her notepad. 'You're a pal. And you got me time off. I'd have screwed up.'

'S'Okay, kiddo. You're the same for me. Help each other, right? And look 'ere you. I told Ma Jones you're going away for a shorthand refresher course. Fact is, she seemed really pleased!' Polly winked.

'Told Dad it's in Kent. Granmarie's given me spending money.' Vivienne mimicked Granmarie's strong, Norman French patois accent, 'Now you mind you spend that on something vrai sensible, ma petite Vivienne.' Bless.'

As the time for London grew closer, Vivienne's plans became more complex. Polly thought she was really going to see Jocelyn. Vivienne hadn't told anyone about Guy.

Just before she escaped, though, Polly blurted out something strange. 'By the way, kiddo,' She suddenly said, leaning skinny arms on the reception desk. Then she took too long a breath.

'What? God, Polly what?' Her heart racing, Vivienne faced Polly's owl-savvy stare.

'Well. Look, it's just – it's just I saw that Guy, you know, that Guy you like so much,' Polly started rubbing her elbow now, watchful and tentative.

'And?' Vivienne sensed Polly's caution.

'Well – he was with that Rita what's 'er face. They were having coffee together, you know, in Le Noury's café?' Polly finished and began tapping a chewed pencil on her strangely whitened and clenched knuckles.

'Oh,' Vivienne forced a fixed, bright smile. 'Oh, Rita? Rita Roussel? Really?'

'Yes, really,' said Polly.

In town it grew dark as Guy waved. Vivienne ran to catch him up, wanting them to walk in step. Taking two strides to his one, she puffed next to him. Guy smiled down at her with amused dark eyes. They headed to the quiet pub they'd found, to make final details of their trip. He wore a long navy coat over a grey striped suit. He was a 'Mod', not a 'Trad'. Guy liked modern jazz, not traditional. And anything at all to do with Teddy boys was definitely out.

'Modern jazz,' Guy said, 'is cool.' As school kids with their gang at his parents' house they all listened to the Modern Jazz Quartet. Vivienne learnt, it was cooler, to call them the 'MJQ'. Charlie Parker was Charlie 'Bird' Parker. Vivienne liked the American names: Dizzy Gillespie, Thelonius Monk and Miles Davis and the funnier ones – Art Pepper, Fats Waller, Cannonball Adderley. She drove her father mad playing Cole Porter over and over and Ella Fitzgerald until her father said he would smash all her bloody records if he had to hear them one

more time. Especially on a Sunday. Didn't Vivienne understand what
the Sabbath meant? A day of rest. A day of prayer.

Walking by Guy's side, Vivienne began to sing softly,

'Every time you say goodbye – I want to die a little
Every time you say goodbye – I wonder why a little.'

She flung Guy an unblinking glance.

'Why the gods above me – who must be in the know
Think so little of me – they allow you to go...'

Guy's eyes half-closed as he smiled at her. Vivienne grinned back,
her heart full of him. Maybe her gods were just sleeping right now,
because gods cannot die.

Guy made a deep, pretend-worried sigh. 'I suppose we're invisible
in a crowd.' He felt for her hand then, still holding it with his, thrust
them both into the navy serge of his warm coat pocket.

Guy really believed that most people rushed about, so intent on
their own business that they didn't notice what others might be up to.
Vivienne didn't agree. She looked around her fearfully. By chance,
though, on that day, through the dwindling late shoppers, emerged
Rita Roussel. She came straight toward them, heading up the street
as they walked down it.

'Hello, Guy,' Rita said quietly, her voice sounding to Vivienne like
simply naked seduction – aimed directly at Guy. 'How are you?'

Rita was tiny, with black, close-cropped hair, an elfin-cap, with
her fringe artfully arranged in strands over her forehead. She had
a pale, heart-shaped face and markedly high cheekbones. She wore
a pink fur coat with the wide collar turned up, framing her face.
Vivienne had to admit to herself: Rita looked very striking.

Then Rita flicked her eyes over Vivienne and Guy's pocketed
hands and looked back up at Guy with her black eyebrows raised.
'Well, maybe see you around sometime, eh Guy. Another time?' She
said, daring a come-hither glance at him, totally ignoring Vivienne.
Brushing past them, Rita walked on, turning briefly to wiggle a wave
back at Guy. Her black mini-skirt barely covered slim, girlish legs in

sheer black stocking that fitted perfectly, without any wrinkles.

Vivienne thought she could have literally encircled one of Rita's ankles between her thumb and index finger. But Guy moved swiftly on, showing no reaction.

'Come on, then,' he said quickly. 'Let's get that drink. Need to talk. In for a penny, in for a pound.'

Vivienne didn't reply but clung close to Guy. They went to the Prince of Wales pub. Guy didn't mention Rita again. But something about the woman wouldn't let Vivienne forget her. Guy went over to order drinks.

Sitting down, Vivienne noticed a ladder had started in one of her tan stockings – 'Damn!' Vivienne tried tugging the woolen hem of her skirt over her exposed knee. Somehow, even through the brown nylon, her legs seemed to have turned into two stone pillars with no hint of nicely turned ankles whatsoever.

Guy plonked two glasses in front of them. Foam spilled onto the beer mats.

'I thought the way Rita wore her collar up like that was so obvious. Didn't you, Guy? And I mean, pink fur!' Vivienne studied his face closely.

'No, no I thought Rita looked quite smart.' Guy gulped some ale, taking thought. 'She's quite a sharp dresser, Rita.'

She heard the words blurt out before she could stop herself. 'Polly thought she saw you with Rita. The other day. In Le Noury's café?' said Vivienne.

'Did she?'

Vivienne's tongue felt stick dry, like when she was scared. Her heart pulsed painfully up into her ears. 'Why was that?'

'Why was what?' said Guy. 'Oh, you mean seeing Rita for coffee? She's just a friend of Amanda's. Rita just wanted to talk.'

'Oh,' said Vivienne flatly. Talk? Talk about what? What had that Rita Roussel shared with her Guy? What did his contained look mean? But Vivienne, sensing his resistance, knew better than to press him.

Vivienne gazed at him, sitting there with his blue, thin knitted tie and navy wool coat; his broad palms with the tapered fingers wound around his pint glass. Light from the window behind him silhouetted his shape. An old-gold light from the frilled glass shade, near to the side of his head, softly outlined his lovely face. All she could see was Guy. Everyone else, although she could hear them, disappeared into the background. They could, for Vivienne, be the only people in the pub. The murmur of voices surrounded her, wrapping her up with Guy in a warm, smoky atmosphere.

Guy lit a cigarette: a Rothman's. The blue-grey smoke curled up into his face and through the haze he smiled at her. Vivienne saw his feather-cut hair, his straight nose. Over his brown eyes frowned dark, distinctively arched eyebrows. Squinting at her through the smoke, Guy unfurled an English newspaper, turning to the Arts pages.

'Ah, this'll interest you, Vivvy. Dorothy Parker. You'll like her writing. We'll go to Foyle's bookshop when we're in Town.' Guy called London 'Town'. 'They've got everything. Then,' he pointed at a photograph 'a piece about Scott Fitzgerald, *The Great Gatsby*, the jazz age. We can get some Fitzgerald, as well. Guernsey bookshops – well it takes hell's ages to get anything ordered from here. And I want to get some sheet music for my father, from Boosey & Hawkes.'

Vivienne could have, quite cheerfully, sat there with Guy for the rest of her life.

After a life-time of waiting, Vivienne and Guy arrived in London. Right away Guy rushed them around Chelsea like a schoolboy let loose.

'Come and see the college, Vivvy. You should be here. You are a good painter. Your parents are so bad not encouraging you. Come on!' Guy grinned, happier than Vivienne could remember.

Vivienne felt the zing, the zest of The Chelsea School of Art buzzing toward her. Like an electric sensation before the storm, of something just about to happen. First thing, Guy took her to the Eight Bells on Cheyne Walk near the King's Road.

As they walked, arm in arm, Guy chattered on, 'London's pavements, some of them and bits of the Embankment are made with Guernsey's granite, Viv. Heard of it? 'Guernsey Blue'? It's unique, our granite. I've always liked the sparkling chips in it. Look like diamonds to me.'

'Like stars,' she said, putting her arm around him. He put his arm around her. They were together, Vivienne wanted to shout out loud. She and Guy were in London and they were alone!

The Eight Bells had a mural painted on the wall behind its long bar.

'See, Vivvy? It's a copy of *A Bar at the Folies Bergère* – by Manet, Edouard Manet,' said Guy. 'It's a joke. The barmaid looks directly at us. There is a mirror behind her bar, so we can see her from the back and we can see her client. Well, us. The model was probably a prostitute, earning extra money. The French Impressionists often used working girls as models.'

Vivienne smiled as they waited for Darius. Guy always went on like that with his mate from their school gang – Darius Swift. Together the two of them would soon be going on about art, Greek mythology, Impressionism, Picasso. Yes, Guy and Darius always talked non-stop. She didn't mind, but it was all so... intellectual: they knew about all sorts of things she didn't Her father, reserved for them his most sucked-lemon expression saying that 'Those two – that Guy Beaufort and that Darius Swift? Proper highbrow college types aren't they?' and 'why didn't they want to do proper jobs? A lot of artistic types were nancy boys...' so he'd heard.

After school, at Guy's house Vivienne listened, absorbed. She learnt about jazz and writers. Vivienne noticed that Guy seemed in awe of Darius. Darius was off to America. Although still a student, Darius had got a deal – something to do with an American celebrity whom Vivienne hardly knew. Maybe Darius would be famous as well. It wouldn't surprise her in the least.

So, here they were. Once Darius and his entourage of students arrived they talked, drank, smoked strange smelling substances, interrupted each other and called out to everyone, Vivienne sighed happily and sat right back. This was her Guy in his element. He'd put his arm around her proprietorily, letting the others know that she was with him. Yes, and he was with her. Guy kissed her gently as they squeezed close together at the cramped table.

All the girls were dressed in long skirts, high boots and wore beads down to their waists. Their hair was long and loose, their eyes expertly rimmed black with eyeliner; lids coated with pastel eye shadow. Their lips were pale pink. They looked nothing like the Guernsey girls she knew. Vivienne thought they were probably models. Jean Shrimpton looked like that and Twiggy and Dusty Springfield. Vivienne decided that, when she got back to Guernsey, she would buy some make-up too and look like them, even if Edward got mad at her.

'Come on, Vivvy,' Guy whispered into her hair, 'let's go to Darius' digs.' He jiggled a key. 'It's not very far.'

They left, leaving the crowded pub, promising to return soon. Darius raised his thin arm, giving a 'thumbs up' to Guy.

'So long!' Darius called out above the noise in a mock American drawl. 'Be good!'

'Oh, she's very good!' Guy shouted back. The others laughed.

'Why did you say that?' Vivienne asked as the cold London air chilled her warm face. The concrete slabs of Cheyne Walk were hard to walk on. Spindly high-heels helped the thick ankle problem, but little else. Stumbling, Vivienne reached out for Guy's arm as he steadied her.

'Nearly there. Oh, I just humour Darius,' said Guy, lightly. 'He likes to pull my leg – you know, about women.'

'What about women? About me?' It had felt bad enough being the backwater islander, a country hick, without them all laughing about her as well.

'Look, don't take it too heart, Vivvy. Darius – all that lot, they'll have forgotten we've gone. Come on, here we are.'

The street was long and undistinguished. Each bow-windowed, terraced house looked, to Vivienne, exactly the same. Guy turned the key in the lock of a neglected door and they mounted the stairs. The flat was very small and on the second floor.

Two single beds lay either side of the sitting room: both unmade. A small kitchen and an untidy bathroom led off the main room. In the middle of the floor was a narrow mattress with a blanket thrown over it. The rooms smelt unaired, of cigarette butts. Something curried and stale came from the kitchen.

Guy didn't need to pull her down. She lay her willing body on to the floor and onto the mattress. He tugged at her coat, kissing her fiercely so his teeth jarred against hers. He struggled out of his coat, shoes and trousers. Vivienne felt his hands riding up her skirt to tug down the see-through and specially bought scarlet briefs. She undid her bra herself and threw it off. It slid under one of the beds. Guy wound his fingers in her hair and kissed her lips so hard again Vivienne just knew they'd show bruises, but she kissed him back as strongly. It had been so long! She devoured him, matching his fervour stroke for stroke. When, at length, he came, he withdrew swiftly so that no fluids would enter her.

'Guy,' she panted, still needing him, 'finish me, finish me.' So, with the lovely hands, warm and strong, Guy brought Vivienne to ecstasy.

Quietly, both lying amongst the debris of clothes and bedding, they breathed deeply to calm themselves. Vivienne glimpsed used coffee mugs under the beds; discarded socks and crumpled, glossy magazines.

'I'll be coming back here, to stay, when I'm a student,' Guy spoke to the ceiling through his cigarette smoke. 'Darius said that when I – when we – when I do, I can rent this place.'

Vivienne drew herself up and began to put her things on, buttoning her blouse, sliding the red briefs back over her thighs. 'When?' she asked, 'when's that?' (When are you leaving me, Guy? When are you leaving Guernsey?)

There would be no point begging him to stay, nor trying to argue with him. No, nothing like that. Guy's mind – his future – was made up. Anyway, she had learnt that trying to catch her butterfly would only damage his wings. If she touched the iridescent gossamer, he wouldn't be able to fly now would he? And if he couldn't fly then he would die. And she would die with him.

'Oh, not long,' said Guy, seeming to struggle with exact dates and times. 'We'll be leaving Guernsey sooner rather than later, though. Not long, no. Got to arrange everything with – with the family. You know, Vivvy? Get stuff agreed...'

Oh, Vivienne knew, all right. Felt the familiar sting. Yes, of course, she knew about 'the arrangements.' That meant when he was married. The 'family' was Amanda. Vivienne lay down again next to Guy where he lingered, lazily, over his cigarette. She took the cigarette out of his mouth, took a puff, then placed it back into his lips. Guy put his free hand into hers.

'I've missed you,' she said.

'I miss you, too, Vivvy. I enjoy us. Really do.' He rolled his head sideways to look at her and drew her hand to his mouth and kissed it, lightly. 'You are such a free spirit. Such a responsive mind.' Guy brushed a hair from her forehead with his hand. 'Now. Listen. You saw the art today – at the college?' His voice tightened with an urgency. 'Please come Vivvy. You've done that self-portrait. Darius says it's great stuff. That would get you in alone. Honest.'

'Guy, don't you think I've tried? Dad – there's no point.' Vivienne moved yet closer to his warm body. Her Guy. Then she said, 'Guy. What about Amanda?'

Guy shifted slightly away from her. 'It's been arranged, Vivvy. Has been for a long time. It's been – it's kind of expected by both our families from as far as I can remember.'

'An arrangement?'

'Something like that, yes. You know what Guernsey families are like. It's been planned until – I've got to say – so it's inevitable. Feels right.' Guy drifted to a full stop and stubbed out his cigarette in one of the used coffee mugs.

Vivienne moved position to be more comfortable. She didn't want to talk any more – especially not about Amanda. Didn't want to go down there – not tonight. 'Shall we go? Let's get back to the Eight Bells. I really liked it there.'

When they did get back, a good hour or more later, Guy's friends whooped with laughter and called out, 'Who's a pretty boy, then?' and 'Better now, dear?' meaning Guy. They teased and teased until Vivienne and Guy laughed themselves, joining in.

Glancing around, Vivienne felt warm gratification at the envious looks on the sophisticated models' faces. Guy had chosen her. In front of all these swinging City girls, it was Vivienne who was with Guy.

Vivienne turned up the collar of her coat – to frame her face – and pulled a few frizzy strands over her forehead to try and make an artful fringe. Guy ordered more pints as they planned what to do next day.

In the morning Vivienne faced a hostile lift. She tentatively pressed a triangular button and jumped as the lift suddenly arrived with a creaking hiss. The doors slid open, revealing squashed, expressionless strangers all staring at her.

No, it was too daunting. City life, city lifts. Not knowing north from south.

Fearfully, Vivienne ran down the dank fire stairs; her footsteps echoed against grubby cream walls. Something smelt of diesel oil. Five. Four. Three. Two. She wheezed as she counted. A shoe came off. She jammed it back on, hurting the back of her heel. 'One...' Vivienne panted, horribly aware she was keeping her Guy waiting. Sweat dampened her reddening face, as, gasping, she landed with a loud clatter in Reception.

Frowning, Guy stood bemused in the foyer, shaking his head at her and pointing at his watch.

'Don't ask,' Vivienne spluttered.

Once at the National Gallery, Vivienne nudged Guy, amused at men in black bowler hats and grey pin striped suits with tightly rolled black umbrellas. Many women wore expensive outfits like Vivienne had only seen in *Vanity Fair* and *Vogue* magazines. Nobody – well, nobody she knew – dressed like that in Guernsey.

Immediately, Guy marched Vivienne around the gallery to see his favourites: Titian, Veronese, Botticelli. They stopped in front of Constable and Van Gogh. Vivienne admired Titian's colours, Constable's rolling ochre fields and dark-leafed trees; Van Gogh's thick citric-yellow oil paint.

'Constable had apprentices to paint a lot of those background leaves, you know,' said Guy. 'But Vincent Van Gogh was totally original. A total one-off – Vincent. Not really an Impressionist nor Post-Impressionist.' Then Guy scolded, 'God, you really must come to London, you know. Can't you find some way?'

But she had been down that fruitless road many times. Sixteen, with neither money nor any support from her father Vivienne didn't know where to start to get, never mind pay for, accommodation. There would be travel expenses to and from Guernsey. No, her father wanted her to get a job: earn some money, end of. The prospect of leaving Guernsey closed around her just as surely as the walls of the National Gallery rooms.

'Anyway Vivvy. Now for Titian's *Bacchus and Ariadne*, an absolute, total, masterpiece.'

As soon as she saw it, Vivienne stood spellbound by the painting. 'Guy, the colours! Cerulean blue, Bacchus' cape. You can hardly believe it's just paint and canvas. Ariadne's plaintive face. She is an actual girl, full of …' Vivienne turned to look at Guy '… of longing and desire.'

Guy smiled down at her. 'Little Ariadne is sweet isn't she, little Vivienne Normandie? Titian used nut oils to get that special sheen of paint. There's lots of classical references as well.' Guy peered closer at the painting.

'You sound like Darius!' Vivienne teased.

'Bacchus – he's the god of wine and fertility, rescues mortal Ariadne flinging her crown of stars into the sky. She may have been married to Theseus or at least promised. The crown could be a bridal chaplet. Or, it might be about Bacchus returning to her. Experts can't agree – perhaps Bacchus cast a spell making Theseus forget his promise to Ariadne. Forget her existence, even.'

Vivienne let her eyes to wander right into the picture. Ariadne's circle of stars, twinkled in the royal blue heaven.

'Wine,' Guy went on, 'brings truth – *in vino veritas* – and pleasure, to us poor old earthbound souls.' Looking somewhat bedazzled himself, he continued. 'This piece was painted for an aristo – Alfonso d'Este. Owning it, he could boast to his rich friends about how well-read he was and how well-connected'. Guy blushed with an embarrassed grin. 'Got that from a book I borrowed from Darius.'

'Can you lend it to me?' Vivienne asked. "And this Alfonso what's 'is name – he was a friend of Titian's?'

'Yup. But better you have your own copy. We can go down to the Gallery shop. They have heaps of stuff about every artist in the gallery.'

They both sat down on the bench in front of *Bacchus and Ariadne*, the more to admire it. Guy put his arm around Vivienne's waist. She leant back into the warmth of his presence.

Guy squeezed her and Vivienne felt for his hand, putting hers on top of his.

'But, look Vivvy. Now, you're off tomorrow, aren't you? Back home to Guernsey? You mustn't – I hope you don't – start fretting if I can't get in touch with you as soon as you might like. We – I – might have to pop over to the States for a few days. Darius is fixing something up. I'm not sure what. I'm not sure of my...plans, okay?'

So: Amanda again. Somehow London, the Chelsea set, the lofty halls of the National Gallery suddenly all seemed like a barred, enchanted world to Vivienne. However could she possibly be a part of it?

On that day, though, Vivienne had Guy sitting right next to her. She burrowed her face into him, feeling the heat of his body right through her coat. Her feet swung, dangling like a rag puppet's from the bench seat. Guy's long legs were firmly planted on the hall floor.

Vivienne deliberately turned a supplicant face up to Guy. He cupped his hands around her chin. He tenderly stroked the springy fuzz of hair around her head. He tapped her gently on the nose, getting some of the pink powder she'd hastily puffed on – to hide the damned freckles – all over his fingertips.

'Best not to take things too seriously, Vivvy. I can't promise you anything. Not sure, really, of where I'm going yet.' Guy said it softly.

'No. No, I don't take things too seriously. Honestly, I just want to be with you, Guy.' Want you. Want you more than anything. Wouldn't tie you down. Wouldn't. Wouldn't.

Guy sighed. 'But that's just it, Viv. I can't be with you like you want can I? I've never promised you that.' Then, quite as an aside he added, 'Bit embarrassing, but you don't happen to have a few pounds I can borrow, do you? I've been getting all these taxis for us...King's Road is a way off – ?'

Of course, Vivienne gave Guy the fare money. She had saved a little for the trip and Granmarie had given her a generous £10, saying 'So, ma petite Vivienne, you'll be just as *toute la patraque*, as good as all the rest, on this course of yours.'

Guy promised to pay her back, 'As soon as funds permit.' He kissed her goodbye, lightly, on the cheek.

On the plane back to Guernsey, Vivienne flicked through pages of the books she had bought with Guy: Titian, Dorothy Parker, Scott Fitzgerald.

'All great stuff,' Guy had approved.

What a clever, beautiful boy her Guy was. Not yet twenty and so clever. As the plane hummed her homeward, Vivienne began to sing aloud. A Buddy Holly song.

Of course Guy needed her. He wanted her. Their sex was so good he must love her, surely? Somehow, something would work out.

Landed home, Vivienne kissed her mother's cheek – smooth and cold as sea-washed stone. Jean, distant with heavy medication said, 'Nin! Oh hello. You're here?'

'Yes, Mum, I'm here.' Jean seemed hardly aware that Vivienne had been away. Jean could always block out any unthinkable absence. Her father told Vivienne that Jean had been on a kind of spiritual retreat over the weekend – with her friends, Muriel Le Croix and Elaine Bordeaux. Thankfully, Edward was far too wound up with how her mother had coped to ask Vivienne much about the 'Kent course'.

Escaping as fast as she could to her bedroom, Vivienne lay on her bed and switched on Radio Luxembourg, tuning her transistor to '208' with Barry Alldis. Alldis played the very Buddy Holly song Vivienne liked. It was past midnight. The radio crackled annoyingly. Vivienne, in striped pyjamas, sat up and put her arms around her knees. She sang along:

'Where you goin' baby? Here am I.
Well, you left me here, so I could sit and cry.
Do you remember, baby? Last September?
How you held me tight? Each and every night?
Well, oops-a-daisy, how you drove me crazy – '

Vivienne changed the last line, singing to herself and waiting for her Guy to come back to Guernsey –'I wish Amanda didn't matter any more – '

CHAPTER TWO

Vivienne always remembered where she was when she first heard that Guy was getting married. It was at Granville, Granmarie's family house, in the sitting room. Jean had breezed in, waving a gold-edged white card.

'Look, Nin. We've all been invited to a wedding. Guy Beaufort and Amanda Le Croix. Now isn't that nice?' Home after one of her stays at thXe psychiatric hospital where she had her own 'Quiet Room', as she liked to call it, Jean seemed more refreshed than usual.

Vivienne said nothing.

'Nin? Vivienne?' Jean shot her a querying glance. 'We must go to it – oh, I do want to go to a Beaufort wedding!'

Vivienne still couldn't answer, but hid behind the heavy book she and Guy had chosen on Titian. She raised its shiny covers to conceal her face. Curled up in a chair, Vivienne saw no pictures, no text, but screwed up her eyes and turned her face to the side as if to glance off a blow.

Jean had moved over to the fireplace, to look into the dun-gold framed mirror, hanging above the mantle. She had hollow spaces underneath the lost blue eyes, mottled with green specks when you looked up close. Sometimes, Jean would look at you with a heavily questioning expression, as if she was saying: 'How did I get to this place? Why did you let me?'

But Jean said, 'Yes, well, a new outfit I think, don't you Nin?' brightly enough. 'And you'll want something? Edward'll want to go. Your father knows both families so well.' Jean patted the back of her greying hair, habitually twisted into a neat figure of eight. Grimacing, she inspected her teeth then applied a slick of red lipstick, absently rubbing her lips together.

'Yes, I expect Dad will want to go,' Vivienne managed. 'Don't know if I will. It's a Catholic do, is it?'

'Don't be so silly, Nin. Your father is quite ecumenical these days. And of course you're going.'

Vivienne didn't think Edward was in the least bit ecumenical but, right now, that was the very least of her worries. Vivienne wilted inwardly. She felt so like a great clumsy bird in her parents' lives. Neither the good little girl nor the lost little boy. Vivienne's place in their diminished nest was as an interloper, hatched out accidentally.

She watched Jean, fussing over her diary, pencilling in hair appointments and muttering to herself about clothes. 'Do show some interest Nin! Do you think orchids will be too much for buttonholes? Must get Edward's morning suit professionally pressed.'

As the day for the Beaufort wedding drew nearer, Vivienne recalled the hushed and hurried phone call Guy had made to her office, some time before. Could they possibly see each other? Say, on his stag night?

Of course, the wedding details were at an advanced stage by then. It was all arranged. But Guy fixed it so he could leave his stag night early. He got Darius to help. Darius understood, said Guy, 'everything'.

So they met, in the gorse-filled fields, high above the sea on the unruly south coast cliffs. Unable to stop herself, Vivienne burst out 'Let's go down the beach!' And Guy had held out his hands – his wonderful hands. She clasped his offered salve, the heat of it drugging her as much as any wine in the blood, surging through her in the hot, sultry night. Hands tightly held together, her craving for him rising like the rolling waves below them, they found the cliff path.

Guy would surely see what her love meant to him?

Then, they had run – joined like a couple as they ran like when they were kids, all the way to Portelet Bay. The lanes were behind them, the shadowy, moon-tipped lanes and the silent fields with their shadowy shapes of sleeping cattle. Vivienne and Guy hurtled down, just like schoolchildren, down, down, down to the beach.

Down the deserted path they had flown, down to the cobbled slipway, across the shoreline and onto the cool, moon-white sand.

Half hidden under a sheltering, leafy bough, they made a makeshift bed. Vivienne watched Guy take off his T-shirt, stamped by his friends with an inked 'V' sign. Added to his shirt rumpled on the pebbles lay Vivienne's carelessly thrown black silk dress, spread out over wet, straggly seaweed.

Guy's bare shoulders folded over her. She could smell his sweated skin and thanked God she had worked to keep her body smooth and tanned. Rough kisses tasted of sand, champagne and each other's tongues. Surf swished over the shore. Yearning flooded in and out of her flesh. Madly clinging to each other, they rolled over and over in a frenzy of need. Vivienne sat astride Guy, splashing stolen wine over his hair, his mouth and then drank some herself, straight from the bottle.

'Guy.' Kissing him, holding back a tangle of her own curled hair brushing over his forehead, she twisted in his dark, feather-cut with knuckled fist. 'I want you. I want you.' And she said it and his name 'Guy, I want you,' over and over again.

'Wild Vivvy,' Guy stroked her breasts lightly and bit gently at her sunned thigh, saying, 'me too, I'm crazy as hell about you.' He rose up, pulling her to standing next to him. Their naked limbs snaked around each other – silver outlined in the moonshine.

Ravenous now, at the silvery water's edge, Vivienne and Guy waded into the sea. They licked mouths, noses and necks. The water lay chill beneath their waists. Kissing him again, midriff high, Vivienne moved further into the lapping, satiny sea, speckled with scattered star-shine. Lost to the world – lost to all sensibility – Vivienne felt Guy's body explore her own, inside and out. She clung to him – they were one writhing creature of the sea. Vivienne stared up at the stars.

They sank below the tide, the tops of their heads just visible. Pushing, pulling, darting like weaving water-beings – like floundering fishes – they came together.

As Vivienne cried out loud, her ecstasy echoed all around the deserted bay. Guy still thrust at her, offering himself. Her pelvis moved in rhythm with the force of the waves and his body. Then she broke free from him and swam to the small pier, teasing him, wet and naked to the night. Vivienne sang out to him.

'Look at those stars, Guy! Come and rescue me!' She twirled around the slippery pole at the end of the pier, swinging round and round, getting dizzy. She dived then, splashing into the sea, laughing and spluttering.

Guy swam up to her, the cool seas had slowly sobered him.

'Don't I need rescuing, though, Vivvy? Isn't it the other way round?'

Quietening, she held his dear, beautiful head gently as they floated on the sea surface. She ran her fingers over his young, sea-sprayed face. Guy was her Pisces, her sea-god.

'You'll be all right, Guy. We'll be all right. Somehow. Everything will be all right, you'll see.'

They rolled over onto their stomachs and, still in the water, hardly causing a ripple, swam in the silver-black sea back to the shore.

Vivienne tried to dry herself with her sand-filled dress, feeling her wet hair drip down her back.

Guy put his arm around her, 'You little sexpot. Crazy little Vivvy. Being with you is like being with nobody else I know.'

'Same for me, Guy,' said Vivienne. 'Nobody else.'

He suddenly held her closer. 'Think you'll regret this, Viv?'

'No, never,' Vivienne said, immediately, hugging Guy – hugging him to her. She felt his wet ear on her cheek. Seawater trickled from his hair onto her face. She caught some of the drips with her tongue and swallowed them like they were drops of finest wine.

'You won't ever hate me, will you?' Guy asked and, in the moonlight, his dark eyes shone. His hair reflected moon-silvered strands in the black, cooling night.

'Hate? No, Guy. Never hate. Horrid word.' Vivienne held him to her. This was her time. This was their time.

To make him laugh, she scrunched up some crinkly brown seaweed to her chin, to make a beard, and pulled a funny face. In a Donald Duck's voice she squawked, 'Look at me, I'm really weird. That's because I was weirdly reared!'

Relief softened Guy's face as he laughed out loud. Finished dressing, they strolled up the beach with their arms around each other. The moon eclipsed behind charcoal-black branches.

Of course Guy was Vivienne's. How could he not be? Hadn't he said that? Hadn't they proved that? Come the dawn, Amanda Le Croix might be marrying Guy. But it would never last.

Everyone – as her mother would keep putting it – everyone was there. The Beaufort wedding reception was a sit down luncheon at the Hermitage Country Hotel. They were served mushroom soup, roast lamb and sherry trifle.

At the top table sat Mr and Mrs Le Croix, looking self-conscious and stiff in their formal clothes. The Beauforts, Guy's parents, totally at ease, joked and smiled all through the meal, leaning over to talk to the Le Croixes.

Guy looked hot and uncomfortable in his grey morning suit. The usual confident set of his head and shoulders, the half-smile of his handsome face did not quite fit this ritual. Once or twice Vivienne caught his eye. Apart from a conspiratorial smile, though, she dared not respond to his wink as Guy raised his glass toward her.

In fact, in the stuffy hotel air, Vivienne felt faint. The mumble of soporific conversation numbed her senses. As she sipped at her wine, the room seemed hazy and unreal. There was an incense of flowers: musky roses, lavender and pink Guernsey lilies. Vivienne felt overwhelmed into a half-swoon.

And Vivienne had not expected serene Amanda Le Croix to look quite so spectacular. Amanda had chosen a long-sleeved, corseted Duchesse satin jacket, rimmed all around the edges with silk. Tiny satin buttons looped from high front neck to dropped waist. The full-skirted ivory gown, stiffened with tulle petticoats, was veiled over with a very fine white organza. A tiered, long white net veil spilled out from artificial white roses, fastened to Amanda's swept-up hair with a silver comb.

Forget Sandra Dee. Amanda was Princess Grace Kelly – marrying her Prince, make no mistake. There were flowers everywhere.

Amongst the cream and white roses and lavender, tables trailed glossy dark green ivy.

Toasts were made 'To the beautiful bride!' And, 'To the happy couple!' Vivienne drank down another glass of wine, then another. She thanked goodness that a young waiter had swiftly noted a real thirst in sore need.

Seated at their table, Edward, her father, whispered like he was giving stage directions to someone. 'See, Nin? That boy was never for you. But you would go and chase after him so. Nin, I told you...'

'Well, all right Dad. Got the message.' Vivienne's face flushed miserably. She could hardly start arguing, openly, with her father but instead studied him as he drank his water and methodically ate his meal. Of course it had been sad, deeply sad, that her parents had lost their beloved blond little boy. Their Oscar – of course it was tragic.

Vivienne pictured how they must have pulled Oscar's lifeless body from her grandfather's quarry. With broken hearts, Edward and Jean had moved from that cursed family land to live with Granmarie and Charles: Jean's parents. They took Vivienne, still a baby, with them. After that, Vivienne guessed, Edward had rather run out of fatherly steam, finding solace with his Gospels. Jean just never recovered.

So, if the Normandie family name was to be carried on – well, it wouldn't be from her father's branch. Edward's place in Guernsey history – the proud and ancient Normandie line – had been stolen from him. It was gone.

They lived at Granville, with Granmarie. Since grandfather Charles Bordeaux had died, Edward seemed content to live on Jean's mother's family land. He had sold his own father's property just as soon as he could – got rid of it. Anyway, the money had come in handy for Jean, since she needed so much medical help.

For Guy's wedding, the Normandie table was set right opposite the Carré's. The Carré family all kept smiling over. Now, they were a really nice lot, a very good family, so Granmarie said, repeatedly, throughout the entire wedding lunch and nudging Vivienne with a practiced elbow.

Jean, in her dark blue costume with matching feathery hat,

suddenly spoke up in an over-shrill voice. 'The Beauforts and Le Croixes have impeccable pedigrees, don't they? Aren't these two well matched? Well, they were engaged for a long time, weren't they? Amanda and Guy?'

'Spoken for,' said Vivienne bluntly.

'Spoken for, yes, Nin. For years. Didn't you go out with Guy once, though, Nin? Didn't we once warn you, Nin?'

'Mum, please! Keep your voice down.' Vivienne reddened until her ears sang. She twisted her hands together painfully. Was this some kind of penance she was being forced to pay?

'Men are such hypocrites, aren't they?' Jean chattered on, 'only marrying good little girls. Men do that, don't they? Such hypocrites.' She folded her napkin neatly and set it down by her plate. 'Well then, this is a pleasant wedding, isn't it? Look at all the people we know, Edward! All these families. Look, there are the Carré's,' Jean waved over then dropped her voice solicitously, 'they have such a nice farmhouse in such a good location. A wonderful family home. Established. Yes, established Guernsey family.' Jean smiled to herself.

Nodding her head toward all the tables then glancing fondly at Edward, Jean said 'And we are the Normandie clan.' She beamed proudly, like a five year old invited to an exclusive children's party.

Almost immediately afterward, Jean's happy smile dropped and she seemed afraid. She attempted a weak smile. 'We are all right, aren't we, Edward? Our clan?'

Edward sipped, grimfaced, from his tumbler. He cleared his throat gruffly and took Jean's small hand. 'Course we are, Jean. Course we are. Just relax, now.'

Vivienne caught a suppressed look pass between her parents' eyes. Thoughts of Oscar? More than likely. 'You look lovely, Mum,' Vivienne said, gently, 'and you've got the classiest hat in the room, by far.'

'That young David Carré is a nice boy,' Granmarie said, pure mischief in her voice, poking Vivienne with her fork. 'Now there's…'

'Oh, for God's sake, Granmarie!' Vivienne's face flooded hot blood again. She crumpled up her white napkin and threw it carelessly over her plate. The waiter poured her more wine.

Now that she was actually witnessing Guy and Amanda together, Vivienne fervently wished that she had never come to their wedding. And she wished she hadn't worn a close-fitting, red two-piece and loads more make-up than she had intended to. Even her scent smelled cheap.

Vivienne looked at Amanda. Amanda had perfectly manicured hands with immaculate pink nails. Vivienne stared down at her own hands – at nails unevenly cut and badly varnished. She had, of course, overslept that morning. She had gone to bed with her head full of Guy, their starry night. His body. Then she had had to rush everything, smearing her nail varnish and slapping on her make up.

Edward had noticed. 'You know, you want to look after yourself a bit more, Nin. Stop wasting you time scribbling indoors with all that art and sitting around, reading. You want to get outside, get some fresh air. Get some exercise.' He flashed an exaggerated look of resignation over to Granmarie. Then suddenly looking resigned, he finished his water and drew himself up. 'That Amanda has turned out to be a stunner, hasn't she Jean? Turned out very nice. Come along then, come on.' Edward offered his arm to Jean.

Their coffee finished, Edward and Jean wandered off. Edward made straight toward Amanda, and, Vivienne thought, any other unsuspecting young woman he might chance to compliment. As Jean left them she had said, doubtfully and much too brightly, that she 'Really must circulate amongst all her friends.'

Vivienne sat, left alone with Granmarie. They drank their coffees in mutual silence. Granmarie put out her roughened, gardener's hand to hold Vivienne's. 'Nearly over, ma petite,' Granmarie said quietly. 'Nearly over.'

The newly-weds went off to change. Vivienne needed a toilet. A dauntingly long queue meandered down some stairs. When she asked him, the friendly waiter told Vivienne that, yes, there was another convenience – outside, 'A little walk away, Miss, but not too far.'

He smiled admiringly at her, saying, 'You know, you're the best looking chick at this wedding, I reckon. Pity,' he dropped his voice to a whisper and chuckled impishly in Vivienne's ear, 'you've only got eyes for the groom.'

A hasty retreat: Vivienne crossed a courtyard, hemmed in with granite buildings on all sides, to find the outside lavatory. It was little more than a shed. No one was around. Squabbling sparrows fluttered and chased each other over the slate roofs, dipping down to peck at insects between worn flagstones.

The toilet smelled cobwebbed and musty. A framed, broken, mirror losing its quicksilver, hung on a nail. But it sufficed. Washing her hands, Vivienne peered closely at her image.

'Good God, what a bloody mess,' Vivienne said aloud. A quick comb of her hair, a rub at slightly smudged mascara then she looked again. 'Damn, not much better.' Pouting, she glossed on some pink lipstick, then sprayed some more scent over her neck and inside her jacket, over her breasts and welcomed the refreshing jet.

Her suit looked hopelessly crumpled. She adjusted the jacket lapels and tugged at her tight skirt. Her nose had caught too much sun from sunbathing in the heat of the day on Herm island. Why had she done that? Well, it had been lunchtime and she wanted a quick tan – because of the wedding – never should do that, not on Herm. Everyone knew how quickly you could burn on Herm. But she had panicked. Couldn't go to the wedding with stumpy, white legs. So, got the ferry and lain for a couple of hours, turning over just once. Not only that, but Vivienne felt distinctly pickled. A sort of helpless mirth began to rise up in her throat.

She could hear her father, "This is not a laughing matter, my girl! Alcohol? Too much sun? It's the Devil's work!" Vivienne attempted to stifle a despairing giggle. What the hell, anyway? She would just have to do. Anyway, what did it matter now? Did it matter how she looked? How she behaved? Who cared? Who bloody cared?

'Back to the fray, then,' Vivienne said as she stumbled out.

It was quiet and sunny in the yard, patterned with shadows. They reminded her of Dutch interior paintings. She'd been studying them at Evening Class: patches of gold juxtaposed with the dark grey of stone. She smiled. Now there's an arty farty expression, Father: 'juxtaposed! Just meant – she told friends, nervous of making a wrong observation, of making fools of themselves – just meant 'contrast'. Just look at the juxtaposition! Better still, what about 'chiaroscuro'? That'd really show your intelligence. 'Chiaroscuro' – means light and shade. Rembrandt style, say and...

'Hey! What...?'Shock jolted through her as, straight in front of her like a barrier gate, an arm shot out.

'Get off. Get off me!' Was it the flirty waiter? Vivienne flailed her arms at the man, yelping in fright. 'Get off me, you lunatic!' As she was bundled into a dusky, dark and doorless stable.

'Shh – Vivvy, it's me!' The dancing dark eyes and half-smiling face could only be Guy. 'It's me!' he said, cheerfully, grinning broadly at her surprise.

'Guy! Guy, you idiot. What – shouldn't you be at your bloody reception...?' Stifled breath threatened to fail her.

By answer, Guy pulled her close to him. He had changed for the honeymoon. Vivienne's face got pressed against his woollen jumper. Woolly fibres stuck to her lip gloss.

'It can wait a minute – I needed to say goodbye, properly, Vivvy. I won't get another chance for – won't see you for some time, will I?'

'Well no,' said Vivienne, forcing her words to sound even, 'seeing as you are going on your – now what was it? Oh yes, your honeymoon. With your wife. Remember her? You haven't forgotten Amanda already, surely – ?"

Then neither of them spoke. Vivienne couldn't. She wasn't anywhere near prepared for this. Birds flew about outside, dust bathing, chirruping and trilling without care. The dank stable, ugly with rusting scythes and rakes, chilled them. What did Guy want?

Then Guy said, 'I just wanted to tell you that last night – well, it was something else, Viv. Head's banging now, though: paying for it. You?'

Paying for it? What, like they were sinners? No – and don't dare mention forgiveness, Guy. Don't. But Vivienne only said, 'I'm all right,' and turned her head away.

'Today can't be easy, Viv. Sure you're okay?' Guy turned her face back toward him with his hand and kissed her lightly. Then he buried his face into her red-suited breasts. 'You smell of violets. Your suit – well red was always magic on you. Bloody hell. This is all much, much worse than I thought it would be – '

'But it was always going to happen, Guy, wasn't it? Your marriage? Always going to happen? I'm fine.' Vivienne swallowed a knotting, tight ball wired up like mesh in her throat.

'No you're not. Look – I don't want you to feel…you know what we have. Last night – well it wasn't nothing. Oh, dammit.'

Vivienne didn't respond. In her mind she saw the vision of Amanda, a princess, dancing and twirling around her new husband. Carefree Amanda had fluttered around the room in her wispy, ivory gown relishing the attention on the biggest day of her life.

'Anyway, you are special Viv. There's nobody like you. You are different from all the others. Even when we were kids – '

'Guy. I can't take this. I don't want this.'

'Maybe if – if we could have, oh, I don't know – a long time ago?'

In the dark stable the open doorway framed bright sunshine. Light outlined Guy's face, the side of his head and shoulders.

'I used to be one hundred per cent sure. That Amanda was the one. Now? I don't know.' Guy pounded the crumbling wall with his fist, dislodging dusty particles of ancient, grey cement. 'Help me, Viv?'

Vivienne coughed with the dust. 'Oh, you'll feel different once you get to Sark. Once you are on honeymoon!" she flapped a hand in front of her face. But she didn't attempt to move away from Guy. She wanted his closeness, however wrongly. She breathed in deeply. If she breathed in deep enough, then, through her body, she would breathe in Guy's very soul. She would keep something of Guy with her – fathoms deep within her.

Then, impulsively, she affected a light-hearted tone, 'Anyway, when you're back – maybe, when you are back from your holiday?

Then...' he heard her voice rising higher '...perhaps we can meet up? See one another...?'

Through his woollen Guernsey, Guy wavered. Like the wriggling of a flat fish, underfoot, Vivienne sensed Guy's fearful withdrawal. It was only fleeting, but enough. She recoiled, damaged.

'Oh what does it matter now?' Vivienne stopped herself from asking any more. Don't ask for more. 'Oh, go away, Guy. What's the point of this? Go to your wife. Go to Amanda. She loves you. This is absolutely pointless.'

For a split second, Guy stayed and lingered. Vivienne kept quite still. Then, as if welcoming her silence, Guy kissed the top of her head and strode out. Vivienne waited until she couldn't hear his footsteps anymore then cried: an agonised, abandoned cry. She bit into clenched knuckles and ran back into the airless old outhouse. Vivienne sat on the lavatory seat and sobbed until her heart burned.

The married couple had left, covered in confetti. The wedding party broke up. In threes and fours people moved to the car park. Laughter rang out amid much back slapping and promises to 'Must meet again!' and 'Soon!'

The Normandies and Granmarie headed toward their polished black Ford. 'Do come on Nin!' called her mother.

Vivienne, alarmed, saw Jean had visibly drooped.

'Wherever have you been, Nin? I was looking all over for you. You can be such a nuisance. Your father is quite right.' Then Jean turned away and, in shiny court shoes, waved her hands about at imaginary flies and picked her way daintily over the gravel. Following her from not far behind, Edward made loud groans of mock despair at his wife's willingness – not his, of course – to leave the party.

'Hello, Vivienne,' said a softly spoken fair haired young man, his hand already holding her elbow. It was David Carré. 'Want a lift home?' He had his own car, he said. David was fair, tall and slender. Not Vivienne's type at all.

David must understand: he was definitely not Vivienne's type. But she accepted his lift, noticing Granmarie raising her eyebrows, grinning craftily. Granmarie had, somehow, contrived to make her wave of 'Good bye' into a thumbs up.

Lord, but she'd be glad to be shot of her family today. Gratefully, Vivienne climbed into David's car.

'I'll take you the pretty way home,' David gave Vivienne an unmistakable, approving smile. He drove around the east coast on the way to Granville, in the north.

On the horizon lay Sark island. Vivienne could see the Sark ferry on a sea swiftly rising from moderate to choppy.

'Might be a rough crossing today, wouldn't you say, Vivienne?' David smiled like a sailor who knew his stuff. 'Yes, really quite bumpy. No way to start a honeymoon, is it? Seasick?'

Vivienne turned to study this man's profile. David kept his eyes on the road, looking steadily ahead. Well, then, David Carré, thought Vivienne, might you be relied upon to offer a girl shelter from bad weather?

'Shall I call you my man of all seasons, then, David Carré?' Vivienne teased.

'Please do, Vivienne. Why not? I'll have you know, Vivienne Normandie, that I am one hell of a fine chap!' Laughing loudly, David threw back his head. His hands, though, still firmly held the steering wheel.

Sark hovered, already shrouded in mist. In these islands the weather changed in wilful seconds. The newly weds would arrive under a rain-filled sky.

But David Carré got Vivienne safely home on that day. The day that Guy Beaufort and Amanda got married: the day after Vivienne's night on the beach with her beautiful Guy at Portelet bay.

But, a few weeks later, Vivienne counted the days on her Italian Renaissance calendar – the one she had bought with Guy in London's National Gallery, a year ago. She flicked the pages back a month, then forward again. It was strange. Vivienne had never missed a period before.

CHAPTER THREE

Vivienne missed a second period as well. Tea tasted sour. Something like it had happened before – with stress, a couple of times, before school exams. When she'd done the round of job interviews, performed shorthand under exam conditions, she had not bled as she should have done. But she had never missed twice before.

Once they returned to Guernsey, Vivienne started to drive past Guy and Amanda's place. They'd taken rooms in his parents' town house, in Hauteville. His father was an optician, an ophthalmic surgeon. Guy's parents had always lived in Hauteville. On this, a growers' island, the Beauforts were 'Townies'.

Vivienne always loved the Beauforts' house. In her warm, olive-tiled kitchen Mrs Beaufort made cakes for their gang of school friends, boys and girls. Her sponges were sandwiched together with thick vanilla butter cream. Mrs Beaufort never complained about them cluttering the place up. The Beauforts preferred classical music, Mr Beaufort played the piano, so the elegant town house lilted with sounds of Bach and Mozart. They had given Guy a studio, losing one of their rooms specially for him. His work stood on a professional artist's easel for everyone to see.

Guy's wedding seemed ages ago now. Once, Vivienne drove past the town house in the dark. It had been raining. Street lamps shone with a dirty yellow consolation, dulled in the wet. Rain blurred the grey, grit pavement. She'd parked in the road and switched off the engine. Steam rose from the car bonnet. Looking up she fancied she saw Guy, moving about behind the open shutters and long net curtains.

In the cold, a slight mound swelled beneath her skirt. He mustn't know about it. Guy had a talented future before him – his new life, even if it was with Amanda. Vivienne had to help him out of this.

Back home in her bedroom. Vivienne set up her own easel, a spindly thing with legs that shot out, unbalanced and fell over if you hadn't tightened the screws hard enough. She squeezed tubes of oil paints, oozing cerulean blue, mixing vibrant pink onto a palette. The oily smell made her feel slightly sick. She began a copy of *Bacchus and Ariadne*.

Carefully, she drew Bacchus' lovely young face - just like her Guy's. She painted his muscled shoulders, his strong legs and flowing, satiny cape as he leapt to Ariadne. She copied the white cloud that pillowed behind Ariadne's head, with hair colour much like her own and just as difficult to control, by the look of it. And Ariadne had the same sturdy calves and thick ankles as hers. Vivienne drew Ariadne's softly curved body, wrapped around in rich blue and scarlet. In the jewel blue sky, sparkled Ariadne's crown, a constellation, flung there by Bacchus. Then Vivienne sketched the writhing, bronzed figure in the foreground, wrapped around with a coiling serpent. 'The suffocating strangle of excess lust,' Vivienne said firmly out loud, probing her top lip with her tongue.

'Nin! Are you ever coming down for your breakfast?' Edward interrupted, calling up the stairs, 'because your mother and I are going to church. Do hurry up.'

Just a bit more? A touch more crimson, maybe, on Bacchus' cloak? Vivienne mixed in a little white, as well. Mustn't make it look too...

'Whatever are you doing? You dreamy girl?' Edward stamped up the stairs and flung open her bedroom door.

'Good God, Nin. What an awful mess!' As his eyes swept over the easel, the oil paints and brushes scattered on her window sill. 'And your bed's not made! And it is a Sunday morning! Sunday is a day of rest! Just wait until I tell your poor Mother. Wait until I tell Jean. Get a grip on yourself, for goodness sake.' Edward shook, adding hotly 'and Edna – Mrs Jones – tells me that you have been giving work to Polly? Because you can't read your shorthand back? I thought you'd been on a course? Don't you ever...can't you ever...what will people think of us?' Then he stomped out of the room, muttering down each stair, 'and do something about your hair, smarten yourself. You look awful!'

Poor Dad. By now he'll be thinking 'Boys are *so* much easier! Oh, if only Oscar was alive! He'd be doing some *real* work! Putting his back into his job and getting *on*!'

Vivienne heard that Edward saw Mrs Jones, Edna, every Saturday lunchtime at the Yacht Club. So all Vivienne's misdoings will have been reported, no doubt? Vivienne slowly put down her brushes and wiped them on an old cloth saturated in turpentine. The smell, like anaesthetic, made her reel back. Her painting wasn't bad, though. It was, at least, a fair enough copy of Guy's (and hers of course) favourite painting.

After breakfast, she made her bed and washed her hair, plastering on some conditioner. Perhaps she should start ironing out the kinky frizz, like she'd read some of the London models did? Except, when she told Polly she had turned white and had said firmly 'for heaven's sake!' Not to even think about ironing anything and especially not her hair, without her being there 'to help you, kiddo'.

Outside, autumn gradually stripped the garden of flowers. Dying leaves crunched forlornly onto the path. There were too many apples growing on their trees, thumping down onto the damp grass with regularity. The birds and mice grew plump.

Vivienne decided to paint in the fields opposite Granville. Wearing a black blouse, long sparkly beads and calf-length black skirt she took her easel, tripping now and then, to the long grassed meadow where the skylarks sang. Flicks of the greens and browns speckled her freckled face and hands. She ignored two boy hikers as they peered over her shoulder. As a painter, you had to get used to this kind of thing – you had to stay aloof and show your professionalism.

Still, 'Cor, that's coming on well,' and 'Wish I could do that!' had her straining a modest smile. And she was glad of their help when the flimsy wooden easel tipped over and they gleefully (just) saved her canvas from hitting the muddy earth.

Vivienne had stopped counting the missed periods. The roundness had moved up a little. She felt vaguely unwell and ate sparingly. Some things tasted vile. Almost everything smelled strangely of cabbage water.

It was Monday so she cycled to work on her blue bike.

'Hey. You okay, kiddo?' Polly peered closely at her.

'Okay. Bit...tired.' Vivienne dreaded Polly's questioning. She was hard to lie to and didn't give up easily. Should she tell her? But then Polly would feel – maybe – responsible for her somehow? Be bound to ask if it was Guy? She couldn't risk it. Couldn't give Polly that sort of burden to carry. It was Vivienne's burden. It felt heavier each day.

'Want a hand?' Without waiting for an answer, Polly began to read from Vivienne's notepad. She frowned then said, 'Just type up the order you did yesterday, kiddo. It's just a repeat.'

Polly slapped the notebook down on the desk. Vivienne took it back with pale hands, hoping her make-up covered the pallor on her face she'd noticed in the bathroom mirror. She forced herself to put a sheet of foolscap into the typewriter.

'Listen, are you sure you're all right?' asked Polly, flicking an anxious glance over her.

'Yes. Yes. I'm fine, Polly,' said Vivienne slowly as her hands feeling clammy and moist. Then, more quickly, 'thanks. Thanks. But, well...' then she swung round, face to face with her friend. 'Actually no, Polly, no I don't really feel so good." (Keep your voice steady, Polly looks alarmed). 'Do – do you think I could go home?' All in a rush now, 'Please?'

The telephone rang, breaking a silent pause.

'Course,' Polly swiftly dealt with the call, covering the mouthpiece with her hand, her eyes not leaving Vivienne. Saying 'Thank you. Bye,' she pulled a lead out of the switchboard then Polly said, 'Course! I'll sort it with Ma Jones. But...' she hesitated, 'you really should see a doc, kiddo. I think so, anyway.'

Taking Vivienne's shorthand pad, Polly went to sit in Reception. Her round blue eyes widened tenderly. Then, with her long, skinny arms crossed in front of her, simply said. 'Look, just take care, kiddo.'

Vivienne headed quickly for the park: get some fresh air, think what to do? Have the baby? That would ruin Guy's life. No, have to find some way, some other way, of helping him. What to do? What to do?

Not seeing Guy, not even touching him or hearing his voice, she couldn't sleep. Sometimes she felt herself levitating like an alien spirit. She had dreams of herself peering into a deep rockpool of normality, full of ordinary people. She circled around them on the untouchable periphery, forever apart.

Right then, inexplicably rising up in her heart but very clear – like some mythical messenger from the ocean's depth – came the answer: Jocelyn. Jocelyn was a trainee nurse, in London.

No more hesitation. Vivienne walked rapidly toward the park's telephone booth. With every step the solution raced through her mind. This was it. This was what she must do. As she opened the unyielding door it creaked, the handle was greasy from a hundred human palms. And, as the dry, curled leaves dropped down, one by one, silently onto the muddied path, Vivienne made a call.

At first Jocelyn had straightaway said, 'Oh no! No way!' Telling Vivienne she'd done some iffy things in her time – but this? This? But then they talked and talked and Jocelyn told Vivienne how much she loved her. They had shared some youthful bruises. Yes, Jocelyn understood. She hadn't forgotten her own miscarriage – and the huge relief when that had happened.

Vivienne told her about Guy: how she felt she was hurtling downhill with no brakes and with no way of turning off to safety. They agreed about Guernsey – such a very small place, with abortion illegal. Asking Edward and Jean for help was out of the equation. Jocelyn said she could see that asking Vivienne's parents for advice was impossible. So then she said yes, she'd ask around and find out what to do, what to get hold of.

It would have been helpful, Jocelyn said, if Vivienne could be a bit clearer about the pregnancy – like dates, maybe? Mmm? But Vivienne gathered all her precious times with Guy together and held them close to her. If she didn't think the pregnancy was happening, then she wouldn't have to think about ending it, would she? See? She just wanted everything to be all right again.

Jocelyn attempted some careful analysis, saying she expected that a degree of detachment was normal, given the circumstances. Vivienne said she didn't know. Didn't know anything anymore, not for certain.

So, after another clutch of deceits, Vivienne found herself back in London. The first thing she really wanted to do when she got to there was to visit Titian and the National Art Gallery. And maybe see the Kings Road. Perhaps Chelsea Art College? Foyles bookshop?

'No, not right now. Best get on with it?' Jocelyn persuaded her, giving Vivienne a doubtful look with worried eyes.

In her small flat, Jocelyn drew the curtains. She boiled a kettle and spread newspapers and a blanket on the bed. Vivienne lay down, feeling no fear, only a kind of numb acquiescence.

'I still would've liked more details, Vivienne, ideally.'

'Don't want to talk anymore,' Vivienne said, closing her eyes. She'd got this far. It was all much too late.

'Well. Here goes.' Jocelyn made the injection.

Vivienne gripped her hand as they began their wait. Jocelyn put the wireless on: first the Light Programme – Perry Como singing *Magic Moments.*

Sorry,' said Jocelyn snapping the switch onto the Home Service and a play. It was some intricate detective yarn.

'That's fine,' said Vivienne, closing her eyes. They became absorbed with the plot. Jocelyn made some tea, Vivienne liked hearing the homely sounds of cups, saucers and teaspoons clattering together with the sound of a hissing kettle as it billowed to a singing readiness.

In time, Vivienne felt no more than a mild contraction. Then some more. Jocelyn monitored them. Then, suddenly, quite without warning, discomfort rapidly escalated to pain – an excruciating pain. Vivienne called out. Then she screamed involuntarily through another wave of agony, and another with an increasingly bearing down sensation.

'Ugh! Jocelyn. God, help me. Help me.'

Jocelyn gave her some Librium and massaged Vivienne's back.

'You're…you're doing fine,' sounding like a midwife should, like they had heard midwives sound. 'Try to breathe deeply, evenly, at each…'

Presently Vivienne uttered a low, gurgling scream – a loud animal howl. Then Jocelyn shook her shoulders, 'Think of the neighbours, Vivienne! Shhh, please Viv. Here, hold this.'

She gave Vivienne a rolled flannel to bite on. Vivienne bit into the soap-smelling towelling, screaming a long, muffled scream – the devil had surely come to claim her. He thrust inside her, punching and cutting at her womb. Had her Father sent him?

Later, barely three hours, Vivienne lolled, exhausted in sweat. Her whole being felt on fire, a great weight moved slowly down her body. A burning, stretching pain pulled her flesh apart. 'Please God make this all stop!'

Jocelyn, white faced, tried hard to show both competence and concern at the same time. With as neutral voice as she could, she said she should measure the dilations now.

'You know, I reckon,' she said evenly, 'this labour is going to be quicker than we thought.' But then Vivienne saw Jocelyn bite her bottom lip. 'I need to see if the… if it's easing out yet, Vivienne. Hold on.'

Vivienne sweated out a long moan, 'Can't hold on. Can't!'

Jocelyn pulled back the red blanket she had put over Vivienne. 'Red is a comforting colour, we're told,' Jocelyn said weakly.

But the red they saw then, the flowing stream of scarlet blood and mucus, the soaked bed and blood dripping onto the rag rug on the floor, flew Jocelyn to the telephone.

Jocelyn frantically dialled for an ambulance.

'What? What's happening?' Vivienne cried out, 'I'm dying aren't I? Oh God. I'm bleeding. I'm bleeding!' She was going to pay for this, for what they had done. There was no way out of it now.

Once the call was made, Jocelyn fled back to her side and held Vivienne's hand again. 'We'll just…just calm down, and they'll soon be here. You are going to get help, now. I'm so sorry Viv. But it's all gone wrong.' Jocelyn, close to tears, patted her arm.

The shock of the haemorrhage unexpectedly calmed them. Jocelyn gave Vivienne some more Librium and made a thick pad of some towels to lodge between her legs.

Soon they sped on their way to Accident and Emergency of the large London hospital. Later, neither of them claimed total recall of that journey. Jocelyn said she thought she was helping Vivienne to get rid of a blob. 'We call them that, us nurses, 'Blobs', embryos, unformed children. You couldn't cope, otherwise. It's our way of coping. It's illegal, yes, but plenty of women terminate. Money can always buy solutions, you know.'

Since Vivienne hadn't even want to admit to it, Jocelyn had no idea that she was over twenty-one weeks into the pregnancy. Vivienne hadn't wanted to count the days. Lost in the misery of not lying next to Guy in her bed at night, of not seeing his lovely face, nor feeling his exploring mouth on hers, his arms around her, she hadn't wanted to face hard facts.

Only when Vivienne felt the blood surging out of her, wrenching her into the horror, did Guy's baby become a reality. Crying out – howling like a mad thing, she had met the woman doctor on that fearful and fateful night. Then, the real agony, worse than any she would ever know again began as Vivienne had drifted in and out of consciousness.

So it was on the Saturday, her wound still raw, Vivienne had returned to Guernsey. They kissed and she left Jocelyn and London in a distant mist.

Mercifully, Edward and Jean had gone to Jersey on a church convention. So, once she'd landed home, the first person Vivienne faced was her grandmother.

If Granmarie had known that Vivienne was pregnant, she certainly hadn't said anything about it. A normally healthy girl, Vivienne hadn't shown early on, just loosened her waistbands for the past few weeks.

Granmarie didn't seem in the least pleased to see her. She waited at the door of Granville, eyeing Vivienne up.

'What's that you've got on, Vivienne?' In her sternest voice.

'Well, ah, it's a Biba dress, Granmarie, all the fashion in London…' Vivienne finished lamely. She put her overnight bag down in the hall.

'That's what Londoners wear, is it? Wouldn't do for cliff walks, would it? Doesn't do much for you. That flighty Jocelyn's idea, was it?' Without waiting for an answer she added, 'and have you lost weight? Why were you such a long time away? That nice David Carré came to call on you.' Granmarie put her head to one side, her eyes narrowing.

Oh dear, here she went. Granmarie was tiny, living proof and the source of Vivienne and her Mother, Jean's, good cheekbones. Her glittering green eyes were lashless, her hair wisp-white. She had somehow shrunk into a waistless, boneless form, wearing a long black skirt, thick stockings and knitted jacket, on an unusually warm spring day. However, 'the Visiting Pearls', an inheritance, and a diamond bracelet were worn with a flourish.

Vivienne noted them. These were only worn on special days, days of *visite*, a part of the old Norman French ways, when people were still 'at home' to invited callers. Granmarie must be over eighty, so she claimed, and in fine condition. She hadn't forgiven Vivienne for wanting to leave the island to go and educate herself at an art college. And, God forbid, to live in London which was full of murderers, muggers and burglars, as anyone knew.

At least, Vivienne had been told endlessly, Jean and Granmarie's sons had stayed to help her. Goodness knows, Vivienne repeated the mantra in her mind, 'there was enough work to do here!'

There was more than enough to do, certainly. What with the business of growing early crops of tomatoes and carnations, chrysanthemums, roses and iris, it was a twenty-four hour a day responsibility. Now that 'her dear husband Charles had died' the boys had taken over most things. But Granmarie continued to rule and run it all.

The property had been whittled down over the years, but there was still a cottage for staff, fields, stables, greenhouses and outbuildings. Granville, the Big House of the parish, was a Victorian granite building, built by Charles' grandfather. It was austere and imposing, much like Charles himself had been, much like Guernsey, so it seemed to Vivienne.

'David Carré called? Did he? Well...I've been busy, Granmarie. I wanted to take a few days off...from my holiday allowance, you know? They work me hard at the office, they do. I have to type, take shorthand, make the tea and sometimes look after Reception telephones...' The switchboard being her special nightmare, having to wear heavy earphones and speaking into a metal mouthpiece, strapped to her chin – 'Well, it's worse than the dentist!' Calls came through on a board with numbered white balls clicking open – like fixed eyes, glaring accusingly at her inefficiency.

Breathing in deeply, filling her lungs, Vivienne sat down.

As they began to take their tea, she slowly became aware that Granmarie was staring – staring hard at her chest. Was a pearl button undone? Did she have a dirty mark?

Instantly looking down Vivienne saw, through her new Biba dress, a stealthily growing patch of wet milk.

Granmarie continued to stare, unblinking, at Vivienne's breasts. But she said nothing, holding her head rigidly, her back straight as a pillar. She smoothed her skirt, not speaking.

Nor could Vivienne speak. She held her teacup in its rose-patterned saucer, quietly in her lap. To have lifted the cup and finished her tea would have shown an unsteadied hand. Vivienne thought she might well have stopped breathing.

Granmarie broke the silence, darting a dark, reproving glance. 'I think it is time you went to your room, Vivienne. To unpack your things.' Granmarie slowly rose up and walked toward the door. 'Don't you?' She bit her lower lip and shook her head, 'And it is time you found yourself a decent man, my girl and stopped...' she hesitated, searching for correct chastisement, '...your wanton nonsense.'

Granmarie fixed her with a gaze that bore into Vivienne's very backbone. Surely, her grandmother's look said, this cannot be true? She'd always called Vivienne strong-willed, but in a proud way. Now did she suspect that she had got rid of a child? Behaved like a common whore? Surely no – Granmarie must think, not her granddaughter?

Vivienne sagged with sorrow. She had disappointed her Granmarie, who had always been there for her. Granmarie who put a banana on her pillow on the days Edward made her go to her room without supper. Granmarie, who had wrapped her motherly wings around and fed her with nourishing words when Jean disappeared again to her quiet room at the hospital.

Vivienne dearly wished she could tell her – or even lie to her, tell her it was a miscarriage, at least. That she had been forced upon and it wasn't her fault. Except…

'Oh, Granmarie.'

But Granmarie questioned her no further. Last spring, Vivienne told her she thought she loved Guy. Granmarie said it was always the same with the first love, the 'Big Love' of your life. She told her how rumours had come back to them about her affair with Guy Beaufort. That she knew Vivienne was not over Guy. But once Guy and Amanda married –? Well Granmarie had attended the wedding: a traditional marriage with serious vows. They had gone to the reception. Vivienne knew Granmarie would only advise she should accept that Guy was spoken for. She had no right to him. The 'Big Love' was over.

All at once Granmarie rounded on her, 'Oh Vivienne! If your grandfather was alive, if Charles had thought, for one moment, that – oh, go away! Go on. I don't want to see you until you have – until you feel better. You'll have to make more of a go of your life, you know, make more of yourself. Vivienne', she steadied herself with a chair, 'see things for what they are. As for your mother, as for Jean – she hasn't been…well…looking after you properly has she? Oh, she's always so unwell, grieving for that poor little boy. And Edward, always pretending to everyone – worrying about what his church people think. I don't know.' She held the door open. A thin shaft of light lit the hallway. 'I thought things would be different with you, Vivienne. I hoped you would be more like me.'

Vivienne needed some air. She brushed her grandmother's cool cheek with a shaky kiss. Vivienne left. But she had wanted to hug her, bury her head in her grandmother's bosom.

Instead, she ran wretchedly down the path, holding her breasts with her hands, where they stained with creamy milk. She ran to her father's car and looked through her bag for a handkerchief, trying to wipe away the warm liquid. She stuffed the used cloth into her dress, spreading it unevenly over her nipples. Then, with still sticky hands, tears smearing her vision, Vivienne started the engine and steered away from her grandmother and Granville. How she needed Guy.

Polly waded straight in, 'What you get up to in London, then?' She waited, coffee cup in hand, sitting on the edge of Vivienne's desk.

'Oh, you know, Polly. Shows and stuff. Shopping. Saw Jocelyn,' said Vivienne avoiding Polly's eyes.

'Uh huh. And?'

'Went for walks, in the parks,' Vivienne blinked away a flash of the labour ward, the woman doctor, the hard, unforgiving bed she'd lain on. Her hands instinctively flew over the grey pleated skirt, covering her stomach.

Instantly, Polly noticed the movement. Her bulging blue eyes widened, then narrowed. 'You look really tired old fruit. All that walking was it?'

Vivienne dropped her cup onto the wooden office floor. It smashed as coffee spilled brown splodges everywhere. After that she couldn't hold back anymore and gave in. Her shoulders shook so that all her damn stupid curls bounced around her face. She tried to cover them all with her hands at the same time, bowing down to cover her face.

Instantly, Polly relented. She put down her cup and closed the office door. 'Shhh! Don't want old Jones come wandering in, do we kiddo?' Polly mopped some tissues at the splashed coffee on the desk and the side of a grey metal filing cabinet. 'It's okay, Viv. Don't worry so, kiddo,' Polly put her arm around her. 'Had a bit of a – do , have we? Mmm? That bloomin' Jocelyn worn you out, I bet?'

Vivienne nodded, trying a wet smile, 'Sort of.'

'Tell you what. We'll go out for lunch, all right? 'Petite Fleure' have just got some lovely new tops in. Okay? We can buy on hire purchase, on tick. Put it on the slate. What the heck! Eh?'

'Okay, Polly.' Vivienne took out Granmarie's freshly laundered handkerchief from her bag. She blew her nose, flicked a 'thanks' glance at Polly and said, 'I'm better. Honestly. I feel better. Thanks.'

But she didn't and wondered if she would ever feel better again? Just couldn't get that woman doctor out of her mind. Straight after the baby had left her body, the doctor had taken savage revenge on Vivienne. Made sure Vivienne would pay for making her – a professional woman – part of an illegal, bloody act.

Could guilt make you go mad? Was that really possible? Time heals, the saying goes. But Vivienne could still touch the scarred track of an unimaginable severance. She was not yet eighteen.

CHAPTER FOUR

Vivienne could say that she was over her pregnancy. Her Guernsey doctor gave her pills to dry the breast milk. Of course there was no more bleeding. Her clothes fitted again, pretty well the same as before.

Her doctor had always been kind to her and was now sympathetic. He didn't question her at all. You didn't get contraception yourself. Didn't have the nerve and, anyway, would hardly have known what to ask for. Only men did that. Of course these rubber things weren't accident proof. Nothing was. Unplanned kids happened all the time. Then a shotgun wedding. Sometimes girls did it on purpose, to get their man.

No, Vivienne's doctor politely asked after her parents, then, more warmly, told her to look after her self and hoped the coming year would be better. He had a wrinkled forehead and over the top of his spectacles gave her a fatherly look, 'life goes on, Vivienne.' Then he called in his next patient.

At Hughes, Vivienne wrestled for normality. She missed Guy and fell into longer silences than she meant to. Polly, of course, noticed. Even Ma Jones told her she thought she was a bit too quiet for comfort.

'You ought to tell your friend to cheer up, Poll. I don't know, these arty types. They make such bad typists.' Vivienne overheard as she passed Ma Jones' office. 'And I let her beat three good applicants, you know, because she was Eddie, er, Edward's daughter. Well, he asked me to – to see if I couldn't find her a job here? He's such a good man. A fine man. Vivienne should be so grateful.'

Vivienne moved away from the door, back to her own cluttered space. She studied the shorthand pad in front of her, not really seeing it but thinking of Guy. She had seen him last Saturday in town, with

Amanda: Mr and Mrs Beaufort. And, once or twice at other times: shopping, sharing a coffee together. Guernsey was getting decidedly smaller.

She thought about Amanda. She didn't dislike her, in fact held her in, well, if not quite what you would call admiration, a kind of respectful envy – in esteem. Same like she had for the head girl at school who always passed academic exams with flying colours yet became games captain as well. But Amanda never fought back, did she? Never seemed to guard Guy against other women. Vivienne began to call Amanda 'frightened rabbit', because of the fixed stare she sometimes seemed to give her. Did she have any idea about Guy and her? Know about London? Perhaps, but didn't mind? Well, Vivienne could understand that. Because, anyway, Amanda had got him. She should care! Amanda was well and truly Mrs Guy Beaufort.

Still, if she had deceived Amanda, well so had Guy. It was his problem as well as hers. She'd sorted out enough for now. Vivienne reckoned she hadn't learnt much, but at least she had managed to realise that.

Once, she tried to talk to Jean about the baby, about the termination. After a really bad night, with dreams of black shadows flying in through the window, touching her face, flitting around the room, brushing her eyelids. She had awoken, sweating in her nightclothes, yet cold to the bone.

In the morning, Vivienne went down into the family kitchen. Granmarie was already outside, busy with the workmen. Vivienne made up a little speech, ready to talk to Jean. She found her mother sitting in the middle of the kitchen floor. Flowers spread all around her; yellow primroses, pungent with spring, violets with bruised stalks. Jean examined each flower, studying them closely. In front of her was a damask red, stiff-covered heavy book, fallen open. Jean lifted a primrose then dropped it like her fingertips were numb. She began to hum to herself. On the stove behind her a saucepan of water burned dry. Vivienne smelled charred tin. Jean picked up a violet now and examined it carefully.

'Mum?' Vivienne called, but Jean didn't look up. 'Mummy?'

Edward bustled in with George, one of the workmen. George held an empty enamel jug. Must have come to get hot water and found Jean.

Jean looked at Edward vacantly as though she didn't know his face. She stood up, letting the flowers and book still lie on the floor.

'Time to go in again, Jean. Time for your quiet room at the hospital,' said Edward gesturing for George, standing behind him, to leave them now. George withdrew, silently. Jean smiled blindly. Edward took the dried, hissing saucepan off the hob.

As her parents left the room Vivienne called out again, 'Mum, Mummy...Dad?' They both turned now, observing her as though she had just walked in.

'Yes?' asked Edward, a tired arm around Jean who'd begun crooning gently to herself. They were two thin shadows, dressed in dark clothes, like silhouettes against the white kitchen wall.

'Nothing. Nothing, really.'

Her parents left for the hospital. Vivienne knelt down and put some of the primroses and violets into the weighty book, so that they could be pressed. She fell into a sitting position, gathering up the remaining flowers for a vase. The violets were already wilting. Violets should be left growing, or they'd quickly die. How to share a lost child with Jean? Share the pain of that with her? The time had gone.

Polly had shown her time and again how to work the Gestetner copier. But all levers and switches always looked exactly the same to Vivienne. They were hostile, metal robots out to get the better of her. She never could work showers. They slipped her up as sure as soap.

Ma Jones wanted fifty copies of the report Vivienne stencil-typed onto a filmy skin, spotted with tell-tale pink varnish to cover all the errors. Polly had the afternoon off to enjoy a sunny day on the beach with her Eric.

Vivienne pressed 'ON' and jumped in her skin as a whizz began, like a dentist drill. The cold steel box sat in a mechanical threat of disapproval. She lifted the flimsy typed sheet and stretched it to fit the studs on the machine. The opaque page slid all over the place on the jet-black ink. Vivienne turned the handle so that the thick liquid oozed through the stencilled words. She fed in a wodge of paper in the tray in front. One sheet disappeared into the bowels of the tin monster and came out the other side. Yippee! It worked. A whole typed page! Only forty-nine to go! The next sheet jammed. And the next.

The afternoon passed as Vivienne alternately printed a sheet or two prizing out bits of paper with a wooden ruler. At length the required amount was completed and she lay them, drying, all around the office.

Ma Jones came in, bristling with shock. 'Vivienne! Look at your clothes! Look at your hands, and your face, they're covered with ink! This stuff is the devil to clean – Oh, I should have let Poll do it. Go and clear up, for goodness sake. I don't know.' She began to make a pile of the dried pages, her senior bosom heaving like bellows. 'Do I have to do everything around here?'

Vivienne took herself off to the tiny lavatory just off the corridor, passing an older man in his glassed-in office, hard at some accounts. Stan looked up at her with a grin of sympathy, 'We all have to learn, sweetheart,' he called out, 'turps'll do the trick,' chuckling quietly.

The car, when it hit her, knocked Vivienne sideways into the verge as easily as if she were a small child. She'd walked that day on the beach, trailing fronded seaweed, feeling salt-air on her face. The wide sandy bay swept her mind clean for a while. She breathed in the salty kelp, trailed her hands in the cold pools, thick with reddish brown anemones and pointy limpet shells. Then up the gritty cobbled slipway, onto the coast road.

The French driver, only over for the day, apologised in mortified French, in obvious, abject horror. Later he brought flowers to the hospital, shaking his young face sadly at Vivienne's plastered leg.

'*Je suis desolé!*' I am so sorry! Of course he was. The doctor said she would be in hospital at least three weeks. The ward looked clean with an empty bed either side of hers. Another hospital, a different wound. She even wished she were back at Hughes (stops you thinking, work). Fruit arrived, flowers and cards.

A funny one from Stan: 'Some people will do anything to get away from...' he'd crossed off 'work' and written in green biro '... the old monster!' Granmarie sent a homemade currant cake and some of her figs.

Edward managed to visit, 'Can't stay long, Nin. Got to see your mother later this afternoon – yes, she's stabilised. Not coming home yet awhile, though.' Then, he gave her a prayer book, with passages he thought she should read underlined in pencil, patted her hand and left her with, 'Saturday today. The Yacht Club. Lunch, must go.' A distracted smile played on his narrow lips.

Ah, yes, Saturday, Edna. Ma Jones. For some reason Vivienne almost felt sorry for her Father.

Then Polly came in, chattering, 'Hurry up and get better. It's no fun on my own, kiddo.' She crossed her bony knees and Vivienne noted the dark brown parting of her hair, like a path through corn yellow.

'I'm so pleased you've come! It's so good to see you, Polly!'

'Me too. Listen,' Polly theatrically pulled a chair close to Vivienne's bed and whispered furtively 'I've had a phone call from that Guy Beaufort.'

Eagle-eyed Polly didn't fail to notice the colour rush to Vivienne's cheeks. Vivienne flew her hands up to cover the hot pink glow and sat up abruptly, dislodging two fat hospital pillows.

'Guy? He phoned. What'd he say?' Vivienne and Polly grabbed at the sliding pillows. Keep you voice steady. Keep calm. 'What did he say?' They stuffed the pillows awkwardly behind Vivienne's back.

'Do you know, I'm really glad I've got my Eric at times like this. This 'in love' thing, it's not for me. No, a nice steady boy...'

'Yes, yes, what did Guy say, Polly, for pity's sake?'

'He wants to come and see you, tomorrow' Polly said, repeating Guy's words in staccato: 'Will that be alright?'' Polly had already started scanning through Vivienne's pile of magazines. 'Ooh! Hey, can I take *Vanity Fair*? Look, they've got an article about Julie Christie. Now isn't she gorgeous', Polly took it without further thought of permission and dumped in into her canvas bag.

'Yes. Take it. 'Course you can. Yes, she's stunning,' Vivienne numbly recalled the Chelsea girls. But what about Amanda? Oh, never mind – answer, answer, quickly. 'Yes, tell him, fine. Tell Guy fine, I'd like to see him tomorrow.' She daren't ask would he be alone? No, daren't ask that.

'Okay,' Polly said brightly, 'I'll tell him. Now, I'm off. I hate hospitals! Ta ta kiddo!' Then she fled.

In the morning it was time for a blanket bath. The nurse sponged her body clean with soap and water leaving 'what's possible' for Vivienne to manage. She asked for some talcum powder and a mirror. Her hair was a bird's nest, her face without the tan that made her teeth and the whites of her eyes look whiter. Fumbling through her make-up bag she found some Woolworth's Tawny Beige foundation and a pink Coty lipstick. They would have to do. The cotton nightdress was flower sprigged and freshly laundered. Nothing more exotic available? Damn. At the last minute she pulled down the frilled neck to show a bit of cleavage, and wet her eyelashes with spit on her fingertips.

About eleven Guy came straight in and sat on her bed, bringing not flowers but books: Aldous Huxley's *Crome Yellow*, about the painter Augustus John, a book on Van Gogh with coloured pictures and an inscription 'Get Well Soon, with Love from Guy'. Guy leaned over and turned the pages with her, so she felt the warmth of his body. In her mind she caressed his forehead, his nose, jaw, mouth. His hair was freshly showered, she wanted to reach out and touch him, to feel the damp, cut hair through her fingers.

'Flowers in a copper vase,' Guy said, with a half-smile, his liquid voice pouring over her parched sanity. 'Vincent paints – contrasting yellows, blues, greens and oranges, setting his colours either end of the spectrum – making each colour the stronger. This was the Impressionists' major trick.'

'Yes,' said Vivienne. 'I've learnt a lot more about Vincent. And Gauguin – evening classes. Remember *Sunflowers*? Our – our London trip Guy?'

'Good, Viv. You have a good teacher?' But he didn't reply on London, their London. 'You're still painting? Get to Venice if you can, for Titian, Bellini, the architecture – then Provence, Viv, Vincent's lavender fields...'

With you! I want to go there with you! Vivienne ached.

'You look well, Vivvy.'

'Don't think so.' She looked well? 'Well' meant buxom didn't it? 'Well' meant fat. She pulled the nightdress neckline up higher.

They talked some more about art. He asked what music she was listening to, had she tried Mozart? She thanked him for the books.

After a pause, Guy cleared his throat. 'The thing is...'

A chill ran through her. A sudden icy draught struck her with foreboding.

'Well, I'm, we're, Amanda and I...'

She blinked at him, speechless.

'Look, we are going to live in America, Viv. Me and Amanda. Darius's found me a sponsor. We're going to LA!' His face shone now in anticipation, 'It's all arranged. We're off next week. It's a big chance. Vivvy. Oh, Christ, now, don't look like that! I've dreaded telling you...'

She felt her eyes stinging. Her splintered leg began to throb. With her hand Vivienne indicated Guy's heaviness on the bed, easing herself away from him. Her mouth sealed shut. Her tongue wouldn't budge.

'Viv,' Guy moved closer, carefully avoiding her leg. 'Come on. I'll write. We'll always be friends. I don't know...can't do anything more. You'll find someone, Vivvy. Someone to offer you more – marriage, kids. I just can't do that for you, can I? Viv, say something.' He bowed his head sorrowfully and took her hand. He stroked it quietly for a while. She felt their pulses beating warmly together. 'I'm sorry. I really am. I'll miss you. But there we are.'

Well then don't go. Don't go! Don't leave me here on my own. But she didn't say it, forcing herself not to fling herself at him, bind him with her empty arms. Please Guy, don't go.

She shifted her wounded leg to the side, hauling herself up a little.

Guy couldn't give her kids? Hell, don't go there. What to say? What could she say?

'Well,' Vivienne jerked her head back defiantly, effecting no effort, 'America! You always said you'd go. You need to, don't you? Can't do anything here. What happened to Chelsea, London and all that?' Her throat stiffened, her chest squeezed tight.

'I've decided not to take the place up. Darius thinks what I've done is probably good enough for the States' market. He's got fantastic contacts, Viv,' his whole face lit up again. 'Film studios, all sorts. The works.'

All at once, she smiled at him. This was her Guy, animated, excited with ideas, looking to his future. 'I just have to wish you well, then, don't I? Hope all goes well for you.' She said it pointedly, not including Amanda and hoped he noticed.

'Yes, and you'll be okay, Viv? Keep on doing what you want to do. Try to get off the island more. Your parents should encourage you to do that, at least. You can have my portable record player. We'll ...I'll get something new in the States. Get Mozart, Vivvy: *Cosi Fan Tutte* – women are all the same. The trio is magic. Anyway. So, look, I'll see you sometime?'

As he got up to leave, putting her new books on the bedside locker, Vivienne imagined the baby they'd shared. The poor, lost little scrap of humanity. Now, all of Guy was disappearing. When they kissed briefly she tasted a trace of toothpaste on his soft lips, his breath smelled of tobacco.

'I'll keep in touch. I'll write – I want to. Little Vivienne Normandie!' He shook his head, briefly stroking her arm. 'Take care.'

Then, abruptly, Guy strode out, with long legs in a striped suit, square shoulders swinging forward. In a moment he had gone and she couldn't see him anymore, just the empty ward doorway and the shiny-clean corridor beyond with health and safety posters pinned on the wall:

'Have You Had Your Heart Checked?'

'Venereal Disease – Don't Die Of Embarrassment.'

A brisk nurse came bustling in with a vase of flowers in each hand. 'Well then, who's visitor was that I just saw in the corridor. What a very handsome young man!'

'He's mine,' said Vivienne, pulling the thin nightgown over her aching leg and up to her chin. 'That was Guy. And he's mine.'

By the time her leg had mended, Guy had gone. She'd kept driving past his house, walking where they had walked. Once she sat on Portelet beach, taking her book on Van Gogh, tracing the message with her finger over and over: 'Get Well Soon. With Love from Guy'.

She picked up handfuls of cooling sand, letting it trickle through her fingers. The pier where she had twirled and danced for Guy stood lapped by green sea, reflecting pools of yellow sun. Fishing boats bobbed idly with the tide. Grey gulls sat importantly on the granite boulders, watching the fishermen's every move with manic eyes.

Presently, taking her book, Vivienne strolled to the Imperial Hotel at the top of the beach and ordered a double vodka and tonic, downing it with two gulps. She ordered the same again. Through the window she imagined Guy splashing in the sea with her, under a moonlit sky. The bar was quite deserted, so only the barman, polishing a half pint glass with a linen cloth, saw the solitary tear run unchecked and drip into her empty glass.

CHAPTER FIVE

'Phone!' yelled Jean from upstairs, where she polished the wooden banisters, over and over again with waxed cloth. A pause then, 'Vivienne! Phone!'

'All right, all right, Mum,' grumbled Vivienne, in no great rush, as she headed toward the hall, a black telephone, hanging on the wall. Her mother hated answering telephones.

'Hello?' Vivienne asked tentatively, not too keen on the blessed things herself.

'Hello! Vivienne?' said a voice softly. 'It's David. David Carré. I was wondering, would you fancy a spin?'

'Oh, hi David. A spin?'

'Yes. Thing is, I've got a new VW. My new Beetle. Oh, come on, Vivienne! It'll be great fun. Go for a drink?'

Vivienne let a silence hover, 'Have you David? A new VW? Well – well, yes, I suppose that would be nice.' Yes, a breath of fresh air, get out of the house. 'Okay, then. What about "Fishpots", the new place – the pub by Town harbour. It's the in-place, Polly says?'

David agreed at once. Then, when they got there, he told Vivienne how lovely he thought she looked and toasted her. They clinked glasses of sparkling wine, although his was a spritzer, diluted with water. David didn't like, he said, drinking much. Summer was in the air. Deep inside, Vivienne felt the laced-in girdle of tension around her heart ease slightly.

They met up every Saturday after that, then each Tuesday as well. At Granville's front door, Vivienne began waiting for the blue Beetle – with the fair David, grinning inside it – with a kind of expectant comfort. David said he felt the same, that he liked her company, very much. Meantime, Granmarie went around with a ridiculous smirk on her face.

When they made love, one sunny afternoon on the secret sandbanks of Oyster Point on Herm island, bleached white by the sun, near the warm Gulf Stream sea, Vivienne shut her eyes, trying hard not to stiffen up. What if she rejected David's body? She hadn't had any sex since the abortion, not since Guy.

But then David stroked her, kissing her briefly all over so that her limbs just let go. Light touches of his hands slowly released pulses of urgent need from her. When he lightly entered her, she felt little resistance, just a moment of searching until fear, that the wounded place might be discovered, passed as she suddenly opened like a sunflower responding to the sun's heat.

'Vivienne, you are wonderful,' David said, holding her tight to him as he finished to orgasm.

'And you, David.' Vivienne held in a deep breath, letting it out slowly with, 'Really, really.' She stroked his face. He had come so close to her special place, where the baby had grown, from where it had been taken away. Now, the place revisited, it closed with relief as he withdrew. After a moment, she loosened entirely and straddled, flat out and boneless in David's arms.

David wrapped them both up in soft, green and white striped towels like babes in swaddling. Now and then they shifted to move off spiky marram grass and onto the sand again. Drowsily, they gazed at the warm azure sea.

'Like being on a tropical island, isn't it? All of our own,' Vivienne said.

'Mmm. And we are castaways.'

'Cast away on Herm, cast away on paradise,' Vivienne smiled at him.

David had brought his portable transistor radio. As Vivienne lay in the sensual sun, eyes closed, *A Summer Place* played quietly in her ear. Vivienne hummed the tune. David joined in. He closed his eyes as well and sent his hand searching for hers, blindly on the hot sand. Their hands linked automatically. Under the searing rays Vivienne imagined they lay, spread-eagled, like two basking starfish marooned, humming a summer song.

Later, Vivienne searched for moisturiser in her beach bag. For some reason a soreness between her legs bothered her. A damp, sanded bathing costume wasn't helping. She recalled the same soreness, after the – come now, stop it. Stop it! Then she'd excused herself to David and went to the toilets, just a hut at the top of the bay. She smoothed some soothing lotion between her legs.

David had fallen asleep. Although he was fair-haired he'd got a deep tan from working outdoors for his father on their land. Lying next to him, Vivienne took some of the blond hair on his chest and twirled some tufted strands between her fingers. He didn't wake. Then Vivienne thought, well you have to carry on, don't you? You can't keep looking back. She peered at an elusive blue horizon, almost lost in a sea mist, then back at the sleeping David. Well then, here they were. He had a fit, outdoor worker's body. She sat up and massaged some stuff on her sunburnt legs that Jocelyn had recommended, olive oil and vinegar mixed. David said her legs were shapely. She had shapely legs! And he actually liked frizzy hair, it was curly he said and he much preferred it to straight.

'What do you think, then? Mr Right?' Vivienne said aloud to the slumbering David and to Guy who was so far away.

Everyone, Polly, Jocelyn, Granmarie answered her question 'What do you think, then? Mr Right?' with: 'David Carré? Oh yes, he's nice, he's really nice!'

Granmarie declared herself so delighted at Vivienne's engagement, she couldn't have been more pleased than if she had arranged the match herself. Edward showed more caution, saying he wanted to know David Carré a bit more – satisfy himself that he was neither a heathen nor a drinker.

David passed both tests, telling Edward he attended Torteval Church every Sunday morning, didn't smoke and drank moderately. In fact, Vivienne had noticed David didn't drink alcohol when he drove. He didn't want to damage the beloved blue Beetle – and didn't, ever, let her drive it, especially, he said, since she got mixed up one day and called the crankshaft a 'cruikshank'.

'Well,' David said 'you wouldn't let anyone that clueless about cars drive yours, now would you, be honest?'

Jean just went along with Granmarie and Edward, since, she said, Granmarie always knew what was right and it meant not having to make a decision herself.

'He's from a good family, though isn't he Nin?' asked Jean, nervously arranging some white chrysanthemums, putting the vase on the top of their polished piano.

'Yes, mum. The Carrés, don't you remember?' Vivienne replied.

Edward still fretted, 'Well, we hope you'll settle down now, Nin. Stop all that lounging about with books, scribbling and fiddling about with paints, neglecting your appearance, worrying your mother.'

'I don't worry Mum! Did she say that? Did you say that, mum?' said Vivienne.

'Not in as many words, no,' Edward lowered his voice, 'and I don't tell her all that Edna, er, Mrs Jones tells me. Still, I can see your Mother does get concerned. I've had to protect her, haven't I Nin? Eh? From some of your…little secrets? We pray for you nightly.' Said Edward, giving Vivienne a queer look that she found faintly ominous.

David took to coming round to Granville to see Granmarie. David's father, Eustace, grew tomatoes and flowers as well. David knew all about horticultural, seasonal work, running a successful growing business. He'd grown up with it.

In her bedroom, overlooking the little meadow with its pond, surrounded by green fields, Vivienne kept a store of vodka in a cupboard. Guy had told her it was the most fashionable drink in Chelsea right now, all the girls drank it. On a wall she'd hung her painting, the copy of *Bacchus and Ariadne*. She'd toast it now and then. She'd shown it to David. He'd ruffled Vivienne's hair and said it was very good, but all that mythology stuff and Greek heroes was beyond him. Couldn't be doing with ancient history. Not his thing at all.

When Vivienne drank, the abortion, losing Guy, the tedium of Hughes all whirled into oblivion. In a sober moment a thought came to her – not exactly what you would call before time – she would leave Hughes. She'd get a job in Town. There would be more life and it would be much more 'with it' – more trendy, even.

Ignoring Edward's angry protestations, Vivienne answered an ad in the local newspaper: the *Guernsey Post* wanted a typist. No shorthand! No reception duties! Less money, but what the hell? Vivienne got the job.

New man. New job. Things were changing. The day she left, Hughes threw a little party. Vivienne swallowed warm white wine and let a lukewarm sausage roll slide down her throat. Polly grimaced as she gulped the tepid wine. They pulled faces at each other in mutual support.

Ma Jones sidled up to Vivienne. 'Well then. Good luck, Vivienne,' she said. 'I hope you enjoy the newspaper work. After all, we've helped you along – trained you. Your father – such a good man – is very disappointed, but I daresay we can fill your place soon enough.' Looking like she could hardly wait to bundle Vivienne out of the door, Ma Jones glanced at Polly then back again at Vivienne. 'Oh, and by the way…'

Parting shot?

'Guy Beaufort came to see you, that time you were in hospital, with your leg, didn't he?'

Vivienne's heartbeat stopped as her face reddened. Oh, God! Would Ma Jones tell Amanda? Did they know each other? What had Polly said? Vivienne's breath faltered and heat rose around her collar. She nodded a wary agreement.

'Mmm?' Vivienne said and stole a look at Polly, where flaky crumbs from the sausage roll had stuck to her mouth as she choked nervously into her hand. Vivienne licked away some sticky pastry flakes from her own lips.

'Well,' Ma Jones stared at Vivienne's discomfort as her mouth dropped open. Polly coughed haplessly behind her. 'Well, Rita was waiting for him in her car. Yes, in the car park. Rita Roussel. My niece is a nurse you know, going to the top, that one. Probably make staff nurse,' Ma Jones blinked rapidly to show her pride, 'anyway, as

I say, she saw them leave together. Shame, isn't it, the way that that Guy Beaufort treats little Amanda, his wife.'

Ma Jones wriggled her rotund body, her pearls swung as she turned to get another glass. Like a painted doll's face, two livid red spots, burnt on Ma Jones' cheeks. Avoiding further eye contact with Vivienne, she turned to talk to Stan.

Vivienne darted her eyes into Polly's. Was it true? Polly's creased brow, down turned mouth and nodding blonde head told her, 'Yes.'

Afterward, in the cloakroom, wedged close together, Vivienne shook as they put their coats on. 'Why didn't you tell me, Polly? Why not?' Vivienne did her buttons up wrong, having to start again.

Polly fetched Vivienne's turquoise scarf from the hook, wound it around Vivienne's neck and said, 'Cos of this. Kiddo, I'm sorry about Rita. Don't leave. It won't be the same.'

Vivienne finished dressing, standing still for a moment. Polly had said that before – that it wouldn't be the same after she had left, that they might not keep in touch. Even on such a small island you could lose track of someone.

'Oh, it's not your fault, Polly. I'd have probably not said either, done the same if it were you and your Eric. We'll keep in touch, course we will. Don't worry. Come in to Town sometimes for lunch? I'll want to know what the new girl's like. How things go.'

'Yeh. Course. See you around, kiddo. See you soon.' They kissed.

Vivienne left with neither another word to Ma Jones nor even a last look back at her cramped office. Goodbye to the sawdust, the noisy saws, the monstrous, inky Gestetner, the dreaded switchboard eyeballs.

By Hughes' entrance door, David waited patiently in his blue Beetle to take her home. Vivienne got in, saying, 'Can we go to The Prince of Wales for a drink?'

David started the engine as a man cycled past them. Stan tapped on the window and blew Vivienne a kiss. Vivienne blew one back to him and waved goodbye. From the back window, Hughes' granite building and the grey cobbled harbour gradually slipped from

Vivienne's view.

Agreeing, David took them. It came to Vivienne, how she had sat there with Guy and listened to the murmur of smoky voices. The place smelled of beer and the vodka shot when it came was good and fiery.

She put up no resistance now to David. She had had enough of holding back. Was tired of it. They held hands and didn't leave until closing time.

Their wedding turned out to be a real family affair. Vivienne didn't want extravagant fuss and anyway, since both David and Edward erred on the frugal side, 'Nothing too fancy' suited fine. As it happened, both Granmarie and Jean had jointly declared 'Quality not quantity', from early on.

Granmarie insisted the reception would be held at Granville. So the Normandies and Granmarie Bordeaux could display to their family and friends that they needed no hotel to cater for them, thanks very much. Their home and grounds were more than capable of entertaining in splendid style.

Come the day, their fresh flowers blossomed everywhere. Granmarie instructed that only the very best blooms from her crops be picked and used for ma petite Vivienne and 'her gentleman', David Carré's, wedding.

They set up a buffet in the dining room, with home-cooked hams, platters of sliced pink beef and the moist white breasts of Granmarie's hand-plucked chickens. Bowls of freshly cut green salad from the kitchen garden and fruit from their orchard vied for space. Jugs of golden Guernsey cream stood invitingly on the table.

For this was a union of two Guernsey families, where sacred vows, Edward said in his speech, had been taken seriously. The importance of hereditary values: of land and of property, were still vital in Guernsey and for the Carrés, the Normandies and Bordeaux. Vivienne and David were the future, linked to the traditions and history of their island.

Hosts and guests toasted them heartily with Champagne.

'A fancy white wedding, just for show, comes a poor second to this sensible match,' said Granmarie, twinkling. 'Ah, I've thanked Charles. Oui, I've prayed to him and the good Lord, Eternel, you know.'

As they stood together, Jean approached Vivienne and David. Her face was worryingly flushed with excitement, 'Dear David, we've known your family for sometime, haven't we Edward?' Jean leaned over and tugged her husband's coat sleeve, as he chatted to another group of people. David and Edward nodded cordially at each other.

'Where do I remember seeing you once, David? It was quite recently.' Said Jean. 'At a wedding, was it...? Where was it? You were sitting at the next table...'

Oh no. Vivienne thought: Guy's wedding.

Jean pushed her fingers over her flushed, furrowed brow. Edward, instantly at her side interrupted, saying maybe Jean should stop worrying herself and think, maybe, of a lie down?

David answered Jean, 'We did meet a while a go, Mrs Normandie. At a wedding, yes sometime ago, I think. And I must say, I am glad you are well again.' David bent and kissed Jean lightly on the cheek.

'Charmed. Thank you David! It is David, isn't it? Your name? Do we know your family?' Jean rubbed her forehead again.

'Yes, well, come along, Jean.' Edward began to steer Vivienne's mother out of the room. 'Your room is ready. Nice and quiet. A nice little rest?' Edward guided her toward the door.

'Want some help, Dad?' Vivienne moved to accompany them.

'No, no, Nin. We'll be alright. You see to your guests.' For once, Vivienne caught a thankful glance from her Father.

Vivienne looked around her at the relaxed gathering, the elegant beauty of the flowers – all that polishing and rolling up of carpets had been worth it.

Granmarie had seen to it that everyone she wanted was there: the Le Croixs, the Bordeaux and all the Carrés, of course. Edward invited their friends from church, and his Yacht Club people. Including Edna Jones.

Polly had come with Eric. Jocelyn couldn't come, 'Nursing

exams, darling. Nearly done now.' Polly, moist-eyed, said how lovely Vivienne looked, dressed in a sky blue silk wedding costume, with matching blue cap caught to one side with silk leaves. Vivienne adjusted her orchid corsage, Granmarie's pearls and diamond brooch. The bouquet weighed heavy with orchids, Granmarie's finest white carnations and a mass of green fern. David looked shy in dark blue lounge suit, a single white carnation with feathery fern bound in silver foil in his buttonhole.

Jean's niece, Janet, eight years-old, was the flower girl in a white silk frock with puffed sleeves and scalloped hem, short white socks and sandals, white gloves and a tightly gripped carnation posie.

Actually, saying their vows had seemed solemn. Vivienne stumbled on 'not knowing any impediment' to their union, just could not get the word out: 'iped...impede...'. In the finish, the priest said it for her, to a ripple of amusement in the congregation behind her.

David had taken Vivienne to be his lawful wedded wife. Granmarie beamed, Edward looked relieved. Jean said she recognised the church – hadn't there been a funeral here – someone young? A child, was it?

Vivienne sipped another glass of the apple tasting wine. David, although laughing, had commented shouldn't she slow down a little? Something like that.

Cousin Tom had been asked to play the shining – specially tuned – ebony grand piano. So, formalities over, *We'll gather lilacs in the spring again* and *Waltz of my heart* tinkled throughout the rest of the afternoon and way into the mild evening. Cousin Tom's repertoire didn't run beyond Ivor Novello but the music lent a gentle air.

Muriel Le Croix found herself at Vivienne's elbow. She was dressed in a dark pink woollen suit. 'Well, congratulations my dear,' she said to Vivienne. 'You look very well. We wish you a long and happy married life.'

'Oh, thank you Mrs Le Croix,' feeling herself going as pink as the suit Amanda's mother wore. More champagne urgently needed, Vivienne swallowed, forcing down the wine in a gulp.

'Oh, and you'll be interested to know...', Muriel Le Croix fixed

a determined expression on Vivienne's face, 'Amanda, well Guy and
Amanda of course, are expecting a baby. Isn't that nice? They are
doing so well, in America. Although they travel, of course – they've
only just come back from Venice again! Guy does so love his art,
doesn't he?'

Muriel Le Croix held her head back, as if waiting for Vivienne's
answer.

Escape! How can she escape? But she had to stay put and say,
'No, no, I hadn't heard about the, the, um, the baby, or them lately.'
Vivienne tried a light-hearted laugh – 'Ha!' But it sounded just like
a mad cackle. At least, though, she did know about the Europe trip,
Guy had written to her ('Love Venice! Saw Titian's *Assumption*! You
must – underlined 'must' three times – get to Venice, Vivvy') but Guy
hadn't mentioned any baby.

Hot, Vivienne tried to move away, 'Well. Give them my
congratulations!' She said. Then, thankfully Muriel Le Croix moved
away to join Amanda's father. Did Vivienne imagine satisfied stares
boring into her back? Possibly – then again, maybe paranoia was
setting in. So, the London trip – when Guy was 'sort of', only 'kind
of', you understand, engaged to Amanda – hadn't gone unnoticed,
hadn't been forgotten.

Polly spotted the whole thing. 'What's with her and Ma Jones?
I hadn't heard either, kiddo. Honest.' They both let their glasses be
filled to the brim. 'Eric's driving. Still, that, you know, that Guy thing.
That's all over and done with now, isn't it? You just look after yourself
now, kiddo. You've got your David now. Mrs Carré! Promise?'

Vivienne thought she had made many promises that day. She
wanted to keep them all. But babies: Amanda and Guy having a little
baby together?

Amanda would have a round, pregnant stomach, like the other
women Vivienne seemed to encounter everywhere. (She had thrown
her baby away, did they know? Vivienne had lost hers.) Oh, to rip out
the pages of that chapter in her life – rip them up and throw them to
the wind!

David frowned at her, looking mildly anxious. A waiter hovered, with a bottle wrapped in a white napkin and nearly passed her by but Vivienne thrust her glass forward. Come on, she mouthed over to David's disapproval. It's our wedding day? With raised eyebrows, she made a silent plea for his permission. David made a reproving smile back

After all, yes, Vivienne may be Mrs David Carré, but she hadn't made a vow not to drink champagne, now had she? You couldn't celebrate your own wedding day and not drink champagne, enough champagne to drown in, now could you?

CHAPTER SIX

The Carrés gave Vivienne and David a lump sum of money as a wedding present. David promptly banked it. Edward approved, telling Vivienne she had a thrifty husband in David and how he never let her mother anywhere near their accounts or bank statements either.

There was a small bungalow for staff on the Carré land, currently empty, which Vivienne and David rented. David said he wanted them to buy a plot and build their own place one day. David insisted they must save and build.

The bungalow was built in their field next door to the Carré family farmhouse, La Colette. Vivienne thought the house was lovely, approached by a long drive La Colette reposed in wooded pastures, bordered by low hedges on cliffs overlooking a distant sea.

For people still in their twenties, Vivienne reckoned they'd started out on married life quite well, hadn't they? David hung Vivienne's oil painting of *Bacchus and Ariadne* in their sitting room, because he thought the colours exactly matched the existing curtains his mother, Pearl had made. The room had French windows, over-looking a flower-filled garden. Pearl was a keen gardener as well.

Guy sent her a couple more letters. Vivienne explained to David that they were old school friends. David didn't pursue the matter further. He was a busy man, he said, he didn't go in for digging around someone's past. David lived for the present – saved for the future, well, you had to. Debt was a terrible thing. Nothing worse, except moral misbehaviour.

Vivienne avoided going to church with David on Sunday mornings, leaving that to Eustace and Pearl. David did ask her to, now and then, but she managed to opt out. She'd still had her evening classes and there was always homework to do, so she found, and research, which she enjoyed.

Once David left for the vinery, Vivienne tore open the air-mailed envelope. Guy wrote that he had attended soirées with Darius in uptown New York. He'd met an artist who was all the rage – 'Andy Warhol, Vivvy! You won't believe what he did with tins of Campbell soup! And silkscreen posters of Marilyn Monroe! Viv. This is all I wanted it to be.'

Though Vivienne envied him, she felt glad for Guy. Maybe what she had done had been worth it? It had to have been.

'David. Let's have some soirees,' said Vivienne one day. 'Perhaps – say, Sunday mornings?' She brought out a wooden chopping board.

'Some what?' David scraped his Wellington boots clear of mud on the scraper outside the back door before coming into the kitchen.

Vivienne chopped red ripe tomatoes, still warm from the greenhouse, for their soup. 'Soirées. They're a kind of get together for artists and musicians and writers, you know?'

'We don't know any. Anyway, Sunday morning is out.'

'Yes we do, there's Peter from my evening class and…' Vivienne thought hard.

'Peter? I thought you said he's doing photography.' Said David.

'Well, that counts, doesn't it? And Polly and Eric could come,' she added, doubtfully.

'Vivienne, what are you on about now? Are you saying we'd have to get a load of wine in and all those cheesy things? No, I think that's daft.'

She finished the tomatoes and plonked them, hissing excitedly, with the frying onions in the saucepan, then added chicken stock. The smell made her ravenous, but at any rate it was a low calorie recipe. 'Well, at least a party, then? A housewarming?'

'We've been here two years nearly! But…' As Vivienne pulled a crestfallen face, 'oh, okay, as long as it doesn't cost an arm and a leg. And not called a bloody soiree.'

'Gooddee! I'll get Polly to help.' The soup tasted sweet and creamy, just like Granmarie made.

They chatted together as the music of The Mamas and Papas and

Karen Carpenter's haunting voice enlivened the party.

'Let me be the one who loves you,' sang Karen Carpenter, 'let me be the one.' The soiree went on until dawn.

For the next one Vivienne phoned all their friends asking them each to bring a bottle. 'I'll make the chilli-con-carne.' She bought breadsticks and Polly brought potato crisps and peanuts and put them in dishes all around. They pushed back the furniture, opened the French windows, not stopping until they were exhausted.

Vivienne did like a drink at lunchtimes. Bet people did in New York at Andy Warhol soirees, and in Venice and London? Be sure they did! It was the 'in-thing', Vivienne would say, to David's frown, 'it's cool, man.'

At least Vivienne didn't have to drag herself to the new job every morning. Getting to know the news first, being in the swing of things lifted dark imaginings.

Straight away, Jessie palled up with her. Newly divorced, 'Sassy, and ready to rock and roll! It's high time, Vivienne,' Jessie said, smoothing her hands down her own slender figure, tossing back her shiny long hair, 'you had highlights put in that frizzy mop of yours.' Jessie wore a red leather mini-skirt and had panda-black lined eyes. 'And, not funny, Viv, but you could do with losing at least a stone.' Jessie marched them off to Bon Marché in Smith Street, St Peter Port, and bought some trendy gear: diaphanous paisley patterned shifts, off the shoulder sun tops. (A small deposit then weekly payments, you see?)

David didn't wholly disapprove, well – not as much as Vivienne feared. He said he didn't think Vivienne needed to change, but if she wanted to, that was okay by him. He said girlies needed to do girly things and he had hundreds of new tomato seedlings to plant out – had to keep an eagle eye on the weather. Oh, tomato growing was a full time job, no mistake. Eustace, his father, really needed him. And, anyway, David liked work.

It took Vivienne ages, well over a year, but she could now get into a size 10, a size 8 if she didn't eat for a week and took pills to get rid of water retention. Even then, she'd slide up to a 12 in a matter of days if she ate anything she really wanted to – like the home-made chips she'd had to give up. And crisps, cheese, bacon sandwiches…

Platinum highlights streaked the curls. Vivienne pulled brown suede and black leather mini-skirts over the top of her slimmed down legs. She learned how to sit down carefully.

Pearl Carré, her mother-in-law, on the church committee, complained and said well things weren't like that in her day. Especially once you were a married woman. David said she'd told him to control his wife. And that their parties were becoming the talk of Torteval parish. The noise, the drinking! This was one of the quietest areas on a small island – what was Vivienne thinking of? Did she think they were living in London? Soho? Or with that bohemian Chelsea set Vivienne always went on about?

One evening as they watched *The Newcomers* on television, David started up. 'Look, Vivienne, mum's right. You're – dressing up – an awful lot lately. You didn't used to. Drinking too much, too. Why can't you…?'

Vivienne lay back on the sofa, letting her hair fall in wavy streamers, 'Come on, David. It's just socialising. I don't want to live like our parents did.' Vivienne didn't want to hurt him, so didn't say 'what about you?' Could it be right to only want sex every other month or so, over in a minute? And then when he wanted it, not her. Even when they did, it seemed – kind of mechanical, like he was polishing his VW or something. Because he needed to, like sex was a necessity, not because he really wanted to do it or really wanted her.

What about the time she'd, on a warm afternoon, taken him by the hand into the bedroom then he'd said he'd just eaten and wanted to rest before going back to work? And, on a picnic, she'd made his favourite pork pie and ham sandwiches. Then, nobody could see them, she'd taken off all her clothes, right there in the grass, and held her arms up to him. He made her put her things right back on, saying what a very common thing to do! David said that sex took place in a bedroom, in private.

Well, what about Herm?

'That was when we were young. We're married now. We don't do it in the backs of cars now, either, do we? We've – we've grown up, Vivienne.'

They were adults, then, and yes, she liked her vodka. But it wasn't affecting her work. So she didn't have a problem. It wasn't a problem.

Often David went down to see Granmarie, in the north of the island. Granmarie was always glad, she told Vivienne, to see David. She liked walking with him to see her orchards: the pears, apples, cherries and the spreading fig trees. Her sons laboured, chin high, amongst thorny red rosebuds and thickly scented carnations. All round the vinery, workmen toiled. Heavy trusses of reddening tomatoes, with hairy green leaves, made a peppery-smelling tropical forest.

The dusty yard behind the stables heaved busy with lorries, loading up for the St Peter Port market, the harbour and airport. David told Vivienne he understood this culture. He respected Granmarie. He and Granmarie talked about the 'vineries' that had once been exactly that, years ago. Grapes had been exported to France and England. Now, these other crops were more marketable, more profitable. David understood the value of generations – of inherited land and family responsibilities.

The Carrés were landowners in Torteval. La Colette was in the south of Guernsey. Vivienne was aware that David knew how important this place of his elders was, of seniority and handed down knowledge. David said they should accept advice from people who knew their soil, knew their produce. He said he listened, properly, to Granmarie as she related her tales with a speech traced through with the Norman patois of the Guernsey French.

'My grandfather,' Granmarie told Vivienne and David, 'employed many more than me. The same men stayed all winter with us – when the soil needed to be cleaned, ready for next season. We gave them all work all winter, all year. That's why they stayed.'

Granmarie showed them photographs of women in starched white lace and black satin, hand-embroidered dresses. They wore rows of jet beads, the men stiff white collars. These were the people that had provided her family with a living and, with that, their fortunes.

'My grandmother had servants. She never washed her own hair, nor took a bus. They had French maids, from Brittany. They were true gentry, with carriages and horses. When Great Aunt Elise took the carriage to St Peter Port, there were no houses either side of the road, until half way to Town.

When Granmarie's Great Aunt shopped in Town, by appointment, shopkeepers pulled out a chair for her. When they visited a beach (only on Sunday afternoons) it was by carriage. Guernsey aristocrats had an allegiance to the British Crown, but not her Government. Here, in Guernsey, aristocracy was your property and how you treated it – how you behaved toward your kin and your staff.'

David understood, telling Vivienne Granmarie came from another age. This woman was to be revered. To this woman, David would turn for counsel.

Granmarie's green eyes twinkled diamante whenever David was in sight. She told Vivienne that David was the only man of hers she ever approved of. All was not lost with her, even if London had, well, tried to tempt her into wicked ways. She hadn't gone and left Guernsey for that awful place, that England. David Carré was la petite Vivienne's soulmate. Granmarie told her so, often enough.

Soul mate? Could David be? What about if her soul was damned already? Vivienne couldn't tell Granmarie about the cold bed, about no more making love in sunny fields or powder-soft sand dunes on warm afternoons.

Granmarie told Vivienne about her own teenage years. The merchant and farming families, the better off, had a tradition for recognising when their boys and girls were coming into adolescence. At sixteen she put up her hair and let down her skirts. After Sunday church, instead of going home with their parents, the unattached young were permitted to meet at their parish church gate. The girls grouped in one spot, the boys nearby in another. A boy would ask to walk you home. But he was not invited into the house until you were certain he was the right one. It would have been thought fast and the boy rushed into marriage. Once the boy had been approved of, the other boys held back, giving him a better chance. After being invited in for a meal, the couple were regarded as engaged. 'That's how I met mon chiaer, Charles.'

One day Granmarie told Vivienne the sad news that Amanda Beaufort had lost the child she and Guy were expecting. Apparently Amanda had been very upset about it. Vivienne herself had had a couple of early scares, hardly pregnancies at all. She was on, then off the Pill. They were, sort of, trying for a child. At the rate David was going she began to worry if it would ever happen. Did not having an orgasm make you infertile? Vivienne felt sorry for Amanda, though. Really. Honestly. She didn't deserve that kind of pain. What did Guy feel? What the hell do men know?

Through their bedroom window the distant sea lay beyond luminous green fields. On sunlit days tall grasses swayed. The fields looked like Van Gogh's cornfields, the ones he painted when he was young, before he became so ill.

Sometimes, though, colour faded and Vivienne felt closed in, as though grey wrapped around her. Then she didn't feel anything she touched nor breathed fresh air. Stop drinking so much, then. Was that it? Tell the pictures in her mind of the baby, of Guy, to go away, leave her alone. Let her be.

The Coal Hole did good pub grub. Jessie took their plates, quiche and chips, to their accustomed nook. They unwrapped the paper towels from around their cutlery. The place was filled with newspaper people, the usual crowd. Bars always reminded Vivienne of Guy; all that smoke and dim lighting, so that she found herself looking for him, forgetting he wasn't on the island any more.

Did he think of all their times: Portelet, London, the Van Gogh book – 'Get well soon. Love from Guy,'? What did he do in America – was he faithful to Amanda? Maybe there was another Rita? Chelsea birds, New York City swingers? LA chicks? She bet there were.

Some of the boys from photography joined them. Vivienne and Jessie bunched up to make more room. Vivienne knew Peter mostly, he was even shorter than she was, always wore open-necked shirts and had sticky-out ears, like an elf. He was doing the O-Level art course. Peter sat next to her from time to time at the evening class.

He needed to get more qualifications, he said.

When she'd first told him about her soiree idea he'd laughed out loud. 'What, in Guernsey? A soiree? No chance!' Then admitted he had been wrong and enjoyed her parties.

She told Peter about Guy meeting Andy Warhol in New York. 'Yeh? Sounds like Guy. Guernsey's not for him. Hardly the United States of America, is it? It's not even as big as a small town in England, let alone a City. Actually I know Guy Beaufort fairly well. We drop a line now and then. Went to the same school. He was a year above. Yeh, he's a talented bugger.' With his wide grin, a line from ear to ear with square, spaced out teeth, Peter looked like a leprechaun.

Vivienne leapt in, 'You know Guy?'

'Well, yeh, as it goes.'

'Tell him you've seen me, next time, will you? And…will you tell me' (easy, easy now) 'what he's up to?'

'Sure, next time.' Peter nodded casually whilst darting a shrewd glance at her.

When Vivienne asked David if she could go on 'a culture vulture trip, David', and see Jocelyn in London, he said they couldn't afford it. And it was the same when she pleaded to see Venice and then an exhibition in Madrid, Spain. Their evening class lecturer had recommended it. Guy said the 'Bacchanals', the two pictures Titian had painted to go with *Bacchus and Ariadne* were in Madrid.

'Can't I go, David, please?' Vivienne stood tiptoe, jumping up and down. 'Some of the other students are going.'

'No, Vivienne. You know how expensive that'd be. Flying first to England, probably an overnight stay in a hotel, then the flight and accommodation. UK Hotel and flight back to Guernsey. No, we can't do it. Not yet.'

'There's the wedding money, it's just sitting there,' Vivienne stopped jumping, standing with her arms hung down.

'That's for our future. Our own place. Trips for art and all that… well, it's not a priority, is it?' said David. 'Is it?'

So, really, that's where she was when the photography boys started teasing Jessie, talking about a party they were going to and did Vivienne want to come too?

'It's going to be a real party. You know, Jessie,' the boys said, giggling stupidly, 'plenty of stuff going around.' Jessie nodded, and said yes, she knew exactly what kind of party.

'Come on, Viv. You like parties. Come on your own. Don't need to drag that David of yours with you. It'll be fun. Promise.' Jessie winked a three-times-mascara'd eye at Vivienne, her straight brown mane hanging over her shoulder like a tawny silk scarf.

'What's all this? Who would you be going with?' David sat at the kitchen table, absently sifting through some invoices, spiking the 'Paid' ones.

'Jessie. Jessie asked me,' said Vivienne, not mentioning the photography boys.

'Where is it?' David moved to the sink, stripped off his shirt and washed his hands and arms right up to the shoulder, then his chest. Vivienne regarded his brown skin, still toned, and the blond hair that fuzzed his arms. She imagined Herm, when they were castaways in paradise and put her arms around him. David pulled the plug out of the sink, let some cold water run to hurry the soapsuds away. He took Vivienne's arms away from him, one by one. 'Not now, Vivienne. I'll be on the go until after ten tonight. I'll get too tired. We've got to ship off by six tomorrow morning. Me and the men have to grade all the tomatoes, you know that and box them up. And Olive's been off today, insisting it's Monday Wash Day! I don't know, that woman…' He sighed.

'I'm not sure where the party is,' said Vivienne, deflated. 'Bit of a mystery, really. But Jessie seems to know the crowd giving it. Oh, go on, David, it'll be a bit of fun.' She bumped into the ironing board, 'Damn thing,' folded it up and put it away in the scullery. Coming back into the kitchen she said, 'I'll do you a really, really, nice roast for Sunday! What d'you say?'

'Oh, alright then. Go on. Will it make up for Madrid and Venice?' He made a tired smile at her as she jumped up and down again. 'But mum and dad are coming over for lunch, after church, don't forget.' He finished drying himself and hung the towel up on the hook at the side of the kitchen cupboard.

'Yes! Okay it's a deal,' Vivienne plopped him a loud kiss on his chest and smelled Palmolive soap.

For the party, Vivienne hooked out a tulip-shaped long black shirt that showed her new waist off, and a white mutton-sleeved blouse with a high neck (courtesy of Jessie's cajoling.) Thank God for hire purchase. She back-combed her hair, swished it up – pleased about her blonde streaks – into a chignon, then outlined her eyes with a kohl black pencil. She caked white powder over her eyelids, like the Chelsea models, adding a brush of pale blue shadow on top. Three coats of mascara and pale pink, almost white, lipstick.

The black coat, just skimming her ankles, had a black, fur-lined hood. It was Julie Christie, Dr Zhivago style (part of the HP, don't tell David). Vivienne jingled her car keys as she went out the door. She was allowed to drive David's VW now, especially since he'd scraped it several times with tractors in the narrow lanes.

'Just off then, David. Won't be late.'

She heard David's muffled voice as he searched in the living room for *Growers World*, 'Okay, Vivienne. I'm just going to check out an article on market prices. Be good.'

Vivienne fled.

On the Crown Pier, St Peter Port harbour, she met Jessie. They'd parked their cars.

'So, where's this party then, Jessie?' Vivienne asked, 'in the Town?'

'Right here, Viv, look down,' Jessie's eyes shone gleefully, like a child exposing a naughty secret.

Moored to the pier floated an obviously very expensive white yacht. It swayed with enticement. They climbed down the iron ladder rung by rung to board the craft. Vivienne noticed the tide was high. The yacht rolled on the dark green swell of the sea. Outstretched hands helped them into the sea-borne den.

Someone threw off the moorings. The yacht glided smoothly out of the harbour, ploughing a wavy trail of shifting colour behind it. Orange lights from the St Peter Port shops flickered reflections.

They pushed their way into the noisy, crowded cabin. 'Hi,' said Peter, the photographer, 'Welcome aboard, Vivienne. What's your poison?'

CHAPTER SEVEN

Several 'poisons' were on offer: spirits, cannabis and something suspiciously stronger as far as Vivienne could tell. The fug reminded her of the Eight Bells in London. She put her vodka on the bottle-cluttered bar. Her full glass spilt as she looked around.

The smoky cabin, stuffy and loud, deafened with chatter. The yacht swayed, anchored some way off Guernsey's coast, out of sight, away from prying eyes and restricting laws. Jessie had, at once, found a bench seat and snuggled up with one of the photographer boys.

Vivienne recognised a retired, elderly doctor, then a couple of professional men, always in the media. Who would have thought it? Some stoned looking faces grinned at her, spliffs in hand as the alcohol flowed. She thought of Edward and what on earth he would say.

Peter closed right in, saying blearily, 'How's you?'

Vivienne felt his hand try to fondle her over the black skirt. 'Have I told you I think you are gorgeous? Did I say that?' Peter took a drag from his cigarette. She backed off from the smell of beer on his breath.

'Don't be so stupid, Peter!' Vivienne didn't fancy him, but, damn, the smoke brought thoughts of Guy. Fact is, more vodka and she imagined Guy here. If he had been she'd ask him, make him tell her things. 'So, the LA birds, the New York chicks – any?' 'Some', he'd say – arching those sexy black brows – 'a few.' She bet. But then they would have talked and talked and laughed together. Vivienne had made a library for her paperbacks and art books, just a small one, a couple of shelves. The books were worn at the edges from all the reading. She pencilled notes in them as well, inserting cuttings from the newspaper Arts pages. These would be things she could tell Guy about, one day.

People drifted off into couples. Some already lay down together on the red leather benches. Some leaned against the walls. Jessie had disappeared with the office boy.

Peter leaned over to Vivienne. Grabbing her arm, he somehow managed to push her through a half-opened door. They fell heavily together on a narrow bunk bed, far too narrow for two people. Peter began to undo his flies, groping at her breasts.

This was ridiculous! 'Peter! You are very drunk!'

'Aw, come on Viv, how about it?' Peter slurred.

Vodka swamped all reason. In a sudden rush of urgent need, she pulled Peter's hair, wrenching his face toward her and kissed him. He kissed right back. She felt his spaced out teeth hard on her tongue.

'Guy!' Blurted out before she could stop it.

'Eh?' Peter sniggered, 'oh well, what the hell!' He stroked her over her skirt, still trying to hoist it up. His grope revealed her fish net stockings and ankle length boots.

'Mmm. Lucky old – David, or Guy – whatever!' He swigged some beer and passed her the bottle. She pushed it away.

'Oh come on, Viv. Don't be a bloody tease!' said Peter, barely able to stand.

'No. *No*! I must get home.' Vivienne felt woozy and sick, 'Oh my God, it's Sunday morning! I'm doing a lunch! What time is it?' Tearing herself away from Peter, she began to smooth down her skirt and fix loose pins back into her unfurling chignon.

'Aw, don't I get another kiss?' Peter slobbered.

'No. NO! Get me out of here, Peter. Get me home. I've got a bloody chicken to cook!'

'Come home with me, darlin' and I'll cook your goose!' Peter laughed, missed his mouth with his cigarette and stumbled toward her.

Vivienne leant on him heavily, pushing him bodily out of the door. She had to find Jessie. Where was Jessie? When she found her, Jessie handed Vivienne her coat, putting an arm through her own.

'Well then, fun or what?' Jessie laughed, roguish eyes sparkling.

'God, what time is it?' Vivienne worried.

'Only three. Anyway, the yacht's already on its way back to the harbour. No worries. You'll soon be home.'

'Okay.' Vivienne warmed to Jessie. Being a divorcee put Jessie in the risqué class, whether she wanted it or not. Jessie was having fun tonight on her own terms. Good for her and nuts to the narrow minds.

In a black sky of early morning, the crew moored the yacht as close to the pier as they could get it. Vivienne saw the tide had all but gone out. She looked upwards at the iron rungs of the ladder glistening wet with sea water and green seaweeds. It seemed a long, long, way up before she reached the top of the cold granite pier.

The craft banged uncomfortably against the pier wall, then drifted out a few feet before being buffeted back again. Jessie went first, holding her hand out to Vivienne. Vivienne felt her long skirt, under her black coat with the fur-edged hood snag on an ankle boot heel. She tore the hem free, then, climbed like a fugitive in the winking lights of the darkened town. Twice she slipped, her boots sliding on the sea-slithery rungs. Someone pushed her onward from behind. She glanced down at the rocking boat, inches from the pier, far down below. What if she fell? She could be killed – wedged between boat and granite harbour wall. What in God's name was she doing here?

When they reached the top of the ladder, Jessie then Vivienne fell onto the pier, giggling inanely with relief and, for a moment, neither woman could stand up. Vivienne hauled herself upward, tottering an unsteady few steps forward. Jessie clung to her. They steadied themselves, then staggered to find their cars.

After hissing 'Night. See you,' to each other they drove home.

Vivienne weaved through the island's unlit lanes, bashing every now and then into an earth-banked hedge. Swerving, she narrowly missed a cat as it streaked across her path. Oh, good God!

At last then she was home. Up the drive (would Eustace and Pearl hear?) Vivienne parked, pocketed her keys and tiptoed into the shadowed hall of the bungalow.

Hopeful birdsong began in the sycamores and, distantly, a valiant cockerel heralded dawn, the night watch over. David was deeply asleep, snoring lightly. The bedside light was still on. *Growing World* lay open, strewn on the pink-flowered quilt.

Vivienne shed her clothes quickly, letting them fall to the floor any old how. Too late to fetch a glass of water, damn, she really needed it but, afraid to wake David, she lay down silently behind him. She switched off the lamp and put her arm around him. In the pearl, early light the bedroom furniture slowly emerged. Lying with wide-open eyes, Vivienne felt their leaked moisture soak in little patches on David's green-striped pyjamas. She withdrew her arm from his body – he always slept dead to the world – and drew the pillow around her head.

Vivienne imagined the woman doctor, agonised at her actions, and bit her lip until it drew blood No, no, no! She tried to banish her thoughts. Then Guy came to her: 'I want to be with you, talk to you.' Yes, Vivienne whispered, 'And I want you, Guy. Not the you I get through letters and other people's bits of news.' If Guy lay next to her he would have awoken by now. They would be holding each other close again, together, rolling over, so close together, like one being. The pillowcase soaked wet under Vivienne's cheek. She turned the pillow over as her dreams revolved around and around. There was the lunch to do in just a few hours time. Before she could think anymore, Vivienne passed out.

In the morning, clattering saucepans made her head bang with dull pain at the temples. Automatically, Vivienne drained vegetables, set the table and opened the misted windows to let in some air. Vivienne avoided David's goading questions, affecting distraction as she prepared the food.

He bent over to prod the roasting chicken with a long fork. Fat spat in puffs from the hot pan. He shut the oven door, putting the oven glove back on its rail.

'So what time did you come in? Must have been late. I didn't get to sleep myself until one. And you look dead rough. Been drinking too much? Don't suppose Jessie was any help? Where did you go, did you say?' David lowered his brow so his blue eyes glowered at her.

He had showered and washed his fair hair and wore a light

blue, crew-necked jumper over jeans. He looked, Vivienne thought, wholesome.

'Thanks for doing the veg, David,' careful here Vivienne, 'er, well, it was a bit of, a sort of, house party…thing.' With her back to him, she put the plates to warm in the drawer at the bottom of the oven. 'A friend of Jessie's. Some – farmhouse or other. Couldn't even ever find it again, don't think.' Should she apologise? Didn't exactly care for lies. 'Then, I slept on a sofa most of the time. Drank a bit, yes.' She straightened and turned to face him, would that do? He continued a steady stare, as if waiting for her to finish. 'Look, David. It was a party! I'll try to cut down. I will. I will.' When this feeling of no boundaries stops. When the mist clears. Her tongue felt the sore in her mouth where she bit her lip last night and she recalled Peter's teeth. Ugh!

David paused, then set out the cut-glass sherry glasses, a present from Great Aunt Harriet. 'Oh, I can't make you out, Vivienne. I don't like you going out on your own. And go and put some make-up on, can't you? You look awful, really hung over. You know what mum is like.' He went into the living room, straightened up cushions on the couch, put away yesterday's newspapers, then lit the kindled fire.

On the absolute dot of one o'clock, they heard the Carrés' Singer Gazelle car pulling up behind David's VW. Eustace and Pearl knocked once lightly on the front door – but they walked straight in before Vivienne or David could get to it.

'Hello darling,' Pearl said to her son. She glanced swiftly all around the rooms. Vivienne really did wish she had cleaned up a bit more, now. Pearl gave David a warm kiss. 'Hello Vivienne,' Pearl hugged her briefly, pecking an in-law kiss on her cheek. 'You look tired, dear. I hope you haven't gone to too much trouble.' Then, with a little laugh, 'not as if we're guests, are we Eustace?' Pearl handed Vivienne her coat. 'Anyway, it all smells delicious.'

David poured the sherries. They sat down in the dining room overlooking green lawns. Eustace wore a herring bone sports jacket, white shirt, dark red tie and grey slacks. His greyish brown hair was parted to the side, as if with a ruler.

Pearl wore a fawn twin-set and tweed skirt, her good pearls and pearl button earrings. Sunday best. Her grey hair was short, in a neat perm. Pearl had the matter-of-fact look of a country woman: she dressed to get on with things – housework, gardening, the washing – with no frills or flounces, but blouses and skirts that wouldn't show the dirt nor get in the way. Her clothes had to take robust home laundering – soap and hot water. Never once in her life had Pearl used dry cleaners.

Eustace at once told Vivienne how fond of her he was, his daughter-in-law. Although getting on a bit. In her twenties now! Eustace teased her that she looked much younger, and that she was bright and David could be too single-minded about saving money. They had plenty of time, he'd made mention, to provide for their future. Eustace said he very much wanted this marriage of theirs to work.

Continuity was still important for property land, and the growing business. In time Eustace wanted to hand over to David. He told Vivienne he wished to prepare them for – one day – running the whole show. The business thrived but he would like to retire perhaps earlier than some Guernsey growers. They might live abroad, who knows? The south of France, perhaps: Provence…? Eustace was very fond of France.

Eustace confided in Vivienne. He understood the problems Jean, her mother, had. And he knew of Edward's, not what you'd call a mania, but certainly something close to a religious obsession. Then there was Edna Jones, Ma Jones. Eustace admitted all the Yacht Club knew about her. It was no secret. Not that Edward was alone in that kind of…duplicity. Far from it – there was plenty of that kind of thing going on and not only at the Yacht Club. Vivienne wasn't to mind too much and Eustace said that Pearl was far more understanding of her than she might think.

The Carré family were not alone, Vivienne knew, in their concern for the future. Guernsey was part of the only bit of Britain occupied by the Germans in the Second World War. The Channel Islands were invaded and under the jackboot for five long years. Some Guernsey men and women had volunteered and joined the United Kingdom forces. There wasn't enforced conscription in Guernsey. The war had unsettled the roots of many a family, many a marriage. Some had not survived.

Some, like Eustace, had stayed in the island. He stayed to protect his father's land. Like thousands of others, he had nearly starved to death until Guernsey was liberated in 1946.

Still, here they all were now. They had picked up the pieces. To Eustace and his fellow Guernseymen, getting the island back on its feet, ensuring stability, was of paramount importance.

How difficult she found dieting! Vivienne was starving. Were three roast potatoes too many, do you think? Too bad. She crunched them into the chicken gravy, feeling a greasy trickle running down her chin as she ate.

Eustace laughed gently, leaned over and mopped up the dribble from her face. 'How's work, then Vivienne. Still like your job?' He cut up his chicken, helping himself to the steaming vegetable dish. 'Yes, and how's your painting coming on? Still going to evening classes? I do like your *Bacchus and Ariadne*, very much, you know.'

Gratefully, Vivienne thanked Eustace, also because he'd changed the subject from Pearl's housework, how one must get into a routine, how difficult that must be when you were a working girl. Pearl herself had never worked for anyone but her husband; she had married young, straight from a private school.

Eustace reminded Vivienne of Guy a bit. He had a similar deep voice, a way of engaging her with his eyes as he talked about art and things outside of Guernsey. Of course, Eustace was cultured – that was, an educated man. He had been offered a place at Oxford before he opted to stay and help his father. And Eustace and Pearl had travelled quite a lot. David didn't want to, not now. He said he'd seen as much of the world that he wanted to with his parents.

With Eustace, Vivienne found herself waving her arms about and chatting more enthusiastically than when just with David. She told Eustace how she loved going into the reporter's room, hearing all the latest news. And she liked the art room. Sometimes they let her finish off some of the artwork and she'd see it printed in the newspaper. And there were the photographers' studios... Vivienne felt hot colour rise to her face, so quickly offered around more wine.

Pearl placed her hand over her glass and refused more. They were going on to the Lenfestys in St Pierre du Bois by three. They had brought the car and she was driving. Their custom was to go every Sunday afternoon, never missed. Vivienne knew old Lenfesty and Eustace would have a whisky or two whilst Pearl and Edith Lenfesty would put the world to rights. Or, more likely, Vivienne thought, the parish miscreants, like herself, in this small and beautiful little island of theirs.

'Now then. I've got a proposition. Would you paint a picture for me, Vivienne? An oil painting?' Eustace queried lightly.

Vivienne regretted how tired she must look, felt the sun lighting her hair as it streamed through the window but she'd just plastered her make-up on. With David grumping at her, she put on whatever was to hand: sky blue eye shadow, loads of black mascara, a dash of pink lipstick. Couldn't do much about the frizz so she'd tied her hair up to the top of her head with a red chiffon scarf. Pearl, by comparison, looked so together – with a mere dusting of beige Max Factor so reputable.

Eustace still smiled benignly over at her. 'You know, I would like a landscape. Of the little harbour near us. Portelet? Would you like to do that for me, Vivienne? I'll, of course, pay you. So, I'm offering you a commission!' He looked amused as she dropped her fork with a clash on her plate.

Stop your shoulders shaking, for goodness sake! She hoped no-one noticed.

'I haven't embarrassed you, Vivienne, have I?' Concerned, Eustace finished his meal, put his knife and fork straight on his plate and placed his warm hand on hers.

Portelet and Guy sprang into her mind like a jumpy silent film. There they were – splashing in the sea. There! Moonlight sparkling on thrashing foam, swirling over their naked bodies.

'Vivienne?' asked Eustace.

'Oh, oh, of course. Eustace! Of course! I'd love to,' Vivienne really would as she dragged herself back to the family table, the Sunday lunch. 'Of course I'll do you a painting. Is there a time limit?' With shaking hands, she began to clear up the used plates.

'No, no, of course not. In your own time, my dear girl. I'd be delighted. Thank you. We both will, won't we Pearl? Time we encouraged this young lady of ours to get back to her painting. She's jolly good, eh David?'

Pearl gave a silent, quizzical smile. Vivienne caught it and moved her chair to where Pearl sat. 'Will you help me choose the angle, the colours, Pearl? I'd want to do something that you think will look well, maybe in your lounge? Will that be alright, Eustace? Is that where you'll hang it?'

'That'll be perfect, Vivienne.'

'Yes, and I do know a little about design,' Pearl said staunchly. 'My tapestry. My gardening. My sewing. They're about design, as well, you know.'

Vivienne readily agreed.

David broke his silence. All through the meal Vivienne had felt the negative vibes coming from him as she rued last night. He spoke firmly, showing no emotion. 'That's a very good idea, Dad. Vivienne needs some goal, something to occupy her spare time. Something to head for.' He darted a glance to Vivienne, heavy with words unsaid like a storm cloud just before it rained.

'I'll set up a studio, in the spare room,' said Vivienne.

'There,' said Eustace, pleased. 'Then that's settled.'

The senior Carrés left for the Lenfestys' good malt whisky. Pearl, no doubt, would have something to tell Mrs Lenfesty, along the lines of young wives these days neglecting their housework, gadding about and – for heaven's sake – oil painting. It had all been very different in their day. But Vivienne could understand Pearl. You just did what was expected in your day. There was no choice. You did what you could. Tomorrow, she would let Pearl have her recipe, Granmarie's recipe, for tomato soup.

As she arrived at the office, Monday morning, Vivienne spotted Peter and Jessie huddled up in a corner. They glanced guiltily her way.

'What?' Vivienne removed the grey plastic dust cover from her new, electric, typewriter. 'What's up?' Joining them, she helped herself at the coffee machine nearby, filling a white paper cup. She sipped bitter, scalding liquid.

'Nothing,'" said Jessie, too quickly, avoiding Vivienne's eyes.

'Nothing,' smirked Peter.

'Saturday was good, wasn't it?' said Vivienne. Let's get it over with, then, forget about it.

'Yeh. It was a gas,' Jessie liked to show off that she knew American slang.

Jessie wore her long hair over one shoulder, white hot pants and knee length white boots. 'There's another special party going – next week. Fancy coming?' Jessie raised a deftly pencilled eyebrow.

'I'm game.' Peter poured more steaming coffee into his cup. Putting an arm around Vivienne he snorted, 'and you are up for it, aren't you darlin'?' He winked, clicking his tongue.

Vivienne wrenched away from him. Bastard! Cheapskate! What an idiot she had been. It would be all over the office. Randy Peter and sex tease Vivienne. What if David found out?

'How's Guy?' Peter asked, nudging her mischievously, flicking a sly glance over to Jessie.

'What? Who?' Startled, Vivienne hurriedly mopped off spilled coffee spots from her blouse, where they'd burnt through.

'Your husband, isn't he called Guy?' Peter kept a straight face.

'You know he's called David.' You wretch!

'Oh, sorry. Oh yes David! It's just that you said…' Peter snorted again.

'Okay, okay,' Jessie covered Peter's mouth with her hand. 'That's enough sport. Leave the kid alone. Come on, let's get some work done around here. He's winding you up, Vivienne, take no notice.'

'Sorreee!' Peter sang out as he sashayed out of their office. He blew an air kiss to Vivienne through the glass door before hurrying off.

All morning they typed furiously, getting copy ready for the editor. A big story had broken – a property scandal. This tycoon had bought half the island but had been arrested for fraud. Jessie had met him at a party he had given at his house. Saturday night was nothing compared to this, Jessie said. Vivienne's fingers flew over the keys.

'Lunch!' Jessie abruptly announced.

Vivienne flung on her black coat as they hustled out of the office. In The Coal Hole pub Jessie bought them shots of vodka.

'Okay,' Jessie began, 'what's all this about Guy? I thought you and David were perfect little lovebirds in your perfect little house? Give.'

'We're fine!' Vivienne fiddled with a beery cork tablemat, glancing away from Jessie's querying stare.

'So?' Jessie persisted.

'So, so-oo, well I had a fling – an affair – with Guy. Before he was married. Before I was married to David. Guy's abroad now.'

'Yes? And?'

'Oh, Jessie! Stop it! I think of Guy, yes…sometimes. That's all.' Vivienne pulled her coat around her. And I got pregnant, had an abortion and the baby was alive and she was Guy's. Okay? The air around thickened, making Vivienne's brow clammy. Was she getting asthma? Suffocating? What to do? She downed the vodka.

Jessie got the same again. 'So you just think of him sometimes, huh?' Then she startled Vivienne, taking her face and cupping it between her hands. They were so close up she could see Jessie's eyelashes, film star lashes, mascara black. 'He's not thinking of you, Viv. No way, honeybun. You are out of his mind. Trust me.'

Vivienne recalled Guy's letters, carefully kept in a shoe box on top of the wardrobe. 'But…'

'But what? It's history, Vivienne. Guy Beaufort is long gone. Is he why you get that dreamy look? I thought it was because you wanted a kid…you look like that, you know, at the baby photographs in the Press.'

'Do I?' No answer to that. Vivienne wished she could just up and run away.

'Look, Vivienne.' Jessie finished her drink, slamming the glass down on the small table. 'Guy Beaufort is totally unreliable. He's, well –.'

'You know him, then? You know Guy?' Vivienne felt the familiar heart thud she felt whenever women – Rita, anyone – were mentioned.

'Sure I do!' Jessie looked around her, to see who else was in the pub. 'Doesn't any red-blooded broad? He's been around, you know. Put it about.'

This was getting uncomfortable.

'Guy likes really sophisticated women – glamorous women, doesn't he?' The Chelsea girls, Rita. Vivienne noticed a button was coming loose from her coat. It was getting old, now, shabby even. Out of fashion. Her glass was empty, it was time to go.

Jessie rose to leave. 'Well, my advice to you, honeybun, is to go home this evening, jump into bed with your David and say 'let's make a baby'!'

Thankfully, Jessie had changed the subject from talk about Guy.

'Listen, they've got a great live band down the Channel Island Hotel. I'm always down there, dancing. Fancy coming, some time?' said Jessie.

'Not sure. Don't think David'll let me.'

They strolled down the hill, hand in hand, back to the office where the morning's work lay corrected by the editor. There was a pile of new work in their in-trays. Vivienne almost welcomed it.

Funnily enough, around this time David started talking about trying for a child. A couple of overdue periods had come to nothing. But Vivienne noticed Eustace started mentioning, in a too-concerned voice, whether 'anything happened, yet, in that department?'

Polly told her she didn't like her new newspaper friends much. Not like the Hughes crowd, were they? 'A bit jet set kiddo, if you ask me.' And then, Polly startled Vivienne saying that David had once asked her questions about fertility.

'David did?'

'Mmm. Well, I'm having another one,' Polly pretended to groan, she only worked three afternoon's now, 'and the toddler's two. Well, what it was, we were walking round your garden and, well, to tell the truth, it was me brought up the subject.'

Vivienne thought Polly's round stomach suited her. Pregnancy suits her. Polly gets these really contented smiles, like when a woman falls asleep with a child in her arms.

'Another thing,' Polly hesitated. 'He mentioned Guy.'

Vivienne turned stone cold.

'Mentioned – asked if I thought you were over 'that Guy business' was how he put it. When you were young. Before you were married. Remember?' Polly's whole face blushed red as a poppy.

'I'll talk to him, Polly.' Over that Guy business. Did Polly suspect? Did David suspect anything – about the abortion? How she felt about Guy? 'Polly,' Vivienne said quickly, 'don't you ever want to...travel, have parties – have get togethers?"

"Uh? Get togethers – you mean like Tupperware?"

"No! More than that. Like my soirees. Don't you still want a bit of excitement?'

'Well, we like Jersey, kiddo. Our little one, he loves the boat trip, the zoo and then we have lunch at the Pottery.' Polly smiled cheerfully.

When Vivienne asked Jocelyn, in London, the same question she said, 'When are you coming with me to Italy? I'm always going to see my grandmother's family – bucket shop flights, package trips. You can even go to America now for practically nothing. Darling, Venice is out of this world! I saw a Bellini in the Zaccaria church. Your Titian studied under him. See? I remember your bloody Ariadne and Bacchus! Come on, Johnnie's dying to meet you. How's David? Bit of a rough diamond, he is. Still holding the purse strings tight, like his mother?'

'We're trying for a family,' Vivienne said.

'Vivienne! Trying for a family? Does David know anything about...?'

'I'm not sure.'

'Well then, tell him. You should do. Not all the details, obviously.

Anyway, must fly, Johnnie is such an impatient devil. Byeee!' Jocelyn
rang off.

Now David said that Pearl had begun encouraging him they
should start a child. That Vivienne ought to think about seeing a
doctor, maybe? Was it natural for a young couple not to start a family,
right away?

Jean, her mother, couldn't talk about babies. Not to Pearl, nor
Vivienne, come to that. And, of course, Vivienne couldn't ask for her
advice or anything.

Anyway, all in all, the idea of having a baby brooded in Vivienne's
mind more and more. Both Pearl and Jean had met their men young,
got engaged, saved for their bottom drawer, got married for life
then made a home and had babies immediately. It was all quite
straightforward. That is what you did. That is what their mothers,
aunties and grandmothers had done.

So Vivienne went to her doctor. It seemed a long time ago, now,
when he had helped her to stop the unwanted breast-milk. He had a
clean, bony face and smiled at her pleasantly over glasses at the end
of his nose. 'I think,' he said, forehead crinkling, 'that you could do
with a little help, Vivienne. Don't you?'

CHAPTER EIGHT

Some of the help for Vivienne included a diet sheet and suggestions like maybe she should cut out alcohol altogether? Her doctor said, not lecturing, but in his normal matter of fact way.

'And we'll do a little spring clean, Vivienne. We call it D&C for short. It's dilation and curettage of the womb. If there is any infection – that type of thing – around the cervix, or whatever, well we can clean it all out you know.'

The doctor handed Vivienne a card, an appointment with the surgeon. He looked at her again, over his spectacles. 'It's nothing out of the ordinary. You'll be out in jiffy. Good luck, Vivienne. You take care.'

All at once, Vivienne could think of scarcely anything else but being able to conceive. She kept rigidly to the steak and salad meals the doctor advised for keeping fit. At least David's love making was for a purpose now, however brief. It even seemed to suit him, for them to be consulting the chart she had pinned to the bathroom door, of best times and best dates to have sex. Vivienne made an effort to encourage David: bathing in scented water beforehand then massaging his feet. But he said that only made him feel self-conscious and bloody silly, so she stopped doing it.

After the D&C, the worst bit came when Vivienne had a test. Air was puffed through her fallopian tubes in order to clear them. It wasn't so much painful as frightening. She always felt vulnerable taking her underclothes off and lying there whilst a stranger, however kind and gentle they were, inserted alien objects inside her.

Vivienne took her temperature every day to check when she was ovulating. They'd been told to limit sex to every other day and she wasn't to shower or bathe immediately afterward. Vivienne tried to make light of it, David getting the actual business of fertilising over as dispassionately as possible. His sperm test had proved that there was nothing wrong with him. The problem was, then, squarely with her.

On her calendar in the kitchen, Vivienne ticked off the days that so relentlessly turned into months. She went into work on a pilot light, shopped for food at lunchtimes instead of going to the pub.

It was a sunny but very cold morning when Vivienne felt nauseous. The smell of freshly made tea made her reel to the bathroom to be sick. The waiting was over.

This time she bought textbooks with photographs of embryos growing in the womb at each stage. She followed every week, every stage of the pregnancy. In bed she read about her own body's change, how it prepared itself for the labour and birth: 'twenty one weeks – your uterus is expanding, your waist disappears...'

Don't look at the picture. Don't.

The day she left the newspaper office, Peter came up to her, kissing her lightly on the nose. 'Ships in the night?' He said quietly. 'All forgotten now, Vivienne. See you around.' Then Peter told her he had heard from Guy. Guy sent his best wishes. He had been to the Blue Note jazz club in Paris and had thought of Vivienne. Cleo Laine had sung Cole Porter's *Every time we say goodbye*. Brought back memories, Guy said to say.

Jessie gave her a tiny yellow quilt, wrapped in Cellophane. 'Glad someone takes notice of what I say! Best thing for you, a little junior. Best of luck, honeybun.' Jessie winked.

When she had a show at five months – a leak of red blood spotting her clothes – Vivienne held a painful, suspended breath. 'It was just a scare,' said the nurse. At nine months, though, the red mucus show was for real and her waters broke, flooding their sheets. At six in the morning, David raced her in to the Amherst Maternity Hospital. Vivienne squelched in with streaming legs and wet flip-flops – all she could find although she had carefully packed her case.

Everyone said how well she had done. The labour felt quite different this time. Vivienne breathed in and out with the rhythmic contractions, inhaling as much gas and air as she was allowed. As the little boy emerged, a healthy full-term son, Vivienne stared in wonderment, sheltering him in her arms, holding him fast as he twisted his reddened face, eyes scrunched shut, seeking her breast. She kissed the top of his still-wet head, scenting the primordial newness of him.

He was perfect. So David said, and the best thing that had ever happened to him. Lying back, exhausted, Vivienne thanked her gods that all was well. She held the picture of her newborn, protected in David's arms, in her sight until the other one, the fragile one, retreated to somewhere where Vivienne couldn't see her.

The nurses liked new mums to stay in hospital at least five days. But Vivienne asked to go home – to get away from steely hospital machines, plastic tubes, the sight of blood. At home they would be safe.

They called him Joseph. 'Our little boy! A son!' David beamed at them both.

'He's just gorgeous. Our baby boy.' Vivienne agreed. Joseph was lovely. He thrived, she fed him and bathed him – it wasn't a dream, was it? She wouldn't believe he was here at last. Not until he was nearly three months old. Then, yes, her baby Joseph was okay. Her baby lived.

Pearl came round with one of her herby casseroles, some crusty home-made bread and a pile of done ironing. She peeped at Joseph as he lay in his Moses basket in their sunny sitting room. Vivienne gently turned the white blanket, edged with satin, away from Joseph's sleeping face.

'He is the spitting image of David, Vivienne. He's a fine little chap.'

Vivienne took Joseph out of the basket, wrapped him carefully in a white cellular blanket and handed him to Pearl, who sat down on the sofa with her. 'Eustace and I, well, I must admit we were pleased he was a boy.'

'I know, Pearl. It's nice to have a boy, your grandson.'

'A Carré,' Pearl breathed quietly, gazing tenderly at Joseph. 'Our David's son.'

Vivienne's father, Edward, was no less delighted. When he first held Joseph Vivienne hovered to take him back, Edward shook so. Then Edward steadied himself and, amazingly, shyly kissed the baby's head. 'Our grandson, Nin. A healthy little boy. Thank the Lord.'

Vivienne recalled the Fair Isle baby hat, patterned pale blue and white, her parents still kept on the hallstand at Granville. And, in the bureau, she had discovered a folder of Oscar's drawings: a square house with four windows and smoke, like wire spirals, coming out of a wonky brick chimney. Then there was one with a cat, round like an O, with no legs but a row of white teeth. Vivienne had seen Edward cry, once, over that folder, really cry, more like sobbing to be honest, but never since.

'He's the picture of Oscar, Nin,' Edward said, so quietly Vivienne could hardly hear. 'The picture of him.'

Vivienne and Edward ensured Jean had had her medication and her midday rest before she saw Joseph. Even then she had cried out, 'Oscar! Oh, My Oscar! Darling boy.'

Neither of them corrected her. Vivienne had taken the fold up pram with its carrycot and yellow quilt down to Granville and let Jean wheel the baby around the garden, watching all the while from the window. Vivienne had no memory of her brother, only photographs her parents had kept. This is how it would have been: Jean perambulating her son around the orchard while Edward oversaw the vinery work.

Granmarie said it wasn't right for Jean to call Joseph, her great grandson, 'my Oscar', but Vivienne didn't reply. After all Granmarie had not lost a child, had she?

Funny how routine so quickly becomes the norm. Vivienne often took Joseph to see Polly and her two boys. They went down to the beaches, watching the children grow in the sun, playing in the sea, making sandcastles.

Joseph had blond hair and tanned easily. Vivienne packed tubs of suncream and a sunhat in her bag. She started making little outfits for her son. Pearl let her use her sewing machine, an ancient Singer. Sometimes, Pearl quietly unpicked seams Vivienne had sewn, hemming them again with 'There, that'll be a better fit, Vivienne.

You did your best.' It didn't matter. Vivienne never minded. Joseph had nice clothes and a new blue cotton suit for the summer.

One day, Pearl invited Vivienne and Muriel Le Croix, Amanda's mother, for afternoon tea. Pearl handed around warm scones, cream and jam. Vivienne poured the tea.

'Oh, and did you know, I must tell you,' Muriel Le Croix stirred a teaspoon casually, 'the latest from Amanda and Guy?' She sipped carefully from her china cup.

The afternoon noises somehow silenced.

'What's that, Muriel?' asked Pearl.

'They've had a little girl. A daughter, born in America. She's called Natalie. Everyone says she's very beautiful. I'm to go over to see her. Isn't that going to be an adventure?' Vivienne knew it wasn't her imagination and that Muriel had scrupulously avoided eye contact.

'Well, that is good news, Muriel. Especially after the trouble Amanda had last time. I am glad for them. Please tell them that, will you?' said Pearl.

Vivienne looked down at her sleeping son, where he slumbered next to her, his head on a cushion, mouth open, his hair fallen back from an innocent, vulnerable forehead. Guy had a daughter. She leant over and stroked Joseph's brow, then his smooth knees, letting her hand rub the soles of his white socks, and cradle his stubby little toes, all curled up.

For some reason a shadow cast itself – a grey mantle swept soundlessly over her mind. It had happened before, when the woman doctor came to jeer – even more since Joseph was born.

'Vivienne?' Pearl asked, 'are you alright, my dear, you look a little drawn. Is it too stuffy in here?' Pearl fluttered a hand toward opening the window.

'No, it's fine, Pearl. Don't worry. Um, yes, Mrs Le Croix, could you tell – could you tell Amanda that I'm pleased for them? Hope she enjoys…' But couldn't finish. Vivienne groped blindly out of the enveloping mist. God, she had to get out of here. 'Sorry, would you mind Pearl? Joseph's tea is due – David's supper?' Vivienne stumbled out, clutching Joseph, heavy in her arms.

Grey, foggy drifts of black and white, like smoke all around her, clouded her mind. What was she supposed to be doing in her kitchen? With shaking hands, she filled the kettle with water from the tap.

'I expect it's the baby blues, Vivienne. I had them,' Pearl said one day, concern in her eyes.

Her father, Edward, in his serious Sunday suit, took Vivienne aside. 'Your mother had that, you know – depression – lots of women do.'

'It clears up,' said Pearl. 'You have to just get a grip on yourself. It will pass, Vivienne. And David will have to… to take more care of you.'

God, that from Pearl? She must look terrible. She did, Polly agreed, 'You look awful, what's up, kiddo?'

But – didn't people realise? – Guy had a daughter. Didn't anyone remember that? And she was beautiful. Every one said so. Guy had a beautiful daughter, called Natalie: beautiful and alive. Natalie was a nice name. Vivienne would have chosen Nicola Jane. Not so far off from 'Natalie', was it? Nicola Jane.

It seemed ages later when Vivienne somehow managed to return to her studio: the spare room. It was an effort but she set up her easel, propped her sketches against a vase on the table and finished the Portelet painting for Eustace. He loved it, he said, showed it to his friends at his club and got her another commission.

One evening class the lecturer said, 'Vivienne, you have really learnt the Impressionists' methods but you have a very individual style. Well done.' He entered a seascape, showing all the smaller Channel Islands, in the Eisteddfod. She won an Honours certificate and the cup. Painting each day, she herself began to notice an improvement. Not exactly perfect yet, not professional, but getting there, including portraits. Eustace started talking about a one woman exhibition for her. Yes, he'd arrange an exhibition. He'd enjoy doing that. 'My artistic daughter-in-law!' he announced proudly, hugging her warmly.

Joseph toddled around the studio, 'Ma-ma, Joffess paint too?' Vivienne had asked David to make a small easel. She set up paper and watercolours on a low table. So Joseph painted next to her. But he quickly became bored, so she gave him one of his picture books from her small library. She'd started collecting children's books for Joseph. He sat on the floor this time.

'Tell you what, Joseph. Mummy's going to do a picture of you. Would you like that?'

'Yesss!' Joseph clapped his hands, grinning with his brand new baby teeth.

'Right. Let's make a start.' Taking a new canvas and a stick of charcoal, Vivienne sketched Joseph's blond head, his wide eyes, small nose and mouth. 'You are a little poppet, aren't you? My little man.' On another shelf, she had a bottle of white wine chilling in its ice bucket. Just a sip or two, you understand, to help the creative juices. Just every now and then. Didn't do any harm, did it, white wine? It comforted. It chased depression – for a while.

Irritated, Vivienne tugged at her blouse, it would keep popping open although it was already a size 12. Same with the jeans she could easily slip on before the pregnancy. Damn things would cut in around the waist. Have to let them out, go on a diet? Yes, stick to a diet.

Not trying for a baby anymore, in bed David turned away from her, leaving her isolated her side of the sheets. He'd come home tired, sometimes even too tired to bathe, go straight to bed and sleep deeply. Vivienne tried kneading his bare shoulders, let her hands drop down to fondle him, but David's responses came less and less.

David started criticising the state of the house. She couldn't go to evening classes, paint and look after Joseph and the house, now could she? He wanted his dinner on the table, on the dot of twelve, his supper at six. Didn't Vivienne understand that in the afternoons there was all the watering of the plants to do, keeping the workmen properly occupied, grading the tomatoes and the all the women in the packing shed to supervise – Olive would keep taking time off on washday. Some of the others started doing the same. There was so much to do! At the very least she could have his meals ready, for goodness sake, and keep the place tidy.

Vivienne asked David for money for oil paints, after all she needed a lot of stuff, preparing for an exhibition. But David told her – in the voice he usually kept for Joseph – 'I'm not made of money. You know we must start to put something by for Joseph's education, for his future.'

So she took out some of Eustace's commission money – David couldn't argue with that – to buy some stuff, neglecting to hear David: if she cut down on the booze then they'd have more money for essentials, well wouldn't they?

'I keep having dreams,' Vivienne told Polly, but not the parts when she dreamed of Guy – of her rousing him, of him kissing her all over until they erupted together, like they always did, like she always had – 'I'm...desolate, not knowing where I am. Like getting stuck in a lift, miss trains, sit on some plane. Don't know where it's going with strangers all around.'

'You're still not right after Joseph, kiddo. Better see a doc?' said Polly, frowning. 'Can't do it on your own. No one can.' Vivienne made a weary nod of agreement in reply.

Granmarie reached her hundredth birthday, received her telegram from the Queen of England, then, seeming entirely satisfied, peacefully passed away. Vivienne had dreaded her grandmother going. Feared that life would never be the same again once Granmarie had gone.

At the funeral, David spoke of Granmarie's wisdom, how he honoured her and how supportive she had been of them. Life, David said, wouldn't be the same for any of them.

So it turned out that Edward and Jean now had Granville to themselves. Vivienne's two uncles said they would remain to help with the growing business, look after the property and land. Edward would still oversee things, though it was obvious that he had a waning interest in it all.

Although Granville was smaller than the Normandie's family house, Edward and Jean hadn't the heart to move, now. They had made a tenuous life on the Bordeaux estate. It wouldn't do to go stirring things up. They extended Jean's bedroom by knocking through into the bedroom next door, thus making her a day room, a sitting room with a bed-settee next to the bay window. After that, Edward was freed up to spend more time with his church people, the Yacht Club and Edna Jones.

Before Granmarie died, David hesitantly confided to Vivienne that he had done down to Granville one day. As usual, Granmarie busily bunched her white carnations in the packing shed. He had wheeled the wooden wheelbarrows full of sacks of blood and bone fertiliser to one of her greenhouses.

'We got talking, like we always did. She asked – if I was seeking her counsel? You know how those bright green eyes could be, piercing you like arrows? I said I didn't know about counsel but it worried me why we – you – had had to have treatment for infertility, you know, before Joseph?'

'You never said that bothered you!' Vivienne said, sharply alert.

'Well, it did. A bit. It's niggled away. I didn't like to worry you. Granmarie said she could tell me little but that she loved you very much – but that something might have happened in London?'

Oh no. What had Granmarie said? Did she tell about the breast milk? Vivienne dug her fingernails into the palms of her hands.

'That…well now I can see something happened by the look on your face! That whatever it was, she thought it might have damaged you, Vivienne? And that Jocelyn might be able to tell me more.'

'Is that it? Anything more?' Her nails dug deeper into the yielding mounds of her palms. Treacherous ground, Vivienne: tell the truth? What to say? But it was going to come to this – with David – someday, sure as eggs.

'And Granmarie said to ask you, to talk to you. She said you and Jocelyn knew more than she did. You must tell me. So what the hell happened, then, in London?'

Vivienne unclenched her fingers. Little half-moon cuts on her palms hurt. What if David did ask Jocelyn? Jocelyn knew some of it. 'Alright. I'll tell you straight as I can, David. But this is very hard for me.'

They sat down outside on a bench in the garden. Joseph rushed around on the grass with a toy aeroplane, as if there were no obstacles whatsoever.

'Okay.' Said David.

'I had an abortion, David,' Vivienne said bluntly, 'It was Guy Beaufort's but he doesn't know.'

David abruptly turned his whitened face from her, as if in pain, as if she'd slapped him. 'Jocelyn helped me, in London. I didn't know what to do. I was so young then. Guy was going away. I got completely out of my depth. Mum was so ill, Dad would have murdered me...'

There was a long silence, with only Joseph's merry cries as he voom-voomed his toy plane upward to the sky. David turned his head away from her, raising his hands in unison toward her, as if to push her away from him. Then David waved to Joseph without reason, saying. 'Wish I didn't know that, now. Wish I had never asked. Wish I didn't know.'

'I wish you didn't know.' Vivienne sighed: wish none of it had happened.

'So. Bloody Guy Beaufort, eh? Can't keep his dick to himself, eh? Didn't he use anything? Bloody fool.'

'It wasn't only him, though, David, was it?'

'No. You surely should have known better – God Vivienne, an abortion? Illegal then? Never mind the morals, and that's bad enough. But you were mad about him, weren't you? Nuts. And blokes know about such things.' Then David gave her a recriminating look. 'Not an innocent then, were you? When we married?'

'No. Don't look at me like that. I didn't know how to tell you.'

'I'll bet.'

'I wish you hadn't gone asking Granmarie.' Vivienne's throat dried. Wish Granmarie were here now, to talk to her. Damn, now don't start crying or you'll never stop. Even now, telling the whole truth choked back in her. Nobody knew the whole truth but her and the bloody woman doctor. She wouldn't tell David the baby was viable (certainly knew what that word meant now) that the abortion was done at twenty-one weeks – maybe twenty-two – she'd never tell David, or anyone, that. Couldn't. Like she couldn't share her nightmares with him, nor the cold hand constricting her heart. Nor that, to Vivienne, all empty cribs looked like someone had stolen the babies away.

'Well, I did speak to Granmarie. And so now I do know.' David stood up and made toward the house.

'David! Say you don't mind. Say I'm a good mum! Say I'm a good wife! Please!' Don't cry. You'll never stop.

'You're a good mum. You're a good wife.' David repeated in a voice flat as becalmed sea. 'And you are a good artist. Trouble is you are such a bloody awful housewife and now I don't even know if I can ever trust you.' He strode to the back door and slammed it behind him.

Vivienne sat on the bench, alone, watching Joseph occupy himself. Making a whirring noise, he crashed his plane into a pyramid of logs that kept falling down, rolling in different directions. Usually, hearing Joseph laugh gleefully warmed her. But she felt a nothingness, wrapped in a speechless white cowl.

Lately, she had been re-reading the books Guy gave her, the ones they had chosen together – she knew them intimately. She had added more: Jane Austen, Dickens and the Brontes.

Johnnie Dankworth had come to Guernsey with Cleo Laine. Polly went with Vivienne to see them. David couldn't: wouldn't. Not his scene.

The Dankworths! How handsome they were. How handsome Guy was. Jazz played in her ears, a slow, sensual saxophone.

'Mummy!' Joseph tugged at her sleeve. 'Mummy. You been makin' me cross! I been callin' you!"

Vivienne got up and went over to inspect the rebuilt log pile, admiring it, telling Joseph what a clever boy he was. But the rough brown kindling shimmered in front of her eyes.

The back door suddenly swung open. David banged it shut behind him with a booted foot. He bore a tray of two blue and white striped mugs of coffee and Joseph's blue plastic rabbit cup, half filled with milk.

Vivienne forced blinks to clear her vision. Joseph went off to the bottom of the garden. He climbed the lower branches of his favourite tree to drink his milk.

Vivienne and David sat down on the grass.

'Thing is,' David began in a low voice, 'Well, I've never much cared for it. Since we're telling truths. Not even a hand job. Mum caught me once, when I was still a kid. It's disgusting. It's dirty.' David stared grimly ahead and drank his coffee.

'Sex is dirty?'

'Well, it's supposed to be for procreation, isn't it? Otherwise... well, we're no more than randy dogs. Animals.'

'I don't think that.' Vivienne said, 'not at all.'

'Well, no, obviously not!'

'You're disappointed I wasn't a virgin?' Joseph climbed too high. Vivienne stood up, 'no higher, Joseph. Careful, darling!'

'Yes. Yes, I am, to be honest. Mum would be, too, if she knew. She always calls loose girls – easy girls – damaged goods.' David pulled at blades of grass, scrunching them up into his fist.

'And you?' Vivienne slowly sat down again on the damp grassy earth.

'We've all got...appetites. Thing is, we have to show some control, don't we? Joseph means the world to me, you know.' Then David's mouth clammed shut.

'And to me, David. And to me,' said Vivienne.

The studio warmed in the afternoon sun. Vivienne worked, upping the white wine in its ice bucket to the occasional vodka shot. Joseph came in so she took a peppermint out of her pocket before kissing him. These days, if she looked in the mirror she saw, if not exactly a beautiful face (never thought that, anyway) at least round, soft skin. Well preserved, she smiled to herself, like some aging actress. Vivienne heard David in her ears, repeating what had become his mantra: 'cut down on the booze'. So why didn't she?

She still had the springy hair highlighted blonde. Tanned to make her teeth look whiter, although her dentist said he despaired of her nervousness. Worst he knew, he said. Whatever experience had she had, he questioned, to be so afraid of the dentist drill? Vivienne didn't tell him – he had a white light on his ceiling, glaring into her very soul.

The portrait of Joseph was nearly finished. She mixed vermilion, yellow and white to add highlights to his nose and chin. Eustace wanted this one, as well. And Edward surprised Vivienne, asking if he and her mother Jean could have a painting of Joseph? He'd even pay her. Goodness.

But shopping, with Polly and Jessie, made her conscious of her weight. They flicked through the rails in the new boutiques in Town, looking for what Jessie called trendy gear. Vivienne dared get some flimsy tops and cotton skirts way above the knee all of which Pearl later regarded with polite, unexpressed horror.

Vivienne reckoned her depression didn't always show outwardly, but some days the sun never shone; everything seemed bathed in perpetual shade. Sometimes she moved like a shadow, herself. When the images bore down on her, her tormentor's face scorned, through round glasses and a mouth so wide Vivienne glimpsed gold fillings.

'Vivienne!' David stuck his head around the studio door, 'for God's sake, didn't you hear? It's the phone! We could hear it way out in the yard. I've had to come all the way in to tell you. It's Jocelyn. She's over in the island, on holiday. For goodness sake, come and talk to her!'

Jocelyn asked how David had taken Vivienne admitting the abortion?

'Has it cleared the air – has it helped? You have an absolutely gorgeous little boy. You and David. That must make up for things?'

'How's Johnny?' said Vivienne.

'Johnny? God, well gone! That second marriage hit some very sharp rocks, darling. I do envy you.'

They booked a meal, at Le Nautique Restaurant, overlooking St Peter Port harbour. The marina jingled full of white yacht masts. Blue-green sea reflected the boats as they rocked to and fro.

'Ah, look at Guernsey's sunshine. Such light. Look at Castle Cornet,' Jocelyn said, gazing over to her right, 'a romantic castle built hundreds of years ago, still guarding the harbour'. Read that in the brochure, coming over in the plane. Wasn't floodlit when we were kids, though, was it Vivienne?'

They ordered fresh lobster, oysters and champagne.

'Mmm. I'd forgotten just how seductive this island could be. London's the place for me, but Guernsey is magic, isn't it?'

Vivienne thought Jocelyn hadn't aged one tiny bit. Her drop of Italian blood showed. She wore her glossy black hair swept up. Her eyes were outlined with black flicks at the outward corners, making them look almost oriental.

'You really haven't changed,' said Vivienne. Jocelyn still had full breasts with a nipped in waist emphasised in a green silk dress.

'Tight fitting as I could find, darling! And you are looking brilliant, Viv. I love your highlights – and boutique clothes, eh? David, what do you think?' Jocelyn waggled her long-stemmed glass from side to side.

The restaurant buzzed, zoomed out faraway, then rushed back, like Vivienne was seeing things through some mad, oscillating camera.

'Nature calls!' David got up, excusing himself. His tall, slim frame disappeared from view.

'Vivienne? Hello!' Jocelyn passed her hand over Vivienne's face. 'Are you with me? You have always been such a dreamer!'

'Sorry, Jocelyn. I think it's the champagne.'

'I've seen that look before, Viv. The blue-eyed longing bit. Not still carrying a flame for flipping Guy Beaufort are you?'

Vivienne made a hurried denial, 'No, no, no. Of course not!'

'Mmm?' Jocelyn leaned nearer to her, placing a red-nailed hand on Vivienne's sleeve. Her raised black eyebrow demanded an explanation.

'Well. I think of him. Now and then, Jocelyn. You know? He's a father now.' Vivienne pushed her plate away, the lobster half-finished. 'He's...they've got a daughter.' She looked out of the window at small boats sailing jauntily out to sea. She recalled the expensive yacht, the cannabis. Peter – she remembered her calling Peter 'Guy' and shuddered.

'Viv! Who the hell cares? Lots of people have daughters. The man hasn't done anything special! Listen, how's your painting going? I'll want to see some of your work and I want to cuddle your little Joseph.'

'I know, Jocelyn. It was a long time ago, I know.' How to admit sometimes Guy's spirit surrounded hers, just as certainly as his cigarette smoke rose in drifts before her face, all those times ago. More than that, she felt him existing – somewhere close at her side, then he would drift away again 'When a lovely thing dies – smoke gets in your eyes?'

'Ah hah! So the flame still flickers? What about David, darling? How's things going there?' This time Jocelyn raised both eyebrows, flashing her eyes suspiciously at Vivienne.

'Um. Okay, all right, Jocelyn. Listen, do you ever feel really, really down?'

'No, never, why?'

'There's times I feel there has to be more. You're lucky – you travel, you're a free agent.'

'Are you sure – David and you...?'

'It's all right. But, well we don't come here often, I can tell you. Sometimes I can't even make it to do my hair, put on a bit of make-up.'

'Viv! You're still such a pretty girl. Look, it's completely different in London. We eat out all the time. It's no big deal. It's cheap. Grass is greener?'

The coffee arrived. David returned. 'What have you two been talking about?' He asked, settling himself down.

'Nothing.' Came the reply, in unison.

David asked for the bill, gulped and paid whilst screwing up his eyes, as if, Vivienne thought, he had just swallowed cyanide. The meal was over.

'Granmarie told me to talk to you, Jocelyn.' David swung his legs

from the hammock, slung between two apple trees. 'Do you mind?'
The leafy trees bordered their lawn.

Vivienne played with Joseph, helping him to load a toy truck with
the grey speckled pebbles that she and Jocelyn had collected from
the beach.

'Me a driver!' said Joseph.

'You are sweetheart. A truck driver!' Vivienne ran on the grass,
bent double to reach Joseph's height. 'Wow! What a clever boy!' She
went back to Jocelyn and David as Joseph tottered indoors to fetch
more toy lorries, dropping some that he already carried.

'I'll make us a fresh crab salad for lunch,' said Vivienne. 'We can
eat it here, under the trees.'

'Idyllic,' said Jocelyn. 'So, David. What do you want to talk
about?' Her white flared trousers streaked with green of the grass.
The red and white top had flared sleeves as well. She wore the long
Chelsea beads Vivienne so admired and her hair hung loose. 'My
signature feature, darling. My hair. Washed and conditioned by
Harrods and Harvey Nichols best. You must come over and see me
soon. David, she must! You must let her come.'

'Well...' David began, 'well, Granmarie told me about London
and Vivienne told me about the abortion.' The hammock swayed
gently in the summer light.

Vivienne saw Jocelyn stiffen as she kneeled on the tartan rug.
She put her hands on her knees. Jocelyn pulled at some daisies,
concentrating on each petal, as if separating them. 'Yes? So what else
do you want to know, David? I helped Viv. Of course. She needed
somebody to help her. I was training at the hospital – you know all
that – then things went wrong. I got her to A&E and then...well, that
was that.'

Vivienne closed her eyes. Don't rake up all this, David. Stop it.

'Will going over all this again help any?' Jocelyn asked, making
the daisies into a posy. 'Do you think it will help? I reckon you're
getting rock fever! You've been living too long on this island, darling.
You're getting too insular. Islands can do your head in, you know!'

'No. There's more too it, what went wrong?' said David. 'There's something more. I don't get it...' He laid back in the hammock, swinging gently, staring at the leaves above him. 'Why the A&E? Jocelyn, what is it?'

'Why don't you ask Vivienne?' Jocelyn stretched her hand out to Vivienne's as she opened her eyes. 'Or maybe we could all just shut up about it? It's history, David.'

Shut up about the baby breathing? About the doctor? Vivienne felt a pressure on the inside of her skull, pushing upward tighter and tighter.

'Yes, please don't keep going on, David. We'll talk another day. Jocelyn's on holiday.' Vivienne said, squeezing Jocelyn's hand in return. How small the island suddenly felt. 'A self-examining microcosm of the world,' Guy called it.

'Yup. Move on, David, ' Jocelyn said. 'Come on, time to move on. You've got your little family. For Pete's sake, let the past rest. I'm off back home, to London tomorrow, Did I tell you, Viv, I've met this really fabulous fella? No, really, fabulous.'

As Vivienne vacuumed the sitting room the lead twisted around her leg, banging the cylinder against her ankle. The phone rang. It was Jessie.

'There's going to be a fancy dress ball, Vivienne. In Sark. It's a staff do. We're all going over to Sark for the weekend. So put that child of yours down, dump the husband and your paintbrushes and come with us honeybun!'

Instantly, David said she couldn't go and he certainly wouldn't, even if he had been invited. He hated fancy dress. They had gone to one or two pyjama parties, beatnik parties and suchlike before Joseph's birth. But he didn't like full fancy dress. Didn't like role-play. He didn't, David stressed, 'play games'.

'Please, David. It's years since we had a party. It's a staff do. I want to go. Just this once?'

David consulted Pearl. Pearl agreed Vivienne could go, saying she was trying – teaching young Joseph to swim, to ride his bike and how to keep a little garden. Maybe Vivienne could do with the break.

Yes, Joseph could stay with his grandparents for the weekend.

'Well, okay. Got my reservations, but still... better than you with a face like a fiddle because now Jocelyn's even been to Majorca on one of her ruddy package trips.'

'It's not 'Majorca', it's 'Mayorka'. I've heard it pronounced – on that telly travel programme.'

'Oh, you are such an ungrateful woman!' said David.

'Anyway, thanks.'

In a surge of lifting anticipation, Vivienne began to plan what she might wear. In Town she rifled through bolsters of material. Shiny satin, pink net, purple chiffon. What could she make? Who could she go as?

Then, of course! Vivienne would be Ariadne.

CHAPTER NINE

'Ari who?' asked Jessie. When Vivienne told her about Titian she laughed, 'well, hope you find Bacchus honey!'

Jessie would be a belly dancer. Her date, Rick, a sultan. Vivienne made her outfit. It looked good. She'd found a cobalt blue cloth to swirl over a loose white shift. Then she made a long crimson scarf to wear over one bare shoulder, the rest to trail over her body and onto the ground. No shoes and her hair to fall naturally, tied at the nape of her neck. Over the whole lot she'd made a pink satin cape – to cover the entire costume from David until she got to Sark.

The heat rose early that day. Standing on St Peter Port harbour, David held Joseph like he was an abandoned martyr, raising little Joseph's hand to wave a goodbye.

Vivienne settled down on the Sark ferry seat. Jam-packed either sitting or standing, almost everyone had taken trouble with their disguises. There were Aladdins, priests, princesses and Roman slaves.

Thank God, Peter the photographer wasn't coming. He had an assignment in Jersey. Jessie and Rick beckoned Vivienne over to their side of the boat. The ferry ploughed forward, rolling alarmingly as it hit the swell of a passing fishing boat.

'Ohhhhh. Ahhhhh!' The crowd yelled cheerfully, pretending to be seasick and passing around bottles of beer. Vivienne clutched her cape around her and held on tight.

The ferry arrived safely at Maseline, Sark's harbour. They disembarked in twos and threes. Merriment carried over the warm summer air. Boarding trundling carts pulled by tractors, they laughed all the way up Sark hill, to the hotel at the top where the ball awaited.

The hotel, 'Aval du Creux', set in lush green gardens, overlooked the sea toward France. Sark allowed no cars, only tractors. Otherwise cycles or horses and carts sufficed. Most people walked.

Mesmerising was the word Vivienne murmured, surveying the island's beauty. The sun lowered to a sultry evening and with that their mood of abandonment and partying got into full stride. Trestle tables, set in the gardens, held beers, wine and spirits.

Vivienne took an iced vodka. The smell of roasting pork wafted over the lawns. Men tended to the turning spit. Blue smoke rose up into the air. Bowls of fruit: oranges, apples and purple grapes, piled high. The night was young, the mood was free.

Vivienne breathed in the sweet smelling bracken, growing thickly on the cliffs in front of the hotel gardens. She smelt aniseed, pine, thyme and camomile. Intoxicating, mysterious, other-worldly Sark – Vivienne immersed into the spirits that seemed to haunt the land. All around the sea lay – clear turquoise shot through with swathes of violet.

Waves in the distance shone with the sunset's golden ribbons. Beyond that, on the other side of Sark, Guernsey slept, far away. Vivienne took another chilled vodka. The greyness, wisps of dark cloud, blew away from her mind in the lulled breeze. Sark's blue sky would not be denied.

Dark green palm trees spiked the air. Lavender scent reminded her of Guy's wedding. This is where he had spent his honeymoon. Vivienne drew the scarlet scarf over her shoulders, thinking of his gorgeous face. What would he say if he saw her now? Would he approve? He'd probably laugh: 'Little Vivvy. You remembered – Bacchus and Ariadne?

'Night and day, you are the one…in the roaring traffic's boom, in the silence of my lonely room, I think of you. Day and night, night and day…'

She heard herself softly singing. 'Wish you were here, Guy,' Vivienne said aloud.

A queue had begun for slices of pork and crisp crackling, hunks of freshly made bread and fresh green salad. Vivienne, suddenly ravenous, joined in. Two men, dressed as leopards, served from behind the table.

With filled plates, everyone sat down in the grass, balancing their glasses as best they could. In the warmth Vivienne hardly needed her pink cape, so she lay it down beside her. Jessie and Rick, fully satiated and holding hands, lay down on the lawn.

'Hello,' a young man said, sitting himself down on her cape. 'You're Ariadne, aren't you?' A dark-haired lad, with perfect porcelain teeth, grinned at her. 'Bet you thought nobody would guess!'

Startled, Vivienne laughed at the young boy's nerve. 'How did you know? What a clever…' she glanced over his fancy dress, complete with reed pipe, 'Satyr…Pan?'

'Oh, and a clever girl as well! Pan.'

Amused to be called 'girl', Vivienne scanned intriguing 'Pan'. He was dark-skinned, with dark, wavy hair. In a crown of ivy he had fixed two short horns. He wore just a brief white toga and a belt of long brown fur, like a sporran, barely covering the tops of his legs. Vivienne guessed he'd be about nineteen.

He reached over slightly to fetch his plate of food and goblet of red wine, set a bit further away. 'Mind if I join you?' He asked with a mischievous smile. 'I think we sort of go together, don't you? Fate has played its fickle way with us!' The boy fixed her with an intense glance.

Vivienne laughed out loud. But she didn't tell him he was delightful and anyway, he probably knew. On finishing their food, 'Pan' went off to refill their glasses. Returning, he put her pink cape over his youthful shoulders saying, 'Bacchus and Ariadne. Yes, I've known that painting all my life. My father is Greek, you know. My mother is a Guernsey woman. My name is Matthias. We owned a restaurant – Aphrodite's – do you remember it? Sold it now.' He moved closer to her. She could feel his bare knee next to hers. 'And you?'

Vivienne had studied Greek art and its stunning Greek boys. Now here, right next to her, sat this fine example. Vivienne let her knee stay next to his.

'Why did you choose Ariadne?' Matthias asked softly. 'Do you, perhaps, want to be rrr-e-s-c-u-e-d?' He put his arm around her, squeezing her to him.

Jessie and Rick had rolled over and gone to sleep, their arms wound around each other. Looking around her, Vivienne saw couples drifting off, over the cliff paths, walking around Sark, finding somewhere to lie down and to drink. Sark weaved its usual spell.

Music seduced the mellow air.

'I don't really know what I want,' Vivienne said to the strong, beautiful boy, looking so like the younger Guy – so like him. 'Well, I do. I want to feel…happy again. Enjoy life.'

'Oh, poor old Ariadne!' Matthias stroked her bare shoulder. 'Come on, what's Ariadne's real name? Who are you?' He began to kiss the curve of her arm. She didn't pull away. Would he make love like Guy? How would it be? Careful, Vivienne, careful! He's nineteen!

'I don't know who I am, but I'm called Vivienne,' she said.

'Who? Didn't hear you.' He leant so she could feel his mouth breathing in her ear.

'Vivienne. Vivienne Carré.'

'Well, I'm going to call you Baby. My lost Baby.' Then he kissed her full on the lips and all reason left her entirely.

Wine on his lips, when he brushed them with hers, tasted of red grape juice. Kisses and stolen wine – just like at Portelet…

'Matthias, I…' Vivienne said.

'Let's go,' said Matthias. 'Let's find a bracken bed.' He pulled Vivienne up with his hands, flinging her cape over his shoulders. 'See little Ariadne? Little Baby? I am Bacchus, after all!'

They ran away from the party, Matthias in front of her, they fled down a gravelled path, past the Windmill to the west coast, leading toward Victor Hugo's Cave and the sea. It took only a few minutes, but, still high up on the lush verdant cliffs, they stumbled, laughing and gasping for their breath, onto a grassy plateau between smooth yellow-lichen boulders.

Matthias lay down his toga and brown fur belt. In the starry night Vivienne ran her eyes over his body. He grinned at her unhidden pleasure.

'You need a treat, and here I am. Little Baby Vivienne. I want you, I'm mad for you!' He thrust toward her.

The grass, mixed thickly with yellow gorse, prickled her back but the heavens shone with shining stars. Matthias wanted her, Matthias – so like her Guy, when they were young and she had him all to herself on the soft sand of Portelet.

Far below on the seashore, waves crashed onto dark rocks. Wild flowers dreamed all around them. Vivienne stroked Matthias' lithe, tanned-dark body. She imagined Guy again. She caressed Matthias' body, so like his. Lying together in the moonlight, near the sun-warmed scattered boulders Vivienne could hear wild birds and the guillemots as they called out and skimmed the violet-dark sea. The ocean hushed as it entered the dark and secret caves of Sark.

Matthias covered them both over with the pink cape.

'But your need is not for me, is it Ariadne? I know. I know.' His hair ruffled in the night breeze. 'One day, though, it will be.'

'Oh Matthias,' she drew him close to her.

'Shhhh. Go to sleep, Ariadne.'

He wrapped himself around her, resting his head at the base of her neck. Vivienne and Matthias slept soundly until dawn.

Rubbing her eyes, Vivienne slowly rose to sit up next to Matthias. He was awake, but lay smiling with his eyes shut. She tickled his still bare chest with a long grass. The morning sun played a gold light onto the island's fissured cliffs. Seagulls called out to each other, whirling overhead. Light shone down through the blue-green sea so Vivienne could see clear to the sand below, even to the shadow-brown seaweed beneath. Matthias sneezed at the tickling.

He opened his almost-black eyes and smiled his perfect Greek smile. She bent down to kiss him. His mouth tasted salty. He trailed a finger down her arm, arousing her.

'Victor Hugo adored this little island. Sark – said it was just like Cythera, the Mediterranean. Cythera, Aphrodite, Sark and now you, Ariadne. How about that? Any better now, Baby?'

Vivienne's hair blew about her face. She felt the early morning sun on her back. 'You're beginning to sound like someone I knew. Better, yes I do feel better. Had a lovely dream. I should start calling you 'baby' though, shouldn't I? I'm a good ten years older than you. actually, how old are you Matthias?'

The rising sunrays made his deep brown eyes speckle like tortoiseshell. 'How old do you think I am?' He asked, looking her straight in the face.

'Well...um, nineteen or so?'

'I'm seventeen!' He laughed, triumphant. 'But, but eighteen very soon! Honest!'

'Seventeen! My God, Matthias, you little terror! I thought...oh my God.' Vivienne started adjusting her clothes, fumbling for the swathes of blue, white and scarlet. Shoes? Oh, she didn't have them – barefoot, barefoot.

Laughing, Matthias tidied his white toga, tied on his fur belt and plonked the ivy crown with its horns back on his head.

'Don't spoil it, Baby. What's the big deal? You enjoyed us, didn't you? I surely have. Come on, let's us be Mediterranean? Huh? Not stuffy, staid old uptight British. Yes?' He helped brush off grass and gorse petals from her shift. 'Anyway. We were wonderful. Sleeping with you was wonderful.'

'Don't say sleeping with for goodness sake – don't go around saying sleeping with me!' Yet, yes, her body did feel good – relaxed and supple. Let this lovely feeling stay awhile, please?

'Hey. Why that sad little look, though?' Matthias asked.

A morning mist drifted over the sea. Vivienne felt it touch her eyes.

'What is it?' Matthias frowned.

'Well...at your age,' Vivienne watched the mist permeate the undergrowth around them, 'at exactly your age, I...I knew someone who had an... She didn't do very much more than we have just done. But you...you men, young boys, you can have your freedom, can't you? And pleasure – no regrets, no babies, no death.'

'Death? How did we get on to death?'

'Oh, Matthias. It's nothing – you are so young. Sorry.'

Matthias pretended to blow his reed pipe, hopping about the cliff like a sprite from the underworld. Vivienne found herself laughing at him. Straightaway he began to sing to her in a mock and surprisingly deep voice. 'Some enchanted evening, you will meet a stranger, you will meet a stranger across a crowded field!'

His antics relieved her, 'Let's go and get some breakfast, you awful boy!'

'Yes. Bacchus and Ariadne, well it's not only about booze, is it. It's feasting, it's forrrnication,' he growled, then 'but only if you're very lucky little satyr!' pulling a pretend crestfallen face.

Vivienne pulled a pretty rueful one right back.

Back at the Aval du Creux nobody seemed to have missed them. Everyone at the breakfast table looked much the worse for wear, anyway. Jessie and Rick weren't even there.

Later Jessie told her they'd stayed in bed, making love until gone four in the morning. It was the Sark thing. Never failed.

In her unused hotel bedroom, Vivienne stuffed some clothes in her overnight bag, ready to go home. She showered and changed into ordinary clothes, then answered a knock at the door.

'There was a message for you, Mrs Carré. Came yesterday evening.' The maid flicked her a suspicious look while handing Vivienne a scrap of hotel notepaper. Vivienne had only read 'from Mr Carré', when the bedside telephone rang loud as a fire alarm.

'And where the hell have you been?' David roared down the phone. 'I've been trying to contact you all bloody night, and this morning! What the fuck is going on Vivienne? Joseph is ill! Mum's beside herself. He's had a temperature. We called the doctor. If you deign to come home, I'll see you at the harbour!' Before Vivienne could say a single word, David banged down the receiver. His words reverberated like a punishment in her ears.

Joseph. Little Joseph! Oh God, please let him be all right. Vivienne immediately telephoned Pearl – simultaneously wishing she had firstly prepared some excuse.

'Yes?' Pearl answered in a timorous voice.

God, this was awful. Pearl would have found it all very difficult to cope with this. 'Pearl, it's me, Vivienne.' She heard a sharp intake of breath. 'Look, I'm so sorry about all this. How is Joseph? What did the doctor say?'

'Oh, Vivienne. I've been so worried! Poor little mite. But the doctor's just been. He says it's just a virus – going all round the island, apparently. He's left some antibiotics. Plenty of fluid, he says.' Pearl's voice quavered. 'It was in the dead of night you know. David came over. Oh Vivienne where were you? And now it's Sunday and we'll have to cancel the Lenfestys – a thing we have never had to do, not in all the years… and then the Sunday lunch. I've still got all that to do.'

'I'm so sorry, Pearl. Thank you for being so good with Joseph, I'm so glad he's alright. You did everything right,' Vivienne wound the white telephone lead round and round her wrist. 'Look, couldn't you take Joseph with you – to the Lenfestys? And…and, why don't you go for a pub lunch – save you cooking? Give you a break?'

'A pub lunch! A pub lunch? Good gracious, Vivienne, Eustace and I don't have pub lunches, especially never on Sundays! No and I'll have to cancel the Lenfestys. Joseph must stay indoors, in the warm. I'm sorry to say this, Vivienne, but you know drinking – well it isn't the answer for us. And we have been out of our minds over Joseph.' Pearl emphasised 'out-of-our-minds' as if Vivienne needed the message spelling loud and clear to her.

'I've said I'm sorry.' But it's never enough, though, is it, 'sorry'? Then Vivienne heard Pearl begin to splutter and cry.

'I'm going now,' Pearl attempted to clear her throat, 'no doubt David will have a thing or two to say to you.' Then she hung up like the phone was too heavy.

Vivienne replaced the receiver. She sat on the bed, seeing her reflection in the dressing table mirror. Just about done it now, then, hadn't she? Poor little Joseph. Poor little man. Yes, she should have been there for him. She'd make it up to him – take him shrimping… buy him an ice cream. He'd like that.

Of course David and Pearl were in the right. Vivienne ran her fingers through the tangled hair. Pouting her mouth in the mirror, she put on some lipstick. Guy thoughts and the warmth of Matthias' body, at least, stayed with her. She'd keep the night close inside her, just for a short while. So long as time would let her.

By the time she got on to the boat from Sark with all the sleepy people, Vivienne felt her dreams evaporate. Matthias, covered with someone's coat, lay sound asleep on the deck near the cabin room. Soon she would see the shadow of Guernsey's coast fall and darken the sea.

On St Peter Port harbour David stood in ambush, arms folded, legs akimbo. What would she say to cover her absence in the night? The Sark ferry buffer shuddered against the granite harbour wall and someone threw a rope, tying the boat tightly up to the quayside like it was tethered, good and proper.

Somehow, Vivienne felt smaller, like she had when her father and old Ma Jones waved her inefficiency at her. 'Well now,' Vivienne breathed, 'welcome back to Guernsey and all who sail in her.'

CHAPTER TEN

'So – you say you got drunk, fell asleep on the cliffs – on your own – nobody knew where you were?' David spat out. 'Do a lot of sleeping don't you Vivienne? Do you take me for a complete idiot? Who else was there? Somebody even drunker than you – looking for a quick one?'

Vivienne never saw David so angry. Could she hide from him – maybe run out of the room?

'Oh, come on David!' she said all in a hurry. 'You know what Sark is like. Once you're there…well, nothing seems real. It's…it's wild, a fantasy world, haunted. You know that. That's really why you didn't want to come isn't it?' A bleak, wafer thin excuse, she knew.

A hiatus engulfed the room as Vivienne cowered from him. David's temper reddened his face. It twisted into a wolf snout as he bore down on her.

'I know what bloody Sark is like! And I know what you are like. You drink yourself stupid the whole time, you don't know what the fuck is going on. And you are *a mother*! Do you hear? Do you think it's right that my mother should be looking after your child, just because you can't behave like a *normal, decent, caring* human being? Like a wife? *Your are my wife! My wife!*' He banged his fist down so hard on the pine kitchen table that it split in half with a loud crack. Cups and saucers slithered off, smashing to the floor. Blue and white striped china, their carefully collected set, rolled into splintered wood, pouring milk and scattering sugar amongst the debris.

'It's as well your son isn't here to see all this.' David breathed heavily. 'I don't know if I want to take any more of this, Vivienne. I really don't.' He ran his shaking hand through his hair.

At the sight of the jagged, broken table, the smashed crockery and David's face, mottled purple with fury, Vivienne surrendered in sobs.

'I know. I do know. Some of it's right, David. I'm sorry. It's just…I don't know what to do sometimes. I do love Joseph, of course I do. And you. We're family. But then…everything gets awful and I…I find a drink helps. Helps to cope.' She sat down on a kitchen chair and cried into her hands.

Outside a fitful wind blew up. Leaves scattered over the lawn. At length Vivienne heard David breathing more evenly. His voice levelled. He said he knew that some of what Vivienne felt was true. But, he ranted, she was wilful. He didn't expect her to be…orthodox. No she never had been that. But she had two sides to her: the loving mother, but then the gypsy. She had demons. David said he witnessed her – in bed at night – something disturbed her. She so easily became unbalanced. It had to stop. Something must be done.

'No more of Jessie's bloody parties. Do you hear?' He kicked at the pile of crockery, sending a whole cup to smash into the door.

'Yes. No.' Exhausted, Vivienne glanced up at David.

'You've pushed me too far,' he said, standing like a conquering Norman soldier, towering over her, 'Jessie's divorced. She has no morals. She's bad for you.'

Vivienne crumpled, all strength deserting her.

'I should never have let you go to that damn party. Mother was right. She agrees with me. She told me I should be reining you in. She's right. She brought me up within the highest standards. She knows what's right and what's wrong.' David strode around the room, just like one of Vivienne's bosses used to – dictating – with her trying to keep up with her bloody lousy shorthand.

'You wouldn't have got Mum going to Sark like that. But then, she never wanted to – not on her own. And she doesn't need to drink like…'

'Oh, alright! Alright! Nor did my mother, come to that. Nor Granmarie. Things are different now. I'm different.' Said Vivienne.

'Look here, Vivienne. Don't,' David's eyes turned to a colourless glass, 'don't you ever do such a thing again, otherwise we're finished. *Do you* understand?'

Vivienne managed to nod, unable to dredge up enough energy
to say, 'whilst we're issuing ultimatums, can you start to make love
to me, properly? Can you learn to please me? Or is that something
else your perfect Mum wouldn't allow?' No, Vivienne couldn't bring
herself to say it. Couldn't say: you're a repressed man, David Carré.
Pity it wasn't Eustace. Cultured, travelled Eustace, who influenced
you most. Pity Eustace didn't teach you to reach out over the parapet
sometimes and see all the life out there – all the fun.

Instead, Vivienne began to help David to clear up the mess.

As it turned out, one day, not long after the row, Eustace came to
see Vivienne. Eustace had praised her recent work. She had finished
several paintings now.

'Right, then. High time we got an exhibition going, Vivienne.
High time your work was shown.'

In her studio, once she got herself going, Vivienne immersed
herself in Guernsey's beauty. She painted pink granite cliffs, angry
grey ones; shimmering green sea with violet drifting through. The
cliff tops enticed her with their yellow and pink wildflowers, thick as
a flowery thatch. She captured the wildness of her island.

When he wasn't at nursery school, Vivienne took Joseph outdoors
with her. They'd trudge along untamed cliff paths, picking sloes from
the prickly hedges, eating ripe blackberries as they walked.

She had done some portraits – quite a few of Joseph. She'd painted
some of her friends' children. Some art she happily gave away but
accepted paid commissions from those who could afford it.

When he reached five, Vivienne took Joseph down to see his
grandparents at Granville. Vivienne reckoned Edward and Jean,
kept the property much smarter than when Granmarie was alive.
Granmarie didn't believe in spending too much money maintaining
properties. She had invested in her land and in her workmen.

Seeing Granmarie's room – where she used to sit, her favoured
cooking pans, great cauldrons, blackened and dented – saddened
Vivienne. Yet, the hand-sewn patchwork quilt still strewn on the

spare bed, the silver-backed hairbrush on Granmarie's dressing table, made her smile.

They went through the conservatory, opening the back door.

'Hello?' Vivienne called out. She had told them she would be coming, bringing Joseph. 'Anyone here?' The ceilings of the airy rooms were high. Though dark at the back, the front rooms were all bathed in western light.

It was a Sunday. All the workmen had gone to their own homes. Edward always went to church early on Sunday mornings, then again later in the evening.

'Hello!' Vivienne called again. 'Mum? No, Joseph, don't play with your granny's ornaments, darling. You know she doesn't like you to. She won't be pleased. Stop it.'

Joseph put back the china figurine, nearly missing the table so it wobbled before steadying to rest. 'Oops!' Joseph grimaced to Vivienne with a gappy smile. 'Sorreee mummy! Where's Granny? Don't like it when she's cross.' He eyed the trembling figurine nervously.

'Go and find something to do, sweetheart,' said Vivienne, wandering into the kitchen. Then she saw her mother outside the lean-to greenhouse. Jean gathered Granmarie's figs where they thrived above an underground well.

Joseph, fair-haired, tall for his age, ran to her. 'Hullo, Granny, can I have a fig?'

'In a moment, Oscar dear. I want us to have these with some goat's cheese. They taste nice like that. And I've specially made some of the onion marmalade chutney you like.'

Vivienne told Joseph about Oscar, saying that Granny's pet name for him was after his dead uncle, her son. Joseph took it in his stride.

'Onion marmalade? Yummy!' Joseph rubbed his stomach and rolled his tongue over his top lip. They laughed.

Well,' Jean motioned to Vivienne to take her shoes off. She had brought in some mud.

'Sorry.'

'Hello stranger. Want some tea?'

Far too early for a gin and tonic? Yes, of course it was. 'Fine.'

Jean took Joseph's hand and led him into the kitchen. They came back with a laden tray. 'Take your food out into the garden Oscar, will you?' Jean asked. 'It'll save making a mess on Granny's carpet. Take your milk, as well.'

Joseph dutifully trotted outside.

'He's a fine little lad, Ninny. A real Normandie.' Jean poured the tea.

'We're pleased with him, mum. Off to school now. Dad not around?'

As she spoke, Edward came in. He pecked Vivienne so she felt his cool, bristly chin on her cheek. He looked smaller – hardened into himself.

'Well then. You brought little,' he looked straight at Vivienne whilst inclining his head toward Jean, 'Oscar. He's a good looking boy, isn't he?'

'He is. Thing is – guess what? I've got an exhibition coming up, Dad. Eustace is arranging it for me and…'

'Eustace? Is he? Tea, please Jean.' Edward helped himself to two spoonfuls of sugar. 'An art exhibition, that'll be?'

'Yes! At the Manor House.' Vivienne felt her heart rush, 'it'll be quite a do, actually. Eustace is…'

'Oh, good! A party! Oh, I'll come to that,' an odd pink colour rose in Jean's face as she began to stir her tea too many times with her spoon. She looked expectantly at Vivienne, like a child wanting to be let into a confidence.

'Now, Jean. Calm yourself. We've not decided yet. Will there be what you might call, a star guest or something?' Edward narrowed his eyes at Vivienne.

'Um. Well, me. Sort of?'

'Oh. So what'll it be then Nin, local scenes? That kind of thing? Will they sell? Lot of that stuff around, isn't there?' Edward stopped talking and looked around distractedly. Then he fished out an English newspaper from under where he sat and spread it out by his feet, scanning the headlines. 'Lot of salacious rubbish, these days. Lot of gossip.'

'Yes, but portraits as well. Been getting a bit of a reputation!'
Vivienne said, as if ashamed. 'And – listen to this – Eustace found a
London agent. An agent! He's interested in my work!' Vivienne did a
'Ta Da!' flinging her arms out extravagantly.

Eustace and Jean regarded her silently. Jean ran a finger absent-
mindedly around her tea cup.

'Eustace has?' said Edward. 'London eh? Well, "that's where it's
all at" is the colloquialism these days, isn't it? Got to be where things
are all at, these days. You'll make sure there's orange juice, won't you?
Not just booze.' Edward folded up the paper and put it on the coffee
table. 'You're encouraging young Joe…Oscar these days aren't you
Nin? With his art? He's jolly good, you know. I've kept some of his
drawings, from when he was a baby. Great talent, I reckon. Course
he'll need training. Get qualifications. That's important, these days.
Go to a proper university, not one of them fancy Art Schools you used
to hanker for. Get qualified, for a good future, eh? Our Oscar.'

'Yes.' Said Vivienne. 'Of course I am.'

'Or, he might try architecture? Yes, an architect. That's a good,
solid profession. Encourage him with his designs, Nin.' Edward got
up. 'Right, I'm off. Got things to do. I'm doing a reading this evening,
St John. Oh, we'd better let you know about your do nearer the time.
See how your mother is, you know?'

'Okay. How are you feeling, Mum?' Vivienne asked.

'She's a bit better, Nin, since the new sitting room en suite. Aren't
you Jean?' Edward muttered as he left the room. 'But of course, we
live from day to day. We are in God's hands.'

Jean collected up the tea things, clattering around in the kitchen.
Vivienne leaned on the door, watching her. 'Now, don't forget our
invitation will you, Nin? I'll have to think what to wear. Don't know
much about art! Don't know where you get it all from. Don't go to
many art exhibitions! Now where is that Oscar?' Jean put some of her
cup cakes into a paper bag. 'These are for him. Where are you taking
him? Don't bring him back home too late, will you? I want him to
help me feed the chickens. It's his special job. Oscar loves doing that.

Then bath and an early night, ready for his playschool in the morning. Got to look after our little man.'

'Yes Mum,' said Vivienne. 'Of course.'

Eustace booked the Manor House for Vivienne's exhibition. They sent out invitations and ordered the caterers. Eustace came over to their house to look over the selected work.

'We'll have to make the framing consistent, Vivienne. Blond wood? Impressionist style, what d'you think? Your style reminds me of the French Impressionists, Renoir in particular. Renoir came to Guernsey, didn't he?'

'Sure did. Painted our red granite rocks with Prussian blue sea. Thanks, Eustace. You do say the nicest things.'

'Not just being nice, Vivienne.'

Vivienne set up each canvas, lining them up around the studio. She and Eustace examined them solemnly.

'Mmm. And,' Eustace held up her favourite picture of Joseph, 'possibly different frames – for the portraits?' They arranged the pictures by height and width, to get an idea of balance.

Vivienne wore a black velvet shirt with her long black corduroy skirt and her hair pinned up. Eustace had his usual light green Guernsey and grey flannels.

'What colour are the Manor House exhibition walls, Eustace? Do we know?'

'Good point. I think we'll need to go and have a look, don't you? And we must see where we'll put the table, for champagne and nibbles. There's plenty of car-parking, anyhow.'

He fished out his chequebook and counted the cheques. 'I'll pay the deposit whilst we're there. And we must get a quote from the printers, for a catalogue. You can get on with those details.' He smiled. 'Don't look so worried, Vivienne. This is something I very much want to do.'

'It all seems to be getting a bit expensive, Eustace.' Vivienne felt concern. And how could she have ever threatened her friendship with this man? 'I'll make an appointment and go and see the Manor House man, Eustace. What's his name?'

'Delas. Cecil Delas. Crusty old bloke, but easy-going. I think we can work with him, Vivienne.'

They parted, Vivienne determined she wouldn't let Eustace down. She opened some wine once he left and poured one glass. Well, maybe just one more.

Vivienne took Joseph to school, staying until he ran off with his mates without a backward glance. Lots to do, lots to organise. She found a decent framer, had her catalogue designed and organised a printer. Lowering clouds hovering over her head had not, yet, descended.

Cecil Delas, in a mustard velvet waistcoat and red polka dot bow tie, pumped her hand telling her he wouldn't charge the highest price he could have for the Manor House showroom. Though she might like to donate money toward his conservation fund? Place would go to rack and ruin if he didn't keep finding ways to renovate it. Delas showed her over the facilities. Vivienne checked the toilets were adequate and the small kitchen clean.

Eustace decided on canapés, 'to go with the champagne reception.'

'Goodness!' Pearl remonstrated to Vivienne. 'All this? I hope he doesn't get out of pocket. Do you know, Vivienne, I can think of a few things I need. New sitting room curtains, for one thing.'

'I know. I'm sorry, Pearl. I have offered...'

David said he didn't doubt her talent, and the project had given her a goal to work toward. But he doubted Vivienne's ability to follow things through. Say she had another exhibition, on the back of this one? Would she cope? Would she work hard enough to get up another stock? It all seemed to take up enough of her time as it was. Far too much of her time.

Blah, blah, blah.

Of course, Vivienne hadn't told him that Matthias had taken to stalking her. He might be handsome, he might remind her of Guy, but only just eighteen? Not the kind of attention she needed, at all. No way, not like this.

Stupidly, with other things on her mind, Vivienne had given Matthias her direct line number. How dumb. When he telephoned her in her studio she put on a specially light-hearted voice.

'What was that about death, Baby?' Matthias wanted to know, insisting she answer.

'I really don't remember saying that. Really, I don't,' Vivienne considered putting the phone down. 'And I really don't have time for this nonsense, Matthias. I'm very busy.'

'Yes you did! You did Baby!' His voice came over even younger than she recalled. Flattered? Yes, but with a kind of nervous relish at Matthias' attention.

'Well, if I did it's...none of your business. Shouldn't you be doing your homework or something? Not chasing after thirty year-old ladies?' Vivienne bit a nail clean in half.

'Did you murder someone?' Matthias pressed her. 'Is that what this is about? Is that what's driving you crazy, Baby? Murder?' He sang over the phone, 'Crazeee Baby!'

'Shut up, Matthias! Just drop it, will you? Stop it.' Alarm shook her words. 'Leave me alone. You don't know what harm you are doing. And stop calling me Baby!' Now she did hang up.

Instantly, the telephone rang again.

'Just to say, I'll see you soon, Baby. Very soon.' Matthias clicked off.

In a glass Vivienne poured vodka, letting the level go over the diamond pattern limit line. Odd how Matthias could disarm her so. In spite of his cheeky persistence, you could say he had real charm – magnetic charm. Vivienne smiled at this thought – young Turk! Well, young Greek, actually.

Her pictures, newly framed, each with a neatly typed label, waited patiently. Tomorrow Vivienne's exhibition opened. Pearl would look after Joseph. She had even bought some of these frozen things called 'Fish Fingers' that Joseph liked. 'And I've bought chocolate – Angel Delight. Whatever next?' said Pearl, looking highly amused at her own naughtiness.

Edward and Jean would try to make it. Jean had made an effort with her outfit, Vivienne had helped her to choose, but lately she had been up and down. Polly and Eric were coming and Jessie: alone. Eustace helped Vivienne with the guest list, unabashedly adding people he thought might be useful to her future.

'It'll be a bit like a soirée,' Eustace teased Vivienne. A *Guernsey Post* photographer would attend. 'A Peter someone,' said Eustace.

Oops. Well, she would just have to deal with that one when the time came. Vivienne shopped with Polly, buying a silk burgundy blouse and a midi-skirt in a darker red. The hairdresser washed and gold-highlighted her hair. He teased Vivienne's curls into a soft mass framing her face. She added diamanté clips either side. She painted pale green eye shadow over a white base, adding black eyeliner with flicks at the corner of each eye. And, just for this do, false eyelashes.

David said she looked nice. Eustace said she looked stunning. 'Good luck. You've worked very hard.' He kissed her hand as he escorted Vivienne into the exhibition hall.

Save for the waiter, they were the first there. Eustace, in dark suit and black and white striped tie, helped to pour champagne into the waiting rows of glasses. The canapés, just out of the caterer's oven, were tiny quiches and mouthfuls of smoked salmon and prawn topped with a skewered caper.

'I'm enjoying this!' Smiled Eustace. 'Cheers!' He clinked his fluted glass against Vivienne's.

Edward and Jean arrived with some friends, instantly claiming their orange juices. A serious Edward took Jean's thin arm as together they circulated the room: he darting surreptitious looks at attractive women.

Polly, pregnant again, beamed over to Vivienne, with her quiet Eric close by her side. Jessie skipped around the room, saying she just wanted to, 'buy just everything, honeybun.' And soon the room crowded with guests. Red spots of 'sold' started to appear. The noise level rose, the champagne flowed.

Eustace winked at Vivienne, smiling a 'Well done!'

'Thanks,' she mouthed back over to him. 'Thanks for everything,' and took another full glass of champagne. What the heck. Time to celebrate.

As she saw David chatting to one of Edward's friends, nodding in agreement at something, Peter from the *Post* arrived. He began to take photographs, the flashlight making pops of blinding white. He worked his way around to where Vivienne stood.

'Great stuff, Vivienne. Risky business, art exhibitions. But then you do love taking a good risk don't you?' Popping a canapé into his mouth, Peter grinned from ear to ear.

'Don't start...' Vivienne hissed between her teeth, frowning at him.

'I know, I know. I won't say anything more. You look wonderful, though. Love the outfit.' Peter ran his hand down the silky fabric of her blouse.

As he did so, Matthias stormed in, walked straight over to Vivienne and slapped Peter's arm away from her.

'Hey! No need for that, chum!' Peter poked Matthias in the chest.

'Every need, I'd say,' Matthias poked him right back.

Vivienne, trying hard not to panic, lowered her voice. 'Who the hell invited you? Matthias?' One or two people looked over curiously. She smiled over at them, brightly as she could. 'Let's get out of here a second,' she prodded Peter and Matthias toward the kitchen and, in a still lowered voice, 'Do you mind! This is my god-damned party!' Then pushed the two of them into the tiny room, slamming the door.

'Now, just stop it. Both of you! Get out! Go home. Leave me to this bloody exhibition, will you? Do you hear?' She shouted, losing her nerve.

'Oooooh,' said Peter archly, 'so is this little boy an item, then, Vivienne? Well, well,' he made to take a photograph of Vivienne and Matthias standing together.

Matthias grabbed the strap of Peter's camera and flung it down to the floor. A lens fell off.

'Didn't you hear what the lady said?' Matthias got Peter by the collar. 'Piss off home!'

'Both of you. You too, Matthias. For pity's sake. Leave me alone. Go away!' Vivienne suddenly felt her stomach knot in a surging pain.

With Vivienne fighting a rising discomfort, Matthias punched Peter, full on the face. His nose began to bleed.

'Why you bloody little Greek!' Peter slapped Matthias' face.

They started to wrestle, crunching over the broken glass of the lens. Instantly, Vivienne knew she would be sick. She just managed to reach the sink and vomited. 'The prawns?' She retched. 'Oh, God help me.' And heaved again.

Matthias and Peter still scuffled. Vivienne spewed once more, tried to grab a piece of kitchen paper and weave past the men to get out of the kitchen. She must get help.

Just as she reached the door, her burgundy blouse covered with sick with the two men punching each other violently, a man opened it.

'Is this the toilet?' He said. Dressed in a black polo necked jumper and black jeans, a tall man came in.

It was Guy Beaufort.

PART TWO

CHAPTER ELEVEN

'Guy?' Vivienne stood stock-still.

Matthias stopped punching Peter. 'Uh?' he said.

'Eh?' Peter let go of Matthias, gawping at the stranger.

Dark-haired, slightly greyer, deep-brown eyes measuring the scene, Guy moved fully into the small, crowded kitchen.

'Hello Vivvy. Need some help?' Without waiting for her to reply, Guy pulled out his handkerchief, damped it under the cold tap and wiped away at the mess on Vivienne's silk burgundy blouse. Under his tender touch, her skin instantly stirred.

'Guy?' Vivienne said again, staring at him. Guy?

'Yes, it's me!' Guy said, as if fairly amazed, himself. 'Wondered where you'd got to!' Then, 'Hi there, Pete. Up to no good as usual?' He slapped Peter hard on the back.

'Hullo mate. How's you?' Peter snickered.

Guy made a pained expression of gathering impatience. Seeing it, Matthias fetched Peter's camera, lobbying it toward his stomach.

'Yes, well, I think we'd best be going, don't you, Pete?' Matthias said. 'Thanks for the party Baby. Come on you idiot.' The two men scarpered, Matthias prodding Peter in the back as he stuffed a white shirt tail back into his trousers.

Vivienne and Guy stood alone. 'Thought this was the toilet.' Guy said shyly. 'God. Hi Vivienne. You're looking very elegant.'

The party noises reverberated through thin partition walls. Someone else came in, saw them and retreated hastily, shutting the door loudly. She should have put up notices 'Toilet', 'Kitchen', bit late now. 'Do I?

'Mmm. Very chic.'

Awash in his beguilement, Vivienne stammered, 'So - So, how... how are you Guy?' (Throw your arms around him. Hug him. Guy is here! No, cannot. Must not.)

'Not bad. We're on a…a sabbatical. Darius's here, too. But they're on holiday. Darius got the invitation. I knew you'd have a really good show Vivvy. Great stuff.'

'Thanks. You look well.' (A sabbatical? How long is a sabbatical?) Vivienne dabbed at the damp on her blouse. 'I must look a complete fright!'

'Course you don't. You haven't changed, still the same free spirit! Even more glamorous, if anything.' His bear brown eyes danced alive in candid flirtation.

You'd think, by now, that it would have gone: the hot potent feel of Guy's hand on her skin. The rushing up inside of her. The intense feeling shooting back from him. The pure hit of desire, if you like. Of all the people in the world, Guy Beaufort, it's you.

'How's America?' Came out way too strained. How black suited him! Vivienne wanted to run her hands under his sweater and feel his body again…

'America's fine. It's me not quite with it.' Guy stepped closer to her.

Through her closing eyes, Vivienne saw him move toward her. She felt his breath on her eyelids. He bent forward so their noses touched.

The kitchen door flew open, banging Guy fully on the back. 'Hey!' He called out, swinging round, thumping his hand on the door to stop the intruder. 'Watch it!'

'Come on, Nin!' implored her father. 'Hah – you,' when he saw Guy. 'Bloody Beaufort!' He muttered not quite inaudible. 'Anyway, come on.'

Vivienne pulled away from Guy, 'Thanks for your help, Guy. Thanks.' She gestured vaguely toward the sink and Guy's crumpled, wet handkerchief.

'Sure.' Guy said, flashing that look at her again.

'People are leaving Nin!' Edward shouted as he walked away.

Vivienne hurried back into the exhibition room, still buzzing with energy. Red spots of 'SOLD' dotted her paintings. Over the far side of the room were David and Eustace, their faces holding identical expressions of doubt.

'What? What?' She mouthed, flinging laughter over the situation, like a fire-blanket. She circulated around the room moving further and further away from Guy, but watching him all the while.

'How are you?' 'Nice to see you!' 'Oh you did? You bought one? Thank you! How kind.' In, she knew, too trilling a voice. But, after all people did like her paintings. All that work had not been for nothing. Good old Eustace.

Over the chatter, departing heads she sought out Guy's. He had joined a pale Amanda at the back of the room. (Oh, Amanda, what are we to do?) Amanda stood expressionless in a white blouse, tailored cream skirt with a pink cardigan loosely over her shoulders. Next to her was Darius and his latest, uber-smart, girlfriend. A native New Yorker? Had to be, in her black tuxedo and baker boy cap.

Vivienne went over to Eustace and David. They all took full glasses from the depleted champagne tray. She put an arm firmly through Eustace's. 'Well then? Everything under control.' She patted Eustace's hand, avoiding David's frown.

'Thanks for coming!' She called out to the departing crowd. 'And thanks,' turning to Eustace, 'for your support and for making this all come true.'

Eustace bowed his head toward her, lifted his glass in a toast and said, 'It's up to you now, Vivienne, my dear,' in studied, thoughtful soberness.

Soon, all the goodbyes had been said and coats gathered. Guy waved 'Bye, see you,' over the top of Amanda's head. If Eustace or David suspected anything, neither said so. Used to the unthinkable passing unsaid, Vivienne pushed regret and remorse from her mind. The feel of Guy's hand lingered on her breasts. Tonight had been hers.

Matthias called to say he was sorry. In the midst of mixing oil paints, telephone in one hand, jar of linseed oil in the other, Vivienne mildly scolded him.

'Don't keep hanging around, Matthias. Sark was wonderful. But that's it, okay?'

'Yes, yes I know. For now Baby. But I will keep trying. I feel it in my heart. You are going to be special to me.'

He seemed cheerful enough, thank heaven. He'd concentrate on his University entrance exams, he told her. He fancied a Classics degree. Well he would, wouldn't he? He had joshed.

'And you have such talent! But,' Matthias sighed in exaggeration, 'I can see you are otherwise engaged, so-o-o to speak?' She protested as he continued, 'Look, promise me you'll keep in touch? Or – if you need any help, any help at all, little Baby. I can't think you did murder someone! Not you. Whatever happened you were defenceless. You don't defend yourself very well, do you?'

So Matthias left Guernsey in a cloud of academic glory to enter Corpus Christi College at Oxford University. He began, he told her later, four years of the best time in his life.

Didn't she? Didn't she defend herself? Was she just another frightened rabbit? Perhaps all Guy's women were frightened rabbits? Except Rita. Nobody less frightened looking than her. Triumphant, more like. Poor Amanda.

Well then. Guy's back in the island for a while? Now you see him. Now you don't. That's Guy. But he's a married man, Vivienne. She should stop it, she knew. Yet, the dreams, the dreams! Lying awake next to the sleeping David – who only needed to make love to make a baby, not because he wanted her – she remembered Dorothy Parker's book that Guy had given her. Vivienne re-read the words. Must she, also 'peer at the night through rusted bars' for the rest of her life? Mmm? That's all Folks?

Natalie, Guy's daughter, played in Saumarez park. Vivienne saw her, sliding down the slides – swinging on the swings. Natalie was a pretty little thing, with Guy's black hair and dark brown eyes.

Their daughter, Vivienne and Guy's aborted daughter, why, she'd be entering her teens by now. She'd be standing next to Vivienne in the park, in the sunshine. Maybe Nicola Jane would be looking forward, say, to a swim this afternoon? Instead of lying dead, who knows where? Without even a Christian burial, or anything.

'The light of my life', Vivienne called Joseph, growing big and strong. 'Seven going on thirty-five!' She liked to tease him. There was such a grown up little head on her strapping young son. He did well at school, often going in to her studio to draw even without her prompting him. She ruffled his fair hair. 'Going to be a Picasso, you!' He'd laugh back.

'Aw, Ma!'

Vivienne stood near the rope ladders, slung between two iron trestles – Joseph's favourite. The little boy swung on the rungs, fit as a monkey. As Guy strolled around the corner of the children's park, Vivienne's heart thudded so rapidly she thought it might well thud out of sync and she would die on the spot. That would look good wouldn't it? Mother dies in park after seeing ex-lover approaching. That would look well – printed in the *Guernsey Post*, wouldn't it?

Guy came toward her with Natalie holding his hand, but Natalie slipped off to join Joseph, looking equally nimble on the ropes. Then the pair of them ran off to the swings.

'Look at them!' he said, but Guy's eyes rested steadily on Vivienne's.

Oh, he looked so good in a grey roll-top sweater (knitted by Amanda?) Yes, Vivienne reckoned, she may well pass out any moment now.

Guy's sabbatical had stretched more than a year – and was now well into two. Vivienne guessed his work wasn't selling but, naturally, you couldn't mention that. Hers flourished.

'Kids are great fun, aren't they?' Guy said, as they fell in step, naturally together, circling the park. 'Amanda can't have any more. Fact is – she's never been right since Natalie was born. Had a very hard time of it.'

They came to an empty park bench and sat down, studiedly apart. Vivienne let her head lean back and breathed in the fresh air, smelling of mown grass. The trees overhead gently fluttered green leaves, fitful in a stirring breeze.

'I'm sorry.'

'Turns out,' Guy let his hand smooth down the metal arm of the bench and looked away from Vivienne, 'Amanda didn't want sex before marriage and is none too keen on it afterwards, either.' As he turned back toward her, his eyes slid sideways to meet hers.

'You can't blame her.' Vivienne stiffened, suddenly wary of this frankness. 'She's probably scared of getting pregnant again.'

'Mmm, probably. Oh, Amanda's a good person. But I do like kids, though.'

Do you Guy? Vivienne thought. Can't tell you what I did with ours, then, can I? She stretched her legs out, crossing booted ankles. Resting her head right back, Vivienne's eyes closed. A long sigh released from her, drifted up through the leafy trees, then disappeared into the sky.

'What about you, Vivvy, you and David?'

With her head laid back, her eyes still closed, Vivienne slowly shook her head.

Then Guy reached for her hand.

Another exhibition in London awaited her attention. Her style, after the French Impressionists, was in fashion. Eustace wouldn't be involved this time. The agent, and someone he knew had begun negotiations.

Eustace said, extra casually, 'Guy Beaufort is in no hurry to go back to America, is he Vivienne? He…he's not like you, is he? You are working so hard, I know you are, toward a career?'

David went on and on, about how much time she took up with her painting. After all, they had Joseph's school routine to think about, David complained and *he* couldn't help in the house much, nor did he want to. His mother, Pearl, agreed. David helping out with housework was quite unthinkable.

At least David couldn't argue that the money from her paintings was hers. Vivienne opened a modest personal account. There wasn't a great deal of money to put in it, of course, but it was a start.

Vivienne and Guy met again. They made dates to meet in the park – sometimes with the children but, once or twice, not. In Guy's company, Vivienne talked of things she didn't even think about, let alone thought she knew about. Like, when Guy said she'd love Venice, Vivienne heard herself saying how wonderful water is as an element for reflective colour.

Guy made her laugh as he relayed stories of Andy Warhol's parties and why he chose familiar objects like the Campbell soup tins for his silks-screens. Vivienne wanted to hear everything and all about the soirées, saying how she understood Warhol challenged traditional concepts of portraying beauty. Get her!

One time, Guy leaned over and kissed her, right there in the open air! Like it was a natural, human, thing to do.

Vivienne found a small, inexpensive hotel in London, overlooking the Thames river. Guy told Amanda he needed to meet up with Darius who had a flat there (full of modern Habitat stuff and red, plastic chairs, apparently). The new exhibition needed organising, Vivienne told David.

Joseph had packed his own rucksack carefully. Camping on Herm island for half-term week with the Scouts was a real treat. Vivienne bought him some binoculars, a book on Channel Island birds, a notebook and a new penknife.

Vivienne took Joseph down to St Peter Port harbour. The other boys had gathered, fresh and eager as colts. 'Bye Ma,' he stretched up to kiss her cheek.

'Bye darling. Take care.'

They waved to each other until the Herm ferry had chugged away right out of sight. Then, stopping only to pick up her suitcase, Vivienne sped to the Airport.

London still excited her. The specialist Art store was simply a sweet shop. Vivienne and Guy bought sable paintbrushes, charcoal and paints. Vivienne browsed through some posters in rack, calling Guy over to look: Titian's jewel colours, Raphael, Van Gogh, Monet's blues and greens. With their heads so close together, his nearness scintillated the very bones of her spine.

Dinner: the Bistro was candlelit. Red wine and brandy glasses flickered in the light of flames. The subtle music played, lulling

Vivienne.

> 'Give me just a little more time
> and love will surely grow
> Give me just a little more time...'

In their bedroom, a king-size bed had clean white sheets and an old-fashioned mulberry counterpane. There was a wide view of the watery Thames. Vivienne went to the windows and opened them out to the night.

'Light reflected on water!' The river lapped below them, dark grey streaked transparent yellows and orange.

Behind her, Guy came close, to see the view. He enfolded her in his arms, hugging her to him. He nuzzled her neck. 'Dior?' (Yes, saved for and secretly hoarded.) Guy rubbed his face into her hair.

She turned around. They kissed greedily, hands stripping off clothes, bodies dangerous with desire, joined together in voluptuous embrace.

Throwing themselves onto the bed, net curtains blew in the night breeze. Guy flicked off all the bedroom lights. Vivienne heard the swish of boats on the river, felt cold river air waft through the windows.

Suntanned, worked out – prepared for these nights – they began to explore each other. Vivienne told Guy they were abandoned children just like they once had been.

'Remember Portelet Guy?'

'Yes, you round that pole on the pier! The moonlight – '

'Yes, yes!' Vivienne's senses overflowed with arousal. 'You – under the sea – you and me under the sea!'

Guy kissed her face, pushing her head and shoulders down on to the pillow.

Resting, delaying an end to their play, they lay quiet. Vivienne heard a tugboat blow its horn, shushing its way up the river. Beginning again, she made love to him, unwilling to stop, not for a single, stolen second.

Time was against them. Vivienne had turned the travel clock face away to the wall, not even looking at her watch. Always, with Guy, time meant nothing. Other considerations – all of them – fled. All defences fell in her willing bestowal.

In the morning and Vivienne cursed fatigue and how sleep claimed her without her consent. Unusually, she ran a bath. Normally, with breakfast to make and the school run, a quick shower had to do.

Covered in scented suds, her hair pinned up, Vivienne splashed Guy. His long legs were bent at the knees with wet black hairs flattened. 'This is really naff! A soppy romantic film!' He gave an embarrassed laugh.

'Yes, like soap opera! Ha, ha! Nothing wrong with romance, Guy.' Washing his hair, she kneaded his scalp, making a lather of bubbles, then rinsed the thick black mop. My God! To think she thought she'd never see him again. Now here, in London, she was sharing a warm bath with him! Vivienne piled on a popping cloud of white froth to cover her legs. She could feel strands of hair pinging into spirals in the hot steam. The tops of her arms were fat no matter how much she dieted or exercised, whereas Guy's body was dark and lean as the Portelet days.

In the taxi, on the way to the hotel, they had passed the dreaded hospital. The doctor. The room. She shuddered. No, No, don't think about it. Right now Guy and she were lovers: god and goddess, with no earthly worries. She let the hot tap run again and soaped his back, kissing his wet, slippery skin.

Now – the art galleries and Covent Garden. In between, Vivienne fitted in the agent and her exhibition. A gay young man, dressed in black T-shirt and leather jacket (The London Media Uniform perhaps?) said, in a positive but flat tone, that the show ought to cover costs, at least. He had seen her Guernsey exhibition catalogue, he sniffed. She would need a decent sponsor, funding and quotations. But she probably did have a market, at least a tiny niche, he said coolly, with an aloof certainty.

Guy strode, Vivienne taking two steps to his one, as they headed toward the National Gallery. 'What if we're seen?' Vivienne asked. 'We're invisible in a crowd,' he said, smiling down at her.

Bacchus and Ariadne awaited them. Thankfully the bench in front stood empty. So they sat, Vivienne recalled, just as if they were the same people as all those years ago.

'Titian's real genius,' said Vivienne, 'was Bacchus looking as though he had that very instant, just as we look, jumped out of the coach. The lightning strike: the French *coup de foudre*. Love at first sight. Suspension of belief. Ariadne points to her future …there and then,' Vivienne hesitated '…for lovers, it's a *je ne sais quoi*…a certain something no-one else can see.' Vivienne sighed.

Guy made no response to 'love at first sight' nor 'that certain something' but agreed on Titian's genius. Anyway, they sat here together again. For Vivienne, it was enough.

'Coffee?' Guy asked.

His wide hand curled around a mug of chocolate, stamped 'T N G' in black capital letters. Guy spoke quietly. To Vivienne, his strong voice sounded like chocolate itself. The table they managed to grab was round and small, really barely big enough for their two coffee mugs. Vivienne felt Guy's closeness.

'You're laying a ghost, aren't you?' Guy said, slowly.

'You mean…getting you out of my system?' He had startled her. No, no, Vivienne didn't like this but didn't say 'Don't Guy, don't spoil this precious time. Our time together.'

'Something like that?' He continued.

'I don't think that, no. No, I don't think of…us like that.' said Vivienne.

At the next table, strangers – a man and woman – nearby, probably up in Town for the day, sat dressed in quality clothes. In identical camel hair coats and Hermes scarves they poured over a National Gallery catalogue.

It was as if the coffee shop were suddenly alien to her and full of people Vivienne didn't know with faces she'd never seen. The air cooled, plummeting her mood downward.

'Don't be sad,' Guy put his mug down and held her hand. She instantly squeezed his fingers around hers, flashing him a questioning look. Stay with me, never go away again?

'There isn't an us, though, is there Vivvy? We're having a good time, yes – even a special time', Guy gave a frustrated sigh, 'You women! But this, us – well, we're both married. Intend to stay married?' Having finished his chocolate, Guy took out a cigarette packet. He lit up, turned his face and blew smoke away from her, through his nostrils, like a dragon.

You women? But Vivienne didn't want to analyse, especially not their marriages and not here! Marriage to David – staying married? Not now, she couldn't think about it, for God's sake. Instead, she said, 'I do love you.'

Guy took a deep drag from his cigarette. This time the exhaled smoke curled in front of him, in a blue-grey haze. Obscured by an ethereal mist, she couldn't control, Guy at once seemed veiled and out of reach.

'Come on, Vivvy. Don't let's spoil things. Come on.' He helped her put her coat on, her brown woollen midi with black fur collar. She retrieved her leather bag from the wooden floor. 'No more mulling.' Guy said. 'Let's go find a nightclub.'

The Flamingo Club was in Wardour Street. Light jazz played as they drank schooners of sherry. A lonely saxophone cried quietly. A drummer caressed his drum with splayed out brushes.

'Dig live music. It all started here and Birdland, New York, as well, of course.' Said Guy.

Laying a ghost? Guy really thought that? This – affair – was a way of getting over him? Well, no point in living then, to be honest. And, of course, Vivienne compelled herself until it hurt, not to ask, 'Have you done this before, Guy – escaped from Amanda?'

'Stop dwelling, Vivvy. Doesn't do any good, looking back. Just enjoy what we have. Look, it's how I am. Never could take life too seriously, see?'

The warming liquid, the soporific jazz lulled Vivienne, her spirit melted to the soothing sounds. So, when they made love their last night, she felt him come back to her: back to how they were. She would keep her love for Guy safe and warm. How could anyone possibly harm it? She would guard it for them. Nothing could destroy true lovers' feelings. It was not possible.

Waking to noisy river traffic, Vivienne and Guy decided they just had time to do the Tate Gallery. Seeking out David Hockney's *Mr and Mrs Ossie Clark and Percy* they laughed.

'You look just like Mrs Clark well, Celia Birtwhistle.' Guy said.

'Yes, well then you'll have to be Ossie Clark. And we both know who Percy is!' Vivienne shot Guy a knowing look. Yes, they had nicknames for each others loins, as well.

They flew back to Guernsey on the same flight but in separate seats in different rows. As they glided over the island, Vivienne mused. How green Guernsey was. How idyllic. Yet those pastures hid minefields of danger and deceit.

A tune from the London Flamingo Club played on in her mind:

> 'You're just too good to be true.
> Can't take my eyes off of you.
> You'd be like heaven to touch.
> I want to hold you so much…'

Wanting to turn and look at Guy, instead Vivienne sang to herself. She often sang, on aeroplanes, it never embarrassed her. Not keen on flying, she preferred boats and ferries – they took longer – she felt no rush to get back home – where a kind of deadening safety awaited. With David, it was like she was somehow suspended in her life, drowning in an invisible amniotic sac.

So: was this how addicts felt? Guy is a drug of choice? His sex, his sexual venom in her veins is her need for survival? Where's the antidote? Who has the cure?

With Guy swarming through her mind, Vivienne prayed thanks as the plane's wheels bumped and screeched over the runway. She knew David waited to take her home.

In the Arrivals Hall, Vivienne spotted Amanda. She wore a tan suede coat, her light brown hair falling straight to her shoulders in separate strands of uneven length. Standing near the exit doors, Amanda jiggled her car keys, standing tiptoe, craning her neck to find Guy. How troubled she looked.

Vivienne felt a stab, a pang of guilt. Because there was more than worry on Amanda's face. Something much more than that. On that day Amanda Beaufort's face showed utter defeat.

CHAPTER TWELVE

Pearl Carré told Vivienne she'd heard of Amanda Beaufort's illness. 'Some bowel thing or other, after the birth of their child. They are quite concerned for her, I believe.'

'I'm sorry to hear that,' Vivienne said, 'Amanda's young…'

'Yes, and doesn't get much attention from that husband of hers.' Pearl flicked Vivienne a sly look.

Vivienne wondered if David had told her right – that if Pearl knew her past she'd label Vivienne 'damaged goods'? Had Pearl heard any gossip? If so, she never confronted Vivienne with anything. Although Vivienne understood Eustace's warmth toward her wasn't entirely shared by Pearl – that she wasn't exactly the apple of her mother-in-law's eye – they got along all right. Well, didn't they? When Vivienne examined her deceits they held no particular triumph for her. It was necessary, maybe, but she did wish she didn't have to lie quite so much.

At La Colette, David was totally occupied, both with his work and keeping the place maintained. There was more than enough, he always claimed, to keep a chap out of mischief. He'd take Joseph around the fields with him, letting him water the plants in the greenhouses, paint the old wooden stable doors, hose down the stone courtyards. Yes, there was always plenty of work for a Guernseyman to do.

'Man's work,' said David.

Their bungalow was but a brief walk from the main house, La Colette. Sometimes, on his rounds of the land and outbuildings – checking what needed doing next day, next week, even next year – Vivienne caught David spying at her through the studio window. So Vivienne kept the wine bottle, and sometimes a vodka shot, under a table now.

Anyway, the lift of the London trip helped for a while. Vivienne worried what Eustace thought – about Guy at the exhibition – what David might have thought. She had tried to ensure them, to hint that nothing untoward had happened. Vivienne just hoped that David believed that the old flame had guttered to an end. David hadn't said as much, not in those words – only reporting that Eustace thought Vivienne would 'Settle down when she's older'. What, Vivienne pondered, did that mean? When she was too old for any straying? So, what age would that be, then?

Eustace apparently said to David that women of Vivienne's creative energy were not usually undersexed? Vivienne would just love to know what David replied when Eustace also pressed him, 'and is everything all right in that department?'

Poor old David, he'd have flushed crimson and denied any problems. Eustace never usually talked about such personal things. So Vivienne could hardly tell her father-in-law that, actually, in that department – their sex life – was completely up the creek. Vivienne couldn't begin to tell Eustace that they often slept in separate beds. She couldn't even start to discuss such things with Eustace, or anyone else. Anyway, it wasn't somehow 'seemly'.

So David buried himself in his work. He regularly told Vivienne how pleased he was with their son. David kept impressing on her how much 'We are a married couple. We are a family.'

In the evenings, David started drinking large whiskies, saying his father, an old Lenfesty, always drinks the stuff and is none the worse for it. David didn't overdo it. He always insists he's in control – that 'one of them has to be.'

'Just popping out for an hour or so, David.' Vivienne called out, lightly as she could, biting the inside of her bottom lip, tasting the drawn blood. The exhibition and London seemed ages ago. Commissions for portraits piled up – no more than she could handle but only just.

Amanda had gone into hospital for extensive tests. Natalie was with Guy's parents for a few days – did Vivienne want to come round? For a drink? This was Guy's invitation.

For their sabbatical, Guy had taken an apartment in St Peter Port.

It had three bedrooms, sitting room – the usual facilities and a terrace with a balcony overlooking St Peter Port harbour.

On the terrace, with potted red geraniums and small green palms, Guy handed Vivienne a large gin and tonic with a lemon slice still fizzing round in circles, ice cracking. 'Amanda sits here most days. She still knits for me, and Natalie. She's extremely skilled.'

'Yes, I can see that. Amanda is very...organised, isn't she? Does she still cut her nails every Friday?'

'Yes she does. She does manicures for her friends, now. They pay her; she goes round to their houses. In great demand. Fancy you remembering such a thing like that.' Guy poured himself more gin cocktail from a glass jug.

From the balcony they could see the islands of Herm and Sark. Vivienne recalled David on the one, Matthias on the other, Guy on honeymoon and Peter and she, all at sea.

'How's your painting going, Guy?' Vivienne instantly wished she hadn't asked.

Guy made an exaggerated frown, shaking his head. He swigged from his glass. 'It's buggered, to be honest. Can't get anywhere at the moment. But I'm getting by. To tell the truth, Viv, I'm working part time – accounts – for my father. With Natalie to think of – Amanda can't work.'

As the sun moved down, casting shadows over the terrace, lights appeared, one by one, twinkling in the dusk. They moved inside, into the sitting room. Guy sank back in a cream-paisley chair, carefully crossing his long legs. He leaned over to his record player, putting on a Dionne Warwick disk.

'If you see me walking in the street – each time we meet – walk on by. Walk on by-y-y.'

'I love her. Got that one. Love Dionne Warwick,' Vivienne began to sing the words.

Guy moved so he could sit with her on the matching paisley couch. He put an arm around her shoulders. 'America wasn't...well, not what I thought it would be. Darius is okay. He's doing very well. His books sell fast. He's making a heap of moolah.'

Guy took the glass from Vivienne's hand then, still holding it, led her to the bedroom. Dionne Warwick's soulful, throaty voice followed them. They undressed to her tender words in silence, save for their breathing.

Lying on Guy's bed – Amanda's bed – Vivienne gave herself up. She'd probably go straight to hell now anyway, so why resist? She had done enough to be damned for eternity already, so what difference would anything make?

Guy closed his eyes and slowly lay back on the pillows. To Vivienne, he looked like a sleeping god she had found in a forest. When she told him that, that he was Mars and she was Venus, easily arousing him with her hands, he grew swollen with need.

'What happened to Pisces?' He said through a half-opened mouth.

'He swam away. Over the ocean and far away. But now Venus needs you, really needs you.' She massaged Guy's body, blowing softly in his ears. He rolled over, heavy on her, thighs pinning her down.

Feeling the brush of his hair on her cheeks and his hands slide down her breasts, her round stomach and her sensitive centre, their sex felt fresh and warm. They came together, easily, without trying, satisfying each other with natural ease.

Then, breathless, coming up for air, Guy lit a cigarette. Vivienne rose to get the glass jug, poured more gin into their glasses then scrambled back into bed with him, pulling the sheets carelessly over them so that their bare feet stuck out at the end of the bed.

The telephone rang.

Without a pause, Guy said, 'Not answering,' removing a speck of tobacco from his lip. 'If it's the hospital – I've asked them to ring my mother. I've said I'm out – with friends tonight.'

'We're awful,' said Vivienne, 'devious people!' But Guy had said that? Just to have time with her? Still – 'What if it's urgent, Guy?' She thought of Sark, how David had raged when he couldn't contact her.

'No. No. It won't be urgent.'

'You don't know that'. But Vivienne let it go. Their time together was urgent as well. She kissed his dark-haired arm, wrapping it over herself.

'You, Vivvy' said Guy, with a mock weariness, 'are insatiable.' But he soundly returned her kiss and put his other arm around her and began to make love to her again.

Afterward, Guy fell asleep. Wide-awake, Vivienne became curious, so got up from the bed without a sound. She padded into Amanda's small bedroom. It was white and flowery and just big enough for a single bed. On the built-in dresser were manicure sets: scissors and pots of pink and crimson nail varnish. Vivienne gently slid open the dressing table drawers. Amanda's things were wifely white knickers, mended bras, everyday tights, colour coded, rolled into balls.

Knowing she wore black, lacy lingerie, Vivienne confronted her own image in Amanda's mirror. 'Amanda. Get well. I don't want to be your enemy. Is that what I am? Really, I don't want to be. I never meant to be that…' Vivienne shut Amanda's drawer softly.

She stole into Natalie's room. Immediately wishing that she hadn't. This should have been hers and Guy's child: their daughter, Nicola Jane. Cotton dresses in pastel shades hung on a white cupboard door. Perfectly hand-knitted cardigans were piled on the dresser. Dolls in different national dress were arranged on a shelf. On another were books. Fluffy toys were arranged in order of importance on the bed's pillow. Vivienne drew in a deep, lamented sigh. She shouldn't have come into Natalie's room.

Withdrawing quickly, Vivienne went back to where Guy slept. She showered, dressed and prepared to leave for home before he could properly awake. In his confused slumber he had kissed her goodbye, wet lips on her chin, mumbling something about seeing her soon.

Then Vivienne drove home. Did David suspect anything? How indecently easy it was – to lie! She headed for the drinks cupboard. Did all this – this sex with Guy make her feel better? Maybe he was making things – depression, remorse – much worse? Vivienne knocked back a seriously full glass, the whisky searing down her throat, clear down to the depth of her being.

Amanda Beaufort wasn't getting better, Guy told Vivienne, adding how very worried he felt about her.

'She's in good hands, but…' Guy fretted.

At the times she couldn't see him, Vivienne started driving past the apartment block in St Peter Port. Sometimes, madly, she had trailed after him on foot. Waited for him to come out of the flat and then just walked behind him. Just to see him. Yes, madness now, David, to add to all her faults. 'Mad about the boy' she sang in Guy's absence. Yes, that was it, definitely. Vivienne was going mad.

She started taking *The Times* since Guy did. She started drinking gin, with tonic, a slice of lemon and ice, instead of vodka. Vodka, it seemed, was a Sixties drink. Gin and whisky were the in-things now, so Guy said.

One day Polly came round with the children: two boisterous lads. After a miscarriage a third baby was well on the way. 'I'm so big this time, I think it's twins.' Polly pulled a tired face. 'Hope they're both girls, kiddo!'

Polly had put on weight with this pregnancy and her legs had varicosed. For reading she wore glasses over the pop blue eyes. Vivienne had helped Polly to dye her hair blonde – worn in a beehive now. All in all, though, Polly looked fine, so Vivienne thought.

'Polly, you are a good person. Hope you do get a girl. Here, put your feet up.'

The children played, making a racket outside with Joseph. They swung in the apple trees, in David's hammock and ran around the greenhouses 'Ack, acking' with toy guns, like pretend soldiers.

'You've done well, haven't you kiddo?' Polly said showing no envy. 'Lovely home. Career going well – little boy, good husband.' The round eyes peered intently at Vivienne.

'S'pose so.' But don't ask about the exhibition thing, please, Polly! Vivienne threw open the French windows, placing two leisure chairs out for them. She helped Polly settle comfortably on a padded green-striped seat. In the sunshine, they sat under leafy trees, filigree with sunlight, dappling the stone terrace.

'Just like a Renoir painting, this. He loved dapples,' said Vivienne.

'Apples? Renoir liked apples? Gosh, you know an awful lot about art, don't you kiddo?' Then Polly pressed Vivienne: 'So... everything's alright then, up here in the sticks?'

'Okay. Yes, alright.' So Polly had noticed about Guy. Vivienne might have guessed.

'Oh, come on!' exclaimed Polly, 'We're alright as well. But, are you happy? I mean, I suppose we are although we've got no money. Eric's unskilled and we've got this lot on the way.' Polly patted her burgeoning stomach. 'Alright is what we are! Are you happy, kiddo? You should be...?' Her question hovered in the warm air.

How to change the subject? What did Polly think? What had she seen? What had she guessed?

'I mean,' putting her orange juice down on the wicker table, Polly leaned over whispering hoarsely 'are you over that Guy bloke?' Then she straightened up, face expectant.

Vivienne couldn't reply. She swallowed some juice, gazing mutely at the distant fields.

'You know...' Polly persisted, 'Look, he's very handsome and all that, kiddo, but he leads that poor Amanda a real dance. You know that, don't you?'

Never can escape from Polly. She takes no prisoners, does our Polly. Still it was unbearable to think of Guy with anyone, Guy with Amanda – Guy without her.

'Well what man is faithful, Polly?' Vivienne simply burst out. 'Given half the chance? Mm? I don't think Guy is any worse than most men. All men, probably.' Vivienne's skin burned, her heart flapped like a caught fish.

'Don't you?' Then Polly broke off, yelling at her son, 'Greg! Put down that plank of wood right now! It might have a nail in it!' Turning back to Vivienne she said, 'Maybe not. But I do know Eric is faithful. It's not all men, kiddo' Polly hesitated, 'What about David? You and he...?'

'We're alright. Polly. And, obviously you and Eric are...okay in bed?' Was that going to far? No, because Polly isn't flinching, but holding her gaze steadily. 'How have you managed that, Polly? How?'

'Keep it varied, kiddo. That's what we do. Shall I tell you...' She again dropped her voice to a strangled whisper, '...our favourite fantasy?'

'Please!' Vivienne begged, releasing a laugh.

'Well, when the boys are asleep, we go to bed early with a packet of chocolate biscuits – digestives are best you know – then we play 'Doctors and Nurses'!'

Vivienne snorted loudly, spraying the back of her hand with spat juice. 'Polly!'

'Well,' said Polly thoughtfully, 'One doctor, you know, one nurse. We're not kinky! We're not swingers!'

A pause: then both creased up with laughter so loud the boys looked over at the sound of them. Vivienne wiped watering eyes with her hands, as Polly sat back with a satisfied look.

'Polly, you are a tonic. You really are!' Vivienne went over and hugged her.

'Aw, so are you! But anyway – remember what I've said, won't you, kiddo, about that Guy?'

Vivienne made no reply. Arm around Polly's pregnant, thickened waist, Vivienne led her friend to see some paintings, and to choose one for her home. Polly chose a view of Les Amarreurs, a bay near where she lived on the island, where she and Vivienne had played as children.

'"Les Amarreurs" means 'moorings',' Vivienne said, giving Polly the painting, gesturing her to take it.

'Oh, ta!' With blue eyes wide open, 'Yeh. I just love Les Amarreurs, kiddo,' said Polly.

'Me too.' Said Vivienne. 'Always seemed like a mooring place, to me. I felt safe on those warm boulders when we sunbathed. Do you remember, Polly – our little gang?'

Polly agreed. Vivienne talked about how they'd learnt to swim there, to catch fish with their hands, learnt how to survive. Presently, they kissed an affectionate goodbye.

With her brood, red-faced and fist-fighting inside the car, Polly left. Her second-hand Vauxhall span a cloud of dust as she rattled down the drive, long arm waving out of the window.

'Be sure your sins will find you out,' the saying goes. Vivienne went and checked after Joseph. He watered his garden plants: some sprouting peas and the green leaves of rows of outdoor tomatoes. Vivienne stirred some gin into a coffee. Sipping the brew, she went into her studio.

A large landscape of Sark lay on the easel. Vivienne had painted the island's spellbinding cliffs: fissured grey and brown granite, falling into clean, transparent sea. It had been difficult to capture the island's mysterious atmosphere of intrigue – of things past. But she felt that, yes, she had made a fair stab at it.

As she painted, Vivienne imagined she saw Matthias' image and smiled to herself. On the bracken and sun-baked grasses she painted a child – a little girl looking like a lost soul.

Finished painting for the day, Vivienne called Joseph in and began David's supper. As she peeled potatoes, then rinsed them clean of starch, Polly's talk of Guy flowed back to Vivienne.

The potatoes steamed a thick vapour, clattering the pan lid, as Vivienne dipped fresh cod in powdery flour. What of infidelity and deceit – why couldn't she be like Polly? Another sip of the gin mix gave her small refuge.

Wiping her hands free of flour, Vivienne took a telephone call. As she replaced the receiver she closed her eyes and smiled. At least, there was tomorrow and the promise of Guy again.

CHAPTER THIRTEEN

'This bloody island stifles me,' Guy complained. 'Can't move. I miss New York – and London, come to that.'

They sat in Vivienne's car, on the cliffs of La Tielle. Locals called it 'Lover's Leap'. She'd parked carefully some way back from the cliff edge. 'You're in a bad mood.'

She had prepared a picnic: quail stuffed with apricots and almonds, soft red fruit, cheeses and red wine. They'd nearly finished the bottle.

'Good job I don't have to drive too far. That's one advantage of living on an island, Guy.' He'd said he liked her navy blue trouser suit (white collar and white zip, neck to waist ending in a white tag – slimming, see?) And admired her hair, liked it swept up and the pink plastic earrings – circles embedded with pink sequins.

'You do take the light well on your face,' Guy stroked Vivienne's skin.

'What, like an aura? Like an angel?' She smiled, this was more like it.

'No – but it is true. Except for the angel bit!' Guy grinned back, finished his quail, fruit and a creamy Brie then helped her re-pack the picnic basket with the remains of their meal. He heaved the basket onto the back seat of the car.

Compliments from Guy? Well, well! Vivienne lit him a cigarette, and, with nicotine still on her lips, placed it in his mouth.

'This is nice.' He kissed her softly on the mouth. 'Trouble is, can't stay long today.'

'No?' His compliment nearly threw her – just as she was thinking what quail and apricots can do. 'Aphrodisiacs – cook your way to his heart.' The magazine article had said. But, hang on – 'can't stay long?'

His breath smelt of smoke. Guy smoke. Vivienne inhaled him to the back of her throat. 'Alright, then. So where to now?

'I know a private place, with a stream. Couldn't bear to drive today. All that traffic! Guernsey roads!'

God, he does need cheering up. Vivienne sped through the narrow lanes to a secluded copse. Guy offered her his hand as they climbed over a loose stone wall. Scrambling through brambles and thickly leaved trees, Guy found them a den. Under a tree, where sunlight flickered through dense foliage, they began to caress each other.

Lying on his back, in white shirt and blue jeans, Guy squinted up at the sky. What did he see? Bright lights winked in flickers of sunshine through dark green shapes.

Guy didn't do compliments. As she shared his sky, Vivienne felt an almost imperceptible prickling of hope: that, maybe, she could be a real part of Guy's life? Properly part of his life?

'I do love you, Guy,' Vivienne said.

Abruptly, Guy rolled away slightly and quickly lit a Rothmans with a clenched fist. 'Why – why do women need to say that? 'I love you?' He puffed his cigarette, hardly taking breath. 'It's…it's so melodramatic! But you do have to say it! Can't we just take what we've got? Vivvy, do you really need 'I love you' back? Commitment?'

Damn it. Didn't expect that. Vivienne sat up, brushing leaves from her hair and her navy suit. Damn, damn. What now? The dewy grass felt damp and sodden under her trousers. 'No, I don't want you to feel – somehow bound to me. I want us to be – I don't know – happy. Us together.' Vivienne felt tearful. Why the hell was she blurting out this Our-Love-For-Each-Other stuff?

'For me, Viv, declarations are a kind of emotional… tethering.' Guy stabbed at the air with his cigarette as he said each word. 'A need for commitment. 'I love you', it's 'get out of that.'

'I don't think that. I didn't say it for that.' Although maybe she did? Guy muddled her up.

'Look Viv, you mean a lot to me. You do. You know that,' Guy said, stubbing out the cigarette butt in the muddy ground. 'But…well, look, I'd much rather we talk about something else. What you've been doing lately. What you've been reading – painting?'

Yes, yes, change the subject. Vivienne wanted to now, as well.

'All right, okay.' She said, hastily casting about, 'I'm just about finished an oil of Sark. And *Dangerous Liaisons* remember we read it together once? Well I've been re-reading it.'

Guy smiled.

That's better. 'Laclos says some interesting things in his book, doesn't he? All about desire and control, education as a loss of innocence.'

'Laclos had some really interesting concepts, yes.'

'And don't you like "a man enjoys the happiness he feels – a woman the happiness she gives"?' Vivienne replied. 'Dorothy Parker agreed with that – "you, being man would have no tears of me…" '

'Exactly. A man on my wavelength, old Laclos.' Guy stroked her hair, picking out a sticky burr entangled in it. 'I like our times together. Just don't like it getting too heavy.'

'I know.' But Vivienne noticed Guy ignored the Dorothy Parker line.

'Glad about your painting. Good. But, look, sorry, I must pick up Natalie from school, now. Amanda has to rest.'

'I'm really sorry about Amanda – really, I am. So, see you sometime soon, then?'

'Course. Look forward to it, Vivvy.'

They scrabbled back over the wall, setting off for their separate ways. Vivienne watched Guy stride out of the wood over a long-grassed field, then hop over a further low, loose-stoned wall, bordering the meandering stream.

Guy seemed to know the place well? He knew of this secret place? Vivienne smoothed down her tunic, flicking off traces of twig and grass. At least mud dried quickly.

What did he mean 'women always have to say "I love you?" ' Women? How many women? A split second only and Rita appeared, smiling, with her damn pink collar framing her face – smiling knowingly at Guy. What about poor Amanda, though? Did she say 'I love you, Guy', any more? And if she did – did she mean it?

Damn! Damn! Damn him! Vivienne leant under the sheltering tree, to the comforting smell of ivied bark. Entwining her fingers flat and hard down over her stomach, she pressed the bruised and savaged place. In the sunny copse the woman doctor sneered right into her face, mocking her. Vivienne's hands were blooded claws – she must never forget that. The doctor would never let her forget that.

She ran now, flying over feathery meadow grasses, to her car. Shuffling through the glove box she found a near-empty gin bottle. Vivienne drank it dry with one long swallow.

Joseph went off to bed, hair tousled, newly bathed. He clutched a mug of steaming chocolate and a new book on sea birds.

'Night Ma. Night Dad.'

'Night darling.'

'Night son.'

Vivienne drew oatmeal velvet curtains shut and sat down on the couch next to David. 'David…'

'Mmm?'

'Have you ever thought of reading something like – well something like *Dangerous Liaisons*?'

'Ahhh…no. Heard of it though. And there was a film, wasn't there?' David took a pile of magazines from the rack under the coffee table and flipped through them. 'Ah!' as he found the *TV Times*. 'Why do you ask?'

'Just wondered – you know – what you thought about the different way men and women think about things. Love, and…'

'Oh yes? It's French, then, is it, this Liaison book of yours? It's in French?'

'Not in French, no. Has been translated. It's about love, women as angels or demons and…'

'What? Oh, it's a highbrow thing, is it? One of your arty books? Anyway, I'm glad you're getting up a library, Vivienne. It's really good for the boy, for Joseph. He'll need good English if he wants to go to University. Not into novels myself. Seem a waste of time to me. They make it all up don't they? I like a good biography – war heroes…'

'I know you do.'

'Look – I really do want to watch the football, Vivienne. Oh, it's started!' David threw the *TV Times* down, got up and switched on the television. He put the volume up loud. 'It's Liverpool against Arsenal, sorry Vivienne – important match tonight.'

Vivienne waited a minute then rose, 'Well I'm off to bed, then.'

'Okay,' said David, eyes fixed to the screen, sitting on the edge of the couch, legs apart, hand on each knee, like he was about to pounce on something.

In her cool bedroom, Vivienne lay quietly. The side next to her was flat: an empty acre of virgin white sheet. The pillow was smooth – ironed and un-dented. Nothing left for it, then, but sleep.

Vivienne's London exhibition went fairly well, certainly better than she dared hope. The Gallery was a tiny room, a broom cupboard, off Pall Mall. Even so, its expense soaked up almost all the income even from her best work. The painting of Sark sold straightaway, gaining the highest price. This time she and Eustace had included some sketches and numbered prints of the Guernsey exhibition paintings. They took very little work back home, content to have made a small profit.

Vivienne felt pleased. She hadn't let Eustace down. With this exhibition she could lay claim to being a professional artist. Even David must agree to that.

Although David said Vivienne seemed to be drifting away from him. She had to, wanted to, spend more and more time in the studio. And David accused her of not always working though, saying how he found her, more than once, on the couch with the cream paisley throw, just lying there looking at the ceiling – gin in hand.

Where did she go, David demanded? Did she always go out sketching, like she told him? He'd seen Polly in the grocery shop – she'd asked David when she could see Vivienne again, it had been ages?

Vivienne suspected David stalked her – at least once. Certainly she'd caught him again, checking up on her, through the studio window. She could just feel those sort of things.

So how could she, then? Drive past Guy's apartment like that? And what about that time her engine stalled, on a dank and muggy night? One in the morning turned to three. When she woke up, cold to the bone, she revved the engine. Nothing. Damn! And Joseph was going on a school trip next day.

'Don't forget our early start, Ma, will you?' Joseph had said. And Vivienne hadn't even gone to bed yet. Suddenly, choking and spluttering, at last the engine burst into action.

Jesus – what did she think she was doing? Driving in a bewildered first light, Vivienne arrived home. She threw herself, her damp woollen coat wrapped around her, onto her studio couch.

Still in his pyjamas, David had stormed in. 'For pity's sake, Vivienne. What the hell is this all about?' He grabbed himself a gin, plonking down next to her. 'Do you know what time it is? You look absolutely bloody awful! Look at you – face all puffy, you're all over the place. You can't carry on like this! There's the ironing – the washing up piled in the kitchen. There's Joseph!'

'I don't know,' Vivienne said. 'I get in a dark place sometimes, David. In a black hole.'

'Oh for pity's sake, pull yourself together, Vivienne. What black hole are you on about? You've got us! You've got your painting. What the hell more do you want?'

'I don't know. I don't know.'

'It's all this bloody art stuff, all that bloody thinking isn't it. Where do you go? You want to get in the real world Vivienne. Get out of that ruddy arty bubble you're in.'

Vivienne couldn't answer. David banged the gin down stonily and left her. This time grey blankness came as a relief.

Worse came as David reported Pearl having a go at him: that Vivienne 'Obviously isn't coping.' The house wasn't being run properly. Vivienne spent far too much time in her studio.

'I agree with mother', David said. 'It's all getting ridiculous. Humiliating. None of our family drinks. Except Uncle Ralph. But then he's always been a loner and an oddball. You are the only one in our family, Vivienne, ever, to drink!'

David told Vivienne that he had even considered consulting Edward and Jean. He then reckoned it would do more harm than good where Edward was concerned. David said even he didn't want the evils of booze ranted at him by Edward. And Jean, well – they all agreed – worrying her was quite out of the question.

'Pity your Granmarie isn't alive. She'd have sorted you out! Her precious granddaughter? Granmarie would have shown you some discipline. Oh, it's all too much, Vivienne. And what about Joseph? He's nearly ten, he needs you. Get a grip, for God's sake, woman!'

Of course David was right there. Joseph, her dearest child, her son, needed her. The school had been in touch with them. Miss Frances had telephoned, asking them for a meeting.

Did they know? Miss Frances had begun, that Joseph was getting teased – about being late nearly every morning, and that was losing him house points? That his homework wasn't always done properly or on time? Joseph had had two lunchtime detentions in one week. Was everything all right at home?

Back at their house, David paced around the sitting room. 'I am appalled, Vivienne! If you can't think of me at the very least think of Joseph!' His voice sagged heavy with contempt, his blue eyes darted rapiers at Vivienne.

'I'll try,' Vivienne raised her hands as shields, 'Of course I'll try to stop. I didn't think…I didn't realise it had got to this. I'll see the doctor. Don't ever say I don't care about Joseph. I do! I do! That's unfair, David.'

'Yes. Too right, you've got to get help. And – well, to be frank – I really think you should stop painting for a while. Get the house straight, as a priority.'

'How can you say that?' Vivienne felt a punch lunged at her body. 'That's so unfair. I want to paint! I can't just do the school run, gossip at the school gate – live a life everyone else wants me to. I can't do it, David.'

David stood rigid with cold fury.

'Look,' Vivienne attempted, 'some people have – like a closed room in their minds. And I don't want to go in, fit in. Be – shaped, inhibited, fitted in, with someone else's life. Can't you understand?'

'You are my wife. Joseph is our son. You have a responsibility to us.' Said David, his eyes glacial. 'And what's more, Vivienne, you have an absolute *duty*!'

Vivienne felt herself slipping, sliding, seemingly unstoppable, on an unknown path. Flinging open a kitchen cupboard, she found a scrubbing brush, a yellow bar of soap and began to scrub a wooden unit top. Clean. Scrub. Clear away the mess.

David sat down and watched her, wordlessly.

'It's just – I want to be a free, flying bird, David. Not a house-trained brown hen – like Pearl, like my mother. They are happy like that. Good for them. But I am not.' The brush made swirling soapsuds, spilling everywhere as Vivienne scoured the top frantically, making her finger-tips red and sore. 'And I don't want to harm Joseph's childhood!' Then she flung the brush down, rapping it onto the floor. 'Oh, this is crazy.' Oh, God! Maybe Matthias was right. 'Crazy Baby'.

'You have a duty, Vivienne,' David repeated, solemnly.

That night Vivienne dreamed. She was watching a circus: dancing horses, grotesque clowns. Brash, tinny music played. Garish, red-sequinned women with red feathers in their hair danced in sequence. Then suddenly, monsters came in: huge black hairy things. Growling, they began to tear the clowns apart then the dancing women and the prancing horses. They tore all their heads off. Blood spurted all over the circus tents, the seats, the audience. Vivienne ran home to find her baby, to save Joseph. When she got there, there was a headless cat on the roof – its blood dripped into the gutter. Granmarie lay in the garden, bleeding. Joseph was dead. His head was torn off.

'Vivienne! Vivienne!' someone called her.

She lashed out her arms, fighting for air, stumbling out of bed and opened the window. Air! Fresh air! As she gasped, slowly the thudding in her heart eased. The room returned to normal. Nobody was there at all. Vivienne was quite alone.

A cockerel crowed, its valour echoing across the meadows. It was six o'clock and she wasn't on her own, after all. There was a valiant little bird, out in the morning air. The cockerel, with the red coxcomb, had kept watch.

All through the next days of threatening greyness, Vivienne made herself paint: shakily squeezing coloured liquids onto a palette. Somehow brushes daubed the mixtures onto canvas.

She made Joseph's breakfast, found his gym shoes, got him off to the school bus.

'Bye Ma. You okay?' He had frowned from under his fair-haired fringe. 'See you.'

'Course, Joseph. Have a good day, darling.' Vivienne blew him a kiss.

The stretched canvas stared accusingly at her. Get on with it, woman! Vivienne turned on the transistor radio: 'Here, there and everywhere...' sang George Harrison and 'Loving you is easy cos your beautiful,' sang Minnie Riperton

The doctor said he wasn't overly concerned. He gave Vivienne a prescription for vitamins. He advised counselling. Possibly a change of scene?

All very well, David had responded scornfully – 'a change of scene', after all they were in the very middle of the season. The worse time. The tomato crop ripened, like it or not. It's like farming. You work all day, every day, until the crop is harvested. So a change, a holiday, is not possible. Not until late autumn, at the very earliest.

Eustace called in regularly. He never stayed long.

'Just popping in while passing,' he'd say, smiling calmly at Vivienne.

That particular day, though, he had said, 'Tell you what, Vivienne. How about we get someone in – to help you with the housework? Our lady that does for us has a daughter, Sonia. She's very young but most willing. What do you say?'

Vivienne thought about his offer, 'Mmm. I'd be grateful, but I'm not sure if David will agree....'

'I'll pay, Vivienne,' said Eustace.

'Oh, no, no! Eustace, I couldn't...'

'It's all right, Vivienne, really. Look your... ill health, it's not good for you, my dear,' he implored with a quick, tender glance.

Dear Eustace. He never mentioned drink to her – or booze. 'Thank you.' It really would help. Would David – would Pearl even agree, though?

They both did, albeit grudgingly. Vivienne didn't blame Pearl. Pearl had led a pretty blameless life, as far as Vivienne could tell.

'Like to see you concentrating on your work, as well, Vivienne,' said Eustace. 'Get on with your painting. And you might think of helping with our administration, say? Me and Pearl, well we aren't getting any younger. And you know, I still think of the south of France. Time moves on, Vivienne, for all of us.'

So Vivienne spent a few days at La Colette, learning some of Eustace's ropes, listening to Pearl, Mrs Carré Senior, on how she ran her household.

Realising Eustace's motives – that she might regain a sense of position, see what a future she might have – Vivienne sighed. Yes, she certainly owed Eustace. He deserved a dutiful daughter-in-law. But Pearl's ways weren't hers. And the doctor's vitamins weren't working very well.

Counselling? Vivienne had put off counselling. Couldn't discuss the abortion or Guy. This was such a small island. Would talking help? No. Forget everything – that was it. Rub out the past. Erase history.

Trouble was, Vivienne had missed a period.

It would be Guy's, of course. David would perfectly obviously know that. Vivienne shredded nerves over broken glass. Ironing Joseph's school shirt, she hovered the iron over her hand, felt the searing metal heat. Press it down. How would that feel? But no, that was no answer. Vivienne finished the shirt, taking another from the pile in the basket at her feet.

In the bathroom whilst she washed her hands she examined her face in the mirror over the sink. Her curled hair and her blue-green eyes looked the same, but her face was pale, the stare was tense and questioning.

Pre-menstrual tension? Yes, of course, that was what it would be: PMT. Pray, Vivienne, for PMT. After all, four weeks have inched by.

Vivienne picked up the telephone, beginning to dial Guy's number. Then slammed it down. What to say? What if Amanda answered? What the hell to say to her?

She would lose David. That's for sure. He's on the edge of his patience already. And she'd lose Joseph – and Eustace. The drinks cupboard offered a grateful numbness.

Two days ago, Guy had rung her on her new studio extension. He had a meeting in town with the family accountant. Then he'd be free – Tuesday evening, any chance…?

Vivienne held her own hand to apply make-up, to steady the shakes. A silky top, black jeans then, over it all, a worn green anorak, buttoned to the chin.

'Just off, then.' With Polly, to the cinema, Vivienne had lied.

'Right. Don't be late.' Said David. 'Joseph's charity walk tomorrow.'

'Yes, I know. He's wearing mufti. I know.' Joseph lay on the floor, watching *Blue Peter* on the television. He turned his open face toward her, 'Bye Ma. Enjoy the film.'

Vivienne had seen the Doris Day musical before, so that was alright.

As soon as she got into the car, Guy handed Vivienne a bottle of chilled, pink champagne, wrapped in white tissue paper. He drove through darkened streets to a deserted farm and parked near the seclusion of an old, granite barn. They climbed onto the back seats. Moonlight shone through the car windows. As they sipped the bubbly drink, the windows misted up, soon affording a veiled screen.

'Hello,' he brushed her fringe away from her forehead. 'Need you. Really need you.'

'Me too.' In the cramped leather seat she felt his chin, pressing down on her neck. She ran her hand over his denims. He kissed her so her head bent down onto the bench seat.

Vivienne gave in to Guy, unrestrained, uninhibited – without hesitation.

His breath brushed her ear. He slid his arms underneath her, supporting her. 'Christ, are cars getting smaller?' But Guy somehow managed to wrap his legs around her.

Vivienne opened her eyes wide: to study Guy's face. 'Not quite your double bed!'

'You deserve better,' said Guy.

'This is better! I'm with you. Can we do London again? Something like that?'

'No, not for a while, Viv. Things at home...you know. Complications.'

Guy's head silhouetted against the blurred pane, moonlight outlined him. 'Like a couple of kids again, we are.'

Vivienne thought of Portelet, but they weren't, were they, kids anymore? Lovers, yes, yet but not a real couple. But, then again, moonlight always became Mr Guy Beaufort so Vivienne kissed him.

In the parked car Vivienne's body chilled outwardly cold. Guy's presence, though, warmed her soul, more than any intoxication. Only Guy would do. The winding, fat python of gargantuan lust strangled her, coiled around her, forcing out all other needs or reason.

Guy cuddled her to him, 'Saw a programme on TV the other evening *Arena*, about Durer – Titian, Vincent. Thought of you, Vivvy.'

'Saw it too. Oils came about because of Venice not suiting frescoes – 'cause of all the sea-salt air?' She snuggled into Guy's arms. 'And I thought of you, too.'

They parted, so heavy with the need of sleep she forgot to mention the overdue period. Nor how her reason fluctuated: that the deep recess of her senses left her tormented and hungry – but not for food. Doesn't Guy know she feels buried alive? Silence rang in her ears.

So – how to tell Guy she's bearing a second baby from him? That she had aborted the first. That it had been alive and that she had killed it? Nor could she tell him that she was thirty-five and probably losing her mind.

CHAPTER FOURTEEN

'Vivienne! Wake up, for God's sake!' David yelling, shaking her violently startled her. 'You didn't get my breakfast! What is Joseph going to wear? It's near eight o clock! Joseph has to leave in ten minutes!' Then David dropped Vivienne's shoulders abruptly so she fell back hard on the mattress. 'Oh, the hell with it. I've got to go. Look! Here's the lorry driver! Yep, he's here. I'm off. For crying out loud. I've been up since six!' David slammed the door behind him.

Vivienne staggered out of her bedroom. Through groggy eyes she saw Joseph in the kitchen, all of twelve years, growing up.

'It's alright, Ma,' Joseph said. 'I've found my Man United T-shirt and my blue jeans with the special rivets, but – help me, yeh? My packed lunch?'

Still in her dressing gown, Vivienne slapped some butter and Marmite on sliced bread, adding a packet of cheese and onion crisps and a wrapped chocolate roll into Joseph's lunch box. 'There you go, sweetheart.' She filled up a plastic sports bottle with water from the tap.

'And some Ribena with it, Ma?'

'Sorry, darling.' Unscrewing the bottle lid, Vivienne added blackcurrant juice to the bottle. Through the kitchen window, Vivienne could see Pearl, in yellow rubber gloves, a white blouse with cameo brooch, tweed skirt and brogues. Pearl was clipping their hedge.

'It's just gone eight, for God's sake!' Vivienne grunted thickly under her breath.

'What?' said Joseph.

'Nothing, nothing.' Vivienne passed a hairbrush over Joseph's hair, found his gym shoes and hugged him. 'Go on then, don't overdo it. Tell Miss Frances if you get too tired – '

'Yeh. You'll be here when I get back? Won't you?' Joseph gnawed his bottom lip.

'Course I will! Course I will, darling.'

'Right,' Joseph held the back door open, 'it's just – well – well.'

'What?'

'Well, look, Ma, other mums they don't…'

'What?' What now?

'Well. They only have – well, wine, with their meals, Ma.' Joseph's cheeks coloured pink. Then he sprinted out of the house, to catch the school bus.

Nobody got to her like Joseph. Vivienne glanced down at her stomach, just under the dressing gown cotton tie. Did anything show yet? And what about 'the wine'? That showed? Vivienne would have to try to get through today without a drink. She must. She must try.

Pearl, clutching the hedge-clippers, came right in. 'Good morning, Vivienne. Eustace told me Sonia's coming to help you? Anyway, her mother welcomes the extra money.' Pearl slid a knowing, critical eye over Vivienne.

'Oh, yes. Thanks Pearl. Yes, I'm glad Sonia's coming.' Unshowered, unlovely, Vivienne let the contemptuous look ride. She had no strength for defence (Matthias, help!) not today.

'It just takes a little more effort, my dear,' said Pearl, more kindly. 'I do realise you have …your hands full, your difficulties. But…organization. That's what I've always found helps. Being organized.'

Sonia joined their household. A young, fresh-faced Guernsey girl, she was both willing and determined. Welcoming her natural energy and enthusiasm, Vivienne drew Sonia thankfully into their home.

All that first day, she showed Sonia round – the gardens, the outhouses, the bungalow itself – and Vivienne didn't drink. Sonia said how she knew her job well and had helped her mother sometimes at La Colette, 'Which is much bigger than this house, if you don't mind me saying, Mrs Carré.'

David, once he knew Eustace was contributing to her salary, gladly welcomed Sonia. 'She's putting the house to rights – and you seem a bit better.' David said it distantly, like Vivienne was a patient and he the authoritative doctor. Then David took Joseph's hand for their usual walk around the vinery.

Another good thing: Vivienne didn't now have to spend any more time following Pearl around, trying to mimic her regime, her idea of organization. Pearl was well meaning, and all that, but – well, her duties seemed endless: Monday and Tuesday were laundry, Wednesday was silver, brass and copper, Thursday was polishing and baking for the weekend. Every day, every moment it seemed was accounted for. La Colette was beautiful, yes, but, Vivienne reckoned, it seemed such a selfless, dedicated routine: keeping a house going perfectly smoothly. Then again, Pearl had always had help.

Eustace took pains to teach Vivienne the business side of his smallholding. 'I can't believe Eustace wants you to learn all that, as well, Vivienne.' Pearl gave them both disapproving, slightly disdainful looks whenever she found them bent over order books and invoices.

'He wants me to learn how to run a business. My Granmarie did, you remember, Pearl – at Granville? I think Eustace remembers.'

'Mmm.' Pearl had said, "Well. We'll have to see, won't we Vivienne? I'd have said you've enough to cope with. Eustace is very well meaning, you know.'

How on earth could she keep this baby? Six weeks now and no show. Worrying tensions seized Vivienne like a Chinese twist. Lately she hadn't felt too good, either. A skin irritation chafed her loins. She showered more often, applying soothing cream, but the respite didn't last long. At least she wasn't lifting a glass all the time – most times, Vivienne waited until Joseph had gone to bed.

David nagged on about her having counselling. He could at least recognize she was trying to take some control. As for counselling, how could some churchy do-gooder take away all the memories, the pain? It wasn't possible. Only Guy would do – or champagne, or vodka – or all three, preferably, all at the same time. Still, Vivienne managed to take Joseph to his football and glued a schedule of his school activities on the kitchen fridge.

Christmas drew near. David bought a raffle ticket at the grocery shop and he won a candlelit dinner for two.

'Never win anything, usually,' David said, grinning widely.

Vivienne tried to be pleased. The prize was to be dinner at Greyrocks Hotel, built on the top of a wooded cliff, overlooking a sandy cove. The hotel offered rooms overnight for those not wanting to drive home.

When they got there, Vivienne saw how the hotel restaurant had been decorated for Christmas: red and green festoons garlanded the fireplace. A log fire, glowing with red and yellow sparks, warmed the room. On the ceiling, tinselled lanterns winked in the firelight.

Wearing a scarlet velvet blouse and matching long skirt, Vivienne ordered her choice. Her blouse was scooped, so the tops of her breasts were accentuated. She decided to wear her hair long, with curls clipped back each side of her face with sparkling glass pins.

Thankfully, the dining room was warm and quiet. David ordered from the menu: chicken soup, roast turkey and Christmas pudding. Spandau Ballet played softly through speakers in the corners of the room: 'I know this much is true…this much is true.'

David glanced over toward her. Vivienne saw questioning on his face. He looked out of place and nervous, holding his knife and fork like he'd just learned how to.

'This is nice, isn't it?' David said.

'Yes, it is. Anyway, don't have to wash up,' Vivienne said, drained.

The other diners looked all dressed up for the Christmas dinner. Vivienne scanned over the room. Some women wore sparkly Lurex tops, shimmering like festive Christmas tinsel. Some wore black satin, some…

Vivienne held her fork stiffly then lowered it slowly. Wasn't that Amanda Beaufort? At a table, almost hidden from them by a wooden pillar, swirled round with green ivy and golden baubles, Vivienne saw Amanda's back. At her side was Natalie, in a lacy, white party dress, her hair tied into a ponytail with a red satin ribbon. Natalie talked excitedly.

Vivienne heard the little girl say she was getting a puppy from Father Christmas. Natalie clapped her hands together. Directly in front of Natalie sat Guy.

Guy didn't see Vivienne. He was laughing with his excited daughter, cutting up her turkey meat, pouring wine for himself, then some for his wife – for Amanda. They all looked relaxed and at ease: a happy, ordinary family out for a Christmas meal.

Although Vivienne chewed it, some white meat stuck in her throat, so she had to swallow hard in forced gulps. The fruit pudding arrived, smelling of hot plums and brandy. Vivienne watched the Beaufort family table, transfixed. David couldn't see them. Vivienne didn't point them out.

David chatterered, hardly drawing breath. Wine sometimes did that to him. From a jug, he poured them both some creamy, brandy sauce, flooding their plum puddings. David dug into his. 'Life is so much better in the winter, isn't it Vivienne? I know the greenhouses and the soil need cleaning – I've booked the boiler-steamer for early January. Then all the hard work starts again of course. Got some new seeds to try for next season. And – but you're not really interested in all this, are you? Women never are. Only Granmarie showed me any interest. She understood horticulture. But then, she was an exception, wasn't she? Granmarie: an exceptional woman all round, really – Vivienne? Who have you seen?' David stopped talking, turning round to follow Vivienne's stare at the table behind the pillar.

'Beaufort? Oh, bugger!'

As she sipped her wine, pushing away her pudding, Vivienne watched the small family party. Presently Guy put his napkin down and got up from the table. In the flickering candlelight, he pulled out Amanda's chair for her and put his hand out to her, assisting her from the table. Natalie danced around them, a dark-haired, happy little girl, waiting for Father Christmas and her new dog.

Guy had a daughter. Her head was full of thoughts: of presents around the tree, a wonderful Christmas day. A lovely family time.

Now Guy put his arm around Amanda. Amanda looked pale. Her shoulder blades stuck out of the plain black dress she wore. In her thinness, Amanda looked taller.

Slowly, they negotiated the tables. Guy said goodnight quietly to one or two people they obviously knew. Natalie ran ahead. They moved out of the room, toward the red-carpeted stairs at the end of the hotel's restaurant. Vivienne saw Guy and Amanda going up to their hotel bedroom.

In Vivienne's vision they walked in slow motion. They climbed the stairs together. She saw Amanda's wedding-ringed hand on the banister. In their bedroom, Guy would lie next to Amanda. In the morning they would wake up together, dress together, eat together. With their little daughter, Guy and Amanda would celebrate a Christmas breakfast.

'Vivienne. Vivienne. Have some more wine – don't spoil our meal. Don't spoil things. Look, we're here to…' said David.

But Vivienne was already lost to David. Tears streamed in rivulets, smearing down over her make-up. She sat quite still, not crying out. A tight ache in her throat spread all around her arms – her heart.

Under the scarlet velvet skirt was Guy's child. Vivienne placed a shaking arm over her waist. She cannot abort the baby – she cannot keep it. Like a hairline at first, the glazed finish on her life was cracking open. The eggshell veneer was breaking. Vivienne ran her fingertips over the severed edges. The two halves of her life were falling apart to expose her duplicity. She clutched at her skirt, like it was a lifeline.

'Vivienne,' David looked around in agitation, 'nobody's noticed anything. They're all partying. Look, I'll tell the waiter. We'll go.' He caught the head waiter's eye. 'Come on, now. For goodness sake…!' David half rose from his chair.

Vivienne beat him to it. 'No! No! *No!*' Screamed out of her. Her chair fell over backwards as she pushed it away and ran to the restaurant door. She dashed into the Reception hall, with its tall green Christmas tree, zig-zagged with white lights. Then out she went, into the garden, into the night, down rough-cut stone steps to the swirling sea below.

Thoughts – ravaged grief, of utter despair – sent Vivienne

stumbling down the gravelly steps. Loosing her shoes, she slid further down, past darkened gorse and cool fronded bracken with pine trees whistling in the night wind.

Briefly looking back, she saw Guy on the balcony of his hotel room, smoking a cigarette. Amanda, his fragile wife, hovered behind him. Crying, Vivienne ran on, across the starlit sand, dotted with pebbles and gleaming white shells.

Almost breathless, great heaves of air forcing out of her, she plunged into the dark green sea. Cold waves lapped around her knees. Further yet she went, and further. The hungry suck of the tide suddenly pulled her off balance. Her long velvet skirt billowed out like a fallen red sail. Vivienne dived her head under the sea. She would keep her head held under – this was the only way. Don't surface – she filled her lungs with seawater. Swallow, Vivienne, swallow, swallow, swallow...

A strong current threw her head up again, so her round face, deathly white, stared sorrowfully at the mindless, starry sky.

'Vivienne! Vivienne!' David raced across the sand. Waiters and diners trailed behind him, all shouting out, all shocked.

Was that David? Without his jacket? And Guy? Where was Guy? Why was she here? It all had to end. Everything had to end. This time, the sea filled her ears, pressed against her eyes, engulfed her in an undulating wall of water as she felt herself sinking slowly down to the bottom of the rocky seabed.

Now she felt Guy and David, struggling with her weight, holding her head up, away from the water. Each had an arm under her shoulders. They were making for the shore. They dragged her on to the cold, wet sand and pulled her away from the sea's lapping, deathly fingers. Her saturated body rolled, a dead weight, on the sand. She was frozen cold, numb, and exhausted.

'She's semi-conscious,' Vivienne heard as if from a distance. Guy and David's clothes were all soaked through. They were both ghostly pale.

'The restaurant manager has called an ambulance,' someone said. Vivienne saw people running down the cliff. They crowded around her, holding thin party clothes close to them in the chill night air.

There was Guy! He was laying her head to one side, listening to her breathing, placing her leaden arms and legs in a recovery position. Vivienne felt his wet hair brush her chin. But, she wanted him to stop trying – yet she has no strength to push Guy away.

David did, David pushed Guy, roughly, from Vivienne's side.

'I know about recovery positions, mate.' David coughed up seawater, it spluttered over his shirt. He told Guy to clear off. 'Why don't you just fuck off?' David cried out.

Guy was gasping in great heaves. He put an arm around David. 'It's all too much. Too much for all of us. Vivvy needs help, David.'

David went quiet, then pushed Guy away again, shouting 'Clear off! Just clear off!'

The ambulance men struggled to bring a stretcher down the cliffs. They got her into the ambulance. David came with her. Guy trailed off, soaking wet, back up the steps. Vivienne tried to make him stay, but she could see Amanda waiting, waxen faced. Natalie was wide-eyed. Poor little thing. Bet she wished this, this – accident – was all over with so she could get back to her Christmas presents and the puppy she'd been promised?

Soon the ambulance sped them through the dark lanes. Vivienne, wrapped in a red blanket, wondered: red. Isn't that supposed to be comforting – a red blanket? Who had told her that? When? When was that?

As the memory came back, of the night when that other red blanket covered Vivienne, anguish writhed around inside her, stealthy as a sea snake. Why hadn't they left her to die? After all, she had killed. Oh, how that doctor can snarl at Vivienne. How pitiless she was in utter triumph!

'Help me. Help me. Somebody help me,' Vivienne cried weakly as a needle pierced her arm.

'Just try and relax,' a voice said. 'Try and let go.'

Through her tranquillized senses, Vivienne heard the ambulance siren as they careered along Guernsey's streets – along roads lined with houses, decorated with Christmas lights.

As the ambulance swept up the hospital drive, Vivienne saw the signs:

'ACCIDENT AND EMERGENCY'
'X-RAY DEPARTMENT'
'CHEST AND HEART'

They arrived at the Princess Elizabeth Hospital and took Vivienne to a curtained ward. A nurse eased her soaked velvet Christmas clothes from her cold body. As she slipped into unconsciousness, the nurse watched over her. Outwardly then, through a benumbed haze, Vivienne had been rescued.

CHAPTER FIFTEEN

The hospital room was sparse, but clean. The curtains around Vivienne's bed were cream cotton, splotched with green daisies. The pillows under her head were too hard and too many. With an effort, she pushed one further down under her shoulder blades.

Was it raining? Everything seemed grey. A pewter sky outside the window, wet with translucent beads, afforded but a pale light. Vivienne tried to lift her head, but her neck ached. There was a barred window in the door. Every now and then someone peered at her.

She heard footsteps outside the door. Nurses chattered and laughed. A telephone rang, unanswered. Then the door swished open, bringing fresher air into the room and her doctor came in.

Holding a file of notes, he sat on Vivienne's bed. He looked at her over the rim of his spectacles. His grey hair was thinning now, the lines on his bony forehead increased. Wearing a dove grey suit with pastel blue tie he talked to Vivienne with his quiet, patrician voice.

'All got too much for you, Vivienne?' His pale blue eyes left something unsaid. 'You are depressed, my dear. Suicidal. But we can sort that out. We're keeping an eye on you, just for a day or two. Then you can go home.'

'Home?' It came out with lifeless inflection.

Vivienne knew he had noticed her flinch, but he continued. 'So you didn't go for counselling? You really should consider it, you know.'

She shook her head, her hair sprayed out on the hospital white pillow. Eyes screwed up, she fought back a swelling wave of refusal.

'There is only so much a busy GP can do, Vivienne. You need a bit of – specialist treatment. It's not nearly as bad as it sounds, I promise. Anyhow, I'm putting you on a course of tranquillisers for a month or two. The rest...' he paused slightly, 'is largely up to you. You have to...come to terms with things, Vivienne my dear. It's going to take time.'

He took her temperature. Then, he said steadily, 'And we did some tests for you. There was no baby. You are just overdue. Probably due to stress, possibly excessive alcohol. Maybe a mix of both?' He was matter-of-fact and calm.

Vivienne sat straight up in alarm. 'How did you know I was worried – about being pregnant?'

'Many patients say things they have been wanting to say for a long time, under sedation, my dear, it's quite common.' He smiled reassuringly. 'Although,' he finished, still maintaining a composed manner, 'you do have a genital infection. Candidosis. The lay term is 'thrush'. It's an infection passed on...woman to woman.' He took his spectacles off, laying them on top of the file of notes. 'Again, it's a very minor complaint and very well known amongst women. Easily cleared up. Now,' he said as he rose and moved toward the door, ' a bit of thinking to be done, Vivienne? A little more care about yourself? Mmm? I'll be back tomorrow.' He left, barely leaving a ripple in the stuffy, still air.

Vivienne lay back, fully awake and gazed at the colourless ceiling. Passed on woman to woman? What the hell did that mean? So Guy did still sleep with Amanda. They did still have sex. Well, of course they did! Look at the hotel bedroom, the family life...oh, dear God.

A loud knock on the door and a face almost hidden behind an enormous bouquet of early spring flowers – 'Bought at enormous expense, let me tell you!' – heralded Polly. 'Well then, you're a right twerp, aren't you kiddo?' She kissed Vivienne heartily on the cheek. 'Got yourself in a right state, haven't you?' Then she quietened and took Vivienne's hand. 'Aw, don't look so down. Can't be that bad? Eh kiddo? Surely?'

'I feel terrible, Polly. Awful. Can't seem to see any point to it anymore. Don't want to be here.' Her voice was flat with a lodge of resignation.

'Hey! Look I felt just like that, after I had Kim. And I'd wanted a daughter so much! Couldn't love her. Not at first. Everything seemed too much trouble. I do know, kiddo, I do, honest. Then I had...you know, pills and stuff. My Eric was a brick. Come on! You've got David and young Joseph. They need you, you know.'

'David. Yes I've got David.' Vivienne said, suddenly tasting stale mucus so reached for a glass. 'And David's got me.'

'Well then.' Polly opened her eyes wide, 'can't have everything we want, kiddo. And no one...nobody's worth this lot, now is he?' Polly indicated at the hospital room: the barred windows.

Vivienne knew Polly's 'nobody' meant 'Guy'. Polly poured them both glasses of Lemon Barley water from the bottle on Vivienne's bedside cabinet. Her bouquet fell off the bed, onto the floor. Polly picked it up and dumped it down on the cabinet top.

'Want to tell me?' Polly asked simply.

'There's more Polly. Things I can't say.' Vivienne just couldn't begin to tell anyone about that.

'You'll have to talk to someone, kiddo?'

'Doctor keeps saying that. But I'm...I'm so scared Polly! If anything, I'd rather forget.' Vivienne smoothed the starched white sheet over her stomach. So, she wasn't carrying Guy's baby. She never would have a baby with Guy, now, would she? And, anyway, Guy had Natalie – and Amanda. Vivienne had lost out to quiet Amanda who knitted and wasn't keen on sex but had kept Guy at her side all these years.

Polly seemed to be fading in front of her: even her hair, usually so yellow had paled. The room retracted; colourless curtains around her bed held an indistinct pattern. Sounds were receding. Vivienne clutched at Polly's hand, squeezing it hard.

'I'm so scared, Polly. What's the point of anything...?'

Polly called for a nurse. 'You're worrying me, kiddo. But you'll be all right, you'll see. I know you will. You'll come out of this. I did. Keep taking the tablets and I'll come and see you again soon. Chin up, old cocker!'

The nurse arrived at the same time as David. David held a bunch of yellow chrysanthemums from his greenhouse. Chrysanthemums sold well at Christmas time. They were, David said, a good, sound product for any grower, at this time of year.

'Right then, I'm off Vivienne,' said Polly. 'I hate this place. I'll probably come in tomorrow, okay? Cheers kiddo!' She winked at David and left.

Polly would tell Vivienne, one day, that, right there that moment at the hospital, she had resolved something in her mind. This situation wasn't to go on. It was time Polly tackled Guy Beaufort. High time. She had one or two things to say to that little bastard.

Guy kept the studio at his parents' house. They were abroad for some months. Polly telephoned Guy first, telling him – not asking him if he agreed – that she wanted to see him. The boys were at school. Polly carried Kim in her carrycot and pressed the doorbell so long that Guy arrived at the door saying loudly, 'Okay, okay! I heard you Polly! Come in, since it seems I have little choice.'

'Hello Guy.' They went up the stairs to his studio.

'You know, you have always remind me of a stork, Polly.'

'Really? I'll take that as a compliment. Storks make wonderful mothers.' Glancing around the studio for a safe place, Polly put Kim's carrycot on the wood-boarded floor, facing the window so that the baby could see the moving branches of the trees and the birds.

'And you've always reminded me of a magpie, Guy. You know – always stealing things, eating other birds' babies. One for sorrow?'

'Well, well. I didn't have you down as lyrical, Polly.' Guy smiled.

'Anyway. I've just come from seeing Vivienne, in hospital,' Polly began. 'Oh – could you put that cigarette out – the baby?' she indicated toward Kim, kicking happily in her pink, one-piece suit.

Guy obliged, stubbing out his Rothmans in a glass ashtray.

'And,' Polly resumed, 'she's in a terrible state. Did you know that she is suicidal?'

'Yes,' Guy said soberly, 'yes, well I gathered that...'

'Oh you did, did you? You gathered that, did you? You little shit. You might be good-looking Guy, but you are one louse. You've driven that woman, a loving woman, to hell and back. She doesn't want to live! What the fuck do you think you are doing? Who the fuck do you think you are? Can't you see she is obsessed with you? You are ruining her life!'

'Don't be so melodramatic, Polly. I'm not ruining anyone's life. We go back years me and Viv. She knows I won't leave Amanda. She won't leave David. But we…we want each other. Get it? Then, I don't suppose you would know much about passion, would you?' Guy raged.

Polly swung a slap across his face, leaving a red wheal. Then she slapped the other side, giving as much force. 'Don't you patronise me you swine! I'm not one of your adoring fans, Guy. I see you for what you are. And, as for passion, I have a loving husband and that's enough for me. I don't need to prove myself. You – you are no more than a…a dog!'

Guy didn't straightaway retaliate. He rubbed the sore place on his face, breathing evenly. 'You don't know what other people's marriages are like. You have no right to judge, none of us do. Vivienne gets depressed, I know that. But she knows the score with me. She's always known, she's an adult. What we have between us is none of your damn business!' He lit up a cigarette glaring at Polly defiantly.

Polly threw the window open pointedly, letting in cool air from the town garden. 'Oh, all men like you spout the same old rubbish. I might not know how it feels to be unfaithful – have a dirty little affair, more like – but I'm not letting Vivienne sink into this illness without trying to help her. She is talented – a bloody sight more talented than you! Keep away from her. Go back to your poor wife. Poor Amanda, she looks awful. I don't suppose you've noticed her either!'

Guy's face blanched in anger. Polly had touched the nerve she'd wanted to since stepping through his door.

Like a wounded bull he advanced toward her, 'I do know how ill Amanda is! Don't you dare come round to my house and tell me what I feel for my wife. Or Vivienne. Sod off home! Go on – go back to your Derek or whatever the fuck he's called. He's more than welcome to you!' Colour rushed back into his face as he began pushing her out of the room.

'Take your hands off me! Don't you touch me!' Polly bent down to grip the carrycot handles.

'If it wasn't for that baby, I'd throw you out!' Guy roared.

'Just bloody well try, you bastard!'

Once on the town street, Polly clutched the cot to her. Kim began to bawl. 'What I'm saying...' she told Guy, about to shut the front door, 'is that if you don't do something, you are going to have a death on your hands, Guy Beaufort. Two deaths! Eh? Vivienne and your wife's. That'll bloody well show you, won't it? Not such a flaming lover boy then, eh?'

Polly left him as Kim began wailing now, hungry for her feed. Guy slammed the front door behind her so hard the knocker flapped brassily of its own accord.

When Guy spoke to her, telling her about Polly's visit, Vivienne imagined his opened window and mist blowing into his studio. It was going to rain, maybe snow. Guy would be looking out of the window, over the gardens of the town houses. The trees were just beginning to show creamy buds at the very tips of their branches.

Guy had telephoned Amanda first, he told Vivienne. He had agreed something with her. He told Vivienne that something had happened. Polly had told him just how ill she had been – how depressed Vivienne was and that he was concerned for her. Amanda really was not well, either – he had, he said, a sense of their lives going out of control. They'd all need to speak to David, of course – naturally – but Guy had had an idea.

CHAPTER SIXTEEN

The new tranquillisers did help – a little. For the first few days, David had to administer them, like she was some child. Vivienne was not to be trusted with the full prescription just yet. Well, you could understand why, Vivienne supposed.

Young Sonia had worked hard to make the house pleasant. She'd put fresh flowers, early daffodils and blue iris, in the sitting room and lit the fire. Eustace popped in and out when he could. David did a bit more than usual around the house and with Joseph. Pearl helped David, saying she was only too willing, as much for Joseph's sake as anything else.

Vivienne just told Joseph she'd got over-tired. Perhaps she had been painting too much. Needed a break. Certainly, another exhibition would have to go on hold for now, at least.

Eustace consoled Vivienne, saying he wasn't completely surprised at what had happened. To be honest, he had seen something of the sort coming – what with her 'depression,' her being 'ill'. How fond of Eustace Vivienne was.

But over the days, once she got home, David's questions and mistrustful looks reproached her. Why then – why there, in the hotel restaurant? Why when she had seen Guy Beaufort? Was it to do with that damned abortion? That was years ago! The man has a family.

'We have a family, Vivienne. We are a family, aren't we?' David questioned, over and over.

'Yes, of course we are a family. Yes, it was…it was because of the abortion, David.' There was some truth in that. 'And I am sorry.'

Pearl didn't exactly say 'See! I knew all that painting – that drinking would one day come to this!' Her face with its withholding expression was enough. Vivienne could imagine the hurt Pearl must have felt – the scandal to which she was subjected. Her son and her beloved grandson, Joseph, had been exposed to gossip: the salacious talk of the parish. Was it possible that Pearl had suggested Vivienne should leave David? That they should split up?

But, during the long history of the Carré family, nobody had ever been divorced. If David's marriage ended in the law courts – well, it would be disastrous for the Carrés. So, it seemed to Vivienne, life must take its course. For the moment, anyway, the Carrés let things pass. After all, wasn't 'Evolution not Revolution' their family motto?

Much worse: for her own parents, Vivienne had evoked memories of Oscar and his drowned little body. Another potential loss of life – to dark, deep water – must seem almost intolerable for Edward and Jean.

They kept their visit to Vivienne brief. Edward had guided a subdued Jean into the kitchen to talk to Sonia. Straightaway, Sonia began telling Jean all about a new polish she had discovered: a cream, especially for antique furniture.

Edward seemed tired, clumsily tipping tea from his cup. Vivienne tried to mop it up, dabbing his saucer with a tissue, making it worse.

'Where on earth do you get all this from, Nin?' Edward put his cup and tea-filled saucer down on the table with a shaking hand. 'All these imaginings and recklessness? Edna Jones told me you were like this, but I thought you'd got it out of your system by now. We prayed for you, you know.' His voice trembled. 'What a spectacle you made of yourself! In front of all those people.' He spoke in a low voice, as if he was in a confessional box. 'You have shamed us. Shamed yourself! Endangered your life! How could you? You and your little secrets. Please, put an end to all your nonsense, Nin, please.'

Vivienne tried to respond, but the numbness, the tranquillisers, stiffened her words. They came out stilted and dry. 'I'm sorry for worrying you...about Oscar...about,' Vivienne's tongue felt heavy and furred, like it had grown too big for her mouth, '...about the drowning.'

'You look like death, my girl.' Then, abruptly, Edward stood up and made for the kitchen. Vivienne followed after him. 'Come along now, Jean, we are going. We are leaving.' Edward cleared his throat and brushed his lapels, straightening up like a soldier on duty who had suddenly remembered to stand to attention.

Before they left, Jean hovered momentarily over Vivienne, touching her arm briefly. 'You looked sweet, lying on that paisley couch, Ninny. Were you resting?'

'Yes, Mum. I was just having a rest. I'm fine.' Poor Jean. There was nothing she could ever do to keep her children alive, was there? No, a mother's love was never enough to do that.

'Yes? Well then, see you Ninny. Do try to buck up? Mmm? Got my little Oscar to look after haven't you, when I can't?' Jean scolded.

'I know. Don't worry.'

All this drinking and throwing herself into the sea and everyone knowing Guy Beaufort will never leave Amanda – didn't they tell her no good would come from loving that man – (didn't they just tell her so?) – this had all been left unsaid.

When her parents had gone, Vivienne thought about what her father had said. Her little secrets? What did Edward know? Ashamed? Absolutely – nobody was more ashamed than she. But not shame for what she felt for Guy. Shame for concerning Eustace, certainly for worrying Joseph – even for shaking David's trust that life moved on, in some inexorable straight path. But Vivienne still loved Guy – she was still in that small boat, tossed about in that wild blue ocean with no compass and no safe shore in sight.

So when she took Guy's call, Vivienne swayed queasily but said, calmly as she could, 'Hi, yes, feeling a bit better, thanks.' Biting her tongue.

'Listen,' Guy said, 'I've had an idea. I've talked it through with Amanda. No, it's all right, honestly, Vivvy. In fact Amanda wants to talk to you. She's not mad at you. We've...well, we'll have to speak to David, of course.' He paused. Vivienne heard him draw a deep breath. 'We wondered if you might like to share my studio – for a little while. Until you are stronger. We could work together? Fact is – well, Amanda's quite keen. What do you think? Change of scene? Get you back to your painting? Yes?'

What did you imagine? Vivienne wanted to agree right there and then, with or without David's consent. The great weight of cloud lightened.

'Sometimes, Vivienne, I can't make head nor tail out of you,' David said. Vivienne saw he had deep lines now each side of his mouth and creases at the side of his eyes. And David's hair was beginning to thin. 'But I have been thinking Vivienne, believe it or not. Maybe we should have taken a break earlier. Perhaps we were wrong not to do that. What about a weekend in Jersey? There's bound to be some bargain break or other going. Mum'll have Joseph, I'm sure.'

'You can't afford the time, David. Let's see how things go. And, by the way, just what did the doctor say to you?'

David studied his hands, gripping then un-gripping. 'Just that you needed a rest. That things had got on top of you.'

'Right.'

'To give you some space whatever the hell that's supposed to mean. Can't think my mother ever needed space, she's always worked...'

'Not now, David please.'

'I just get the feeling there's more, something you're not telling me, Vivienne.'

'Let's just see how things go, David.'

David shrugged his shoulders. 'Yes, well I do have a lot to do. The new plants need bringing on for the season. Can't put them on hold. The cold snap hasn't helped. I'd hoped they would be further on by now.'

'I know. I know.'

So, David eventually agreed that part of Vivienne's space could be to share Guy's studio. Eustace had talked the idea through with David, and told Vivienne that he could see some good points.

'For one thing,' Eustace said to Vivienne, 'everyday life soon tempers an over-active imagination.' He gave her a wry glance, 'and for another, we want you back at your painting, Vivienne.'

David said he could see what Eustace was getting at. 'I'm not a believer in all this counselling lark myself. A change of scene – space

– well we can give it a try, I suppose.' David sighed deeply. 'But it wasn't like this in my mother's day.'

The Beaufort town house was still the same to Vivienne. Its familiarity, and the palliatives she took, soothed her. She fancied she saw Mrs Beaufort in the kitchen, making her sponges filled with soft yellow butter cream. Here were all the old gang – school friends chattering like town sparrows as Mozart bathed their ears. Upstairs was Guy's bedroom and his bed, where they had first made love. She expected he shared that with Amanda now.

Guy had canvasses on his easel. His work was abstract and linear. He always wore Amanda's knitted jumpers with blue or black jeans. Vivienne put her hair up and wore plain blouses with the sleeves rolled up to her elbows. For work she liked cropped trousers and inch high pumps (more flattering to the ankles, you see, than flats.)

'I've always loved the view from this house. Beaufort house,' said Vivienne, ' – look at the gardens.' Sometimes they were fresh with rain, other times filled with sunny spring blossoms. Lately Vivienne had detected a curious feeling – an almost forgotten anticipation for the morning's first light.

Vivienne began to make a small stack of finished paintings, her side of the studio. Guy worked more slowly. They'd break for coffee and examine each other's canvases. Vivienne accepted Guy's criticism and he hers in an easy companionship. Now and then they would crack open some wine, sit on the floor and just talk. Vivienne thought how funny Guy could be and actually found herself laughing more often than for a long time.

'What do you think of Turner?' Guy asked her, one day.

'He used too much white,' said Vivienne.

'Yes! You are the only person I have ever met who thought the same as me about Turner. I've always thought that. Too much white. Impressionism is fine but I actually prefer Constable to Turner.'

'Not *The Hay Wain*?'

'Not only that one – but why not? Since we're criticising the World-of-Art's sacred cows!'

Vivienne laughed. What a shame it was that Darius had lost

interest in Guy. Darius liked fresh ideas and projects. He thought Guy had become outdated, difficult to market. Right now, though, Vivienne thought, Guy could do with Darius in his life.

One gentle summer afternoon Amanda called by. Guy was away in London, buying more brushes from the specialist shop he and Vivienne had found. Amanda sent Natalie and Joseph downstairs to the sitting room to find drinks and biscuits and watch the Beaufort's television.

Vivienne felt shy in Amanda's company. Aware of her embarrassment, her limbs feeling stiff and strained, Vivienne sat down next to Amanda on the low-slung, much used canvas couch. On the coffee table stood their empty mugs.

Amanda's cheeks were hollowed out; her skin was white and stretched tightly over her cheekbones. Underneath her pale grey eyes were dark grey smudges. Her fine hair had thinned to a wispy brown. Bony arms and legs were not disguised by a blue satin blouse with pussy cat bow and a pleated, ankle-length skirt.

'The thing is, Vivienne,' Amanda came out directly, 'the thing is…I haven't got very long to live. I want to say…I'm glad you can be…a good friend for Guy.' Amanda stilled Vivienne's protest with a wave of her hand. 'No, no, I have advanced cancer. It's gone too far, it's spread. They can't do anything.'

Amanda rose, going over to the window, looking at the trees in full green leaf, rustling in a summer breeze. 'Guy is unfaithful. It's always been like that. But…well, I don't really want to go into any details. I haven't been enough for him. To tell the truth, well I knew I wasn't from day one. You…you know, Vivienne you are much more his type.' Amanda's gaze looked straight at her.

If Vivienne could ever have imagined that, one day, Amanda would be talking to her like this! Well, she would have denied it could ever be possible.

'I won't see my grandchildren. That's the hardest part – leaving Natalie.' Amanda wiped her tears with the flats of her hands, that, Vivienne saw, were still beautifully kept. 'Guy would say I'm being melodramatic now, wouldn't he?'

They both gave a rueful laugh.

'But I want you to know,' Amanda continued steadily, 'Vivienne – that you being his…friend. Well…it's okay by me.'

'I – I, Amanda. I am so sorry about everything.' Vivienne filled, welled up, with compassion, guilt and sorrow all at once: all together. Amanda, the young bride, fluttering around her guests in her floating ivory gown was nearing her end.

'Surely there's a chance, isn't there? Mightn't there be? New treatments come along all the time. Just the other day someone told me…' Vivienne halted, unable to talk through a tightening throat.

'No, no. Don't trouble yourself Vivienne. Don't get upset. I have had plenty of time to think about what I wanted to say. I just wanted to tell you this. Cancer – well it brings things out of oneself you wouldn't expect! I certainly never thought I'd be saying these things to you!' Amanda gave Vivienne a quick smile of both recognition and resignation.

Tears stayed in her eyes as Vivienne put her arms around the paper-thin Amanda. They embraced awkwardly, then withdrew from each other.

'We chose a very unusual man, didn't we?' Amanda asked her with soulful eyes.

'Very. Although I don't know how much choosing I did, Amanda. Guy sort of happened.'

Then Amanda hesitated before saying, 'And, well, look after yourself, Vivienne. Guy…'

'Yes?' Vivienne prompted…was there something else Amanda wanted to say?

'Oh, oh I don't know. Guy can be selfish, you know. He wants independence, yet he wants a family.'

God, this must be difficult for her. Amanda talking about emotions, about Guy. Vivienne sure had underestimated the frightened rabbit.

'You haven't been…very well, yourself, lately, have you Vivienne?' Amanda looked down at her immaculate hands, thoughtfully stroking the fingers bearing engagement and wedding rings. 'There is such a thing as, well, caring too much, you know.' She shot Vivienne a candid look. 'Anyway, look, I didn't mean to come here and tell you what to do. It's just, well take care, Vivienne. Take care'

'You know Guy loves you very much, don't you Amanda?' Vivienne felt emboldened to say. After all, the woman was showing such courage and thoughtfulness toward her.

'Yes. Yes, I know he does. He loves Natalie as well. The trouble with Guy is – he's like two people wanting to be in two places at once, if not three.'

At this, Amanda engaged Vivienne with a frank stare. Vivienne nodded in agreement. She sensed there were many things she and Amanda cannot and would never share. But Amanda had no obligation to show friendship toward her. Vivienne felt chastened, humbled, even, at Amanda's strength and her leniency. Possibly, in other circumstances, they might well have been friends.

Presently Amanda fetched her tasselled string bag. She called out to Natalie that they were leaving now. They went down the stairs with the worn carpet and Vivienne opened the front door.

Vivienne and Joseph stood on the top step of the Beaufort house as they waved goodbye to Amanda and Natalie.

'Why are you crying, Ma?' asked Joseph.

As her tears spilled out Vivienne managed, 'Just a bit sad, darling.' But she thought, 'I'm crying for all the women who ever loved Guy Beaufort. They do a lot of crying, do Guy's women.'

As they painted, absorbed in their work, the telephone in Guy's studio rang. Taking a long drag on his cigarette, still looking at his painting, he answered, 'Yes? Oh…' he glanced at Vivienne. 'Well I'll ring you later about that. Okay?' Guy rang off. 'People always think you have nothing better to do, don't they, when they ring you,' he said, sounding apologetic.

'Yes, they do.' What's to apologise for? Vivienne looked at Guy. His thick, dark hair needed cutting: it fell over his forehead in a loose wave. The sweater today was a sort of maize brown, the denims frayed navy blue. Guy peered at a minute section of his painting, dotting on vermilion paint with his new sable brush.

Like missing a step, thinking you are going to fall headlong – then stopping yourself in the nick of time – Vivienne shook off a second's doubt. Putting her brushes down, she went over to Guy.

'You do like bright colours, don't you?' How glad she was! Colour – the enjoyment of colour was beginning to return!

Guy suddenly put an arm around her. Unabashed, she kissed him vigorously, full on the lips. His flesh tasted salty and warm. Still kissing they sank to the floor. She lay on her back, Guy covered her, smothering her with his body. They were one again. She tasted his saliva and breathed in through the smoky wool of his sweater.

'I've missed you, Guy, hold me.'

'You've been far away,' Guy kissed her neck.

'I've been so lonely.'

'We're here now,' Guy whispered, 'Vivvy, I'm here now.'

'I'm not mad am I Guy?'

'Yes. We both are. Mad as hell,' said Guy.

Each day they painted, feeding each other's needs whenever they could. David started complaining, resenting her time away from the house. But Vivienne felt her strength returning. It was like a thirst being satiated. Still, at home with David, even with Sonia's help, things were not right.

Vivienne would just have to try harder. For Joseph's sake.

Poor Joseph. Vivienne hated Joseph telling her: 'Today the bread of my sandwich had black bits in it, Ma. And it tasted like it had been on the floor.' Oh, dear.

Yes, so room for improvement? Vivienne would try: Must Try Harder.

Then Amanda Beaufort died. Expected for so long, she died quite suddenly, at their apartment. Guy found her, sitting on the balcony, overlooking the islands on a gloriously sunny day. In her lap she had held a piece of knitting: a blue sweater for her husband. The pattern blew about on the balcony floor.

Vivienne didn't go to the funeral. At the Roman Catholic Church a

Requiem Mass was held. Guy had done all the arrangements himself, especially asking for Faure's *Sanctus* to be played. Eustace and Pearl represented Vivienne and David. Edward attended, representing Jean.

They told Vivienne the church had been absolutely packed. There had been great bouquets of flowers everywhere: cream and white roses, lavender and glossy green ivy. Eustace reported that the Catholic Mass had been extraordinarily moving. All the Le Croixs family and friends, and all the Beauforts filled the pews. There wasn't a seat left, people even stood at the back.

Little Natalie had sat with Guy in the front pew. She held her father's hand all through the ceremony. Guy had held his head bowed down throughout the service. There was a private burial.

Guy, they told Vivienne, was inconsolable. He looked utterly bereft. They all said it would be a long time before Guy Beaufort got over Amanda's death.

'Of course,' Pearl told Vivienne when she got back to La Colette, wearing her black costume, pulling a hat-pin from her black veiled hat, 'he relied on her for all the practical side of his life. Muriel Le Croix told me Guy can hardly boil an egg. She put up with such a lot, that girl. Amanda was a wonderful mother. Amanda was a wonderful wife.'

CHAPTER SEVENTEEN

Vivienne moved back to her own, smaller studio. David told her he did not think Guy's experiment had worked that well, anyway. The move back to the house allowed Vivienne's memories to sneak their way into her mind again. Not always so intense, maybe, but she could sense them there, silently lurking, like the elusive black fish they had hunted in rock pools, way back, when they were kids.

In articles about drinking, Vivienne read of alcohol as a self-medication, alcohol actually causing depression. Alcoholism was depression. So it was all a question of control, then?

One thing Eustace had been right about was that seeing Guy, day by day, had helped her equilibrium. Trouble was, what now? At least she still found her painting absorbing, with talk, maybe of a New York visit? Almost by chance, her style was in vogue. Vivienne had finished a body of good work from her time in Guy's studio. That was something, at least.

So, maybe things were slowly working out? Even though David complained that she was still volatile, 'You get so inflamed, Vivienne. Disturbed.'

Yes, well, David, sometimes flames take a long time to burn out. Vivienne couldn't begin to talk to Polly about Guy. Polly couldn't ever believe, she said, that Vivienne had shared Guy's studio with him in the first place.

'I went to see Guy, kiddo,' Polly confessed to Vivienne. 'I suppose he thought you being together was his way of helping? I told him a lot of things, you know. About being heartless. That he was a two-timing…'

'Polly! I don't know if I wanted you to say all that!'

'Well I did. And I'm not sorry,' said Polly firmly. 'What now, with poor Amanda dead? He's not going to change, you know. Little prick.'

'Polly!'

'Anyway, I've got my own lot to look after. They don't half keep me busy. But I'm keeping my eye on you, kiddo. If ever you want advice, you know? One old married lady to another?'

'Is that what we are now?' Vivienne's eyes widened. 'Old? Old ladies?'

'Reckon so, kiddo.'

Jocelyn had been in touch, as well. She had phoned and written more since the 'near drowning thing'. Jocelyn had long ditched husband number two, 'Blame my hot Umbrian blood darling!' Her passion overflowed with excitement when she told Vivienne more about her gorgeous Italian boyfriend, Enrico.

'Darling he is the business!' Jocelyn exulted. 'Twelve years younger than me and sensational in bed. You must meet him! You must come over to London.'

Jocelyn had, many years ago, qualified as a nurse. She'd decided to buy and run her own – 'Exclusive, darling!' – alternative medicine practice.

'Complementary medicine,' Jocelyn enthused. 'Homeopathy. It's the thing to be in. My practice has everything, darling. I provide everything: massage, acupuncture, aromatherapy. The works. I'll give you a free treatment when you come over. You won't believe how good you'll feel afterwards. Promise.'

When tackled about Vivienne seeing Jocelyn in London, David relented. He said he felt that he should have let Vivienne have a break before now. They had had a good season for once. The new plants had, after all, been a sound choice, if difficult to propagate. David was getting very good prices for his crop this year. So yes, she could go to see Jocelyn. 'But not for long, mind? A long weekend at most. Joseph will miss you and Mum's not getting any younger.'

Yes, yes, Vivienne realised all that, David, she was quite aware of her obligations, thanks. And her GP still went on at her. Just the other day he had shaken his head reproachfully at her when she avoided committing to counselling sessions. 'I'll still take the tranquillisers?'

She offered, tentatively.

'It's over a year now. And I want you off those, Vivienne. They are not a long-term solution.'

As Vivienne walked with Guy on the flat, wide beach, the sky a Mediterranean blue, high and cloudless, she recalled that terrible Christmas. The sea was calm now and welcoming, winking with sunny sparkles. Creamy foam flopped lazily onto the sandy shore.

'Thanks for rescuing me, Guy. You know? That Christmas, all – that?' Vivienne threw some round pebbles into the sea, watching them skip, drop and radiate increasing circles until they disappeared.

'Not only me, Vivvy. David was there. He's strong, isn't he?' said Guy.

Vivienne didn't answer. She didn't want to think of David, nor how strong he was or wasn't. Guy thinks of David as strong?

'Not just physically, Vivvy. David is consistent.'

Another compliment about David! She would much rather they talked about their relationship. Because Polly had been right: Vivienne did play with the idea, probe the notion of how it might be, living with Guy.

'David's, okay, he's only strong in some ways. Weak in others…'

'Like most men, then.' Guy turned his head and avoided her fierce gaze.

What was all this about? Vivienne wouldn't walk straight out of her marriage, no, not just like that. But if it came to a choice – if Guy actually asked her – actually made a proposition to her, well then, yes! Of course she would be more than tempted.

They sat on tufted, springy earth spiked with spiny grass. Sea pinks dotted the turf. In the light breeze they dug their hands into the pockets of their overcoats. They watched Natalie as she played with her Christmas present, her white West Highland puppy: Fraser, her Westie.

'Growing up, isn't she?' Vivienne smiled. 'Same as Joseph. Soon be taking GCEs at this rate!'

Guy nodded in agreement.

'We hope Joseph gets through his exams alright. We want him to go to college. What about Natalie?' Vivienne said it more just as something to say, rather than want of a discussion on education. Guy looked into the distance. He seemed oddly aloof. It must be because of Amanda.

'Actually, Vivvy.' Guy said levelly, 'actually I wanted to see you today because I have something to tell you.' Now he looked grave.

The nape of her neck tingled with a dreaded apprehension. 'What?' God, Guy suddenly looked awful. Her mouth dried, 'What is it?'

He took her hand, squeezing it hard so it hurt.

'Thing is, I'm going away. I'm leaving Guernsey. I'm taking Natalie. We're going to live in Cyprus.' Guy gazed forlornly at the blue horizon, with troubled eyes. 'I want a fresh start.'

'Fresh start?' Vivienne cried out. 'Guy! Don't, don't go. Not again, please!' Words twisted inside her head, her heart constricted. She began to breathe rapidly. 'What will I do without you?'

'Viv. Little Vivvy,' Guy held her close, wrapping her with his coat, muffling her protesting words. 'You must let me go. I must let you get on with your life. We have children to bring up, work to do.'

Vivienne wept into his coat.

'Christ, Viv, I am finding this hard enough. Don't be like this. I miss Amanda. I've got to get stronger Viv. I must. I want to do it. I want to go away, far away.'

'But what about us?' Vivienne cried miserably, 'what about us?'

The little white Westie ran up to them, his coal-black eyes beseeching that they play with him. He shook his coat, spraying them with wet seawater. He dropped the red ball at their feet, his tongue hung out with a quizzical pant. His tail wagged expectantly, without him trying.

Natalie, so unmistakably Guy's daughter, scrambled to join them, hugging her dog. 'Naughty, naughty boy!' She chuckled, running off with him again, down over smooth stones to the sea's very edge.

'Why Cyprus?' Vivienne said in a tight voice. Why anywhere? Anywhere away from her, it seemed. Any plans she had, any thoughts she had about their love together lay dashed on the hard rocks below.

Guy sighed, 'Well my father knows a bloke out there, an old friend, who has a pottery. Tourist stuff, you know. And he's looking for a manager who knows a bit about art. He'd like me to paint, to sell my paintings.' Now Guy frowned uncertainly at the distant sea.

'What, commercial art? Postcards? You can do better than that, Guy.' And, it was worth a try: 'you can do that here, surely?' She stumbled, clutching at him. There must be some way to keep him.

'I know, Viv. But it's not only that. I must get away for a while. Guernsey stifles me. I want to...I want to try something new.' His voice rose now in earnest, 'Natalie will love it! She loves islands and being in the sun. It will be good for her, to get away from it all.'

So, then, it was all settled. All planned.

It turned out that Guy had found a house in Nicosia. Natalie was enrolled at an English-speaking school. The flights were booked. He told Vivienne he wasn't taking much furniture. He'd put most of it in store, would be selling it or he might bring some stuff over as time went on. The apartment in St Peter Port was gone. He and Natalie stayed at his parents' house once Amanda had died.

So there would be nothing much left then, for her to mourn. For Vivienne to remember him by. 'You'll keep in touch?' She asked fearfully. 'Please give me that much?'

'Of course.'

As life's colours seemed to haemorrhage from her, Vivienne sorely needed a drink. Taking some vodka from the fridge, she poured a long one: her glass dripped, brimful, over her fingers.

'Well I think it's the best thing he could have done, kiddo,' Polly said with satisfaction. 'Best thing. Bugger off, I say. Tell you what, I'll have one of them vodkas. Got any lemon?' Polly downed the shot of vodka in one go. 'No more though. I'm driving and I've got my little Kim to think of.'

Vivienne didn't go to the airport to see Guy and Natalie off. Their last night together had harrowed her to the bone. Clinging to him through the night, feeling his thighs next to hers, Vivienne inhaled his smoky scent. They didn't talk. Guy looked tired and sad.

When would she see him again? Vivienne had asked, feeling hysteria unstoppable, uncontrollable, rising in her words. Guy hadn't mentioned her to going to Cyprus to see him. He clearly wanted a break from everything, everyone, 'Just for the time being anyway, Vivvy,' he had said. As if that was, somehow, going to help.

From the cliff top, standing in a gusting wind above Portelet, Vivienne watched the plane fly overhead. She didn't wave. She just watched the silver aircraft flying away, until it was a speck over the wind-furled ocean. Then it was gone.

Vivienne wandered into St Peter Port town. She faltered around the shops, hardly knowing why, not buying anything. Once back home she prepared supper, scraping carrots and parsnips, cutting her finger. She ran it under the cold water tap, watching the blood wash away. Joseph began to question her about his homework.

'What's a dyke, Ma?' Joseph flicked through a dictionary with a pencil.

'It's a term used for the butch side of a lesbian relationship,' Vivienne said vaguely, winding a plaster over the cut finger.

'I'm doing geography, Ma?'

'Oh, well – look it up then!' Tense, Vivienne put the television on. Some actors were saying things they couldn't possibly mean. Advertisements were loud and trivial. Then came the news. Vivienne switched off. Didn't need drama. Pain and sorrow in the corner of her sitting room, blasting out of a television box? Vivienne didn't need that.

David came home. 'Something smells good. Jocelyn phoned again. She wants to firm up about this London trip.' He poured himself a whisky. 'Still want to go?'

David drove her to the airport. 'Jocelyn's meeting me at Heathrow,' said Vivienne. 'Then, we're off to the galleries. She said she's excited about the possibility of New York.' Vivienne tried not to sound so flat and lifeless. 'So, take care then, and Joseph?"

'Of course,' said David. Vivienne gave him a light kiss on his cheek, but he had gone before she went through the Departures

Gate.

Now that she was on her way, Vivienne felt pleased she had made an effort. The black trouser suit looked good, and the white shirt with extra wide lapels. She and Polly had gone to the hairdresser's: had her hair piled up into a chignon. Polly even had her roots done.

'Normally do my own, cheaper from a box,' Polly had grinned happily at the hairdresser.

'You don't say,' he replied, flicking horrified eyes to the ceiling.

They sped from Heathrow, then immediately took a taxi to Harrods. Jocelyn spent, in an hour, what Vivienne might have in a year.

'Here.' Jocelyn threw Vivienne a bag full of Yves St Laurent make-up, Dior perfume and Chanel No.5.

'Jocelyn! I can get these much cheaper in Guernsey!'

'Who the hell cares? Carpe diem! Seize the day, darling!'

Jocelyn looked wonderful, even though she'd gone forty. She clutched a very pretty young man, glued to her side. Enrico had black wavy hair, long-lashed brown eyes and a calm, amused grin. Enrico looked like some kind of youthful sage. He wore a purple silk shirt, unbuttoned – so Vivienne could see some of his toned, tanned chest – no tie. Midnight blue chinos.

'Hello Enrico. You are gorgeous just like Jocelyn said!' Vivienne laughed as Enrico gently kissed her hand.

'I am most pleased to meet you, Vivvyon. Enchanted.'

'And he's no fool,' said Jocelyn throwing them both a decisive glance, 'Enrico is nobody's fool.'

Vivienne virtually ran to keep up with them both. They tore around London: Harvey Nichols, Selfridges, Fortnum and Mason. You had to enjoy it. London's city pace energized Vivienne.

Feeling swept along in Jocelyn and Enrico's slipstream, Vivienne tried hard not to remember. Yet there was an undercurrent – the almost but not quite forgotten London of the sixties – the termination. Vivienne wondered if the woman doctor still practiced?

And, of course, the galleries reminded her of that time here, with Guy. The £10 he never did pay back. The Chelsea School of Art. All the promises that had held. It seemed so long ago – when youth and her dreams made all things seem possible.

Aware now that Jocelyn was speaking, Vivienne pulled herself back into their company. 'You've done wonderfully well, hasn't she Enrico? America eh? She's a star! Let's go celebrate!'

They linked arm in arm and strolled into the nearest oyster bar, soon shucking back delicacies in a chrome and glass restaurant. Vivienne had never seen the like of it. David would die when she told him the cost.

Jocelyn took Vivienne to see her Complementary Medicine health suite. All was quiet and luxurious. Jocelyn had decorated all the rooms in white and green. There were glass tables, white-tiled booths and massage tables. Everything smelled of fresh cut grass, camomile and mint. Mood music: birds in a forest and tinkling streams, played from speakers in every room.

After her massage, warm and cosseted in a fluffy white dressing gown, sipping iced tea, Vivienne felt her body positively uncurl itself.

Smiling triumphantly, Jocelyn booked tickets for the theatre. A gay musical would do them all good, she said. In the taxi home they sang the show's song, all the way, clear to Jocelyn's home in Putney.

Next day, a relentless Jocelyn with an amused Enrico decided to take Vivienne shopping in Putney High Street. Traffic bustled about. People thronged the pavements. Vivienne made the effort to keep up. It was all so way busier than Guernsey.

As they neared a zebra crossing a handsome, young man bumped into Vivienne. He immediately began to apologise, saying, 'Oh, I am so sorry! I do apologise'. It was Matthias.

CHAPTER EIGHTEEN

'Hello!' Vivienne and Matthias cried out simultaneously, 'Well Hi!' They embraced in surprised delight.

'Matthias! Am I glad to see you!' Incredulous, Vivienne introduced Matthias. 'This is Jocelyn, and this is Enrico. I'm in London for a few days – and you?'

'So am I! I'm down from Oxford. Just for a day or two – the bookshops – you know. It's Kismet, Baby. It's fate!' Matthias hugged Vivienne, swinging her around on Putney High Street's busiest day.

'Hey! Where have you been hiding this dish, Vivienne?' Jocelyn said, her eyes wide, appraising Matthias.

The dark-skinned, dark-haired lad with perfect teeth smiled, but kept his arm firmly around Vivienne.

'We go back a way,' said Vivienne.

'Come on, Jocelyn,' said Enrico suddenly. 'We must make ourselves – what is the correct word – scarce?' He winked broadly at Vivienne.

'There's no need… ', Vivienne began.

'No, no, it's okay! Don't need a second hint. We'll shoot off to look for goodies, Vivienne. See you later darlings.' Jocelyn and Enrico wafted off in a cloud of Chanel and Gucci as they whisked into the milling crowd of shoppers.

'So – coffee?' Asked Matthias, guiding her toward a café nearby, barely touching Vivienne's elbow. 'Now, what's been going on with you? I want to know all about it, Baby.'

Was Guy's absence in her life noticeable – the missing of him…?

'Not much to tell,' said Vivienne.

'Nonsense.' Matthias gestured toward a door. 'Something's up. Shows all over your face. But you're still completely wonderful, my little Ariadne.'

'And you are still completely impossible, Matthias,' Vivienne scolded with a smile as they entered the coffee shop, 'quite impossible.' She shook her head.

'Now then,' Matthias said, pulling out wooden chairs with spindle backs, 'what's the matter?' He plonked a battered, grey leather folder onto the table. They ordered two coffees: black, no milk, no sugar.

Vivienne thought Matthias still looked incredibly young. He wore a beige raincoat, a size too big for him, with the belt flapping about and the buttons undone. His checked tie hung loose and his shoes were scuffed and in need of a polish.

'No. You first. Tell me how Oxford is going?' Vivienne sipped the thick, hot liquid, burning her tongue. Every table in the steamy coffee shop was taken. Bursting shopping bags littered the floor. Vivienne and Matthias had to talk loudly, above the noisy chatter.

'Okay then, me first. The research I'm doing takes in Latin scholars – Ovid. Ovid's *Ars Amatoria*, the art of love. Greek mythology. It comes easier to me than most.' He smiled at Vivienne, showing his white rows of clear, even teeth.

Vivienne sat back, easing down her tensed shoulders. Matthias hadn't lost any of his impudence. Serious study hadn't bowed him down. He was still the clever, intriguing boy that lifted her spirits, shooing away the demons.

'Guy's in Cyprus now,' came out almost inadvertently from Vivienne. 'His wife died. He's gone to live there.' She let her gaze wander to the café window, at the preoccupied shoppers hurrying by. Then her eyes cast back down to the cooling brown pool in her coffee cup.

A party of noisy customers left, all at once. They took their bags with them, with much scraping of chairs and rustling of white plastic.

'That's better,' said Matthias, loosening his tie even further. 'Didn't like shouting at you. So, that's what's up. Ariadne still pines for Bacchus?'

Vivienne said nothing.

'You still eaten up? Poor Baby.' Matthias drank his coffee, clattering the cup back into the saucer, not taking his eyes off Vivienne. 'But you're not still going around thinking you're a murderer are you?'

Her eyes lowered again, and her face chilled, although the café was, if anything, too warmly heated.

'You mean to say you've been in pain all these years? It's never gone away? Jesus, Baby!' Matthias exclaimed.

'Yes to the first. No to the second.'

'Didn't anyone help you? Hasn't anyone tried to – ? Have you never talked about all this, Vivienne?' Matthias took both her hands into his, kissing them. 'Jesus, Baby.'

'Yes,' Vivienne said, dully, 'people have tried, Matthias. My doctor tries. David – his father, they have tried, I must say. I cannot, though. I just cannot. There's too much…too many things…'

Matthias gripped her hands, kissing them in light dabs. He leaned so close to her that their noses touched. 'One day, Vivienne my Baby, my Ariadne, when you want to defend yourself, I'll be there. That I promise. Do you think you could tell me? Tell me all about it, yes, one day?' His mellow brown eyes scrutinised her carefully.

'Maybe. Maybe one day, Matthias. Maybe. Yes, I will remember what you said.' Yes, if Vivienne could tell anyone in the world about this malignant, pulsing ache, it would be Matthias. But all too soon she would be back in Guernsey, facing her gremlins without him. So she said, 'Tell me about Bacchus and Ariadne, Matthias. Tell me about Titian and mythology, anything. I want to hear your voice!'

Gently, slowly, Matthias took his hands away from hers, looked up at the ceiling then back down to her and sighed. 'You mean about the passionate love between Bacchus and Ariadne, don't you? You're still very pretty, you know. All that curly hair and dazzling blue eyes!'

'No, I'm old. I'm getting old.' He's got lovely eyes himself: brown eyes that turn tortoiseshell in the early morning sun.

'Nah. It's what's going on inside, Baby. You should see some of our students!'

'Wish I could have gone to Oxford, Matthias. And Guy's

always said I should have gone to the Chelsea School of Art,' said Vivienne.

'Well then, he was right about that. And possibly you should have gone to both. But there's time. Time for everything, don't be sad.'

'No, I certainly don't want to be sad now I'm here with you. Carry on, please?'

'Okay. Right, well in the foreground of the painting is a man, fighting off snakes. They writhe around him.' Matthias made exaggerated twisting motions with his hands.

Vivienne nodded, smiling at him.

'Snakes can be a symbol of evil. But they also can signify the power to heal. The sloughing off of a snakeskin symbolises rebirth and healing. A snake with tail in its mouth – a perfect circle – was a religious symbol of eternity. Of Father Time.'

'Oh, that I didn't know,' said Vivienne, although she did. Matthias' voice was like a balm: he was a Mediterranean zephyr, sweet and warm.

Matthias took Vivienne's hand again and cradled it in his. She could smell his warmth and his youth. His fingers were like a schoolboy's, not much longer than hers. 'One day, your evil snake, your python, will die, Vivienne. And then you will heal! You will, you'll see.'

The café clock ticked: a clock with Roman figures, a circle surrounded by polished wood.

'There is an ancient saying,' Matthias asked for the bill. 'It's familiar to the Renaissance, *Veritas filia temporis* – 'Truth is the daughter of time.' Mercy and truth are the daughters of time. When they meet together, justice and peace have kissed each other.'

'Yes, and sleeping gods can lie, but never die. Oh, Matthias.' Vivienne fumbled in her bag for a tissue. She dabbed her eyes and blew her nose. 'Thank you. That was lovely. Thanks. I'm so glad we met again. You are so lovely to me!' With both tears and laughter, Vivienne kissed his youthful cheek.

'So are you. You're special.' Matthias brushed away wet from her eyes with his thumbs in a light, tender touch.

Then Vivienne told him about the possible New York show. How Joseph was a young schoolboy now – growing so tall and talking about going to University. She talked to Matthias about Polly and Eustace and life in Guernsey.

When the waitress had given him his change, Matthias placed a tip on the plate.

'Oh no, I can –? Won't you let me –?' Vivienne protested, fishing about in her purse.

'Nonsense. All done. Listen though,' he looked at her thoughtfully, 'have you ever thought of doing a degree yourself, Vivienne? You could do an Arts degree – say an external degree – with the Open University, for example. I can see it's difficult, living on an island with no university faculty. But, will you think about it?'

Vivienne said she would. And, actually, that thought had occurred to her. They swapped addresses and telephone numbers. She had mislaid his. But this time, Vivienne said, they would not lose touch again. 'I really mean that.'

Through the café window they saw Jocelyn and Enrico approaching, laden with designer store bags and laughing together. Matthias and Vivienne kissed goodbye. Vivienne lingered in his healthy embrace: his raincoat enveloped her. 'Thanks, Matthias.'

'That's okay, lovely Ariadne. I'll help you, one day, help you to defend yourself, Baby. I'll help. You'll see.'

Then he was gone. Matthias ran across the road, hopping on to a number 22 bus, heading for central London. Vivienne saw him, his face at the window, as he waved from the back seat. Vivienne's Bacchus, with the lovely face and the wondrous mind.

So, back to Guernsey, Vivienne decided to do exactly as Matthias had suggested. She sent away for an Open University prospectus. Also, there was the New York show to be thinking about. She didn't have nearly enough works to show for an exhibition like that. There'd be the frames to sort out – the exporting, the catalogue. There was loads to be getting on with.

Sonia had been a real find. With a clean, airy, sweet-smelling home, David too busy to be getting at her as much, then meeting young Matthias – the missing-Guy-days – the bad days – were at least, almost controllable. Their growing business, David's work, was beginning to pay off. Life inched forward. Even some sense of purpose in Vivienne's life, if tenuous at first, felt detectable.

When the phone rang, it was Pearl. Eustace had had a heart attack. He was rushed to Southampton Hospital. Guernsey's medics used Southampton for cases the island couldn't cope with.

Pumped with clot-busting medicines, Warfarin and aspirin, Eustace lay in his hospital bed, pale and weak. Pearl couldn't fly over with him. She detested flying. So she had asked Vivienne and David to go. They sat at his bedside.

Vivienne shivered with frantic worry. There was a very dangerous chance of Eustace having another – serious – heart attack, they were told. He had been lucky to survive this one. It had been massive. The damage would have been extensive.

'Eustace, Eustace, my friend. Be strong,' Vivienne held his hand.

'Your lovely eyes… you cheer me, Vivienne.' Eustace had never touched her lovingly before, but stroked her unruly hair fondly. 'Don't worry, my dear, it will take more than this!' He winked at her. His hair stuck flat against his head. His skin seemed papery white. Vivienne held back a rising sob as hard as she could. She bit the inside of her mouth.

'It's just…Vivienne, just…look after David, will you? And Pearl and our Joseph. My dear, it's all I want from you. Promise me?'

'Of course! Of course Eustace. Don't say that. You are going to get better.'

Eustace smiled a watery smile. His eyes seemed faded.

'Eustace,' Vivienne said urgently, 'thank you. Thanks for everything. You are my dearest, dearest, kindest friend.' Her throat constricted.

'I know, Vivienne,' he whispered, very tired now. 'I know. I am so proud of you. Now you go and I'll have a little chat with David. Okay? Is that okay?'

She kissed Eustace on his cheek, suddenly more lined now, tucking him up with the sheets, straightening his pillows. She brushed away a hair from his forehead. He smiled at her through half-closed eyes.

Then Vivienne turned and ran out of the ward. She glanced back through the door. David had taken her chair, holding his father's hand. Eustace grew limper and stiller as each moment passed.

In the corridor, Vivienne stuffed her clenched fist into her mouth, letting tears flow over her knuckles, onto her blouse. What the hell would she do without Eustace? It wasn't fair. He was such a good, fine man. First Guy, then Eustace. She was losing two men in her life. Vivienne was over forty. Eustace – Guy – they were needed – sorely needed. She wanted to rush back to Eustace and hold him to her – warm him back to health.

David strode straight out of the ward and put his arms around her. 'I don't believe it Vivienne. He's gone.' He collapsed and sobbed into her hair in agonised cries, so breathless she thought David might faint. Crying like a little boy he repeated, 'My father. My poor father.'

'He never did get to the South of France,' Vivienne cried, holding David. They clung to each other, leaning on the walls of the hospital corridor. 'It's so unfair. He was a gentleman. My loving friend. Oh, David. I am so, so sorry.'

They rang an utterly devastated Pearl. Vivienne got Joseph to ring all the numbers she gave him: her parents, all Eustace's friends and relations.

The funeral of Eustace Carré was a parish affair. Eustace, his father and grandfather before him were well known. Eustace had always been referred to as 'the clever one', involving himself in parish matters: a douzenier – elected to ensure good husbandry of the parish. Eustace had told Vivienne his father held the meetings in Guernesiais, in Guernsey French patios, until quite recently. Then there was all Eustace's work for charity and the church.

Vivienne saw to the Order of Service, the Hymn sheets and all the arrangements for Eustace. This funeral was to go without a hitch, everything was to be perfect. David and Pearl chose the hymns: *Abide with me* and *Rock of Ages*.

Pearl grieved with an upright stoicism, taking to her bed for three days and nights. Each day, without a word to disturb Pearl, Vivienne took her mother-in-law cups of tea and bowls of tomato soup. Silently, she put the trays on Pearl's bedside table, leaving the calico curtains drawn closed, the window unopened and took away yesterday's used dishes.

When Pearl could speak again, Vivienne quietly consulted with her which readings she wanted from the Bible. Pearl whispered she wanted David to read from St John, Chapter 1: Verse 14. *Verbum caro factum est.* 'The word is made flesh and dwelt amongst us, and we beheld his glory, the glory as of the only begotten of the Father, full of grace and truth.' Pearl wanted David to make the address.

The parish priest came to see them. Vivienne sat with Pearl, listening to his words of comfort. With stricken face, Pearl said she just wished this part could be all over with.

David went through Eustace's papers, paying immediate expenses. He sorted anything urgent from that which could keep. The growing business couldn't stop – even for this.

Vivienne saw how many people had been affected. David said he was constantly amazed how many came up to him, telling him of kindnesses Eustace had done.

'He was of the old school,' they all said. 'A proper gentleman.'

In the church, Vivienne felt for David as he, somehow, got through his reading and the address with an ashen face. Joseph read his poem:

'We planted seeds together and watched them as they grew.
Alone, I'll have to reap, Grandad. But always just for you.'

Vivienne smiled in tearful admiration for Joseph. He had managed it. He had been quite certain he would break down. As Joseph returned to her the seat next to her, Vivienne hugged his arm, 'Well done sweetheart.' Joseph smiled shakily, brushing his fair fringe to the side. David muttered, 'Thanks, son,' with a hushed, choked voice.

At Eustace's graveside, David tearfully sprinkled the rich earth of his beloved parish onto Eustace's coffin. Joseph supported his grandmother. Pearl wore her black costume. Her hat with black veil covered her entire face. Toward the end of the burial she had to be supported. To Vivienne, Pearl seemed smaller as she leant on Joseph's young arm. She wondered how Pearl had been able to bear the whole of the service, and then all this. But she had coped beyond tears.

Vivienne knew how heartbreak did this: stopped tears in your eyes, left you beyond emotion. Poor David. He looked devastated. Vivienne, too, would be glad when it was all over.

In unsaid deference, Vivienne avoided close contact with Pearl. She stood slightly apart from her. People would see that Pearl was the senior Mrs Carré. Eustace would have wanted that: his family, united in public, with David now at the head of the Carré clan.

As the priest completed the service, Vivienne looked out and over the open grave to the headland. She could see the sea from this grassy hill. It was just a slightly deeper blue than the sky. Gulls glided above, calling out over the gathered funeral crowd, with long, mournful sighs.

The funeral over, everyone headed to La Colette for the wake. Vivienne, Sonia, and Sonia's mother had made freshly cut ham sandwiches, sponge cakes and tea. As soon as she could, Vivienne left.

She returned to the church graveyard. Vivienne laid some white roses, picked from Eustace's garden that morning, on the newly replaced grass turf. On a handmade card Vivienne had written, 'Thanks for everything, Eustace. My dear friend, thank you for everything.'

Vivienne cancelled the New York exhibition. David protested, saying that Eustace would have wanted her to go ahead. But Vivienne didn't budge.

'No. No, there's too much to do here. It can wait.' She flicked a conciliatory look at David, and noted the nod back, expressing his thanks.

Sonia got married to Henry Brehaut, a fine young man, a sturdy grower from the Vale parish, from Vivienne's parish. They enjoyed a modest wedding, but none the less sincere for that. Sonia's mother told Vivienne they had saved up for this very day since Sonia was a child. Eustace – and Pearl, of course – had always been generous to them.

'Not many people give their cleaners bonuses at Christmas and paid them when they were off sick, or on holiday, now did they?'

So, the Vale church, an ancient landmark in the north of the island, was duly decorated with their own flowers, their own produce.

Indeed, Sonia's white wedding to Henry had all the traditional trimmings. The reception was a warm and lively party. The best party that Vivienne or everyone else could remember for years.

Soon, David became engrossed in his father's business. He had decided to handle both properties: his own and his father's, making one large estate. Pearl told them she was worried that the house, La Colette, was much too big for her, just for herself.

'Has been for some time, really, too big. You know?' said Pearl.

So La Colette was offered to them, to 'David and his family,' as Pearl put it. Eustace would have wanted that. He had told her, she said, more than once. Vivienne wondered what Pearl's own thoughts were? But she could understand: that Pearl always honoured her late husband's wishes, down to the last word.

'Eustace would have wanted it,' Pearl said implacably.

David agreed with enthusiasm. 'Best thing, of course it is.'

Vivienne pondered, what would it be like? Living under the same roof as Pearl? You could say it would be a bit like moving back with mother. Still, she loved La Colette. They would be company for Pearl. Also, it won't be too much of a move for Joseph, the main house being literally on the same property. So, Vivienne agreed.

For a mere peppercorn rent, they let their own bungalow to Sonia and Henry Brehaut. Sonia said she was delighted. Now she was to live in the house she had so carefully cleaned. And Henry, a true Guernseyman, knew a 'bloney good deal' when he saw one.

The move was time-consuming and exhausting, Vivienne told Polly. Eustace and Pearl had gathered massive amounts of stuff over their long marriage. There were inherited items from both sides of their families: mahogany tables, dressers and sideboards; china and lace, silver and brass; clocks and ornaments.

After taking stock of their own home, David and Vivienne decided to sell some things. They consulted with Sonia as to what she would like left behind. Sonia plumped for some of the larger pieces: a sideboard, the new scrubbed pine kitchen table and the sofa with the paisley throw.

At La Colette, Joseph immediately bagged the top bedrooms in the attic. These would be his bedroom and study. He had plans in hand to go to university and become an architect. His grandfather Edward Normandie said he was delighted. Vivienne just smiled wryly as her father took full credit for Joseph's idea

'Very sensible decision and an answer to my prayers. I saw his talent from birth, Nin.' Edward said to Vivienne, 'He's a bright boy. A designer. Didn't I always say so? My grandson will have a good future.'

Vivienne had never thought about the day, that one day she would live and be mistress of La Colette. Edward said the same and that he and Jean thought the house was quite grand. Grander still than Granville. Let's hope, Edward said, Vivienne could finally put "all her wilful nonsense" in the past at last?

Jean still questioned Vivienne about 'that night in the sea'. Jean said her friends still talked about that sometimes. She would ask curiously, why had Vivienne done such a thing? Then she would forget what she had said, why she had said it and change the subject.

The worse job, David said, was cleaning out all the sheds and outhouses. Eustace had a huge collection of growing, farming and gardening equipment. David couldn't possibly keep it all, maintain the stuff and store it. But he wouldn't sell anything just yet. Anyway, there was so much else to do.

David took over Eustace's study. Initially he said he found this very difficult. He told Vivienne that he felt Eustace's presence all around him. Vivienne sensed this aura as well, but welcomed it, finding Eustace's spirit comforting.

Together, Vivienne and David went through Eustace's papers.

Eustace had taught Vivienne well and she catalogued invoices into files, carefully going through legal papers and journals. Eustace had built up a fine library of maps of Guernsey and all the Channel Islands. And, David discovered, saying it was a totally unexpected bonus: a very good cellar. Malt whiskies included.

Vivienne tentatively suggested that the money they had been saving for their own place might now be – well, at least some of it – be used? For travel, say ? Or a new car?

David blanched, saying, 'God no! This place will take an awful lot to maintain, Vivienne. I'm going to have the roof looked at. I have two vineries to update now. Some of our tools and machinery needed replacing anyway. Matter of fact, I've been really concerned about it. No. We'll have to plough a lot of capital back into the business. And of course, there's Joseph's education – he wants to go to university and...'

But Vivienne had already switched off.

Shocking, even more shocking, perhaps than Eustace's death, was Pearl Carré's. She simply died in her sleep, just six months after Eustace's funeral. So David buried both his parents within months of each other. As the family stood once again in the same church graveyard, over the grave of Eustace and Pearl, Vivienne threw flowers for them: deep pink gardenias, white carnations and blood-red chrysanthemums.

So they lay together, dear Eustace and Pearl, thought Vivienne, on this quiet hill, overlooking Guernsey's turquoise sea, streamed through with purple swirls. Vivienne thought about Pearl's steadfastness to Eustace's wishes and she made a vow. Now, she must try, really try to be what Eustace had always wanted her to be: Mrs Carré Senior, of La Colette.

For a start, Vivienne invited Jean to La Colette for afternoon tea. Arm in arm, she took her mother around the gardens, lit that day with a butter yellow sun. Vivienne thought Jean seemed frailer. A pair of grey doves cooed at them from the roof of the house.

'Ah, it's so peaceful here, Ninny. So elegant.' Jean stopped and admired a rose, taking a cream, pink-edged petal between her fingers, leaning down to smell the scent. 'That's a Peace rose, isn't it? Oh, and Ninny, did I tell you? Do you know that Guy Beaufort has married again?'

CHAPTER NINETEEN

Vivienne stiffened, 'What? No, I didn't know that. Who told you that? Who…who has Guy married?' They stopped walking. Vivienne felt the sun baking down on her head. Slowly, they began to move indoors.

'Oh, some Catherine or other,' Jean absent-mindedly leafed through some Carré family lace Sonia had laid out on the dining room table for Vivienne to sort and decide what to do with it.

'Very nice stuff. Fetch a good price, I'd imagine,' said Jean. "Oh…sorry, yes: Catherine. Her family's been in Cyprus for yonks, apparently. They're English though. That'll be nice for – Nicola, was it?'

'Natalie,' said Vivienne numbly, watching her mother turning over the handmade lace. 'Guy's daughter is called Natalie'.

'Well, anyway. A stepmother for her. Guy always needed someone to, well, run around after him, didn't he? What colour would you call this, Nin? Ivory? Ecru? Parchment? Anyway, now. Is Oscar here? Where's Oscar, where is my darling boy? I'd so like to see him before I go!'

Vivienne drove Jean home. Jean chatted on about how nice La Colette was, how well Oscar looked… But Vivienne hardly took in what her mother was saying. Guy had married again?

Yes, okay, it was some years now since Amanda had died. What the hell did Vivienne think Guy had done? Become celibate? No, but at least he could have let her know. Surely he could have told her, not left her to hear from just anyone: as passing gossip?

Arriving back, Vivienne walked around La Colette gardens. She must distract herself: there was always work to do. Wielding Pearl's secateurs, Vivienne clipped the hedges, yielding the scissor edges like a guillotine. Keep to Pearl's routine, she urged herself on. Concentrate. Don't let it get to you. Where would that lead to? There was so much to do here. Damn the man. Damn Guy. Yes, keep the routine going. She and Sonia needed to keep La Colette just as Eustace had liked it.

Sonia knew La Colette well. Her mother retired once Pearl had died, saying she worked for Mrs Carré, senior, and, no offence, but she didn't want to work for anyone else, if that was alright?

Then there were all the men and women working on the land and in the greenhouses of the vinery. As they moved into their forties, Vivienne took stock. Neither she nor David had seriously entertained the idea that one day Eustace wouldn't be around, or Pearl. David's family had a history of long living – late eighties, nineties, even one or two one hundred years-old. David said he had just assumed that his father would be the same.

Joseph grew tall: taller than David, with the same easy lope and fair hair. Sometimes Vivienne wondered if she loved Joseph too much – adored – him? Yes, you could accuse her of that. Joseph was the one thing in her marriage that Eustace and Pearl, Edward and Jean all agreed on: he was a fine young man.

Sunny natured and a natural student, Joseph spread himself out in his attic rooms. Every day Elton John, David Bowie and Phil Collins belted out, very loudly, from the top windows of La Colette.

Vivienne didn't mind at all, humming the latest pop songs as she went about the house. They didn't hold the parties that they used to when they first married. Now, Vivienne planned occasional dinner parties, quite formal ones really, using the fine china and silver of La Colette. She wrote place-cards and arranged flowers, blue and white to match the Italian Spode.

She wondered what life would be like in Cyprus? Did Guy hold dinner parties with this Catherine of his? What was their life like together? Did Catherine like sex? Vivienne bet she did. Bet she and Guy…Oh, God – this Catherine someone, making love with her Guy?

Then Vivienne wanted Guy again: lying next to her. She wanted to be with him. Her new bedroom was far bigger than her last – big enough for an en-suite bathroom – Vivienne moved around it, taking in the double bed with all-white quilt and sheets. She liked plenty of space, she told David, half the time waking up spreadeagled right over the edge of the bed.

The wanting of Guy never left Vivienne. Even now, she felt somehow incomplete. Even now, when she drew the heavy pastel curtains, and poured some vodka, thoughts of him and her poor little scrap of a lost child dwelt on her mind. 'Guy,' she found herself thinking, 'how different your life is from mine. How far apart we are. What strangers we have become.'

From Joseph's rooms she heard Phil Collins' words playing, over the still, night air.

> 'Take a look at me now,
> oh there's just an empty space.
> And there's nothing left here to remind me,
> Just the memory of your face...'

Matthias' advice about Vivienne enrolling with the Open University proved to be sound. She listed the subjects she'd studied over the years: Egyptian icons, Byzantine art, the Italian High Renaissance, French Impressionism, Dutch interior art. It still captivated and interested Vivienne. How she wished she could have shared it all with Guy. Think how he could have helped her with the essays. Little by little, essay after essay, Vivienne worked hard toward gaining her degree.

She still painted, just selling locally for now. Sometimes she held a small show, selling to tourists. The paintings fetched good prices. People began pressing her to do more.

Vivienne's studio at La Colette was a high-ceilinged attic room on the other side of the house – well away from Joseph's loud music. Her room had Velux windows in the ceiling and two long windows, almost the length of the tall walls. She had a view over their fields and meadows and the long winding drive of La Colette, with granite pillars half-hidden by trees in the distance.

Did Guy still paint? Vivienne thought about the picture postcards of cats sitting on plant pots: of red geraniums in window boxes. Well, she didn't know. He hadn't communicated with her for ages. Was Catherine an artist? What had attracted Guy to Catherine? This her heartburn over Amanda, starting all over again. Was Catherine another of his timid rabbits or a strong young woman? How old was she? Who was this god dammed Catherine of Guy's?

'Vivienne, can you come down?' David shouted up the stairs, 'Vivienne?' with an increasing volume. 'Joseph wants us all to look at his UCCA form. Do come and help. Which University is best for architecture? Any ideas? Come on.'

Vivienne roused herself, putting down her brush, concealing a glass with its vodka dregs behind a jar of pencils. She descended the stairs and went into the stone-flagged kitchen. David and Joseph sat on a long bench, with papers strewn all over the sturdy oak table. Coming from the cooker, Vivienne could smell the oniony lamb stew she had put on to simmer early that morning.

'Come on Vivienne,' said David, sounding exasperated.

'Alright, I'm here now, aren't I?' said Vivienne.

Joseph looked up at her. Vivienne recognised disappointment in his blue eyes. 'Too much booze,' the look said. 'Too much booze, ma.'

She sat down opposite them. To Joseph, David made one of his 'What are we going to do with her?' looks he used to do to his mother. They made lists of pros and cons: the suitability of the course; the time it would take to travel to and from Guernsey; the availability and cost of residential accommodation. Eventually they all decided on a university in Wales.

As fully expected, Joseph did well with his A-levels: gaining an A and two Bs. He got accepted at his first-choice university – the Welsh one. Vivienne was just astounded, she told Polly, at how quickly Joseph has become a fully-grown student and, not only that, was travelling and living away from Guernsey three times a year.

Vivienne could scarcely comprehend where the time had fled.

Their little Joseph, off to university! All their friends said the same: where had all the time gone?

Some five years on, after all that commuting to and from Guernsey, Wales and London, Joseph qualified. They celebrated. Vivienne didn't object at all when Joseph said he would like a holiday.

'Course you would, darling. You've earned it!'

Joseph had been offered a position with a firm of architects, hoping, he said, for a partnership one day. But, anyway, for the time being he wanted a break. Say a month or so?

'Of course,' agreed Vivienne and David. 'Anywhere you want!'

'Cyprus,' said Joseph, smiling.

'Cyprus?' Oh no, anywhere but bloody Cyprus! Vivienne groaned inwardly.

'Yup! I want to study the ancient ruins there, Ma. See how it was done, perfectly, once before.'

Nothing Vivienne said would change Joseph's mind. She implored him to visit Crete, for its ancient Minoan remains, or Rome or Athens – surely he wanted to see the Parthenon? But Joseph said, no, he had made up his mind. So, he packed his gear, booked his flights and was off.

David returned from the airport. 'He's a fine young lad, isn't he? We were lucky, there, Vivienne.'

'Yes. He is. We are,' Vivienne said mournfully, missing Joseph already. 'I wish Eustace could have seen this. And Pearl, come to that. Anyway, mum and dad are still around to see him turn out like he has, that's something.'

Joseph rang them every Sunday night. He loved Cyprus. He was swimming every day, sketching plans at the historical sites, visiting the Paphos mosaics. 'Great! It is great, Ma.' He sent them all sorts of amusing cards and letters, enclosing dried herbs. Cyprus was full of history.

'Ma,' Joseph said one Sunday, 'you should come out here. Come on! Dad, too, he'd love it.'

'No. I don't think so,' Vivienne said, hastily, 'I'm...I'm allergic to mosquitoes.'

'Rubbish!' Joseph laughed down the phone, 'You can get loads of stuff now, for mosquitoes! Don't be such a wimp!'

'Well. We'll see,' was all Vivienne felt she could say.

'Nearer fifty than forty, now.' Vivienne grimaced, joking with her friends. The Open University courses engrossed her, taking up a lot of her time. 'Memory isn't what it was,' she kidded. They all agreed. They felt the same.

Vivienne looked at herself in her bedroom mirror. Her figure had rounded. She had to let out some clothes. Her hair, still a pretty tangle left to itself, was grey but streaked blonde, coloured by professional hairdressers. She'd developed a taste for good make-up: Dior, Yves St Laurent, Chanel. It was all Jocelyn's fault; Vivienne teased her and said she was lucky that the stuff she liked was slightly cheaper in Guernsey.

Once she met up for coffee with Jessie. 'You're looking very feisty, Vivienne,' Jessie said. 'Love that dress.'

'And you!' Vivienne exclaimed automatically. But Jessie looked very changed. The sassy girl with the brown silk scarf of hair flowing down one shoulder was thin, now. Her hair had somehow lost its luxuriance, her skin its healthy tan.

Jessie worked in a hotel now. 'I'm manager,' she claimed, staunchly. But Vivienne knew Jessie was working at the hotel bars, doing some waitressing, with just a few administration duties. It didn't matter. Money. Position. It didn't matter that much. Though Vivienne thought again, that maybe it did and that Jessie could do with some. So, if she was honest then, Vivienne couldn't say money didn't matter. Not having enough plainly did.

Vivienne noticed lately that David had become – just slightly – more stooped. His fair hair had thinned and showed a sheen of white under a strong light. His eyes were still a clear blue, though lined either side. Were they getting old? Vivienne shivered.

One especially balmy summer evening, Vivienne threw open the windows of La Colette to let in the warm scents of the garden – lavender, late roses and night stock. The evening stars sprinkled a dark blue sky. She put on Mozart's trio from *Cose Fan Tutti*.

'Must be all that Open University,' David always muttered when she played classical music.

Yes, but it wasn't only the OU. This particular music reminded Vivienne of her favourite film: *Sunday Bloody Sunday* where Mozart's *Cosi* trio had played throughout the film. Peter Finch was handsome, yes, but the scenes of Murray Head – a young man showering naked, lathering soap as the music played, thoughts of Guy...

The telephone rang. Vivienne reached out her arm to the side table and took the call.

'Hullo?'

'Ma! It's me! I've got some news!' Joseph sounded excited.

'What? What is it, darling?' Vivienne sat up.

'Ma! You'll never guess what! I've found her! The girl of my dreams. I've fallen in love!' Joseph laughed in hearty gusts down the telephone. 'She's absolutely lovely. You'll love her!'

'No! Wow! Darling, that's wonderful. Are you... are you sure?' Vivienne gasped, trying to take in Joseph's words, spilled out with such eagerness.

'Absolutely! Absolutely sure!'

'Well, who is she? When did all this happen? It's marvellous for you, darling!' Vivienne straightened up on the chintz couch, and began playing with the pearls at her neck. 'Tell me! Tell me,' she bounced up and down.

'Well, I was exploring Apollo's sanctuary – in the heat of the day...'

'As you do!' Vivienne laughed.

'As you do! Taking photographs, you know, making pencil sketches. Then I stopped to drink some water. I always carry water now...'

'Yes, yes, get on with it!'

Joseph had heard a voice, as if it was coming toward him. A light, melodic voice that he found entrancing. Through the ruins came a slight, very dark haired girl with wide brown eyes. She was a teacher, surrounded by six or seven students. She was telling them all about the underground cisterns and the history of Apollo's sanctuary.

'Then, Ma, then we had a…a *coup de foudre*, just like that! A lightning strike, just like in your painting of *Bacchus and Ariadne* you know, in the sitting room? Both of us. Right at that exact, same second! We had fallen in love. It was love at first sight!'

He stopped, breathless. Vivienne could hear him swallowing in rapid gulps. Then Joseph continued. 'It is just magic. I've hoped and prayed to find someone like her. Someone like Natalie, Ma. Natalie. Natalie Beaufort is her name.'

Vivienne gripped the telephone so hard she thought it might break clear in two. 'Who did you say?' Please, not Natalie Beaufort, please! It was a punishment. God was punishing her. Be sure your sins will find you out.

'Ma, you alright?' Joseph sounded anxious at her silence. 'You've gone a bit quiet! Didn't expect that! Be pleased for me? Aren't you? You believe in love at first sight, don't you? The thunderbolt?'

'Yes, yes. Of course I do.' Stumbling, Vivienne took a deep breath, reaching her very diaphragm. Lord, this was going to take some act. 'Thunderbolts,' she said. 'Yes, I believe in thunderbolts, and lighting darling.' She just wished it wasn't this wretched one. 'This…this Natalie…I think, well I think we know her, don't we? Do we know her?' So nervous, Vivienne pulled at her pearls so the rope snapped and some beads bounced onto the floor and under the coffee table. Vivienne grabbed at one as it rolled onto her lap.

'Yes. Fact, Natalie said she remembered you. You knew Guy, her dad, or something? When you were young? And that,' he gushed on rapturously, 'is one of the other reasons we got talking – sharing Guernsey as a place we knew. Remembering each other from childhood. Oh, Ma, isn't it a fantastic coincidence? Isn't it wonderful?'

Before they could gather their senses, before they could fully comprehend what Joseph had told them, Vivienne found herself planning a wedding. She felt a dazed incredulity, the exact same feeling as when Joseph had been placed in her arms for the first time. She begins to organize a wedding for their only son in what you could only call a trance: a catatonic state of pure disbelief.

As the days passed, Joseph phoned with an increasing urgency.

'We want to get married straightaway, you see, Ma. We are potty about each other. And we want to do it right, though. Do the whole white wedding thing. Sorry it's such short notice. What d'you think? Mmm? Soon as poss? Oh, I knew you'd both be pleased! I knew you'd approve!' Joseph sighed. Vivienne had to admit, he was deeply, deeply happy.

And Joseph told her he had never been so content. He had found the girl of his dreams and at the same time made both his parents happy and proud of him. Could anything be better? Joseph had asked Vivienne. What could possibly be better than that?

PART THREE

CHAPTER TWENTY

'If it is any consolation,' Guy said, 'I'm as shell-shocked as you are. Catherine's pleased, but of course she doesn't know the half of it.'

No, Vivienne wanted to scream at him, it was of no consolation to her, none whatsoever, nor of what bloody Catherine thought! Did Guy really have to bring Catherine in to it at this stage? Catherine! Catherine's pleased! If only they weren't talking on the telephone, Vivienne would have liked to punch Guy: hard on the nose.

Faced with the *coup de foudre* and Joseph's obvious determination to marry Natalie, Vivienne decided she had no choice but to agree to the union. But it was with a heavy heart that she began ringing the marquee people; the florist's and the caterers.

Of course, Guy was conveniently in Cyprus. Vivienne seethed through her teeth. He even got out of the arrangements for his own daughter's wedding. Catherine did offer to come over to Guernsey – 'to help?' Vivienne refused, as politely as she could.

'So kind, but I can perfectly well cope.' She felt her heels digging in, 'I can manage. I'm good at administration.' Vivienne laughed a strained, tinkly laugh, wondering if this Catherine recognised maddened intransigency when she heard it.

Yet, the odd thing was, Vivienne thought, Catherine sounded like Amanda, mark two. Quiet and self-effacing, she didn't push herself onto Vivienne. Catherine kept her distance. She was quite nice, in fact. Catherine was nice – you know, like the women Guy always married.

Vivienne strode around the house, simmering in vexation, snapping dead heads off flower arrangements. She emptied the kitchen waste bin, tying up the black plastic sack so fiercely it tore. A blackened banana skin and torn cardboard packet stinking of stale tomato sauce fell out limply onto the floor. 'Sod it.' She placed the ripped bag inside another one and dumped it in the bin outside. 'Sod him.'

Guy had barely contacted her all these years. Vivienne had missed him sorely. Now here he was, ringing up every five minutes to see how things were going, as though nothing, nothing had happened.

The bloody man has said he was looking forward to seeing her. He had thought about her often – often! What, so often he upped and married Catherine?

David went about looking furious and confounded. Vivienne thought of the impossibility of it all. She could hardly tell Joseph the truth about her and Guy. If they opposed his marriage, purely because of her past relationship with Guy it would be – even on the simplest level – unkind. Anyway, these two were going ahead, whatever happened. So what would be gained by hurting Joseph?

In fact, when they met the grown-up Natalie, Vivienne and David liked her very much. Vivienne was taken aback at how like Guy Natalie was. Slim, dark-eyed, shoulder-length glossy black hair. She had the same mannerisms: a half smile, and she even smoked Rothmans.

Joseph was, quite clearly, besotted with her – cuddling her, stroking her hands, never leaving her alone. Yes, it was true: Joseph and Natalie did go well together. Perhaps – Vivienne attempted to drum up some conviction – things would be all right?

There were some attractive flats being built in St Peter Port, with fine views over the harbour – the most beautiful in Europe, it had been called. The view included the ancient Castle, Castle Cornet, and even France, on clear days.

The flats were fitted out with all modern equipment. Joseph would be near his architect's firm in St Peter Port. Natalie had been offered a teaching position and had accepted. She would teach history and art. She soon met up with her old school-friends, asking two to be her bridesmaids.

The Beauforts had long gone: sold up and retired to New Zealand. They wouldn't be coming to the wedding. They sent their best wishes and a handsome wedding present.

Edward, Vivienne's father, treated Joseph's engagement with huge caution. 'Is this some kind of joke, Nin?' He rasped coldly when she told him. 'Whatever would Eustace and Pearl made of it, d'you think? And us – what about us, having a Beaufort for our clever Joseph?' He glowered darkly at Vivienne. 'Another Beaufort? No good will come of this. Another lamb to the slaughter?' Edward glared at Vivienne. Of course, once he saw Natalie, he completely changed his mind and said maybe it was God's will.

Natalie charmed them all. She had an alert, quick mind and easy manner. Vivienne warmed to her. She would, after all, have a daughter-in-law now. A girl that she could choose clothes with and gossip. Did Natalie paint at all? At least they could chat about art. Maybe, then, if they were all careful...and sensible – things might work out.

Joseph had hired a mini-bus for his stag night. His best man and ushers settled down for some serious drinking.

'I hope,' Joseph told them, 'to have a long and happy marriage – like my parents have had.' He did not miss the knowing looks the boys exchanged, raising their amused eyebrows.

'Well, okay,' Joseph downed a pint in one go. 'Not always a happy marriage exactly. Whose marriage is?' He gulped more warm ale. 'In fact, sometimes I think I've been living, walking Elastoplast, sticking plaster on my parents' marriage! Keeping them together. Keeping us all together.'

The boys slapped him on the back in camaraderie, ordering more drinks. Then they moved on to the next pub. Andrew, best man, was the first to move. 'Can you get us to L'Ancresse Bay, now, please driver?' he asked.

As soon as they hit the beach, they had all stripped off, running straight into the sea: spirited, healthy males in the midsummer surf.

Acting on request, the driver obligingly switched on full headlights and then his car radio. 'Simply Red' blared out, serenading the bare men. They hoisted nude Joseph onto their shoulders, charging deeper into the warm sea.

'I –I 'm gonna fall from the s t a r –r- s – straight into your arms,' the boys all yelled, singing loudly along with Mick Hucknell.

'And that,' Joseph slurred drunkenly, splashing out in the water, 'my lovely Natalie – I am longing for you Natalie – is our song!'

Vivienne had agreed with Guy that they would meet, alone, a day or so before the wedding. She would meet Catherine later. David was more than happy to go along with the idea. He told Vivienne he wanted to put off seeing Guy as long as he possibly could. So far David said he hoped he had behaved like a civilized human being. But once he saw Guy…well Vivienne wasn't to think he could contain his utter dislike of the man.

When they met, Guy openly appraised Vivienne with that searching look she remembered well. She knew her waist had thickened, that expert make up didn't quite hide the fine lines, fanning the sides of her eyes. But at least the lines flicked upwards. The grey in her hair and the frizz were under control, (only yesterday streaked platinum). Vivienne had carefully selected – taken ages to decide on – a deep pink suit with shoulder pads and a cream satin blouse, its broad lapels spread over the collar of her suit jacket; gold drop earrings; gold chain. She could taste the Baby Pink lipstick on her lips. If she could only stop shaking it might help her get through this meeting.

Guy bowed deeply, making her laugh self-consciously.

'Well then, little Vivvy with the sizzling blue eyes. Very fetching. Very attractive. And still wearing Dior perfume?'

With a clear vista of the dazzling harbour, they sat on the balcony of the restaurant. They ordered chilled white Chablis and lobster thermidor.

As he sat in front of her, the view of the sea interlaced by a leafy tree fluttering behind him, Guy was, Vivienne scarcely credited, very nearly the same man.

Yes, there was a flecking of grey in the black hair, worn longer now with groomed slicks curled behind his ears – a style Vivienne wasn't sure she liked. But his jawbone was still keen and his eyes still beguiled her with a seductive shine on the dark brown, drawing her immediately into his pool. It took just one beat of time and she wanted to swim to those eyes again, willingly, with no lifeline. There was no golden thread to rescue her – as Ariadne had given to Theseus. No, instead Guy's eyes threw out a spellbinding noose to her, and she reached out and clung to it.

Instantly, Vivienne knew that she and Guy were far from over.

Guy, in casual black suit and open-necked pink shirt, began telling Vivienne about his life in Cyprus. Catherine and he had sold a house in Nicosia, 'Far too noisy,' and had moved into a small village in the hills, an hour or so from Limassol. He and Catherine joined in the village community life. There were several British ex-pats living in the district. They often had gin and tonics with them. Catherine had lived in Cyprus with her parents from some years. Her father had been in the Army, stationed in Cyprus and stayed on when he retired. It was a good life, Guy told Vivienne. They enjoyed it.

And his work? Well, the pottery business and his painting – that hadn't lasted long. Although, yes, he still painted for his own pleasure. He did a bit of teaching – English – in the village school. Catherine's first husband had died: she was a widow and she had inherited a good deal of money and also, later, from her parents' property. So, they got by – did Vivienne see? – they lived well enough.

Guy cut into his lobster with his knife. 'This is as good a Thermidor as I have ever tasted. They've got the sauce just right.' He ate, then raised his head to look at her. Vivienne noted he was thicker on the neck and shoulders – but no less handsome for that. She dug her pointed shoe into her own ankle. Stop it! Stop it! Not again. Not after all that's happened. But kicking herself – trying to warn herself against dangerous, sublime Guy, using her intelligence and backing off – didn't work. It never had.

After sugar-crusted crème brulées and perfect filter coffee – not too bitter – Vivienne said as casually as rising desire would allow, 'David's away for the day. He's gone to Jersey to look at a market garden. He… won't be back until seven. Would you…would you like to see, ah, La Colette?' She gestured for the bill, ignoring his protests. 'My treat.' She threw Guy her wickedest smile. There, now she had done it.

Guy had twisted around looking at the view behind him, admiring

it, but now turned back to look at her. He shook his head from side to
side, indicating, 'No, Vivienne. Naughty, naughty!' but the voluptuous
look in his eyes, the full black of his pupils, the amused smile on his
lips said, 'Yes. Yes please.'

At La Colette, Vivienne poured them drinks. She knew Sonia
was out of the house, helping, down at the wedding marquee. They
had put it up in one of David's finest fields, bordering the southern
cliffs.

She showed Guy around the house. He spoke quietly, in
appreciation of the well-proportioned rooms: the pastel colours she
had chosen, the polished antiques and the lovely location.

As she poured liberal second drinks, she waited. She knew
what Guy was going to say. Her mouth, dry as rice-paper, stilled in
anticipation. Her hand spilled her drink on the Axminster carpet.

'Well then. When can I see your bedroom, Vivvy? Still sleep
alone?' Guy showed no culpability.

'Yes. We sleep separately. David snores…you know?'

'I know.' His eyes softened.

Ah well, always enjoyed the thrill of the chase, yes? They
mounted the stairs. 'Do you remember us, Guy? Our stolen times?'
said Vivienne.

'All of them. I remember the good times, Vivvy.' Guy stroked
her arm.

As she gave that flicker of reaction, Guy's eyes glanced at her
quivering with a lizard's alertness. Yes, she thought, why the hell
not? They would have a little afternoon delight, she and Guy.

Was she still attractive to him? Was she over the hill? Past it – past
desire? Could she be more exciting than Catherine?

They entered her bedroom, swiftly closing the door behind them.
'You, little Vivvy Normandie, are still such a sexy, sexy little bird!'
He caressed her hip curve with his index finger, sliding it down to
her knee.

'And you, Guy! But why didn't you… why…?'

He stilled her words with his hand. 'Not now. Not the time.'

Crossing to the window, he pulled the curtains close together. Only a thin beam of sunlight chinked through the Sanderson chintz. Then he lay down on the bed, pulling her toward him and kissed her gently as a child on her neck. 'Been wanting to do this all lunchtime.'

Vivienne shivered. This was ridiculous! How easily she surrendered, giving herself up to him. Dear God, how she wanted him. 'I've wanted you...I've missed you.'

'Not now. No worries now, Vivvy.'

True. This was hardly the time to remind him he has been gone from her side for years. He was here now, Vivienne.

Silently they lay together on Vivienne's white, embroidered bedspread. Guy unbuttoned her pink jacket and cream satin blouse. She felt the silky material slink off her and, with her eyes shut, slipped him easily out of his suit and shirt.

She was damned glad she sunbathed to an even tan: was pleased her flesh was still firm as Guy slipped off her bra.

'You don't sunbathe topless? Good, I like that. You're lovely.' He kissed her breasts and let his fingers brush against her fine hair, rounded stomach and back. 'I want you, too.'

Vivienne felt her body lifting up in arousal. Guy's light fingers tingle-touched in rippling sensations all over her skin. She sought his lips and brought them down over her, feeling his soft, moist mouth exploring every part of her. She followed his body exactly, to and fro, like they were practised dancers, knowing each other's every move.

Slowly, he entered her in sensuous rhythm together. 'We're sea beasts – my sea lion.' Vivienne said, crushing him near her. It's Guy! She smelled the familiar shoulder, the Armani in the crease of his armpit. He weighed heavily down on her. The heavy weight of his body on hers, his very maleness, excited her. 'I'm your lioness, Guy. Yours!'

They came together. Vivienne called out with the delight released in her body, until a drowsiness overcame her as the unaccustomed orgasm faded.

When she opened her eyes, she found Guy's own, looking at her with his dark brown gaze. Unhurriedly, he moved so that he held her head in his arms.

As they lay back, exhausted, Vivienne brushed the hairs on the back of his hand with her mouth. Now Guy closed his eyes. She untangled herself from him and raised up on one elbow the more to look at him. Dark eyelashes, slightly curled. Pinpricks of black hair were beginning to show on his jaw. This close, his hair had more silver in it than she had first thought. But that made the black hair that there was look even darker. She stroked his chest, feeling the wet of him between her legs.

Soon it was time to bathe together in her bathroom, with its tiled frieze of full-blown pink roses. Vivienne lathered Guy softly, lovingly, just as she had in London, when they were younger and full of the juice of youth.

They towelled each other dry with her fragrant bath towels. Guy gently kissed her ears, her hair and chin as she dressed.

'You and me. Like we used to be?'

'You'll always be a young boy, you know. I always think of you – of us – as young. Daft, isn't it?'said Vivienne.

'No, it's not,' smiled Guy.

Yet Vivienne felt a painful tremor, a distant lightening shot through her heart – this would have to stop, right here and now. What if Joseph knew? What if he found out – or Natalie! They would be heart-broken. It wasn't fair. This was Joseph's time, not hers. She must restrain herself – and Guy. It was all up to her. 'You know we mustn't…you know…we shouldn't do this, don't you Guy?'

Guy blinked at her, expressionless. 'Oh come on Vivvy. Not now. Tell you what, make us some coffee? Don't look so worried! No harm done.' He strapped on his watch, finished dressing himself and laced up his shoes. 'You can think about it, once more at least? Before I go back to Cyprus?' He shot her a quizzical glance.

Fearful now, combing her hair Vivienne managed faintly, 'What about Catherine? I feel awful about Catherine. You should, too, Guy.' And she did feel anxious – that she cannot resist him – wouldn't be able to say no if he asked – if Guy pushed it.

'I never feel bad about having sex with a woman, Vivvy. I don't feel guilt toward Catherine. Come on! Sex…it's natural. It's…the human condition. Anyway, Catherine can take care of herself, believe me. Don't you worry about our Catherine!'

Guy never asked about David, Vivienne noticed. And she herself hadn't thought about any guilt toward David. So, fine one to talk, then, wasn't she, about fidelity? Still.

Over coffee Guy lit a cigarette. The lingering smoke drifted around the sitting room. Vivienne would just have to say she had had a smoke, if queried.

'So, why all that long silence?' She asked, offering Guy a glass ashtray.

'Many things, Vivvy. I was in a sort of wilderness.' He rubbed his eyes with his knuckles. 'Just concentrated on bringing up Natalie, not wanting to even think of Guernsey. I started drinking. Had a couple of flings, nothing serious, still got my bad habits,' he gave her a boyish grin. 'No point in worrying you, or anyone.'

'I would rather have known,' she said.

'You had your own life to live, Vivvy. I could see that. Always known that.'

'I've…well, it can be lonely.' Vivienne said, then noticed Guy began to look uncomfortable at that, so she changed the subject. 'Do you still manage to travel?'

Guy told her, yes, he had been back to Paris, Venice and America. They talked of their paintings; of films and plays; of writing and books. Until Vivienne thought it was as if Guy and she had never been apart.

Lulled, Vivienne said, 'There hasn't been anyone else, for me, you know.'

Guy frowned, 'I guessed that. But it's your life, Vivvy. Maybe men have different ideas on what is infidelity? And women are so…'

'Melodramatic? I still like Dorothy Parker's writing, though,' Vivienne said. Yes, well, so treachery wasn't so hot a subject, either. But that was just what they were being, weren't they, treacherous? But Vivienne made herself let it go. She had Guy back. She had held Guy Beaufort close to her bosom, in her own bed. That was more than enough melodrama for her for one day, thanks.

Vivienne drove Guy back to his hotel. They kissed perfunctorily on the cheeks. Then, promising they would see each other soon, they parted.

Vivienne returned to La Colette in a maelstrom of conflicting feelings. Common decency was being strangulated out of existence by this inextricable attraction. This unfathomable need for Guy: was she really so dissatisfied with David? Well, maybe that was not the best comparison, especially not straight after sex with Guy, for goodness sake! But David didn't see the need any more for what he called copulation. In fact, when he put it like that, used that horrible word, she didn't want it, either. But what of the kind of unfed feeling – a lurking hunger? A splinter of ice divided her soul and it wouldn't go away.

And there was Joseph, the wedding and Natalie to think of, let alone Catherine and David. One thing, though, for certain: Guy the charmer, Guy the snake charmer was back in Vivienne's life. And worse: she felt sedated with him. Guy hypnotised her – she swayed to his tune, captivated, not knowing where to start, where to turn to be free of him. Did she want to be free of Guy? Yes, she did. Then, no, she didn't. The lovemaking she had just had was deeply, ravishingly satisfying. And, did you notice? Vivienne had not said, 'I love you.' No, not once.

CHAPTER TWENTY-ONE

Most of the arrangements had been finalised. Invitations had been sent, flowers, cars, cake and wedding stationery ordered. The marquee would include portable loos. Buck's fizz would be served to the reception queue. Vivienne had finally chosen which outfit she would wear. She had attended to it all.

She felt a little surprised at not feeling a damning shame about Guy. Although a tinge of guilt remained. But, if anything, Vivienne felt full of vigour – quite energized, even. She was fancied! She was a young girl again, feeling quite skittish! She caught sight of herself in the hall mirror and bared her teeth at her image, as if she were her own confidante: a conspirer to the intrigue. Vivienne wore her nicest lingerie and an extra spray of Dior.

It was early morning at La Colette and they were all restlessly preparing for Joseph's wedding. Joseph, bathed and calm, had eaten a soft-boiled brown egg. He ate it while reading Vivienne's *Gardens and Interiors*. Vivienne and David both fidgeted, bumping into each other as they hurried between one room then the other.

At length, Vivienne went into the scullery. She needed to check the white rose buttonholes for them and her own corsage. The florists had done well. The church flowers were perfect. They were all green and white – to Natalie's strict specification.

David walked in. 'Vivienne,' he said stiffly, as though he had rehearsed, 'I'm not finding this easy. We'll have to stand by each other today, alright? We must get through this, neutrally, for Joseph's sake.'

It must have been hard for him. She knew David must dread seeing Guy, that Guy's presence distressed him. 'I can't tell you what today means to me,' she said. 'And, I know, David. We'll have to put things on hold, sort of, won't we? Joseph's my whole life.'

'I know he is. Mine too,' said David. 'Big day.'

'Yes.'

'Well, let's finish breakfast with our boy.'

Vivienne nodded. She hoped David noticed she didn't have a G & T on the go, or any wine. He had said he had noted she was attempting to cut down. Mind you, there was all the wedding champagne to get through and, later, Eustace's fine malt whisky. God, she wished the whole thing were over and done with.

When they joined a beaming Joseph, he held out a hand to each to them. They both smiled at him. 'Here we go then,' Joseph said happily, 'D-day!'

Guy nursed a drink. It was early, even for him, but he couldn't get through this sober. He watched Catherine as she dressed carefully for the wedding. She was slender, with short blonde hair, in an unfashionable pageboy cut. Catherine had chosen a primrose coloured suit in boucle, and matching yellow straw hat. Everything about Catherine was understated: small hazel eyes, very little make-up, delicate nose and mouth – coloured peach with lipstick.

Catherine was rather a cool chick, Guy thought as he observed her – the type of bird to be relied on. He sometimes wondered what Amanda would have made of Catherine and what little Amanda would have given to be at her Natalie's wedding. Guy finished his drink and adjusted his tie in the mirror. Surely he would behave himself – just for this one day?

The guests began to arrive at Torteval parish church. Vivienne was wearing Nicole Farhi, a suit David told everyone he would still be paying for when they were grandparents. Jocelyn came with Enrico, easily outdoing all the other women in her dark green silk Jean Muir.

Edward and Jean were seated in the front pew. Edward acknowledged all and sundry formally, shaking hands with people. Jean fidgeted with some new gloves, asking how Oscar was all the while.

Polly came, wearing a red hat. Yes, she afterward told everyone she knew the joke: 'red hat, no knickers,' thanks very much. But she'd got it in a sale at Creasey's and liked red, so there! Her Eric and their three children – two boys and a girl: Greg, Glen and Kim, all in their twenties, sat stiff-backed and smartly dressed.

When she had told her weeks ago, Polly had rounded on Vivienne, her round eyes wide with disbelief. 'You're not going to let him marry Natalie Beaufort, are you Vivienne? Guy's child? Couldn't Joseph have found someone else, kiddo?' Polly had told Vivienne that it was all way beyond her, but then, sometimes Vivienne was quite beyond her, as well. In the end she had agreed with Vivienne: best go along with it all. After all, there was nothing more attractive than forbidden fruit, was there?

The old Lenfestys came. Vivienne and David knew they made the effort as much to honour their friendship with Eustace and Pearl as for anything else. 'We last met up at Eustace's and Pearl's funerals," said Mr Lenfesty, 'but it is a happy occasion today, isn't it? Joseph is a good boy.' David thanked them for coming.

The Le Croixes politely sent their regrets. They couldn't attend. Amanda's father had been ill recently. Though, since Natalie was their granddaughter, they sent a cheque with their wedding card, welcoming Joseph into their family, and had left things at that.

Vivienne couldn't blame them. Muriel Le Croix would have had to witness Catherine at Guy's side. Amanda had had such a sad end to her young life. And, maybe Muriel had suspected Vivienne's affair with Guy all along? Probably.

The church organist put her foot down as slowly Natalie, on Guy's arm, walked down the aisle to a nervously awaiting Joseph.

Natalie wore a white satin bustier, embroidered with pearls, showing off her tanned shoulders and breasts. In her black hair, pinned up to a French pleat, she wore white roses. The dress skirt had layers of white net. She carried a bouquet of green and white flowers. Her bridesmaids' ensembles exactly matched.

The service began. 'For as much,' the vicar's voice boomed, 'as God has joined together this man and this woman, Joseph and Natalie, as man and wife – let no man put asunder!'

The bride and bridegroom kissed to cheers. They all left the church amidst photographers, cheering people with confetti at the church gate and much commotion. People drifted to their cars and to the wedding reception at La Colette, overlooking the cliffs and the calm blue sea under a sunny sky.

Vivienne's guess about Catherine had been correct. She was nice. Catherine even seemed self-effacing. Amongst all the peacocks Catherine could easily be lost.

David didn't agree. 'That Catherine is banked fires, I reckon. No push-over like that poor little Amanda. And she's got her own money, I'm told. Good thing, I'd say, married to that bloody man.'

Vivienne sighed and went back into the church to retrieve her bag. She had left it on the church pew. Nearly empty now, the church seemed quite different. A child ran in and out of the wooden pews, singing breathlessly, clattering on the tiled floor with her new black patent party shoes.

A man stole up to her, grabbed and kissed her hand. Vivienne jumped, 'Hey? Guy! For God's sake!' She glanced hurriedly over to the stone, arched doorway. 'Not now!' What the hell was Guy thinking of? They were going to be discreet. Guy had agreed. People would be looking for her.

Vivienne glimpsed a red-hatted head, with a face bearing a curious expression, peep around the stone door then withdraw, soundlessly.

Guy laughed in hearty delight at Vivienne's discomfort, 'Hello, in-law! Just wanted to say, hope to see you soon.' He winked broadly.

'Guy, you are drunk,' she smelled the whisky, 'Go and find Catherine, for goodness sake!' Vivienne said, making herself forcibly pull away from him. Though she felt half-frightened, half-pleased at Guy's nearness.

Still laughing at her, his devilish dark eyes dancing, Guy backed toward the door. 'Don't forget Vivvy, no harm done!' he blew a showy, flagrant kiss.

The noisy wedding party, posing for final photographs, were about to leave the church. Vivienne glanced around and found her bag. Polly, in her red hat, walked swiftly toward her down the aisle.

'So, kiddo? This is why you are looking a bit…cat got the cream today? Guy?'

'It really isn't what it seems, Polly. It's…Oh, tell the truth I'm in a proper muddle!'

'Don't worry, kiddo. Not a word to anyone. Big day for you.' Polly linked arms with Vivienne as they left the church.

Never in her life did Vivienne feel less like attending a wedding reception. The fact that this do was her own son's did not help the situation, whatsoever. No, not one bit.

The marquee was set in the Carré's tree-lined field, bounded by banks of wild fuchsia, honeysuckle and Maythorn. It overlooked Guernsey's south coast where the land sloped toward a wooded cliff. Beyond was a curved bay: a small harbour for fishing boats.

Vivienne asked for the canvas sides of the massive tent to be raised: it was getting so hot. Collapsible wooden chair legs sank into rich, grassy earth. A local band played with perhaps more enthusiasm than talent, but valiantly – if slightly heavily – on the drums.

'I've forgotten who half these people are,' said Jocelyn. David told her they were the salt of the earth. Jocelyn waved at Joseph, raising a champagne glass to him. 'Don't you mean the fat of the land?' She said wickedly. Then Jocelyn smiled at Vivienne. 'You look wonderful today, Vivienne. Simply lovely, darling.' Enrico nodded in agreement.

Vivienne found it hard not to keep looking at Guy. Catherine, sitting near him, looked a fragile, porcelain figure in her new, primrose outfit. Now Vivienne did feel sinful.

Guy was chatting to Edward and Jean – the three of them as if they had been pals over all these years. What wretched deceivers we all are. Vivienne thought as she watched the scene, wrestling with such conflicting thoughts, her head shook involuntarily.

David got up from the table: to circulate amongst the guests. Sonia and Henry were there and Sonia's mother, Amy, with Frederick, David's foreman. All their workmen and women seem relaxed, cheerily waving over every now and then.

Jessie came to the wedding alone. Rick was long gone. Jessie was a single parent now, and looking, Vivienne thought, not slim but alarmingly thin. She was chain-smoking too, so that Vivienne wondered if the cigarettes contained just tobacco – or another substance? Yes, Jessie had lost far too much weight and looked somehow unkempt. Her chestnut hair fell like a curtain still but lay flat and lank.

Had anyone else noticed that Polly and Guy were studiously avoiding each other? Polly took no prisoners. She had told Vivienne how she felt about attending this wedding. Yes Guy was handsome, Polly said, but he didn't fool her, not Polly. Still, even for Polly, Vivienne thought her glares at Guy were particularly icy today – frowning at him at every opportunity.

Most of all, for Eustace's sake, Vivienne felt remorse at being with Guy at La Colette. What on earth would Eustace have thought of her if he had known? Vivienne felt hot under her Nicole Farhi suit. Was it too late to make some kind of amends? How could she stop wanting Guy? 'Help me, Eustace, help me,' Vivienne muttered under her breath.

A hardwood gavel rapped loudly three times. A toast was proposed: 'To the Queen. And to the Duke of Normandy!' Everyone rose and raised their glasses.

'I didn't know you and David were from a titled family, Vivvyon,' said Enrico, innocently.

Vivienne burst into laughter. 'No! Course we're not! Guernsey was once part of Normandy, France. "The Duke of Normandy" is one of any reigning English Monarch's titles. Prince Charles will be "Duke of Normandy" one day, see? Maybe you'll have to look up Channel Island history, dear Enrico!'

Jocelyn immediately filled Enrico's glass, 'You weren't to know, darling,' she said protectively, barring her extravagant teeth at the Guernsey guests' looks of amusement. 'I'll tell you all about our history sometime. It's very French.'

The reception eased as people began to leave their own tables and move around, greeting each other. Wanting to know what they were saying, Vivienne sat next to Sonia who was chatting to

Catherine. Sonia was saying she didn't know Mr Beaufort very well but remembered the first Mrs Beaufort. Vivienne shot a worried look over at Catherine, but she seemed composed, somewhat preoccupied even.

'This wedding must have cost you thousands Mrs Carré,' Sonia said.

Vivienne nodded in agreement, 'A fair bit, Sonia.'

'Although marriage, it in't about money is it?' Sonia broke off a bit of bread roll as she contemplated. 'I've found it don't really help. Not in the finish.'

Catherine responded at this with a small smile, as if warmed by Sonia's blunt philosophy.

'It's a struggle, though,' Sonia continued, 'tryin' to keep the old man happy, all the time! I find it a struggle, for sure. Men are just big babies aren't they?' Sonia's cheeks turned pink. She fanned her face with her hands. 'Sorry. Not used to red wine daytime. But, I am enjoying myself!' Sonia's look to Vivienne sought, and received, her encouragement.

'So what do you think marriage is all about, then, Sonia?' Catherine leaned forward as if not wanting to miss a single word.

'Well, same as I say, it in't about money.' Sonia shrugged. 'No, I reckon marriage is about...lookin' after each other, I suppose. Especially when you're really fed up with each other!' Now Sonia beamed.

Catherine laughed, 'Well, that's certainly true!'

Catherine had a very nice laugh, and a very nice manner, Vivienne noticed, ruefully. Damn it.

The view from the tent, Vivienne reckoned, was as intoxicating as the steady stream of wine and champagne. People had drifted out and onto the mown field where they sat and lay down. The sun and sea breezes caressed their faces. Aromatic air and the soothing sounds of the waves far below transfixed them all.

'Come and sit with us,' Jocelyn called out to Vivienne. Then Jocelyn caught one of Catherine's hands at the same time. 'Come on!' she encouraged them.

The three women, well wined, hats off, shoes discarded, sat carelessly on the shorn hayfield. They all watched a sailing boat in the distance, no bigger than a cockleshell, trail across the bay. A triangle of white sail made for the misty pier.

'We've been talking,' Vivienne said, hesitating with Catherine so near, 'about marriage – with Sonia. We think it's the little things that aggravate, what about you?' Vivienne felt uncomfortably close to Catherine. Vivienne could clearly see Catherine's ringed finger. The rings were plain: both white gold with the engagement ring a single diamond set in a platinum heart. Catherine's hands were dainty and tanned the pale caramel colour of those who lived in permanent sunshine.

Then, Vivienne found herself saying, 'I think you change passion for compassion in a long marriage...don't you?' Immediately she realised that neither of the other two had experienced a long marriage. And, anyway, Vivienne really wanted to get out of this type of mulling. She became shamefully aware of being next to Catherine, Guy's wife.

'There has to be love, though, don't you think?' Catherine suddenly said, gazing wistfully toward the distant bay.

Jocelyn immediately raised both eyebrows over to Vivienne who returned the same with hers. So. The Beauforts had problems.

But neither pressed Catherine further. They had all drank far too much. Vivienne believed there were certain limits to female curiosity. And, anyway, Jocelyn had already suggested a post-mortem, in the pub, later on. Everything was to be up for discussion – the wedding, the reception, 'everything!'

Enrico came bounding over, looking anxiously at Jocelyn. Jocelyn got him to sit next to Catherine. They soon fell into conversation about Cyprus, which Enrico said he was familiar with and liked a great deal.

With Enrico engaged in talk with Catherine, Jocelyn asked Vivienne quietly, 'So, what happened to your little *mezze*, your little Greek dish of delight, then? Mmm?' Jocelyn chewed on a stalk of hay.

'Shh...Jocelyn! You are awful! Matthias...he's not my little anything. He's a – close friend.'

'Close young friend,' Jocelyn snorted, 'Very close?'

'No. No, he's not. Not like that. Honestly. I can see you don't believe me. Well, all right...nearly. Once. And that was years ago. Now, he's a kind of – adviser'

'Adviser!' Jocelyn threw back her head, her glossy black hair falling loose and cackled loudly. But she didn't say more then. Vivienne knew that Matthias would be one more item for the post-mortem put firmly on Jocelyn's agenda.

A strengthening wind wafted over them, carrying with it a sea-weedy smell. The country air was thick with herbal scent. The canvas marquee soughed in and out as though it were breathing.

'Yes,' said Vivienne, almost to herself, but not quite. She didn't know if Jocelyn, Catherine or indeed Enrico heard her. 'It's not marriage that is so difficult. It's life.'

CHAPTER TWENTY-TWO

The next day, wedding over, Joseph and Natalie prepared to leave for their honeymoon. They'd go to Cyprus and stay in the Beauforts' 'Zephyr Villa'. Guy and Catherine had a couple more days holiday in Guernsey. Catherine wanted to see something of the island: Guy and Natalie's homeland.

At the airport, waving goodbye to the newlyweds, David firmly linked arms with Catherine. He told Vivienne that he had taken rather a liking to this lady. Yes, Catherine made up for him having to tolerate 'that bugger Guy'.

'Would you like to come back to our house, to La Colette, Catherine?' David said. 'I'd like to show you my Channel Island antique map collection. My father, and his father before him, began it. I'm not saying it's a unique collection. But it is important, in its own way. There are some maps of when Guernsey was split in two.'

Smiling her quiet smile, Catherine agreed. 'Well yes, David, of course. That would be ever so interesting. I'd really like to see them!' Catherine's page-boy hair bobbed emphatically as she spoke.

If it weren't such an out-of-use word, Vivienne thought you might call Catherine 'gracious'. She had a gracious way of being. Nevertheless, although she managed a bright enough smile and said, 'That's a good idea, David!' Vivienne thought it was a terrible idea. All four of them at La Colette?

'What?' Guy mouthed silently at Vivienne's frown, gesturing what could he do about it?

Vivienne wished Guy would stop looking quite so gleeful at her discomfort. She began to feel nervous. Guy merely continued to smile broadly, like some beatific choirboy.

As soon as they arrived at La Colette, David whisked them all around on a brief tour. Then he steered the compliant Catherine off to his father's library.

'I love the house,' she enthused to David as they left the room, 'and Guernsey is stunningly beautiful! And the wedding, David...it's all wonderful.'

Guy sat down in the sitting room. Vivienne opened the French windows. Fresh air poured in, cooling her nerves.

'Couldn't you have refused, or something?'

'Oh, do stop fussing, Viv. Life's for living. You are a sensitive little soul, aren't you?' said Guy. 'Little Vivvy Normandie.'

'Carré,' said Vivienne, putting on her sternest voice, 'Vivienne Carré.'

'Oh dear!' Guy pulled her to him and kissed her full on the mouth. 'You know you look fabulous?'

Vivienne pulled away from him, at the same time wishing she could hug him. She wouldn't see him again for – well, who knew how long? Months? Years?

'Might not see you for some time, Viv.'Guy said, more quietly. 'We've always taken chances...?' His frown creased the lines in his forehead, making his dark brows arch.

'There's so much to...so many people to think of, Guy. Joseph, Natalie, Catherine, Eustace...David,' said Vivienne.

'Well, they're not here, are they?'

'Always out of sight out of mind with you, Guy, isn't it? That's you all over! You never contacted me. I was so lonely! Now you come back – just when I'm getting my life back together and...'

'I know that. Didn't I say that? I wanted you to lead your own life. You are. Well, okay, I can see David isn't what you...'

There was a light knock on the door. Sonia came in with a tray. She began to set tea things out on the wax-polished table.

'Tea, Mrs Carré? Mr Beaufort? I've put your favourite chocolate biscuits, Mrs Carré.'

The French windows had blown shut. Sonia glanced at them. 'I'll open them, bit hot in here.' Sonia said.

Sonia opened the windows, fixing the catches either side. Soft, clean air filled the room. Vivienne heard the faint crow of a cockerel in the farmyard nearby.

'You didn't need to come in just for us today, Sonia! It's good of you. Did you enjoy the wedding? You looked lovely,' said Vivienne.

'Oh, it's nothin'. I'm only just over the way. I wanted to, Mrs Carré. What a lovely day! Hope they'll be as happy as me and my Henry.'

Vivienne saw Sonia survey Guy suspiciously. He had some pink lipstick smeared on his lower lip. But before Sonia left, she looked back at Vivienne and there was no trace of judgement in her eyes.

On the table was a book: *Art as Illusion*. Guy picked it up. They started talking about it and soon Vivienne was lost again, deep in Guy's velvet company. He asked about the Open University, saying it had a superb reputation. He might take up an external degree himself – it would keep him out of mischief!

'What subject would you take, Guy?' Vivienne asked.

'I don't know. What do you think, Vivvy? 'Self improvement'? 'Popular Myths of Modern Marriage: the impossibility of monogamy'. Mmm? What d'you reckon?'

She laughed warmly. 'You are an impossible man.' Yes, Guy could always bewitch Vivienne with his words: Put a spell on her without having to try. And of course, she agreed, they must keep in touch.

David came in, with Catherine behind him, closely studying a map. 'Look, it's a copy, Guy. David has said I can keep it. It's a map of Guernsey when it was divided by the sea. Isn't that interesting?' Catherine's small hazel eyes sparkled with enthusiasm. David looked as though his shoulders had broadened, his back straightened and had such a satisfied look on his face, that he even seemed younger.

Once Guy and Catherine had gone back to Cyprus, Vivienne reflected. With Guy she had the deepest pleasure. With Guy she had deep guilt. Either way, she didn't want to be without him. But, then there was Catherine – did Guy always have to marry women Vivienne didn't want to hurt? So she cannot be with him. Damn him. Pour a vodka, Vivienne. What the hell?

'Well, then,' Jocelyn, all agog, ordered sweet white wine. 'Must be very chilled, please.' She instructed the waiter. 'Enrico wanted to be with us, didn't you darling? Enrico feels a bit disoriented in Guernsey.'

So they sat there, Vivienne, Jocelyn and Enrico in the restaurant at Jerbourg, perched high above the pine-tree'd hills.

The islands were clearly visible today: Sandy Herm, Jethou, the caves of Sark, even little Alderney. In fact, the day was so clear that France was a faint grey-blue strip spreading far over the horizon.

'Firstly: Catherine and Guy,' Jocelyn started straight away, adjusting the thin straps of her silk top from under her jacket. 'What d'you reckon? He's up to something, I'll bet. He's such a good-looking rogue, isn't he? Still the business, though. Heavier, but just as handsome. Bet he's screwing around.' Jocelyn decided to slip off her jacket, handing it to the patient waiter to hang up.

They sipped their wine like conspirators, considering Jocelyn's words, watching people on the lawn outside. The visitors relaxed at scrolled white tables. Each table had a sun umbrella, striped navy and white, poled through its centre. Green palm trees, exotic against the blue sky, waved their fronds above them, like fluttering fans.

What could Vivienne say? Yes, Guy is certainly screwing around. Yes, we went to bed together. Yes we are an item. So she just smiled, albeit weakly. Enrico's eyes narrowed fixedly on hers. Vivienne hastily brought the subject round to Natalie. 'What do you think? Do you like her?'

Enrico said, 'She is pretty. But she has a hardness I don't care for.'

'Really?' Both Vivienne and Jocelyn replied in surprise.

'Hard?' said Vivienne. 'No, I don't see that. She's a career girl, perhaps. But…she seems very much in love with Joseph?'

'That doesn't make her soft, Vivienne!' Jocelyn said.

'No, well I realise that. But I expect…' Vivienne thought a bit, '…she's toughened up? Losing her mother so young. Better to be a bit harder than Amanda was, say? Catherine's stronger, though, don't you think?' What did they think of Guy's new wife?

'Catherine is quite a lady,' Enrico smiled effortlessly. 'And no, Catherine is not a doormat as you call it. I didn't know Amanda Beaufort, of course.'

'No, Catherine's not about to be walked over. David would agree with you.' Vivienne ran a finger around the rim of her glass. 'David thinks that Catherine is bright. That she has hidden depths.'

After Vivienne saying she thought Catherine was too good for Guy, Jocelyn suddenly dissolved into a fit of giggles and nearly choked on her wine, 'You'll never guess what one of your guests told me, Vivienne! I didn't get her name. She looked as though she liked her gin. She was in a tweedy get-up. Must have been baking in that marquee!'

'What?' Vivienne and Enrico implored.

'Well, she was really tipsy and she told me – "My first love didn't love me back. My second wouldn't leave his wife. My third couldn't do it and my fourth left me for another man. So I just decided to stay married!"'

All three hooted out so loud with laughter, heads turned. Vivienne spat out some wine, having to wipe her mouth, staining a pure white linen napkin. Still joking and laughing, they ordered their food: Vivienne the fresh mackerel in a lemon sauce and Jocelyn the now obligatory lobster. Enrico had a whole cooked crab, 'caught that very morning', still in its shell, which he picked clean into a creamy, fleshy pile with expert aplomb. Although mayonnaise was supplied, Enrico asked for some vinegar. 'No fresh crab should be eaten without vinegar.'

Jocelyn made appreciative remarks about the restaurant: its wooden floors, windows on three sides of the rooms, and the wood decking running outside as far as the lawns.

Vivienne didn't tell them she could see the beach below, where she had waded into the sea in abject misery, that long ago Christmas. What if she had succeeded? She shuddered, returning to her lunch, pushing away the incubus – the leering woman doctor's face, Guy and Amanda in the hotel that dark night. Vivienne shoved it all back into the haunted attic she had formed in her mind. Time and again she had searched for light on those lingering shadows.

'Hey, Vivienne, are you with us, Vivienne?' Jocelyn was calling out. 'Your David's aged well, hasn't he?' She cut up some mature Guernsey cheese, spreading golden butter over biscuits. 'You two are the only people I know still married after all these years.' Jocelyn bit the laden biscuit. 'What did you say, at the reception? "It's not marriage that's difficult, it's life?"'

So Jocelyn had been listening, after all.

'Yes, well,' Jocelyn continued, 'I agree with you. Life can be very difficult. Bloody difficult.'

Enrico reached for Jocelyn's hand, his long lashed eyes admired her fondly.

'Finding the right partner, to start with, is not only difficult it's bloody near impossible! Still, I've got him now.' Jocelyn kissed Enrico's cheek with a sound affection.

'Bambina,' Enrico sighed theatrically, 'we are for life!'

'But you still haven't told me about this Matthias,' Jocelyn eyed Vivienne mischievously, 'why the mystery?' She bit another biscuit with her expensive teeth.

'No mystery. Not really. Matthias...understands me. He's someone I can talk to.'

'About what?' Jocelyn wasn't relenting.

'Um, things.'

'Things?'

Vivienne felt herself redden. 'Oh shut up, Jocelyn. He's of no interest to you. There's nothing going on, I can tell you that much.'

Butting in, Enrico said, 'Of course not! I know that for certain, not with Matthias. Leave her alone, Joss. She has private thoughts, this one. Deep and very private thoughts.'

Vivienne responded quickly, 'Enrico. Do you believe in love at first sight?'

'Of course!' Enrico beamed, 'Naturally! Happens all of the time!'

'Well I don't,' Jocelyn claimed, 'get to know each other over time, I reckon. I've had my heart broken too many times to trust first impressions.' She dabbed at her mouth with the cloth napkin.

'Oh, I don't know. I believe in Kismet,' Vivienne drained her glass. 'Fate. Fate always takes a hand.'

Enrico smiled widely, boyish in his agreement. 'You know, I give all Joss's clients Tarot readings. Whilst they relax in her capable hands. Vivvyon, I am always right!'

Sensing how on her wavelength Enrico was, Vivienne deftly steered him to his thoughts on Guy.

'He is, Vivvyon – you understand art very well, don't you? Guy Beaufort is the French term *trompe l'oeil*. Guy is not only easy on the eye, he is also a 'triumph of the eye'. Guy is not what he seems. *Trompe l'oeil* is...taking that which is painted for that which is real. Your – that Guy, he is an illusion.'

'God, you can be so Italian,' Jocelyn teased him fondly.

Vivienne felt Enrico's fixed, steady gaze laser back toward her. Then he solemnly said, 'I see a snake, Vivvyon, a serpent in your beautiful Guernsey paradise. Now Matthias – your Bacchus...'

Both Vivienne and Jocelyn stopped drinking their coffee. They listened attentively to Enrico's every word.

'Now your Matthias. I liked him very much! You know he is going to be a very important philosopher. I believe that Matthias will go down in history!' Enrico fairly erupted in kisses: first Vivienne's hand, then Jocelyn's, then both women, twice, on each cheek.

'Matthias will?' Vivienne exclaimed, open-mouthed.

'Will he now?' said Jocelyn, 'How intriguing!'

'You have, Vivvyon, in Matthias,' Enrico finished, 'a true friend in your deep and great, great need. Now, Joss, no more questions of Vivvyon. I want to go home. I want London. I cannot breathe here!'

Jocelyn wasn't put off, 'What deep and great, great need, Vivienne? What?' Jocelyn implored her. 'Not the – the you know what – still?'

'Not now Jocelyn,' insisted Enrico. 'This is not the time. Vivvyon will tell you when she is ready. Now go, go. Let's go.'

As they said their goodbyes, Vivienne made a decision. All their talk of difficulties, relationships, love and life had made her think.

What about Natalie? Did she need advice? Vivienne should help her: help her with her marriage to Joseph. Amanda was dead. Catherine was in Cyprus. Yes, it fell to her. Vivienne must be the one to advise Natalie. Granmarie, Eustace, and certainly Matthias would expect no less of her. Time, then, for Vivienne to get to know her new daughter-in-law.

Jocelyn had commented on how alike David and Joseph had become. 'He's the spit of the younger David, Vivienne.' Joseph was fair-haired and tall.

Her Joseph, Vivienne thought, how grown up he was now and how studious. He wore spectacles and sober office suits. In her heart, though, Joseph was still Vivienne's placid little boy. It was so difficult to think of him as married, mortgaged and an architect. Vivienne told Natalie so.

In her modern flat, one of many in newly-built blocks, Natalie agreed. 'Yes, they are alike. I've thought that myself. David, on your wedding day, could be Joe. I just love your black and white photographs, Vivienne! Our generation forget, don't we, what life was like without colour?'

Natalie couldn't know the nerve she had hit, touching Vivienne's bruised place where colour wouldn't enter. Vivienne realised it was a quite unintended hint toward her depression. Natalie could know nothing of that, after all.

Natalie busied herself around the flat. She went in and out of her spotless tiled kitchen, complete with its microwave, dishwasher, washing machine and tumble drier. She switched off the flat screen television and logged off her computer.

'Now then, Vivienne, you've got my full attention!' Natalie hugged her mug of green tea as she curled up on the cream leather couch. She had lit expensive, scented candles – gardenia with cardamom and myrrh – putting them on the windowsill.

Vivienne always found it difficult to look at Natalie without seeing Guy, her father's dark eyes and hair. Natalie wore a simple white T-shirt over blue denim jeans. She had long, slim legs, wore little make-up and pinned her hair up in a tortoiseshell plastic grip, so that bits deliberately stuck out at the back. Natalie's clever eyes were wide and slanted: so big that they made the rest of her face seem small.

'Well, anyway...' Vivienne said, 'I just popped round, you know, to see how you are, Natalie. Working like you do, I wondered how you cope. If you needed a hand, ever?'

'Oh, God, no! We're fine, Vivienne. I've got time in the evenings, after marking and stuff,' she indicated toward the piles of papers and books on the desk she had made in the corner – a little office with her computer, answering phone and stainless steel lamp. 'Joe does his bit. We eat out a lot. That's one thing in Guernsey – plenty of restaurants!'

Lighting a Rothmans cigarette, Natalie pulled the glass coffee table toward her, flicking ash into a deep blue ceramic ashtray. 'We've got all our friends, as well. We don't do dinner parties like you all used to. More like one-pot suppers in the kitchen, everyone digging in! We make life a lot easier for ourselves than you lot did!'

Yes, she could see that, Vivienne mused. Natalie didn't need her anything like as much as she had needed Pearl to show her any domestic ropes. Even Edward had said how he approved of Natalie and Joseph's flat. Everything, Edward reported, seemed very tidy.

'Pity you can't have pets in these flats, isn't it Natalie? You used to love your little West Highland dog, your Westie – what was he called now: Fraser? Whatever happened to him?' Vivienne recalled Natalie as a young girl, running after the doggy white streak, chasing a red ball.

'Oh, little Fraser? My Christmas present? Yes, he was so cute! When we left to live in Cyprus, Dad gave him away, to a friend of his.' Then, rather pointedly, Vivienne thought, Natalie looked at her watch.

'Well, look, Joe's going to be home late this evening. He's got some huge design project going on – down at the new shopping centre at Admiral Park. I've got quite a lot of work to do – but would you like to stay for supper?'

The question was, Vivienne discerned, made more out of politeness than of any real desire to entertain her. It was vaguely disappointing. Natalie didn't appear to need much mothering. At least, if she did, not from Vivienne.

'No, no, it's alright. I have to get back for David,' Vivienne evaded, thinking of the meal Sonia had prepared for David, in case Vivienne did eat with Joseph and Natalie. 'By the way, don't mind me saying, I mean I don't mind you smoking, Natalie, we all did in our day. But, after all, we didn't know the dangers, then.' Vivienne sighed, wishing she would not keep on sounding quite so much the mother-in-law.

'No. A lot of stuff changed. We don't have to get married any more; living together isn't a sin.' Natalie took a long drag at her cigarette, blowing the smoke out through her nose. She finished her coffee, putting it down with a decisive chink onto the coffee table. 'Don't you think it's better for us, Vivienne?' Natalie raised alarmingly familiar, dark-arched brows.

'In many ways, of course, Natalie. Restrictions have stopped. Life for you is much more...it's much kinder than it was for us, in the fifties and sixties.' Lord, Vivienne hadn't meant to get into such discussions like this with Natalie. She really must stop all this talk about difference in society through the ages. She'll talk about Natalie's work, Joseph's work – art, perhaps. Not all these potentially risky comparisons. Soon she feared they would be talking about abortions and divorce laws. She needed to change the subject.

Natalie changed it for her. 'You knew my folks when I was young, didn't you Vivienne?'

God, this was no better. Vivienne began fiddling with a long bead necklace she wore, over her maroon tunic. 'Well, yes. Knew them both...both of them, from very young. Your mother was a nice lady, Natalie. Amanda was a good person.'

'Yeah, but didn't you have a fling with Dad?' Smoke drifted past her face but Vivienne could clearly see alert – amused even – brown eyes through the flapped-away haze.

'A...a fling? Well, yes – but it was in our youth, Natalie. He was my…my first love, yes.' Vivienne strained to breath evenly with a gulp in her throat. It was bound to come out at some time. This was Guernsey for Pete's sake! What had Natalie heard? What did Joseph know?

'Joe told me.' Natalie stubbed out her cigarette nonchalantly. 'That you had had…a bit of a thing about Dad. It's okay, Vivienne. I'm cool about it. Okay, it's a bit gross, maybe. But I'm not bothered about it.' Natalie uncurled and rose from the couch, stretching her arms. Then she walked with bare, crimson varnished toes to where Vivienne sat. Vivienne tried to get up whilst hastily bundling her bag and car keys together.

'The way I see it, Vivienne,' Natalie said, with her arms crossed in front of her, 'women should make their own choices, live their own lives. Women should be able to do that. Joe and I – we're nineties people. It'll soon be the Millennium! Everything's changing. Things are changing all the time.'

Now she was sounding just like her father's daughter. Weariness overtook her as Vivienne asked Natalie to give Joseph her love. She said she hoped they might come up for Sunday lunch. Would she like her to invite Muriel Le Croix, her grandmother? Would Natalie like that?

Seeing Vivienne to the door, Natalie agreed. She said she'd like that. She didn't see nearly enough of her gran now that her grandfather Le Croix had died. The Beauforts were in New Zealand and both frail now. Natalie didn't expect to see them again.

Joseph had told Vivienne they saw more than Natalie ideally would like of Edward and Jean. Natalie didn't tell Vivienne that, though. Mind you, Natalie wasn't telling her a lot of things, was she?

Maybe it was just as well, Vivienne thought. They were a young married couple now, with their own lives to lead. But then, Natalie did have some news for them. At the Sunday lunch Vivienne had prepared at La Colette.

Natalie delivered it in her usual matter-of-fact way. She had just helped herself to broccoli and carrots. Natalie replaced the china vegetable dish back onto the table and said she was cool about it, but that 'Catherine has left Guy'.

CHAPTER TWENTY-THREE

Her studio at La Colette let light stream in from the long windows, with the Velux lending more from above. Vivienne wore her painting shirt to mix oil paints onto her palette. She had decided to start a landscape: the view from the studio.

It was a clear day. Sunshine bathed the lush green fields. Violet shadows underlined burgeoning hedges. The land sloped down gently toward the sea, stopping short at rocky granite cliffs. Vivienne wondered what Van Gogh would have made of this view of Guernsey. Renoir emphasised the red rocks of the west coast in his paintings, making the sea look vibrant royal blue. Vincent would have focused on the stubbly, cut hay and gorse; drawn a wide sky with cerulean sea. She dabbed vermilion and yellow onto the canvas: tall poppies, vivid wildflowers.

Seagulls constantly whirled and dived, stopping now and then to gobble a snatched lunch from the warm earth. Sometimes they landed, like important sentinels, in rows, when a tractor pop-popped along the ploughed ridges – unearthing special treats.

As she mixed, adding linseed oil or turpentine for thicker or thinner paint, Vivienne turned Catherine's call to David around in her mind. Could Catherine borrow him for a few days? She much needed his advice. 'Could David come over to Cyprus, d'you think? Would that be possible?'

Pressed, Catherine said that there were several reasons why she was leaving Guy: that he was uninterested in her. That he was drinking, not working, and that she had had enough. Catherine simply wanted to do something else with her life.

Vivienne felt relieved that Catherine had rung them. Well, if she suspected anything between Guy and her she wouldn't have phoned, would she? So Vivienne agreed, yes, okay, David could go. David made it clear to Vivienne that it was an excellent opportunity for him to show that bugger Guy how to behave toward this wife or any woman come to that, even if it was too late for Amanda. Catherine deserved David's help. She was a good person. He liked her.

Catherine wanted to start a business in Limassol. She had had, she told them, her eye on a Taverna for some time. Her two close friends, male partners, were to run it for her. More than that, she wanted to start growing salad vegetables: tomatoes, cucumbers, capsicums (peppers), for the Taverna. Her father had left her some land. She had the capital. It was a project – something she very much wanted to do. Something Catherine had had in mind for quite a long time.

Vivienne carefully applied her paints. She had sketched first, deciding where to place focal points of the background and how to achieve the foreground. The Mediterranean blues of the sky and sea in these islands were a gift. Absorbed, her grinning demons were held at bay. Painting was her palliative, along with the wine she sipped as she worked. Alcohol, Edward's evil substance, was, for her, a painkiller. So why not?

Vivienne had her BA Honours degree in art history. For her thesis, she had chosen the myths in Titian's painting. Matthias was both delighted for her and helpful with advice. Although Vivienne had phoned Guy a few times, he was either too inebriated or too forgetful to be of much help.

'Why don't you come to Cyprus, too?' David asked Vivienne. 'I don't much fancy travelling on my own. You can see – what was it? The Icon Museum in Paphos, Joseph told us about? And the Apollo thing and all that stuff? Just up your street, I'd have thought.'

'Cyprus history is rich in mythology and classical art,' read the travel brochure. Vivienne smiled as she read. As if she needed persuading! She'd visit Guy – see how the silly man was. No need to tell David that. And, if he had guessed, he wasn't saying anything. Trouble was, she really did attract bloody mosquitoes. She would have to get really effective medication.

For his part, David told Vivienne he was both flattered and pleased to have been asked for help by Catherine. Lately he was going about with an expression on his face that Vivienne had never seen before. So, it was settled: Vivienne and David were both going to Cyprus.

Natalie confided with her in-laws that she was glad that they could help her (soon to be) ex-stepmother. In turn it would help her father. Guy and Catherine both seemed to be in need of friends at the moment. Questioned, Natalie said she wasn't in the least surprised that Catherine was separating from Guy. Guy was a difficult man to live with, Natalie said, she had found that out for herself. Liked his own way far too much, did her father.

Not particularly close to Catherine, though not disliking her, Natalie said she had far more to do than grieve the loss of her. Anyway, she would see her now and again when she went to Cyprus. They certainly weren't enemies. No, it was Guy Natalie was more concerned about. He was useless domestically and hopeless with money. So, maybe David and Vivienne could help? 'After all, it could do…' said Natalie philosophically, '…no harm.'

At first, Cyprus seemed dry and barren after the green lushness of Guernsey. But it had, possibly, the only sea in the world to match Vivienne's island – caught as Guernsey was, in the Gulf Stream. Dense blue, swished through with rainbow green, the Cyprus seas were clear and deep. Faced with such beauty, Vivienne forced down her depression, tried to let it run right through her, and out the other side. Surely Cyprus would offer respite. Cyprus might offer that?

Landing at Larnaca without a hitch, David promptly went off with Catherine, taking from her some scrolled plans that she had brought. Catherine looked slim, healthy and young, with her light caramel tan, white shirt and shorts and baseball cap. Her blonde hair, still in a page-boy cut, curled in tufts over the rim of her hat.

It had been agreed that Vivienne and David would go their separate ways. Ostensibly, Vivienne was staying in Paphos: for the Icons museum and important Mosaics. Vivienne wanted to visit all the ruins. Naturally enough, David wanted to put his time to Catherine. He was taking her request for his help, and her projects, very seriously, 'about time,' he said 'someone did.'

Guy, Catherine told them, was going to look for an apartment in Nicosia. She would be keeping their villa. She had paid for most of it, anyway. But, for now, Catherine was based in Limassol whilst she oversaw the new businesses.

But Vivienne had no intention of staying in Paphos. She immediately took a taxi to the Beaufort villa: to Zephyr Villa.

'Zephyr Villa?' It means 'a spring breeze bearing flowers,' Guy explained when she rang him. 'I'll be glad to see you, Vivvy. I'm a mess.'

The whitewashed villa was a box, built on a hillside, set among bark-brown, carob trees. Tissue-thin, purple bougainvillaea shaded a porch. In the garden grew scarlet geraniums, pink oleanders and tall, dark green palm trees.

The taxi had bumped over a dusty sand road, running through the village. Hung about with unhurried washing, people sat under their trellised porches. The community of British exiles, at their ease, peered from white chairs on burning concrete patios. Cicadas sissed incessantly. Vivienne applied yet more cream on her arms. The mosquitoes bided their time: poised, invisibly, awaiting their evening meal.

Vivienne paid the Cypriot driver. He revved up his ancient Mercedes and swept away in a cloud of dust. Guy came out onto the porch. He wore a creased white shirt, in need of a wash, with the sleeves rolled up. His khaki shorts revealed bronzed legs and bare feet. His hair fell in a fringe over his tanned face. His eyes looked glazed. He was, Vivienne realized, pissed.

Inside the cool villa, Guy had placed bowls of green olives, oranges and lemons. There were baskets of purple aubergines, courgettes and sweet potatoes. The maid who, Guy told Vivienne, lived in the village, had washed the stone tiled floors. Pine furniture reflected clearly on the cleaned surface.

Beyond the blue shuttered windows was the foot of the Troodhos mountains, showing peaks of yellow ochre, but grey-blue in the distance; brick-red nearer the rubbly road.

The plains were dotted with olive, carob and eucalyptus trees; charcoal brown branches jutted out from desiccated soil. A sheltering family of lizards scuttled over the walls, whipping their tails. Catherine had placed terracotta pots on the porch, planted with bright red geraniums with their dark green leaves.

'Hello Guy,' said Vivienne. Zephyr Villa is lovely. I can see why you live in Cyprus. It's wonderful. But you, Guy, are you alright? You look – ill. You don't look well.' Vivienne, in a sleeveless blue top and white shorts, already tanned from Guernsey, still felt an insistent heat on her body.

'Well, you look fine. You always took the light well. You haven't changed, Vivvy.' Guy loped around the tiled room, holding a bottle of beer, swigging from it all the while. 'Want a drink?' He grinned but his face kind of drooped at the same time. He rummaged around in the fridge, found some beer and flicked off the top. 'G'wan. It's hot today. Cool you down.' Offering the drink to Vivienne, he came up close to her.

She accepted the beer. God knows, she needed it. 'Guy. What have you done to yourself?'

'Don't you bloody start, for God's sake!' Guy passed the back of his hand over his moist mouth.

'Why are you drinking?' But, even then, there seemed little point. She would talk to him tomorrow, when he was more sober. Vivienne had booked a room in the village, just a short walk away.

Guy belched, hiccupped then said, 'Will you help me look for an apartment? Seen one in Nicosia. It'll be alright. Catherine's all taken up with David.' He winked, tapping the side of his nose with his index finger. 'Maybe got a little something going on there, eh Vivienne? D'you think? Eh? Old Dave and Lady Catherine?'

'Don't be ridiculous, Guy. For heaven's sake.'

'So…we might as well,' Guy lunged at her. Vivienne quickly stepped aside so that he fell, sprawled onto a striped divan.

With him so drunk, Vivienne thought she would be turned off. But no, Guy was still ravishingly attractive, damn the man. He put the empty bottle on the cold floor and lay full length, on his back.

'Come and make love to me, you sexy woman.' Guy held out his long brown arms. His eyes swam liquidly with alcohol and desire.

'Guy,' Vivienne softened. He was still her Guy. Her lovely young boy at Portelet – in London – in Guernsey. Sober or drunk, how she loved to hear Guy talk to her of things that David never did. Things that no-one else did, save Matthias. But Vivienne must resist him! This was all wrong …

'Look, Guy, I'm going. I'll come back tomorrow morning and then we can go to Nicosia. All right? Go to bed and – in the morning, well, clean yourself up. There are empty bottles everywhere, for goodness sake. No wonder Catherine…'

Suddenly angry, Guy sat up. 'Oh, no. That's not why. Catherine wants me all to herself. I told her. I can't. I cannot be one woman's man. You know that! You've always understood that. So…there,' he became muddled, 'so that's why…' then flopped back, out of consciousness.

Obviously, she wasn't going to get anywhere with Guy today. So Vivienne let herself out and walked in to the village. She went into the village shop and bought water, stamps and postcards. She asked if she could use the ancient telephone, dust covered, near the till. She telephoned David. He said all was going well. He and Catherine had sat down in her rented flat and worked out a business plan. Later he was going out to see her land and to help her to start preparing for the growing Catherine was determined to do. Catherine was very grateful, David said, and that he liked her company. They were going out later for a meal in Limmasol.

David didn't ask Vivienne if she wanted to join them. She felt slightly put out. He asked after her day. She didn't have to think of what to say for too long, David clearly needed to get off the phone. So they told each other to take care and hung up. Vivienne looked at the receiver, buzzing emptily, then shrugged. She was hardly in a position to lecture David Carré.

The survivor of their break, thought Vivienne, must be Catherine, because Guy looked dreadful. The normally even-featured face was getting to look haggard. His hair was greyer.

Next day, as they sat in a sunny quadrangle in Nicosia, Vivienne and Guy carefully embraced. He had found an apartment on Hippocrate Street. It had looked gloomy to Vivienne, and dusty. She found the fug too depressing.

'Come on, then, let's have a drink in the courtyard,' Guy suggested. So then, there they were, sat on a bench under a spreading myrtle tree, tubbed in an earthen-brown pot.

Guy's anxiety got to her, making her tense. 'So what are you going to do, Guy?' Vivienne asked.

'Tell the truth, Vivvy. I'm seriously thinking of moving back to Guernsey.' He brushed a hand through his hair, raking damp black strands off his forehead. The planes of his cheekbones stood out, his half-smile looked sad. Guy had made an effort, though: showered and wore a clean navy sweatshirt, jeans and sandals. Vivienne told him she'd noticed and complimented him.

'That's better, Guy. You look better. It's not like you to neglect yourself.' It was too worrying. Guy's state was the most worrying part of this whole trip. 'Look, why don't you just take this apartment, clean it up – do it up nice whilst you can think of what to do next? Catherine's keeping the villa?'

'Oh yes!' He glowered, 'our Lady Catherine has fixed herself up very nicely! Taken the villa, got a new business – got money. Doing very nicely. Doesn't give a shit about me!' Guy knocked back his drink, pouring more from the wine bottle they had secured in the plant pot's earth.

'I think she does. Of course she does. Catherine cares for you. Amanda did...' but, at this, a lingering pain in his eyes warned Vivienne off. Don't talk about Amanda. Not today. 'Look, are you still painting, Guy? Doing any work at all?' She felt growing alarm at his condition. How would he manage, could he exist now that Catherine had gone?

'Nah. Like you so cleverly said, years ago,' Guy lapsed into a sarcastic girl's voice, 'Why paint postcards of idyllic blue shutters, red geraniums in flower boxes, dear little pussy cats asleep in the sun?' Well, you were right. Nah, can't do any of that any more.'

Casting about for lifelines, Vivienne asked, 'Do you still hear from Darius? Could he help to market your...'

'Darius!' Guy exclaimed loudly, 'Huh! He's on his third or fourth heiress! Rolling in moolah. Best seller after best seller. Have a look on the Internet. We send Christmas cards. I'd rather die a pauper on Limmasol beach than ask Darius Swift for help.'

'Just a thought,' Vivienne said lamely.

'Oh, I know, Vivvy. I know you're trying to help.' Guy put his hand over hers. They drank their wine in the sweet-smelling shade in the stone courtyard. He sighed, 'And yes, you're right. I'll take this place and really think about what to do. Now,' he patted her hand, 'I want to show you those Icons, the Byzantine Museum in Paphos and the mosaics you should be seeing instead of wasting your time with the likes of me. And,' he returned her smile – Vivienne enjoyed hearing him being positive –'did you know that Ariadne died and is buried, here, in Cyprus? There! Now I do have something interesting to tell you, little Vivvy!'

'No, Guy! No, I didn't know that. Yes please, show me her burial place.' It was good now, talking about art, Titian, Ariadne. It was good to be together again. Maybe she had helped Guy – just a little?

They left Nicosia and headed for Paphos. Cyprus, with its warmth and beauty, was doing Vivienne some good. Her peace, though, was short-lived. All the way down to Paphos, Guy insisted they stop at every other Taverna. As she drove the hired car, Vivienne became uneasy. Guy drunk, Guy dishevelled was getting harder to bear.

As the day wore on, Vivienne began to think Guy didn't even register her company. She knew that if she started to drink too much herself, they really would be in turbulent waters.

The Byzantine Museum had uniquely important Icons. Enthralled, Vivienne studied the old gold and dark red pictures: the Pantocrator, Mary with the baby Jesus, holding the gospel in his hand; Hodegetria with Mary pointing to the child 'He who shows the way'. Each icon had its own unique meaning.

With Guy, Vivienne weaved her way around the ancient mosaics, marvelling at the intricate skills of the craftsmen at the Tomb of the

Kings: fascinating and eerie at the same time. Though how much better for her if her head was clearer and she didn't need to support a heavy, staggering Guy. Vivienne would come back one day, on her own, to see it all again.

As he attempted to inform her of all he knew, about everything he had ever known, Guy stuttered and slurred. He attracted disparaging looks from other tourists, especially the Brits. No wonder Catherine had called it a day. Guy, like this, was decidedly hard going. And Vivienne hadn't come all this way to exhaust herself, propping up the man. Certainly not physically, anyway.

They left Paphos. Vivienne badly wanted to see the Apollo Sanctuary, at the top of Episkopi Bay. She wanted a word or two with Apollo, god of beauty, music and prophecy. She knew from her OU studies that the laurel, myrtle and palm trees were sacred to him. Apollo was a classical Greek spirit: the rational, civilized side of man's nature. He was the other side of the coin – of Bacchus – who represents mankind's darker, passionate side.

They crossed over the searing hot stones of the Sanctuary. 'This is where Joseph and Natalie met,' Vivienne said to Guy, 'remember?'

'Yes,' he said, 'I think I do. Vaguely.'

'Apollo is the sun god. His light reveals the truth about everything. Light reveals truth,' said Vivienne pleased she'd remembered her course. Standing by the pink twin pillars, gazing upwards to where the stone entablature rose, Vivienne whispered to Apollo. She closed her eyes. 'Will everything be alright? Will I, one day, be rid of my mortal sins? Give me your answer, Apollo, will you? I am in need of you.'

Vivienne stayed, not moving but sitting silently on a broken step in the sunshine at the foot of the fabulous columns. Guy amused himself, chasing a lizard, leaving her alone. 'Don't know anyone else who speaks to Apollo! You are one wild woman, Vivvy!' He called over, chuckling to himself.

Through the still air, distantly, but unmistakably, Vivienne heard a valiant cockerel crow. She had been given her answer. She had heard the sound of hope.

'Thank you,' Vivienne said out loud to the pillars, standing proud against the royal blue sky. 'I thank you, Apollo.' Then she bowed, turned and caught up with Guy, rejoining him. 'Now, Guy, what was that you were telling me – about Ariadne?'

'Ahh, yes,' Guy said dreamily. 'Ariadne, Ariadne. The little lost mortal, buried here in Cyprus.'

'Where, Guy? Take me to see the place. Is it a shrine?'

His hand felt clumsy and damp as he ruffled her hair. It had frizzed in the heat, the tips of it sun-bleached as Vivienne had trudged around the Sanctuary.

'Let's go, then.'

Vivienne drove them swiftly on the well-kept Cypriot roadways to Amathus. Near Limassol, lay the burial site.

Guy sat down and Vivienne did, too. 'Ariadne, known here sometimes as Aridela,' he grinned. Vivienne had to admit that she liked Guy showing off, it slaked her thirst, as she put her face to the sun and drank in his words. 'Pregnant by Theseus, Ariadne died here, in childbirth. She was buried in a sacred grove and it's dedicated to Aphrodite, goddess of love and fertility. One of her symbols is the cuttlefish because of its eight tentacles. Figure eight is a significant mythological number for reproduction. Anyway, the women of Amathus treated Ariadne kindly. After she died, they buried her here. Ariadne's festival is still celebrated on the second day of September.'

Enthralled, with her eyes shut and feeling the sun burning on her, Vivienne asked, 'What happened to the child?'

'Er, well I don't think there is a record of the child,' Guy replied. 'I expect historians haven't found that fact, well... important enough.'

'No,' Vivienne felt tears mass into a prickling behind her eyes, 'I don't suppose it is. It was, after all, just one more dead baby born from the pain of an abandoned woman. Poor Ariadne. She didn't deserve such an end. She had tried so much to help Theseus, helping him to overcome the monster – to escape from that labyrinth with her magic golden thread. It was hers. She just gave it away. What did he do? Dumped her so she fell into Bacchus' arms. Ariadne was a princess,

Guy, the crown of Crete, a lovely young girl, strong and brave. So much for having your bridal chaplet thrown to the heavens to join the bloody stars. Where the hell was lying Theseus, forgetting his promises? Where was Bacchus? She was left all alone in childbirth. Gods don't die. Were they asleep?'

'Steady on, Viv!' Guy said, looking at her in surprise at the tears flowing freely. 'It's only a bloody Greek myth. Only a story, Vivvy? Christ, I need a drink!'

CHAPTER TWENTY-FOUR

Vivienne rang David again. He said they would need to meet at Larnaca airport, the following morning. 'Don't be late, Vivienne.' He said. Then he told her Catherine and he were pretty much done. He'd seen the Taverna and met her gay friends. He liked them very much, thought they would be just the right people for Catherine to be in business with. They had all got on just fine.

Catherine's land, the soil, was of good quality although she would need to install underground irrigation. They'd gone to the nursery to select plants and seeds to get her started. He was sure she would do well. Catherine was a hard worker. That evening David was being treated to a trial dinner, by Catherine's team. They wanted him to judge their local cooking and perhaps decide what would be the best things to concentrate on – to cultivate for the dishes they wanted to provide. David was much looking forward to it all. He'd see Vivienne tomorrow, then.

The maid from the village had been in again, taking away a veritable glass mountain of bottles and a heap of empty cans. Vivienne helped herself to a fresh orange, smelling the pungent juice burst on her face as she pulled at the peel with her fingers. She bit into the fragrant segments. The Troodhos mountains looked close enough to touch as she walked through the glass sliding door to the terrace. In the dry field next door a dog, tethered in a roughly built kennel, barked noisily and repetitively, like brief questions – as though he knew no-one was going to respond to him.

Guy was still asleep. So drunk the night before he had forgotten to lock his door. The maid had walked straight in. She couldn't have been more than eighteen. Dark skinned and round, she kept stealing glances at Vivienne. Vivienne wondered how the young girl would like working for Guy alone – had she had liked Catherine or not?

Pushing a soft-haired broom, the girl went into Guy's bedroom. Vivienne heard muffled giggling and words in Cypriot that sounded very close to 'Not now!' said by the maid. Guy clearly didn't know that Vivienne was there.

What an absolute dope you are, Vivienne scolded herself. Would the pretty young maid mind just working for Guy? Well, obviously not! How long had that been going on? Is that what Catherine had found out? Guy Beaufort was utterly incorrigible.

Before she left, the maid shot Vivienne a triumphant smile. Shades of Rita, Vivienne thought. All his conquests looked triumphant. All the women who love him wept.

Out on the terrace, in her straw hat, Vivienne let the sun warm her. She could hear Guy showering, then moving about the villa. He clattered in the kitchen, opened the wooden shutters, then came out to join her with red wine and two glasses, but no food.

In the strong sunshine, the ravaging of Guy was quite clear. Vivienne accepted a glass. After all, she was on holiday.

'Why didn't you tell me you had arrived?' Guy said, without a trace of embarrassment.

'Even bonking the maid, now?' Vivienne couldn't resist. 'Honestly, Guy. Don't you have any pride left?' This time Vivienne didn't think of the young Cypriot girl as competition. Just as an easy lay for him – another chick that Guy was taking advantage of.

'Don't be such a snob. I think she's sweet. You should be careful, Viv. I don't need a woman to have money and position to be attracted to her,' adding meanly, 'and you're not getting any younger, are you?' Guy lit a cigarette.

Stung, Vivienne lashed out, 'Maybe not. But I'm not going to pot like you are! Look in the mirror, Guy. You've become a lush!'

'Take's one to know one,' he retorted.

'What are you going to do with yourself, Guy?'

'Look, what is this all about? Why have you come here at all? But, look, let's not argue Viv. I didn't sleep well...'

'Huh! Wonder why?' Vivienne snapped. Perhaps she was jealous of the goddamned maid, after all. Guy always did this to her. She thought one thing, then, with a click of his fingers, she thought something else.

Yet she did feel pity for him. His looks had been so special. It wasn't good to see him looking like that. He had washed his hair, yes, but it was badly cut and he looked, somehow, run down. But he had hurt her.

Guy sighed apologetically, 'I'm sorry. I'm sorry about what I said. I hardly know what the hell I'm doing these days. Look, I'll fix some lunch. And, in fact, you have kept your looks. You have... preserved yourself well.'

Vivienne laughed, 'What like jam? I'm "in lovely condition" – like Shelley Winters in the *Alfie* film?'

'Something like that!'

The air cleared, the sun shone warmly down and Vivienne laughed. Guy did as well. They drank their wine.

'This is a really nice area you have created, Guy,' said Vivienne. 'Private, sheltered, lovely views. You are going to really miss all this when you go to Nicosia, aren't you?'

'Yes,' Guy's dark eyes danced with a wicked familiarity, 'won't even have a maid!

Don't worry about me. As I say, I might come back to live in Guernsey.' He rose. 'No, stay there. Enjoy the sun. I'll make us some food. You might not believe it, but Limassol has some truly excellent supermarkets – British names. They do good quality food. Catherine shops...Catherine used to shop there all the time.' He went inside, taking the wine bottle with him.

Returning, with a new bottle and some salad, Guy placed all the things on the table in the garden. They had ripe red tomatoes, olives, salty anchovies, cucumber and sliced red onions. Guy had found some cooked red mullet and cold new potatoes. He cut some bread for her, offering butter and firm, white feta cheese.

'I do love the Mediterranean sun,' said Vivienne with appreciation, 'it lifts the spirits. Warms the bones.' She absent-mindedly rubbed the swollen mosquito bites on her arms and legs. Every idyllic place had its devil, after all.

'Yes, it does. Guaranteed sun is always a treat for us Brits, isn't it?'

'You do know that property prices in Guernsey are sky-high, don't you Guy? Even very tiny apartments are well over £100,000, considerably over that.'

'Yes, I know, I know,' he said tetchily, the wine starting to show effect. 'But Natalie's going to look around for me. She is good at spotting bargains.'

'I imagine she is,' Vivienne agreed, coolly. 'Well, I hope she can find you something reasonable. She and Joseph seem to be getting on all right, don't you think? They seem to be happy? Working hard?'

'I hope so.' Said Guy. 'Natalie has had a lot to put up with. First Amanda, then Catherine going. She hasn't had an easy childhood.'

Vivienne noted Guy didn't mention herself in this, nor their relationship, although she had known Natalie since she was a little girl. Guy must be very good at keeping secrets: keeping his life in compartments. For some reason 'He is an illusion, Vivvyon' leapt into her mind. Enrico said that. Guy was not what he seemed.

They finished their meal. Guy stacked the dishes and took them from the terrace into the kitchen. He brought out some whisky and two cut-glass tumblers.

'God. It's a bit early for that, isn't it?' Vivienne said, looking at her watch.

'Not for me,' Guy proceeded to make them whisky sours.

'Guy! That's a sundowner drink!'

'For me it's a sun-upper drink. Who cares?'

He had allowed himself, then, to become this lazing drinker. His ambitions had gone, he had let his talents die. Guy had opted out. What on earth had happened to him along the way?

'Tell the truth. I've never wanted the nine to five thing, Vivvy. Once my painting didn't exactly set the world on fire I have become a disillusioned old bastard, instead of a hopeful, young one.' Guy chortled into his glass. Vivienne saw him beginning to draw into himself.

This was too dismaying, too disconcerting. Vivienne wasn't going to sit there, matching him drink for drink, though. And she had a plane to catch tomorrow morning.

'I think I might go into Limmasol, Guy. Do a bit of shopping. Want to come?' He'd settled down to a day's drinking, she thought, drumming up an excuse why he might not interrupt his, obviously, daily routine. Vivienne stood up.

Guy squinted up at her, the sun in his eyes. 'Why did you come here, Viv?' he asked.

'Well, actually, Catherine asked David and David asked me.'

'Well! How very neat and tidy!' Guy said, thickly. 'Lady Catherine beckons and old Dave comes running! Still, bet he's pleased. Time he showed some balls. Do you still sleep apart?'

'Yes,' she tugged at a loose strand on her sleeve, 'as it happens. We do.'

'Cor! So old Dave's gagging for it then, eh? He'll have one hell of a shock once he finds out how frigid the Lady is!' He guffawed loudly. 'Poor old Dave eh? Never gets it right!'

Startled as to how quickly the conversation had turned round to her marriage with all its faults, Vivienne said, 'As I said. I'm going shopping Guy. Are you coming?'

'No! Don't go. Don't go. C'mon. Sit down next to me. You've only just got here. I want to talk to you. To look at you – lovely Vivvy.'

'No. I'm going,' she said, weakening.

He pouted moodily, looking like a hurt little boy who had been told off. She couldn't hold back a laugh.

'Well, come back soon. Tell you what, we'll go out tonight. I know an absolutely divine fish Taverna. I found it. It's right by the sea. It's heavenly. You'll love it Vivvy.'

'Well, alright,' Vivienne sighed in agreement, 'but only if you promise to lay off the booze for the rest of the day. I'm not going out with you if I have to lift your face out of the soup.'

'Don't like soup,' he smiled impishly. 'I promise though...' he added quickly as she made to go, 'Promise,' he made a cross over his heart, 'to be a good, good boy. There. Will that do?'

Guy stretched out his feet on the padded lounger, putting his hands behind his head. 'See? Look Vivvy, no booze!' he waggled an empty glass and smiled a broad smile.

It was quite true, there were many good shops in Limmasol. Vivienne wrote out a postcard to Polly. 'Found fabulous shop on St Andrew's street. Stuffed full of antiques and soft furnishings, mostly from the Eastern Mediterranean. Not touristy tat at all.'

Vivienne pottered around the supermarkets and, indeed, they had every kind of fresh fish, meats and cheeses. She imagined herself living in Cyprus, shopping and buying groceries. There were many British voices and families on holiday, with a fair sprinkling of ex-pats.

Walking as far as the old harbour, she surveyed the tourist strip of beach, stretching for some miles. A far cry from dear old Guernsey, she smiled. But then, guaranteed sun and warm blue sea would always attract large hotels and many thousands of visitors. Still, Vivienne reckoned her island had its own unique and unspoilt charm.

Returning to the villa, she found Guy had kept his word and gone to bed with a plastic bottle of water at his bedside. A slumbering god, she thought, wanting to stroke his hair, to touch his sleeping face, but she didn't.

Vivienne placed some cheeses in Guy's fridge and some melons to add to his baskets of fruit, some fresh bread and milk. On the tiled window sill were photographs, mainly of Natalie as a little girl. There was one of Fraser the Westie, with Natalie hugging the off-white dog with the coal-black eyes.

Another photograph, smaller, was one of Natalie with a younger child. Vivienne couldn't tell if it was a boy or a girl. They held hands, standing in a pool, surrounded by the blue granite rocks of Guernsey. There were no photographs of Amanda, Catherine or Guy. And Vivienne and he had always been careful not to be photographed together, so she wasn't among his souvenirs either, she thought ruefully. No record of her here, then.

Tired now, Vivienne lay on the couch in the cool tiled room, welcoming the shade from the outside heat. The neighbouring dog still barked mournfully. She slept for an hour.

At seven in the evening, Guy woke her as he came bounding in, full of energy. He shook her and made aperitifs with a practiced aplomb. They took them outside to the same terraced spot. 'Only here can you sit out in such warmth in the evenings. Isn't it civilized?' said Vivienne.

Guy clinked her glass as they both said, 'Bon Sante'.

'Very, very civilized. I love it. Now, can we get to this Taverna?'

'I'm starving,' said Vivienne. She put her hand over her glass as Guy made to top it up with his cocktail shaker.

'Oh dear, you have become quite the little saint, haven't you?'

'No, of course not. It's just that...I'm not going to be much use to you if I'm half-cut, am I? I'm trying to help you, Guy.'

'But you're making me feel self-conscious. I'm not going to change just because you are here.' With some flourish, Guy drained the cocktail shaker into his glass.

'I didn't expect you to change,' said Vivienne. 'But, then, you must let me be myself, as well.'

'Christ, this is getting too heavy. Let's go.' Guy reached for his sweater – one of Amanda's, Vivienne noticed. So, he hadn't got rid of all his past, then?

The Taverna was all Guy said it would be. It was charming. Set so near a sandy beach, its stone-flagged floor all but fell onto the shore. Check-clothed tables with ill-assorted wooden chairs faced the bay. Each table had a small glass lantern, glowing amber with lit candles. The air was heavy with jasmine. Cicadas hissed their hypnotic racket.

They both wore cool cotton shirts and shorts. Guy had liberally splashed on some Armani after-shave, Vivienne, her travel-sized Dior. They grinned openly at each other. They were being naughty and they both knew it.

The Cypriot waiter took their order: the full *mezze* – a huge oval plate bearing calamari, prawns, lobster, langoustine, oysters and three different sorts of crab. The chef had surrounded the dishes with wet seaweed. Vivienne even spotted some tiny, live winkles clinging to the shiny brown sea plant.

'You'd think the whole lot has just come out of the sea this very moment!' Vivienne said, tackling her prawns. Guy ordered red wine. It arrived in a brown stone jug with two matching goblets.

Vivienne tasted her wine, her body mellowing in the evening sun. She watched Guy eat his food, a sky, darkening to magenta behind him. They heard the sea gently drawing out and then returning with a swish of sapphire tide.

Across the flickering glass lantern, in a split-second, each caught the other's eye. All the years – all the longings – were there, Vivienne knew, for Guy to read. Returning to their meal, they ate quietly. Each time they looked up, the same understanding played between them.

Finishing, thanking the waiter, paying the bill, Vivienne reached out for Guy's hand. It was warm, sending the same surge of desire through her that it always had.

Vivienne became aware that her voice would expose her need, 'Shall we...' she tried to steady it '...ask them to let us have some champagne – to take with us?'

A cork popped and the waiter returned with their bottle. Then Guy turned to Vivienne, saying, 'Come on, then.'

They left the Taverna. The night air warmed their legs, tanned and bare in their cotton shorts. Guy linked his arm into hers and, wordlessly, they began to run to the beach.

'This way,' Guy steered her toward a secluded cove. Soon enough, the Taverna disappeared from view. They could hear melodic Greek music: the bouzouki and soft male voices singing, drifting over the curved headland from where they now lay. Above them was the canopy of the night: like some sequinned gossamer silk, stretched clear across the black, velvet sky. The sand was a white powder underneath them. Wordlessly and straightaway, they took off their clothes. They lay, motionless at first, he on top of her, kissing open-mouthed. She rolled him over, then he the same, their mouths never left each other's. Soon their naked bodies were dipped in floury sand.

Looking down at themselves, Guy and Vivienne laughed into each other's sanded shoulders. She could feel his erection. Not for the first time the thought of being damned to Hades came to her. But infidelity? It didn't count, on holiday. Nothing did. Sleep, eat, drink, have sex. Holidays were a licence to leave all man-made rules behind. And Vivienne was on holiday – in remission from her demons. Let them all go to hell.

Guy surprised her. He was still a strong lover. He entered her as she pulled his heavy shoulders down over her full breasts. Vivienne bit the flesh on his salty neck, licking it better when he winced. He ran a demanding hand over her sanded hair.

Face to face, sitting up cross-legged, they shared the champagne, passing the bottle to each other. Then Guy stood the nearly emptied bottle in the sand. He pulled her up and led her into the sea. Silently, hand in hand, they waded into the warm waves that enveloped them in violet swathes.

Vivienne's hair streamed out as she floated on her back. She could see the stars: she could see Ariadne's crown of stars. Floating next to her, Guy washed seawater over her body, splashing her face, teasing her.

Then they clung to each other, managing to keep afloat, entwining their legs around. Vivienne felt Guy enter her. She clung to him, holding him closer and closer to her. He wound himself around her so tightly she felt close to swooning.

Afterwards, panting, they lay back, flopping onto the soft sand. A night breeze slowly blew them dry. When they dressed and finished the last drops of champagne, Guy kissed her, brushing his mouth over her nose and eyes. Still, after all this time, Vivienne's senses welcomed him, received him into her, accepted his caresses. She wanted no one else.

'Guy, what now? Whatever must we do?' Vivienne hugged him close to her.

'Try to live our lives, I suppose, little Vivvy, as best we can,' Guy brushed away a strand of untidy hair from her eyes. 'Take what we can while we can,' he said quietly.

'So you are like Pisces, aren't you?' Vivienne said, faintly. 'Always swimming in two directions.' And then, as she felt the inevitable, familiar withdrawing of Guy – away from her, she wanted it settled. Was he swimming back to Guernsey? Would they – could they – become anything more? She knew, though, that if she asked he wouldn't reply: he would be evasive. Maybe couldn't say? More than likely he didn't have any answers.

Still promising he would think about coming to Guernsey, promising he wouldn't drink as much, Vivienne left Guy in his Cyprus home. As she left, the dark-haired man on the arched terrace of the white box villa, on the carob tree hill, looked smaller and smaller. Then Vivienne couldn't see Guy properly as the olive trees got in the way.

On the plane back home, David, in his pale blue sweater and pale blue denims, looked as though he was about to nod off.

'So?' Vivienne quizzed him lightly, unbuckling her safety belt, taking a flight magazine from the net in front of her. 'So, Catherine? Banked fires? Hidden depths?'

'A lady,' David said drowsily, peering at Vivienne inscrutably through half-closed blue eyes, 'of extraordinary qualities. The only real lady I ever met.' His smile drew a firm line.

'And?' Vivienne pressed him.

'Cyprus,' David said thoughtfully, 'has given me something I thought I would never have – it's a once in a lifetime.' Then, as the pilot dimmed the lights, David's head dropped back as he fell fast asleep.

But Vivienne stayed fully awake in the throbbing, muffled cabin. She watched the shifting clouds, obscuring the earth, far below. She glanced at David as he slept. There was a French belief: 'Everyone is entitled to their secret garden.' She'd let him be.

As Vivienne left Cyprus behind, as the miles distanced her from Guy, the well-known feelings crept back and threatened to overwhelm her. Yet, instinctively, she felt something more than that: something different. Something was moving out of her life. It was slipping from her hands into an infinity where she could not follow. She sensed a kind of harm in the air. Perhaps, as she recalled Matthias' words, she may be learning to defend?

CHAPTER TWENTY-FIVE

Two years, almost to the day of his wedding, Joseph, his face fixed white with dismay, stood in La Colette's conservatory. He had phoned Vivienne and David, asking if he could come and see them. He had something to tell them.

Outside, rain swept across the gardens. Raindrops scattered over the conservatory roof. Vivienne put her hand out, to hold her son's. Joseph's hand was icy cold.

'Darling! Whatever is it? What's the matter?' She scanned his face, taking his wet jacket from him.

'Do you want,' his voice was deadly serious, cracked and hopeless, 'the bad news or the really bad news?'

'Natalie?' Vivienne asked, instantly.

'She's left me, Ma,' Joseph broke down, 'she's gone off to London! And, Ma,' he cried now like a child, his cheeks shone white and streaked with tears, 'she's pregnant with our baby!'

'Oh God,' Vivienne sat down heavily on a wicker chair. 'David! David! Come quickly!'

When he heard the news, David put his arms around Joseph, 'Oh my Lord! Son, whatever has happened? What is this all about?' He held Joseph close to his chest.

Joseph took off his glasses, wiping his cheeks with his hand, 'I haven't got a bloody clue.'

'Well – well, what did she say?' Vivienne put her arms around them both. 'She can't just walk out!'

'She has, Ma. She's packed and gone.' He started to weep again, sitting down on the floor. Rain spilled in great rattling flurries over the conservatory windows.

'David. David, get us some whisky. It's all right Joseph, sweetheart. Tell us exactly what Natalie said. I don't understand this. I spoke to her only a few days ago. We were going to go shopping tomorrow, for goodness sake!'

David returned with the whisky and glasses then sat in a chair opposite them. 'We are in our fifties. We should be having some peace and quiet. I was thinking of working less…this is dreadful. It is dreadful.'

As they drank from their tumblers, Joseph told them that Natalie said she simply found life with him too boring. He was too much like David. She didn't want Vivienne's dull life, thanks very much.

'Charming!' Vivienne retorted. 'No wonder I couldn't get close to the girl, if that's what she thought. Silly little thing. What does she know? And what did she expect from marriage? Excitement? That's not happiness.'

'That's not helping, Ma. Natalie won't be told what to do or what to think.' Joseph looked desperate.

And,' Vivienne suddenly recalled, 'she's pregnant? How far gone?' She felt a sick, ominous dread rising from her heart into her throat.

'Just a week or so. It's the pregnancy that seems to have made her mind up to leave. She said she was going away – to think.' Joseph knocked back his whisky.

'To think? Think about what?' Vivienne shot David a fearful glance. He returned it with a look of disbelieving horror.

'Well I don't bloody well know! What the fucking hell does any woman think about anything? I'm beginning to think I haven't got the first idea!' Joseph railed. 'I thought we were happy,' he cried, 'everything seemed to be alright – in bed, you know, everything…' A blush crept up his neck, spreading across his cheeks.

Poor Joseph. Vivienne remembered how Eustace had asked them just that. She and David had never been 'good in bed', but here they still were.

Vivienne held him to her, stroking his hair, as Joseph sobbed. He put his glasses back on and blew his nose. 'I thought we were getting on alright. We were going on holiday, to Brittany. It's having a baby. It seems to have thrown her.'

'Well, maybe her hormones are all over the place, darling. Some women get really peculiar, honestly. Ask Auntie Polly.' As the news began to penetrate, Vivienne realized that they were talking about a potential grandchild. A chill of alarm prickled her skin. God, she must talk to Natalie. She must.

'I'll go over to London. Anyway why is she in London?' Vivienne already began to plan the trip. She'd stay with Jocelyn. Jocelyn and Enrico would help. And so would Matthias...she would phone them all.

'No, no. Please don't Ma. It'll only make Natalie more determined to do her own thing. I know her – well I thought I knew her. She's stubborn and defiant. If she's crossed...well then she gets even more determined.'

'Well, what are you going to do, son?' David asked flatly.

'Do? I don't know. She wants to sell the flat. It only happened a day or so ago. But I guess...well I guess I'll have to come back here – at least for a while. Can I? For a start?'

'Of course! Of course!' Vivienne and David said at once, and together.

'So, she's been planning this, then? She has already said she wants to sell the flat? Scheming little monkey!' Vivienne's temper flew out of her control. 'Little madam! With her life all tidy and exactly how she wants it – hurting my son, running off with our grandchild! I do want to see her Joseph. I've got one or two things I would like to say to the little cat!'

'Now, don't start getting yourself in a state,' David said, maddeningly calm. 'Listen to what Joseph is saying, Vivienne. He's right. It won't do any good ranting at Natalie. No. We'll have to think rationally about what to do. Alienating Natalie is not going to help. She must be feeling isolated and lonely, as it is. Let's all think rationally about this, okay?'

'Oh, it's alright for you to be so bloody rational...so unemotional.' But Vivienne did see the sense in what David said. She took deep breaths, to steady her heartbeats and quietened down. She moved into the kitchen. 'I was just starting supper, darling, you'll stay?'

'Thanks Ma. I feel lonely and isolated too, you know.'

'Course you do,' Vivienne kissed him, 'you don't deserve this, you really don't.'

'I dunno so much, Ma,' Joseph said miserably, 'takes two to tango, doesn't it?'

'Just you remember that this child is yours as well. She can't just go off and live in London. Why we'd... you'd never see it!' Vivienne drained some peas in a sieve, then began mashing up steamed potatoes with butter and a little milk.

David came into the kitchen, opening a bottle of wine. Joseph set the table, automatically, without being asked. Then he said, 'I haven't mentioned up until now Ma, but...well, Natalie is talking about whether to keep it or not.'

Vivienne dropped the bowl of cooked potato onto the floor, where it crashed and broke. David fetched a dustpan and brush, scooping up the broken china and steaming mash, saying nothing.

Taking some pasta from the cupboard, David put a saucepan of water on the hob to boil. All the while he watched Vivienne.

Vivienne felt pain seizing her. Natalie really couldn't do this to them. 'So that is why she's in London?' It seemed like a block of ice had formed around her.

The men sat down and began their meal. Vivienne stood, unable to eat, drinking her wine. She held the wine glass so tightly that David slid his eyes over it in alarm.

Well, if it breaks, Vivienne thought, too bad. It will be in smithereens, won't it? Just like her life had suddenly become.

'Do sit down, Vivienne. You are doing yourself no good at all. Come on, now, sit down.' David kicked a chair away from the table so it was ready for her to sit on.

Still, she couldn't sit down nor face the meal. 'Didn't you see any of this coming, Joseph? Have any idea? Weren't there any signs?'

'One or two, looking back,' Joseph's eyes moistened as he ate his food slowly and deliberately. 'A couple of times...you know, our friends hinted Natalie wasn't, well, happy. We've both found it difficult to settle back in Guernsey. I've been working really long

hours, for a long time. I'd take work home at the weekends as well
as the evenings.'

'But she works as well,' Vivienne replied, 'she told me. Natalie
works weekends and evenings as well! That's not a reason to leave
someone, surely?'

'I don't know, Ma. Maybe I didn't take enough notice of her –
she's so full of vitality, always on the go, bags of energy.' Joseph
pushed his plate away, placed his elbows on the table and held his
head with his hands. 'She likes "girly evenings out" – you know.
God knows what they talk about. And she's had one or two weekends
away: that pop concert, Paris? Maybe I've just let her drift…we've
drifted – Oh Christ!' He began to sob. Great gulping cries tailed off
gradually into a hiccupping silence.

'Well, I don't know, Joseph. But like you said, it takes two to
tango and Natalie has to take some responsibility for all this mess.
Do you think she'll come back to you?' Vivienne fumed. What the
hell did Natalie think she was playing at ? Girly nights off? Weekends
away? How dare she treat her Joseph like that? She hadn't worked
at her marriage. Vivienne's mind raced ahead. Yes, she'd make those
calls tomorrow, whatever Joseph said. If Natalie Beaufort thought
she could just go ahead and decide whether or not to carry Joseph's
child, with or without his permission, or Vivienne's or David's –
well she would just have to think again. Vivienne would get hold
of Guy, as well. What did he, a Catholic, have to say about all this?
Mmm? Did he know about it? Did he even care? No, he's probably
too drunk to care about anything! He hadn't even remembered where
his daughter had met Vivienne's son! And she'd contact Muriel Le
Croix and Edward and Jean. They were all involved, for God's sake.
Natalie – Vivienne stiffened – Natalie, my girl, you have a fight on
your hands.

When Vivienne told Polly, she commiserated. Her son Greg
was getting married next year. She feared for him. His girlfriend,
said Polly, was a right little clever-clogs, earning a fortune in one
of the banks. She had a string of qualifications. They were going to
have a huge mortgage. But there was no telling them. So, yes, Polly

understood. Thank God, she said, her daughter Kim was a home bird. She'd done domestic science, cookery, at school and was going into catering.

'These liberated girls, kiddo, they won't put up with things, same as we did at their age. No way. They'll put up with nothing!'

Upon hearing the news, Muriel Le Croix blamed the Carrés, especially Vivienne. Edward blamed the Beauforts, and especially Vivienne.

Guy said he'd lost his faith years ago but would be coming over to Guernsey. He wanted to see his daughter. He was now seriously considering life on the island. Catherine had sold Zephyr Villa and had been surprisingly generous toward him. So Guy had a little cash now and Natalie said she'd sell the flat to him at a reasonable cost – seeing as he was her father.

'It just gets worse and worse!' Livid red, Vivienne told Joseph. 'Now she's involving you with legal property rights! I certainly underestimated your wife, Joseph. Someone once told me she was hard and I denied it. But they were right, weren't they?'

Joseph, still looking miserably in love with Natalie, merely nodded. He said his life had gone pear-shaped overnight. He was back at La Colette. He told Vivienne that the family life with the girl of his dreams – all he yearned for – was gone. Joseph plunged himself into more work, spending hours in his attic study, looking, Vivienne found, paler and thinner by the day.

As if, Vivienne considered, things weren't complicated enough, Jean died. Vivienne had noticed that Jean was even less worldly aware than usual of late. She had retired to her rooms at Granville more and more. In her late seventies, she seemed to have just given up.

The funeral was held at the Vale parish church, on a hill overlooking the meadows, the pond and L'Islet bay. As she walked in the funeral cortege, Vivienne glanced over from the brow of the hill, to the view of the fields, imagining her brother playing all around there when he was a little boy. And she pictured Jean running to meet Oscar now, arms open, and taking his hand to pick wildflowers with him in the meadow's long grasses, so at last together, they entered into an untroubled peace.

Edward said he wasn't surprised at Jean's death. He himself was getting tired. He thought he would leave Granville. Now that Jean had passed on, it was time to do something about moving. Anyway, Jean's brothers and their families had been patient enough for all these years. They wanted their share of the inheritance which, Edward said, was fair enough.

Granmarie and Charles's day, when Guernsey family houses and land passed intact to the children, was all but over. Jean's brothers would get a tidy profit from the sale of Granville. And, anyway, Edward had quite other plans for his future.

Vivienne went down to Granville in an attempt to pay her respects for Edward's loss. The orchards were still full of fruit trees, though the tomato crops were much reduced. Vivienne reminisced: there was still some fruit produced on the island but Guernsey's finance sector had taken off. The island, so Joseph concluded, was a globally important centre for banking, insurance, trusts, pensions and the like. As Polly had ruefully reckoned, all the young people were practically guaranteed jobs. Vivienne's little Guernsey was attracting financial professionals – people from all over the world.

'So,' Vivienne said, as they strolled around the vinery, 'my uncles are going to sell?'

Edward, skinny-limbed and white-haired, walked with a stick. He shook his loose-jowled head. 'Yes. You can see Nin – it's all too much for us now. Granville will fetch a good price. Someone will do it up. It's the land as much as anything. I expect it'll all go as building plots or flats or something.'

'Yes. It's a shame, but of course, put it on the market. Get a bungalow – much easier to run.' Vivienne found talking to him, without Jean around, awkward. At least Jean would have interrupted the silences with her chatter, however vague. 'So, what do you think about Joseph, then? About Natalie? Her being pregnant and talking about an abortion?'

It was as though Vivienne had poked a stick at a heaving hive.

Lowering his brows, Edward glared at her. 'Well, I'm not getting worked up about it, like you are. It's not formed yet, is it? Why shackle poor young Joseph up with a child he'll hardly see? And no doubt he'd have to support if that Beaufort girl stays in London? No, I can see getting rid of it as an answer, Nin, tell the truth… I told you, didn't I? Those darned Beauforts are nothing but trouble.'

So surprised, Vivienne stopped in her tracks. A lorry drove noisily into the yard, sending off dust, petrol and exhaust fumes. Then they moved away from the vehicle and the yard, back toward the house.

'Dad! You a Christian! What about the moral side?'

Vivienne waited, not breathing.

Edward frowned at her blackly, with hooded eyes, 'That's not the point, Nin. Abortion is legal now, girls aren't even damned now if they have bastards. There isn't the same shame on the family.'

Incensed, Vivienne snapped, 'as a Christian I thought you would say that termination was immoral, even if it was legal!'

Coolly, Edward said, 'Let's say, I'd never have forgiven you if you had a child out of wedlock and shamed us.' Edward's cheek mottled red. 'We brought you up properly, with Christian morals. We wanted you to marry a man who expected… an unsullied wife.' He opened the back door, gesturing with his walking stick for Vivienne to go in. She declined.

'That's it then? It was my fault for having normal teenage desires?' As she stood there, Vivienne recalled when she lived at Granville. From where she was she could see her old bedroom window. She remembered counting the days on the calendar, alone, all those years ago. Consuming regret stole over her. She had terminated her love-child because of what the neighbours might think. Yet now, her father agreed that an abortion was an accepted convenience, after all. 'Shame? What about your shame – what about you and Edna Jones all those times behind Mum's back?'

Edward shook his stick at her, shouting, 'Don't you talk to me like that!'

'Yes, damn old Ma Jones! How can you preach to me about morality? What about you and your deception and lies? You are a hypocrite, Dad.'

Spluttering viciously Edward said, 'Don't you dare bring Edna Jones into this! You've made a cock-up of Joseph's life – all that drinking and throwing yourself into the sea! You have been nothing, nothing, Nin, but a disappointment to me. Don't you ever forget that!'

'I never have.' Vivienne's arms fell to her side. 'I have never forgotten anything about living at Granville.' Then Vivienne raised her voice above Edward's protests. 'I wasn't Oscar – how could I be? But I am strong in spite of you.'

'Huh! Daubings. They don't mean a thing to me. Oscar would have been a son to be proud of.'

Vivienne breathed deeply to steady her voice, 'I knew,' she said, still shaking, 'from when I was nine that you resented my talent. Resented my being alive, even.'

'Oh, bugger off,' Edward backed toward the door. 'You and your creativity and dopey, dreamy ways. I never know what the hell you're on about!'

'Good luck. Dad. You'll need it, what with all your disappointment and conscience. Okay for you to sin was it? As long as nobody found out?'

Then Edward faced her full on and fired his wounding bullet: a practiced crack shot. 'Conscience is it? Conscience, eh? Look at your own, my girl. You look to your own.'

Suddenly Vivienne froze and stared back at her father. 'You mean – you knew? You knew, all along I was pregnant? But you never tried to help me?'

'Of course I knew. Why should I help you? You got yourself into it, you got yourself out of it. You didn't need me. You never listened to me. I had to protect Jean, I had to protect your poor mother. Why should I have bloodied my hands with your wicked, carnal sins?'

'Bloodied your hands? You left me to bear all that on my own just so you could say you didn't know – didn't have anything to do with an unwanted child? I was your daughter. I was your child.'

Edward looked so hard at Vivienne, with such naked contempt, it made her step back with fear. But he said nothing more. Instead, he turned and went, without looking back, into the house, slamming the door shut behind him.

Vivienne ran then, clambered into her car, slamming her foot down on the accelerator, to put as much distance, as fast as she could between her and Granville.

As she covered the miles, driving toward her home at La Colette, the tide of rage against Edward gradually fell into a running stream. Along the coast road to home, Vivienne wound down the sea-spattered car window seeing the beaches where she had played and swam as a little girl. Today the sand and rocks were swept over with a green but uneasy, rolling sea. Clouds on the horizon filled with grey rain blowing across the sky in a misty silence. Vivienne felt the cold haze enter her spirit, blurring her vision.

CHAPTER TWENTY-SIX

Joseph let Vivienne into the flat. He wanted to clear out some of his things. It was dusty, but still clean and tidy. Natalie had extricated herself so efficiently she might never have been there.

Seeing the cream leather couch, where Natalie had curled up with her mug of green tea once, Vivienne felt sorrow. On the windowsill the expensive scented candles sat: the black wicks looked mournful, waiting to be lit again.

There was food to be thrown out. Vivienne took a plastic sack and began throwing out of date microwaveable cartons into it. There were half empty jars of tapanade. She drained olive and caper jars into the sink, adding them to a box for recycling.

'This is just gross,' Joseph sighed. 'The sooner we sell the flat, the better.' He folded some shirts into a suitcase and put shoes into boxes.

'Joseph. What a real shame,' Vivienne said. 'I do sympathise, darling. I really, really did think you and Natalie would make it. What with your *coup de foudre* and everything.'

'Looks like your Titian and his myths isn't always right, eh Ma?'

'No, Titian was mortal, just like the rest of us. I just hope all this is for the best. Maybe…maybe you and Natalie would have been unhappy, trying to stick it out – oh, I don't know.' Vivienne sighed.

'You did, didn't you?' Joseph stacked some books into a cardboard box, 'stuck it out, you and Dad? I always felt that it was me that held you together, though. 'I'm sticking plaster on their marriage!' I used to say.'

Vivienne whirled round, 'You used to say that? You used to feel that?'

'You weren't that happy with Dad, were you – when you were younger – when you were drinking?'

Her face heated with hot blood. Red-faced. Vivienne blurted, 'You never said anything, Joseph!'

'I did. I did Ma! You were always on some spaced out planet. Don't get me wrong. I liked you being different from other mums and you were – you still are – such a pretty lady. Just like your Ariadne you always went on about.'

'I did?'

'Ma, don't you remember any of this?' Joseph stopped stacking the books and went over to Vivienne, where she wrapped ornaments in bubble-wrap.

'Not every detail, no,' she felt winded, 'you make me sound like a complete air-head.'

'You were! Look, it isn't important, now. We've got too much else to worry about. Anyway, it wasn't all your fault. Dad…he should have shown far more…oomph!'

'Oomph?'

'You know, taken you out more, travelled, taken a bit of interest in the arts himself, maybe. You were obviously not cut out to be a housewife, now were you? Still aren't!' Joseph grinned at her lovingly.

'Possibly not,' she felt defensive, 'and I don't know that Guernsey men have 'Oomph'. They have…they are strong and honourable, though. You'd want a Guernseyman next to you in battle. They stick to their guns; have comradeship and loyalty. Comes from being an islander, I suppose. Eustace – now he was a wonderful friend. He understood me.'

'Am I like that?' asked Joseph.

'Course you are.'

'What, strong but oomphless?'

They both burst out laughing. 'There are worse things to be, darling!'

'Well, I love grandpa Eustace, too. But then you see he married the right person. Grandma Pearl, she was born to be a housewife, she…'

Yes, alright, alright, Joseph. Don't push it, I've got the bloody message!' said Vivienne, both irritated and aggrieved. Things 'weren't all her fault'. What was that supposed to mean? So she said, 'So, do you think you are like your father, Joseph? That, maybe, you should have gone along with some of the things Natalie found important?'

'Yeh.' Joseph Sellotaped his cardboard box thoughtfully. 'Yeah, yeah. Maybe I do. Mind you, I think Dad is great. He's been a fantastic father.'

'He has,' Vivienne agreed. 'But good fathers don't always make good husbands.' She was reluctant to give David all the damned parental laurels. What? Whilst she herself has been some kind of bohemian gypsy, wafting in and out of Joseph's life, high as a kite? It hadn't been as bad as that. Had it?

Trouble was, Vivienne needed a drink. And there was the increasingly worrying fact that Joseph might not even be allowed to be a father – good or bad. They finished their packing for the time being and left the flat.

Joseph gave Vivienne a spare key. She promised to pop back later and do the final clean. There were still a few remaining things to clear away.

The La Colette sitting room was peaceful but Vivienne sat in a mull, fretting how time was passing and they hadn't heard a peep from Natalie. The pregnancy must be some weeks now and Natalie still had not confided in Vivienne, nor asked for her advice.

Lately images of her own new-born baby and the woman doctor had begun to appear in Vivienne's waking hours as well as her sleeping. In their frequency the doctor's face frightened her with its macabre distortion: grotesque and inhuman.

As for Natalie – Vivienne would appeal to David. They simply must do something. Or she'd go mad: become unhinged with inactivity. It wasn't sane, was it, to have such terrifying – what? Hallucinations?

Up in her studio, Vivienne looked out at the view and drank from her glass. The landscape she started had not been touched for days. Surely there was something constructive she could do?

Apparently, Vivienne next discovered, through Jocelyn this time,

Natalie had got all the medical agreements she needed. She awaited an appointment in a London clinic before finally setting a date.

When Vivienne asked her, Jocelyn wondered how much help she could be. It was not strictly her – well, not even Vivienne's business, was it? Jocelyn said that kindly, but added that the situation wasn't the same as it had been for Vivienne. And wasn't Natalie, after all, her own woman?

But, Vivienne was relieved that, in at least an attempt to help, to leave doors open, Jocelyn invited Natalie to visit her Alternative Clinic. She gave her some free treatments: a Facial and Complimentary Manicure. Jocelyn told Vivienne that both she and Enrico had grown fond of Natalie. She said, obviously, Natalie looked strained. She wasn't taking the situation lightly, if that was any consolation?

Enrico, Jocelyn reported, said that whilst Vivienne was a deep thinker of things, she was up against Natalie – a much harder do-er of things. He knew what the outcome would be. But he would not be persuaded by either Jocelyn or Vivienne to say what he thought that was. Natalie must make up her own mind.

'And you,' Enrico said when he phoned her, 'you, Vivvyon, have to make a vairy painful journey. Only you can do that. I must ask you to talk to Matthias. I urge you. Matthias will want to know about all of this.'

Indeed Enrico was right. Matthias certainly did want to know of the difficulties Vivienne faced: Natalie also. For, wasn't Natalie going through some decision – the same that Vivienne had had to? And she was on her own, with no Amanda to help her.

Matthias offered to come down to London. He suggested that Vivienne meet him there – as a kind of starting point? Vivienne must persuade the family that she had to see Natalie. Then Matthias would help her from there on.

'Be strong, Baby. You are going to need to be very strong.'

Beating Vivienne to it, Natalie flew over to Guernsey. 'Just for a couple of days. To sort out my bits and pieces – the legalities and so on.'

Taking a chance, Vivienne went to the flat. She knew Natalie was there. She let herself in.

'Vivienne,' Natalie rounded on her, anger stiffening her slim frame, 'this does happen to be my private space.' The flat was nearly empty now. Their voices echoed around the pastel-coloured walls that Natalie had so carefully decorated with abstract stencils. The view from the picture window was still sunny, lending a bright, curtainless light.

'Natalie. I'm not here to cause trouble. Really, I'm not.' Natalie was still her daughter-in-law, with her wide, anxious brown eyes, face paler and drawn but body still slender. Except Vivienne saw the undeniable slight swell under pin-striped trousers. Natalie wore a white, polo-necked sweater. Her black hair was cut to chin level so it swung in a thick, glossy sheaf as she moved and spoke.

'So what have you come for, then?' Natalie folded her arms. There were just two easy chairs left in the room. They both sat down. Natalie wore no shoes. A navy holdall spread open on the floor.

Vivienne had pinned her gold frizz back in a French pleat. She wore a loose print blouse over blue denims. The two of them sat opposite each other. Vivienne longed to take the younger woman's hand in hers, to comfort her.

Defiantly, Natalie lit a Rothman's cigarette, shooting a hostile stare at Vivienne.

'Should you be smoking...?' Then Vivienne bit her lip.

Natalie glared at her, taking a long, deep draw of the cigarette, 'I want to. Next question?'

'It's just...just that,' Vivienne stumbled in tension, 'just I want you to be...quite sure of what your options are. No, please, don't look at me like that, Natalie. After all, you are still Joseph's wife. I do have a right...', Lord, this was not going well.

'Listen, Vivienne,' Natalie coughed in the smoky, empty room, 'you do not have a right to come here, to my house and interfere.' She got up and opened the window, flicking ash outside where it blew away like the remains of a cremated body.

Vivienne shuddered. Joseph was quite right. Confronting Natalie was not the answer. She would become entrenched in her own opinion.

Vivienne thought hard. She would have to try a quite different tack if she wasn't going to be counter-productive.

'I can fully understand you not wanting to be a single parent. Believe me, I can.'

'Of course you can't!' Natalie snapped at her. 'You've got your country house, your boring David. He lets you get away with murder! You have had a long marriage. You, Vivienne, you can't possibly understand how I feel!'

Fearful, lest the fragile contact with Natalie severed too soon, Vivienne tried hard to sound calm and rational. 'Abortion may be legal now, Natalie. But, but the...consequences are no less... destructive than when it was illegal, in my day.'

'So?' Natalie crushed her cigarette out on the outside wall of the window, reaching a long arm to the outer sill. 'So, now it is legal. So I can do what I decide to. What's with you, Vivienne? Suddenly the all-caring mother-in-law? What's behind this? If I need advice I'll ask my father, thank you. I'm surprised you haven't mentioned him yet. You usually seem only to keen to bring him into the conversation. Guy, precious Guy! I mean you are hardly a role model for stable upbringing of a child within a marriage are you?' Natalie's dark eyes glinted at Vivienne through slits of accusation.

'Don't be so bitter to me, Natalie. Don't be so angry with me. You can say these things to me – probably I do deserve it. But this...this baby...'

'Foetus,' Natalie said, bluntly.

'Potential baby,' Vivienne didn't waver, and she detected a tiredness in Natalie's voice. 'It is more than a blob, you know. Look, we'll help you to bring it up – if that's the problem. If you don't want to be a single parent. I can understand that. You want to get on with your life – without Joseph. I can even understand that, too. I can, honestly. But once the baby is gone – well, it's gone forever.'

'Christ! Don't you think I realise that? You don't understand. I don't want part of Joseph growing inside me. Get it? I don't want to play happy bloody families with Joseph and you and David and all your fucking clan! It's me that will have to carry it. My life that'll be held back. I want to move on, Vivienne. I want a complete break.'

Tearful, Vivienne reached out and held the struggling woman. Natalie resisted her, trying to wriggle away from her. 'I think,' Vivienne said softly, 'you could still be friends with Joseph, Natalie. And with me. You don't hate him. I know you don't. What if you end up hating yourself?'

'Don't be so melodramatic, Vivienne! For pity's sake. One sex act and I'm bound to the Carrés forever more? Forget it!'

Natalie wrenched away from her, knelt down to her navy holdall and began stuffing clothes into it. The zip stuck: a pair of navy tights caught in the zip teeth. Natalie tried to tear the tights away.

'Here,' Vivienne knelt down beside Natalie, to help her. They both pulled at the tights, eventually easing them away so that Natalie could finish the zip and close her bag. Vivienne ached for her. She looked so vulnerable: so young and proud. Was Natalie so proud she couldn't take advice from an older woman who was past it? From some old bag who did not understand the modern world?

Her voice hushed, Vivienne said, 'It's just, Natalie, don't let pride – don't let society push you into a decision you haven't had time to think through, darling. Yes, of course you have your whole life ahead of you. Don't let it be full of regret.'

To Vivienne's surprise, Natalie didn't move away from her this time. For a second she let Vivienne hold her. As they stood up, Vivienne could feel the rotund swell of Natalie's pregnancy against her own womb. At this moment Vivienne prayed silently and deeply. She used all the strength she had to wish for the life of the baby, for Natalie, for Joseph and, for that matter, Vivienne considered, the whole of unloved humankind.

Guy breezed over to Guernsey, plonked himself, fully at home, in Natalie and Joseph's empty flat and promptly phoned Vivienne.

'I feel full of the joys of spring.' When she asked how he was. 'Why not? I've the flat and a bit of money to jingle and Guernsey is a beautiful place to live. What's not to like, eh? C'est la vie, Vivvy, c'est la vie!'

'That bloody man is impossible,' David groaned. 'He's still drinking, I suppose?'

Vivienne spotted Guy out shopping in St Peter Port, going in to one of the supermarkets. He had put on a bit more weight. Guy strolled about the shop, filling his trolley with ready-made meals. Vivienne watched him, thinking how she preferred to shop in the local parish stores. Family-run, bringing over Welsh lamb and Orkney beef, stocking freshly caught local crabs and lobsters, brought in by Guernsey fishermen. You could buy bread, baked that morning in St Malo.

Yes, Vivienne must tell Guy about the shops that sold locally grown food. Alderney and Sark butter; Herm oysters and people took in their home-grown herbs and salad things; pellet-shot rabbits and game birds. In spring there'd be Jersey Royal potatoes that Vivienne liked to cook with grilled Guernsey mackerel and garden peas. Yes, she must cook something for Guy.

They grew all their own vegetables. David wanted to do as Eustace had always done. They had tried to interest Joseph but had no luck so far, he being so busy with his architect's career.

Not satisfied that he had merely 'lost his faith' and that was that, Vivienne asked Guy if she could meet him. Did he want her to cook for him sometime? Surely he wanted to help his daughter? What about Joseph and her splitting up – what about the pregnancy?

'Sure. Okay,' Guy yawned. 'Although I don't think anything I say will persuade Natalie, one way or the other.'

But Vivienne pursued him so much that he had to agree a meeting. Once she was in the flat, she noticed that Guy, along with the ready-made meals, had stocked the fridge with beers. He had bought some things over from Cyprus and purchased more furniture in Guernsey. 'Just enough, you know Vivvy, in case I want to entertain!' He laughed in satisfaction as, thoroughly annoyed at herself, she blushed.

And yes, the weight showed. Guy's neck and shoulders had grown heavier. His face was smoother. Still, Vivienne reckoned, Guy had kept enough of his good looks for any entertaining.

'You just don't change,' Guy slid measuring eyes all over her.

'Bit more trouble to cover the grey, though, eh? Getting a tad solid around the waist? But you have certainly kept those fiendish blue eyes, Vivvy!' He kissed a noisy 'Hello' on both her cheeks.

At least he didn't mention her ankles. 'I'm so worried about them splitting, Guy. It is heartbreaking to see Joseph looking so lost. And I'm not sure Natalie is as in control as she makes out.'

Guy nodded. 'I'm not completely without concern for them, Vivvy. I do talk to her. But she never tells me private, you know, intimate stuff. Never has. This is where we miss Amanda. Amanda would have sorted all this out.'

'Yes, I agree. I believe you're right. Amanda loved her daughter. Poor Amanda. We'll have to try and do what she would have done. What do you think Amanda would say about this…this,' how Vivienne hated the word 'termination'.

Guy kept wandering about the room. Vivienne had trouble keeping him on track. To her irritation, he started sifting through a stack of CDs.

'I don't know, Vivvy. This isn't something she could have envisaged is it? Natalie was just a little kid when Amanda died.' Eventually he stuck a Take That disc on the player.

'Whatever I said, whatever I did, I didn't mean it. Take me back, take me back again?'

Guy moved around the room, singing along with the words, grinning at her. His eyes were still the charming blackest of dark magic.

'Guy, you really are a dreadful flirt! What happened to Mozart and Cole Porter?' asked Vivienne.

'I like to keep up with the kids. Keeps me young. Still like all the other stuff, though: Miles Davis, Ella – you know.'

Then, curious, Vivienne asked, 'any more little maids around, Guy? Did you bring anyone with you to entertain? Or are you going to look around for some local…fancy?'

'Ahh!' Guy boomed, coming right up, looking at her face to face. 'Now, then, little Vivvy, that would be telling, now wouldn't it?' He put the sound of the music up louder, went to the fridge and opened a beer. 'Cheers!' He toasted Vivienne with the raised can, a wide smile and that devilish glint in his eyes.

CHAPTER TWENTY-SEVEN

Joseph went down to Granville to help his grandfather Edward Normandie with the move to his new bungalow. Joseph reported that the house was quite small, had two medium bedrooms and a box room. The lounge was about a quarter of the size of Granville's but there was an easily managed fitted kitchen diner and a neat and sunny conservatory. Edward could sit and look at the view over the grassy L'Ancresse common and the sea in the distance. It would suit him just fine, so Joseph said. Edna Jones had moved in. She would cook for them both and look after Edward.

Joseph told Vivienne he was, frankly, in no mood to judge anyone and popped down to see the old couple when he could. Sometimes he took some architect plans for Edward to see. Joseph said Edward always greeted him gladly and sang his praises to Edna, saying he was 'a really clever lad, like Oscar. Someone to be proud of.'

Muriel Le Croix told Vivienne Edward didn't know how lucky he was. That she rarely saw Natalie, her granddaughter. The girl was always busy when she was in Guernsey and spent far too much time in London. Muriel prayed for Natalie to keep the baby and was sorry about the whole affair: her leaving Joseph. But she wouldn't beg Natalie, just she hoped that, if she did have it, then she would bring it to see her: her great-grandchild, after all, Amanda's grandchild. Wasn't anyone guiding poor Natalie?

Muriel did tell Vivienne though, that she thought she was doing her best and Guy was useless. She missed her dearest Amanda ever more each day and had never got over her passing. Amanda's father was gone now, too, but she had her friends from the various clubs she belonged to and the Day Centre. At least, Muriel said, she had some small comforts.

Feeling it was crucial to keep in touch, Vivienne took to phoning

Natalie. She didn't always reply. Natalie had taken a rented apartment, close to Jocelyn and Enrico in Putney. Vivienne thought that, if she kept things fresh in all their minds, then time wouldn't keep slipping by so dangerously fast.

She wanted Joseph to keep his lines of communication open with Natalie as well. He should try to see her. Surely the split need not be so drastic? So final? Some of their young friends and work people kept asking after the both of them.

It got so that, once, when Natalie had flitted over to Guernsey to finish her move, Vivienne arranged a girly evening at La Colette. Sitting in the midst of them she joined in the chatter. Joseph was sent off to his attic den with the boys. Vivienne opened chilled bottles of Chardonnay and put out canapés, bought from the supermarket, not made by her, on the kitchen table for everyone to dig in. She played Madonna music and agreed Hugh Grant was good arm candy – had charm in spades. So, you see, Natalie? Vivienne wasn't completely out of touch.

Taking her aside, Vivienne said, 'Natalie, we do care about you. It's not just about the, the... We – I – want you to know, Natalie, that we love you. We do. I know now your marriage is over, but you are not nothing to us. Oh, I probably sound like an interfering old cow and you think David is a boring old fart – but we offer you help. We want to. We really do.'

But Natalie shrank away from Vivienne and looked uncomfortable. 'Things have been said…things have been done…I'm sorry Vivienne.' Then Natalie upped and left the party.

The days passed with fear and foreboding. Soon, Vivienne dreaded, Natalie would have the abortion. It didn't seem that she could do any more – let alone remotely begin to prepare for Natalie's final decision.

Meantime, she kept visiting Guy: a two-pronged attack. Each time she talked about Natalie and Joseph, pressing him to listen. At times he seemed to hear her, sometimes he had obviously been drinking. Vivienne still had Joseph's key. Guy never asked for it back.

Then, Vivienne thought she might ask Sonia if she knew of anyone who could clean the flat for Guy? Would he like that? And Vivienne asked him if he would like to go to a concert with her? The St James concert hall had been established and thrived since Guy last lived in Guernsey.

'We have all the big names coming here: Ronnie Scott, Andrew Lloyd-Webber, Jose Carréras...'

'I had heard,' said Guy. 'We'll see, Viv.'

One day, to get him away from his bottles, Vivienne arranged a day trip for them: to Herm. The little sandy island looked perfect in the shimmering sunshine. After climbing up the steep, white harbour steps, Guy at once suggested they might get a drink.'

On the way to the Mermaid Inn, they passed The White House Hotel looking colonial with its wooden balcony and green palm trees. Its garden flourished with the scent of exotic flowers.

'Great place for a weekend?' Guy gave Vivienne a broad grin.

'Would be, yes.' She smiled back. Guy still thought of her like that? Well, well! He was undeniably bigger, yes, but still attractive in his navy blue Guernsey and jeans. How would it be to hold him again...?

'Vivienne?' enquired a woman's voice.

Guy had popped in to the gift shop to buy cigarettes. Vivienne had stayed outside, looking at postcards with her straw hat tipped over to shade her face from the sun.

'It's Jessie,' said the woman eagerly.

Vivienne wouldn't have recognised her. Thinner still than she had been at Joseph's wedding, Jessie wore her hair coloured a lifeless black, tied back into a pony-tail. Her simple white sheath dress showed arms that were brown, but not the tan of lying in the sun – more that she worked outdoors. Her eyes were still heavily emphasised with black eyeliner. 'And this is my son.'

A handsome lad, probably in his twenties, black-haired with wide-apart brown eyes, shook hands with Vivienne.

'And you're...?'

'Adam,' he said in a pleasant, deep voice. He put a strong, protective arm around his mother's shoulders.

'Hi, Adam. Nice to meet you. Well, Jessie – haven't seen you for ages. Not since the wedding. You know Joseph and Natalie have split up, do you?' Vivienne didn't mention the pregnancy.

Jessie sympathised and asked how things were. How was David? How was Vivienne's painting going? Did she remember all the gang from the *Guernsey Post*? They chattered on. Adam hopped from foot to foot, looking impatiently at his fashionably cheap plastic watch from time to time.

Guy came out of the shop with his cigarettes, then dipped back in again. He must have forgotten something, Vivienne thought, possibly a lighter? Guy was forever losing lighters.

Jessie followed Vivienne's glance. 'Sorry, are you with someone? We're holding you up?'

They could see Guy through the shop window, buying what appeared to be a brightly coloured scarf.

'Well then,' Jessie said, linking arms with Adam. 'Better be off. Don't want to miss the boat back to Guernsey. See you sometime, Vivienne. Take care.' Then she left to catch the ferry, hurrying down over the pebbly hill toward Rosaire Harbour, some fifteen minutes walk away.

When he rejoined her, Vivienne asked, amused, 'What on earth are you going to do with a paisley silk scarf, Guy? Do a Noel Coward impression?'

'Just an impulse, Viv. You know me.'

A prickling of unease, the same she had sensed on the plane coming back from Cyprus, swept over Vivienne's skin. She felt this when storms were around: at the advent of a silent lightning flash before thunder – a crackle of electricity, a sharp tingle of her senses. Something was impending, perhaps a gale or a storm? Vivienne hoped that the sea wasn't going to be rough: rocking boats, disturbing people.

On the ferry back to Guernsey Vivienne could see the town: St Peter Port, rose in gentle tiers. Terraced white buildings stepped ever higher to ochre spires, rising to greet a cloudless sky.

Guy said the view always reminded him of some ports in the

Greek islands. They disembarked and climbed the slippery stone steps of the White Rock harbour. Vivienne breathed in the pungent salt-sea smell. Yachts from all over Europe jostled for space. As they parted, Guy promised, at Vivienne's insistent entreaty, to see her again, 'soon.'

Matthias had phoned. It was time for them to meet. Perturbed, Vivienne called him back straightaway. She wanted Matthias to meet Natalie. Surely, with his persuasive powers, Natalie would listen to Matthias?

Enrico repeated that he knew the outcome of Vivienne's troubles. Well, she just wished he would tell her what it was! Now Guy was back in Guernsey. Joseph was miserably unhappy – everything twisted all round and round in a tormented tangle.

Vivienne couldn't paint and David berated her for drinking too much because one evening she had fallen and cut her face. It was only a graze and healed quickly, but Vivienne knew, full well, thanks, that it could have been far worse. She could have sCarréd herself. Even Sonia had taken to giving Vivienne alarmed looks.

Matthias insisted that, 'of course' he would get down to London as soon as Vivienne wanted to meet her and Natalie. He had been waiting for her call. When Vivienne asked her, Natalie refused to see either of them in London or anywhere else. She wasn't to be summoned like some errant schoolgirl.

'I don't know exactly what you are scheming, Vivienne, but I can guess. And I can assure you that I will do as I feel right. In any case, I have got a date for the abortion now, if you really must know.'

Had she felt the foetus – the baby – move yet? Vivienne fretted, wildly tugging at and twisting her hair between her fingers. Had it quickened or was it still just growing steadily? Was it male or female: a little girl or a little boy? Did Natalie think about any of this?

Natalie told Vivienne that she wasn't going to discuss anything further with her. She said she was not going to talk about it anymore to anyone. She would continue part time as a supply teacher and work out a future for herself.

When she thought about the impending appointment, Vivienne, horrified, questioned her 'When, Natalie? Where?' Vivienne shook, her very veins shrank flat with cold fear.

'In London,' Natalie had said, neglecting to say which hospital, 'in a few weeks time.' Nor did she mention a date, either. 'I know what you are trying to do, Vivienne. But this really is my business.' Then she added with a resigned voice, 'Please don't be so unhappy. It's just a...'

'Foetus? But it will be...it's growing...' Vivienne couldn't hold back a sputtered cry.

'Don't keep going down that road, Vivienne! Stop tearing yourself apart over this. I know what I am doing.'

'But you don't, you don't. Natalie – that's just the point! You don't know what you are doing.'

'Well what makes you so damn sure, Vivienne?' Natalie challenged her.

Yet, even now, even at this stage, Vivienne couldn't tell Natalie. She could not release her demon wolves. What if she went mad? If she revealed the woman doctor's actions toward her and told Natalie? – Then Vivienne would let loose her hounds of insanity.

So Vivienne only said, 'I know, Natalie. That's all.'

At La Colette David made a pot of tea. He had overseen his staff and the growing estate. They were in a quiet time of the year when the crops were all but gathered; the soil was rested: the grass in the fields grew more slowly. David put a striped woollen cosy on the teapot and took the tray into the sitting room. Vivienne sat fidgeting, flicking through the pages of *Quarterly Art*.

'Don't get so stressed, Vivienne. Things will work out.'

'Well, that's just so easy to say, isn't it David? How can things work out – what with Joseph, Natalie – their baby...?'

'Another thing,' David added milk and sugar to his cup, stirring it slowly with a spoon. 'I don't like you seeing so much of that sodding Guy. You went to Herm with him? Sonia told me she saw you.'

'For heaven's sake! Seems half of Guernsey went to Herm when I went with Guy. It wasn't a tryst. I'm trying to get him to think –

involve himself – take some responsibility for all this.'

'That'd be a first.' David handed her a cup of tea. 'But Guy Beaufort – well, let the stupid bugger do his own thinking. If he's drinking, well then how can you help?'

'I know. Even Joseph is beginning to think I should 'Let things go,' Vivienne drank her tea, 'but I'm not giving up. I can't.' There's a lot more to it', she darted a nervous glance, couldn't tell David the truth, either. 'It's complicated.'

'More complicated than an abortion when you are seventeen, with no support and it's illegal? Still, us blokes. What do we know?' David finished his tea and got up to go.

Rattled, filled with a consuming anguish at Natalie's words, Vivienne drove blindly over to Guy's flat, not even knowing if he would be in or not. Incensed, she arrived and turned the key with a hot indignation, and walked right in.

'Guy!' She called to him. 'Guy, I want to talk to you!'

Although the flat seemed empty, he had plainly been here recently. Cigarette butts smouldered in the ashtray. Vivienne could smell coffee coming from the kitchen. Cigarette smoke wafted from the bedroom.

'Guy?'

'Oh, hi Viv. Coming,' Guy's muffled voice came from the bedroom. Vivienne looked at her watch. It was four in the afternoon. She threw open the lounge window. None of Natalie's neatness evident now, then. The room was a mess – with tins of Strongbow in the wicker wastebin. An opened tin perched on a cheap wooden table. Empty plastic sandwich boxes, labelled 'BLT' and 'Prawn and Mayonnaise' lay on newspapers, strewn on the floor.

Guy came into the room, looking sheepish, rubbing his wet hair with a towel. 'Sorry…just washing my hair.' He smiled a half-smile gingerly.

Vivienne knew, immediately, that someone was in the bedroom. She had interrupted some afternoon delight. Vivienne felt energy drain out of her. Oh no. She hadn't come here to witness this. This was about the last thing she wanted to face: Guy's latest conquest.

Wearily, Vivienne said, 'Oh, I'll come when it's more convenient then, Guy. It's just – I had some urgent news.'

Vivienne couldn't hide her disappointment: her exhaustion.

Guy tried to smooth things over. 'Sorry, Viv.'

'Are you?' she nodded her head toward the bedroom. 'Still, you don't have to apologise to me, do you? Free agent now and all that crap. Give me a ring. I want to talk to you – it's about Natalie.'

'Sure. Sure,' said Guy. He shrugged his shoulders at her, holding his palms uppermost, as if to say, 'This is me, I'll never change.'

Yes, of course, yes, he was free to have affairs. Vivienne glanced at herself in the car mirror as she drove home. She hoped the scarcely contained tears didn't show to other drivers. So, what about she and Guy, then? In the car mirror her face pictured not only disappointment, but a kind of stultified grief.

Polly laughed out loud, 'Of course he's bonking someone! Guy bonks anything that breathes doesn't he kiddo? I'm surprised the fat old soak's got it in him!'

'Polly!' Vivienne protested weakly, 'he's not that fat.'

'He is.' Polly insists. 'Your trouble is you see him through rose-coloured glasses, kiddo. I reckon he's lost the plot, myself.'

Vivienne wondered how much Polly knew about her and Guy. She was always tolerant, but Polly was shrewd. And, had she suspected Vivienne's abortion, all those years ago? If she had, then she had never questioned Vivienne about it. No, Polly always waited for Vivienne to tell her things like that. Things that had happened when they were young that lay buried: barely concealed in the shallow grave of yesterday.

CHAPTER TWENTY-EIGHT

Joseph moped so much about the house – nearly driving Vivienne to distraction – that she decided to take a short break away with him. They'd pop over to France. After all, Dinard was only thirty minutes away by Aurigny airline. Always alarmed that the Trislander 'plane Aurigny used had only one pilot – passengers seated in twos with no aisle, so locals called the plane the 'flying cigar' – Vivienne found relief when Joseph claimed these were amongst the safest aircraft in the world. Joseph said the planes could land on a beach, if necessary. In fact had had to, a couple of times.

Their hotel was on top of a busy hill, overlooking Port de Plaisance and the bay of St Malo. This place was Vivienne's haven. She could, at the very least, postpone her worries here.

'Vous desirez?' asked the polite waiter. 'What would you like?'

'Je voudrais le petit dejeuner – I would like breakfast – s'il vous plait. Est-ce que nous pourrions de l'eau? Could you also let us have some water?'

'Avec gas?' The waiter wanted to know.

'Sparkling? Oui, merci.' Vivienne ordered water quite deliberately. Best to keep her senses sharpened. And Joseph's accusations about her drinking were not forgotten.

'Why does absolutely everything taste better in France?' Vivienne asked, biting into hot croissants.

'Dunno,' Joseph replied, dully. 'Can't relish anything much at the moment.'

'Did you really think I wasn't there for you, Joseph? When you were growing up?' worried Vivienne.

'I didn't say that exactly, Ma. Just…you weren't cut out for the housewife bit, particularly. You weren't, were you?'

Vivienne added a curl of yellow butter to her roll, heaping French jam: rich and sweet, on the top of it.

'No,' Vivienne agreed. 'No, not that bit.' From the restaurant window she could see several yachts, their white sails purposefully billowed out as they raced toward the Channel.

'Just look at this view, Joseph. It's so lovely. We are fortunate to live in these little *Iles de la Manche*, our little Channel Islands, aren't we?'

'Mmm,' Joseph said doubtfully. Got its drawbacks, though.' He drew his mouth down.

'Come on, Joseph. Cheer up. You'll find someone else,' though Vivienne said it without much conviction. She recalled holding Natalie to her, feeling her swollen womb. Poor Joseph, poor lamb, he looked so dejected.

The other diners were all French. Vivienne noticed two tables where dogs sat patiently underneath the white tablecloths. An old man, who didn't say one word to anyone throughout his meal, wiped his mouth on the tablecloth occasionally. Then he surreptitiously fed his poodle hidden underneath the table. All the while the waiters took not one bit of notice.

Joseph smiled at the old man then turned to Vivienne, 'Not like you to say a thing like that, Ma. That I might find someone else. Right now I can just about get through the day. I love Natalie, you know. I am just stupidly in love with her.'

'I do know, darling. Life is hard for you at the moment.' Vivienne ached for him. 'Falling in love – well, you almost wished you hadn't don't you? Wished you didn't inflict such agonies on yourself. But then, falling in love is out of your own control.'

'Did you love Dad, when you first met?' Joseph queried. 'I've always wondered.'

'Of course!' Vivienne answered, immediately. But she didn't want to sit here, talking to Joseph about her and David. She was trying to both stop thinking, dwelling, about the past – and about the impending total disaster.

'But you weren't in love?' Joseph persisted.

'No, alright, Joseph, since you keep going on and on about it! No,

I wasn't in love with your father when we married.' She was getting a bit fed up of this scrutiny of her marriage and the rotten job she'd made of bringing up her son. 'But I…I do have great respect for him. I did for Eustace, as well, yes great respect for that man.'

'Bloody hell!' Joseph chewed furiously on a bit of croissant, 'is that all men can expect then, bloody respect?' He reddened. 'I hope you know I love you both. Dad and you.'

'Of course I do, we do, my love. Well, alright then, I feel a…a fondness for David, as well.' Vivienne plucked some green grapes, one by one, from a basket on the table. She licked her sticky fingers. 'And your father can be very kind. Kindness is a much underestimated quality in a man.'

'Well, that's a bit better. Yes, Dad is kind and quite wise, in his own way.' Sighing deeply, Joseph said, 'So you reckon I'll find someone kind, that I can respect and be fond of?' He picked at the grapes as well, eyeing Vivienne thoughtfully.

'You could do a lot worse, darling. Don't you think?'

'Maybe. Can't say I meet many girls at work, in pubs, that fill me with fondness, exactly. Might want to have a quick shag with one or two. But there isn't anyone like Natalie. If I do find someone, I can't think where.'

She couldn't let the subject go yet, so Vivienne asked, 'You keep saying I wasn't a good housewife. Are you really meaning I wasn't a good mother, Joseph? It's really bothering me.'

'You were pretty well wrapped up in yourself, Ma, to be honest. Sometimes I found it really difficult to get through to you. You did… well you still do, go off in a trance. You know?'

'No! I don't remember being like that at all! Off in a trance? And still do?' Vivienne flashed Joseph a quizzical look.

'Yeh. You do go off in a dream. Then, well you don't listen to me or Dad.'

'I do!'

'No. No, you don't Ma. You don't.'

Vivienne's eyes stung. 'Was I…am I, really such a failure?'

Then Joseph smiled gently at her. 'You look so sweet, you know.

Young for your age. Your hair is always so springy and I like all those clips you use, to try to keep it in place. And you have very sparkling turquoise eyes, Ma – you've always been so…effervescent,' he laughed.

'Effervescent? When was I effer vozent?' She laughed with him, enjoying their shared, old joke.

They decided to take a walk around the town, strolling onto the wide, sandy beach: Plage de l'Ecluse. Taking their shoes off, they paddled their feet, admiring the gothic looking houses, perched high overlooking the bay. Near the Casino, they sat at a table in a sunny square. Vivienne ordered chilled apple juice and watched the holiday crowds thronging by, enjoying the late summer sun.

'So, what do you really think Joseph – about the baby, about what Natalie wants…?' Vivienne turned her face away from him, ostensibly studying the passers by. She might not like his answer.

'It's hard for me to visualise, Ma.' Joseph puzzled behind his glasses. 'I don't know much about babies.' He poured them both more juice.

The liquid glinted golden in the sun's rays. Vivienne, straw hat pulled down, listened to her son's words.

'If I think of it now, I can only see a sort of unformed collection of cells. Not really existing as a person. But if I think,' he raised his glass slowly to his lips, 'of a baby – a son or a daughter…well, yes, I would like one. But I don't have to go through nine months of carrying it, do I? Or disrupt my life. I imagine a woman's life changes forever, when she has a baby? Was it like that for you, Ma?' Joseph stared at Vivienne intensely.

'Of course, everything changes – when you…when you…when you have a baby.' Then Vivienne said, 'actually, do you think I might have some wine now? Order some wine, would you Joseph? Red.' She closed her eyes tightly. God almighty.

'You had trouble getting me, didn't you say?' In the sunlight, Joseph's fair hair shone as he poured Vivienne's wine.

Vivienne thought how boyish Joseph still looked at times. 'Yes, I had a bit of treatment. But then, thankfully you came along at last!

You've always been a good son, Joseph. No trouble.' She swallowed some of the wine, feeling the red tannin warming her throat.

'Until now?' He replied quickly, 'bit of a bugger now, though, aren't I? All this,' Joseph gestured fruitlessly at nothing '...bit difficult now, eh?'

'Your father says it'll work out. It'll sort,' Vivienne attempted a weak smile. France was always sublime, but, for once, she could not entirely lose herself in its beauty. She could not shake a growing trepidation.

They walked to a viewpoint. Sitting on one of the only two benches was an old woman, dumpy in a headscarf and thick woollen coat. She had spread out a pink-flowered silk cushion, filling the entire bench. From her copious bag she lifted a freshly bathed, miniature dog. It had a diamanté necklace for a collar and a pink satin ribbon tied a single tuft of hair on its head. It flopped onto the cushion and fell asleep.

Vivienne and Joseph stood with some other onlookers. None of them complained about the seat being taken up. As the animal snored gently, the woman sang softly to it.

'Only in France,' Vivienne smiled at Joseph. But it made her think: another culture, a different society. How freely one could behave given a different time – given a different place.

'Ahh....France!' Vivienne and Joseph sighed together as, hand in hand, they headed for Dinard airport.

As they arrived back in Guernsey and La Colette, Sonia called out to Vivienne from the landing, where she vacuumed the carpet. 'Mr Beaufort telephoned, Mrs Carré. He said could you ring him back. He said "Soon as".' Sonia leaned over the banister, giving Vivienne a brief but decidedly old-fashioned look.

Vivienne felt the familiar tingle, the rapid pitter-patter, stinging her heart at hearing Guy's name.

'I think I owe you an apology, Guy began, as they met in Cambridge Park, St Peter Port.

'Not really,' she said, looking away from him.

'You are only trying to help Natalie, I know. And you are worried about your Joseph. I can see the least I could be doing is ensuring I don't worry you any more than I already have.' He kicked some leaves so, in a gold flurry, they danced to the base of a tree.

'Remember here? Used to play in this park – when we were kids.' Vivienne said. 'A town park. It was so different from playing in our fields and the beaches. We always kicked the leaves, looking for conkers and acorns. Children still do that. Funny, isn't it, how children so naturally do the same things, generation after generation?'

'You really are such a thoughtful soul, aren't you?' Guy said.

They sat on a green wooden bench with peeling slats, slightly sloping to one side. On the far side were town houses, worth millions now, so the Estate Agents said.

On their left, over a high wall, branches were already beginning to shed yellow leaves. Beyond that was the grey sea and the smaller islands: asleep on the horizon. Vivienne felt a sudden chill. They both hunched into their navy wool coats and drove gloved hands deep into their pockets.

'Thing is,' Guy said, 'I wanted to tell you I was sorry about the other day. And…to say I do appreciate you're trying to look after Natalie. I know now she has set the abortion date.'

Vivienne was gratified that Guy at least looked concerned himself, now. He frowned and cupped his hands over a lighter's flame to light a Rothmans. 'Does seem a bit final, now, doesn't it? Oh, perhaps it's for the best, Viv. Get it over with. Then we can…'

'I don't think like that at all,' Vivienne tensed, 'not at all! I can't believe she's going ahead. And you,' she rounded on him, her voice raising 'all you can think of is sex! Men and their blasted penises! Is it all you ever think of?'

'Steady on, Viv,' Guy looked taken aback, 'look hear, I don't have to be celibate just because my daughter is taking her own life – her future – into her own hands. I don't want or need to be celibate. Come on now Vivvy. We are all grown up. We are adults.'

Alarmed, Vivienne watched him pull out a leather-covered flagon from his coat pocket. He lit a second cigarette and downed a dreg.

'Want some? It's Napoleon brandy. Lovely stuff. Warm you?'

She pushed the proffered flagon sharply away from her. 'Good heavens, Guy, it's eleven in the morning.'

'Yes, well, I feel the cold. Plus, I need it.'

'Like sex,' Vivienne scorned.

'Yes, actually, exactly that. Human needs, Vivvy. Human desires. You've certainly got them. Even poor old Dave's probably got them…then again, maybe not…' Guy jerked out a short laugh, taking another swig.

'That is so childish. Do you really think that helps? No, David doesn't screw around. Doesn't need to prove himself all the bloody time.'

'Still jealous, little Vivvy? Well, well! I'll take that as a compliment. Anyway, Catherine is besotted with him, I'm told. Can't shut up about him. I'd watch that, if I were you, Viv, Lady Catherine gets her own way. Likes a challenge, she does.' Guy blew cigarette smoke into the cooling air.

'Yes, well maybe she isn't as frigid as you claim. But then, each woman reacts differently to each man, in bed.' Somehow, saying this stopped them quarrelling. Vivienne thought of all the beds they had shared: how good their lovemaking had been. They must mean something together, they must surely?

Guy's reflective expression seemed to confirm her thoughts.

'Tell you what, Vivvy,' Guy said, 'what about if I do us a lunch? At my place? What d'you think? We can talk then. I'll do something Cypriot, something Greek. What do you think?'

Yes, well that would make up for things, make up for this squabbling meeting, wouldn't it? Might be better to talk to him when he was more sober, and somewhere more private? They fixed a date for the following Friday.

Running into Vivienne's studio, Joseph waved some papers about. Vivienne was finishing off the landscape view from her La Colette window.

'Wow,' said Joseph, 'that's really, really good, Ma. The sea, the sky... But, look, Natalie has started the divorce. I got these today.' He thrust the papers toward her.

Vivienne put down her brush, wiping her hands on her old shirt. She took the papers and began to read. 'Have you spoken to Natalie? Did she tell you to expect these?'

'Oh, sure,' Joseph sneered, 'she told me how she's hating involving lawyers, but this is what she wants. A legal separation.'

'Well, maybe you'll feel better once things are – final, darling?' Said Vivienne, unconvinced.

'What like after a funeral, when someone has died?'

'A bit. Yes, what the Americans call closure?'

'Oh, God,' Joseph stomped off, telling Vivienne he had a lot of work to do. At least that bit was going well, he said, his career was flourishing. He'd even saved up a bit. He left Vivienne to her painting.

The flat was a good deal tidier than when Vivienne had last seen it. Guy had obviously made an effort, even placing a glass vase of white lilies on the table and washed all the ashtrays. Something tasty cooked in the kitchen. Vivienne smelt kleftiko: a Greek lamb casserole with rich meaty juices.

Wandering in, she found Guy fussing with some herbs: chopping and cutting thyme and oregano on a wooden board. He wore his navy Guernsey with jeans over which he had tied a navy and white striped apron. Just like a little boy, Vivienne smiled to herself. Intent on his task, a flop of black hair fell over his forehead. His tongue licked his teeth.

Guy was, Vivienne thought, pleased, worried that all would be well for her lunch with him. Saucepans steamed on the hob. The table was laid, complete with a single orange gerbera in an ochre coloured vase. Guy threw open the kitchen window, brushing his sweated brow with the back of his hand.

'Open the wine, will you Viv?'

She pulled white wine out of its ice-bucket and opened the bottle with the red corkscrew Guy had lain next to it. She was charmed.

He really had gone to some trouble for her. He did care, it does help. She glanced around the kitchen. Okay, it wasn't spotless but Guy had attempted to clean up the flat.

At length, Guy left the food to finish cooking and joined Vivienne in the lounge. 'Christ!' he said, 'there is so much work in entertaining!'

And it's me he's entertaining. Vivienne felt warmed. She relaxed and sat back with her head on the couch. 'Yes,' she said, 'there is always more to do than you'd think, isn't there? Even...even when it's just for two. Thanks, Guy.' And he didn't look too sloshed, she was pleased to see.

'High time,' he returned her look of pleasure, 'so, how's things?'

'Natalie has sent Joseph divorce papers. But he seems to be getting a bit more used to the idea.'

'Yes? I've got mine, as well. The Beauforts are in a mood of change. One dumping, the other being dumped.' Guy downed his wine, pouring another one. 'I had hoped though,' he said quite wistfully, Vivienne thought, 'that Natalie's marriage would last. I'd like to see her settled. Perhaps she's too much like me?'

'Natalie is very like you Guy. She'll be alright.' Yet an inner nagging made Vivienne wonder if any of them would be alright again after all this?

'Anyway. I think everything's ready. Shall we eat?' Guy helped Vivienne to her feet. She'd worn her flimsiest silk blouse with a thin-strapped camisole underneath. Guy would notice she was wearing a strapless bra and had tanned her shoulders. She'd clipped her hair up as he liked it best and sprayed Dior liberally. They went into the kitchen diner and sat down.

'I know it's daytime, but I like to do it. Natalie left these behind.' Guy lit the scented candles. Their musky perfume filled the air.

Vivienne sat down, entranced, and unfurled a fuchsia pink napkin, placing it neatly over her silk skirt. She began to eat. 'This is really delicious, Guy. It's really, really good.'

'Ta! The meat is tender isn't it? Do you know how...'

Guy didn't finish his sentence as, just then, they heard the grating metal of a key in his door. Someone entered in a waft of cool outside air, calling out to Guy in the kitchen, 'Sorry I'm late. Couldn't find a parking place! Hope I haven't ruined the food?'

It was Jessie.

'Jessie?' Vivienne sat, open-mouthed, holding her knife and fork in mid-air.

'Jessie!' Guy choked, blushing a fierce red, 'what the hell are you…?'

'What?' Jessie came into the kitchen, surveyed the meal, the candles and – Vivienne. 'Oh my god. Sorry. What's going on?' She stopped unbuttoning her raincoat.

'Next Friday, Jessie! I said next Friday.' Guy hissed. He looked aghast at Vivienne's stunned face. 'You've got the wrong date, Jessie.'

'Jessie?' Vivienne said quietly, the room swayed. She suddenly felt quite ill. 'You've come for lunch?' She couldn't, in the circumstances, think of anything else to say to Jessie. Her old friend?

'Look, I'm sorry, Vivienne,' Guy said, flustered, 'Jessie, well yes, Jessie comes for lunch,' he sounded embarrassed, 'sometimes.'

'And dinner?' Vivienne snapped. 'And afternoon tea?'

'Free country…' Guy tailed off.

'Yes, but you never mentioned her. Jessie, you never said.'

God, now Vivienne was going to cry. They bewildered her – look at them standing there, like a couple as she sat, alone, at Guy's table, on her own.

Jessie pushed her lank dark her over one shoulder. She wore it long today and she was still too thin. Her black eyeliner was heavy, circling uneasy eyes. For the lunch with Guy she wore no jewellery. Under her raincoat Vivienne saw just a plain cream shift. Jessie had brown sandals on and no tights, although it was a cold day.

'Well then. I think,' Vivienne's breath heaved painfully, 'I'll leave you both to it.' She was mortified. 'Here Jessie, have my place. Don't let the food go cold. After all, Guy has gone to so much trouble!' She would not cry. She must not cry. Not in front of them. Not in front of Jessie.

'Viv!' Guy tried to stop her leaving. 'Viv, don't go like this. Don't leave like this. Have some wine...'

'Get out of my way, Guy. Fuck you!' Vivienne ran to get her coat, her bag and keys. 'You are a pair of bloody liars aren't you?' She stopped still, turning on Jessie who stood, pale-faced, at the kitchen door. 'Did you see Guy that day in Herm?'

'Herm? In Herm? Um, well, yes, I did Vivienne but...' Jessie stammered.

'And Guy?' asked Vivienne pinning a blazing glare on him, 'you saw her?'

'Yes, but there's no need...'

'So. There I was, stood there, a complete idiot, while you two had your little secret between you?' Vivienne said, incensed.

'Let's be adult, Vivienne. We're adults, for Christ's sake.'

As he tried to appeal to her, still in his striped apron, Vivienne railed, 'You can take that sodding scarf you were forced to buy in bloody Herm and tie it around your bloody neck. Tight as you can!' She shouted, 'Go strangle yourself Guy! You're welcome to each other, you bloody pair of liars!'

Vivienne fled from the flat, still smelling the delicious stew, with the scented candles still glowing. Jessie? Guy and Jessie? How stupid she had been. How long had that been going on?

CHAPTER TWENTY-NINE

'I had seen them together, kiddo yes,' Polly admitted, levelly, eyes virtually popping out of her head at Vivienne's interrogation. Fuller in the figure now, midde-aged, Polly would cheerfully agree.

'Where?' Vivienne demanded, 'where did you see them?' She hadn't spoken to Guy since that lunchtime in his flat. Sonia had called her to the telephone several times, but she wouldn't speak to him. A couple of letters from Guy lay unopened on Vivienne's dressing table.

The two women sat in La Colette's warm conservatory with its view over the garden. There were autumn colours: purple Veronica amongst the green and late lavender. Vivienne had some Christmas decorations she was sorting through, in a box at her feet.

In her hand, Polly held a bright bauble, embellished with red glitter. She twisted it round holding it up to the light, 'Isn't that pretty?' Polly asked.

Sonia had prepared coffee for them, then gone home. She had all her own baking to do for the Christmas celebrations. Vivienne had heard Polly having quite a chat with Sonia, sharing recipes with her: telling her how her Kim was qualified now and working at the College of Further Education as trainee chef.

'You know,' said Polly, 'saw them walking on the beach...once, at Portelet, I think it was...' Polly frowned, concentrating as she untangled some tinsel, trying to remember. 'Oh, yes and my Eric saw them – at least he thought it was them – when he was playing for the darts team, at the Kosy Korner – you know, pub on the corner by the Town Church?'

'Portelet?' Vivienne's head shook in seething disbelief. 'Polly, when was this? Why didn't you say?' Christmas decorations dropped back in their box as Vivienne, all enthusiasm gone, let them fall.

'I try not to tell you things about Guy, kiddo. You always get so upset. Like I didn't tell you about that ruddy Rita woman. If I told you every time I saw Guy Beaufort with another woman – well then, we wouldn't get to talk about anything else, I reckon!' Polly laughed shortly, then leaned forward. 'Hey, what difference does it make now, kiddo? Come on. That…well that's all in the past, now isn't it?' Polly raised her eyebrows as if surely awaiting Vivienne's denial. 'You're not…you're not still holding a candle for Guy Beaufort are you?'

'It was just such a shock, Polly. I mean Jessie, of all people. And that silly game they played in Herm. Of course I'm hurt, of course I am. My God, after all I've gone and done…!' How to express the rawness, the wounding betrayal she felt? Right now, as Vivienne dissected her exposed thoughts, there was hardly room, even, for Natalie's pregnancy.

Now that she knew, Vivienne determined to find out where Jessie lived. When she did, she began driving past her house. It was a narrow two up, two down Town house in a rundown part of St Peter Port. A few times Vivienne saw Adam coming and going. He'd probably got a job in a bank or something, Vivienne decided.

Once, she trailed Jessie to a supermarket, following her around the aisles to see what she was buying. When Jessie put ready-made meals, pasta and bottles and cans of Strongbow into her trolley, Vivienne just knew these things were for Guy.

So, what was she: Jessie? Guy's little maid replacement? More? Was she yet another of his frightened rabbits? How long and how deep went this blasted affair?

Rattled, Vivienne told David what had happened. He shrugged, looking nothing more than bored. 'So what? Guy and Jessie are having an affair. Doesn't matter to me. Doesn't matter to you, does it?'

Doesn't matter? Here she was, a successful artist – a University student, a mother and, yes, even a wife, and Vivienne was stalking Jessie. She was driving past Jessie's house and Guy's flat day after day. It'd be dementia, then, it'd got to her after all. She was in her fifties and she was slowly becoming quite demented. Damn you, Guy.

Damn you to hell.

Far worse: Vivienne longed for Guy. Why didn't this wretched yearning die down? After all, she knew now, about Jessie.

David had started nagging again: cut down the booze, Vivienne. Her nightmares deepened: dark tides swept her to a perilous ledge where she could see her depression – lying at the bottom of its crevice, staring up at her through black cracks, with the mad red eyes of a sea serpent.

In the glove compartment of her car, Vivienne began keeping a leather-covered flagon of Napoleon brandy. Good for the cold, didn't Guy say? She took a fiery nip.

This was the park bench where she'd sat with Guy. Autumn bit deeply now. Branches, darkly damp, veined a greying sky. Near the path she watched an elderly man enter the telephone booth she had used, making her call, all those years ago, to arrange her abortion. She had been seventeen. The brandy seared her throat. Vivienne had only just left school that year: the year she aborted her daughter.

The brandy tasted good. Muffled against the brisk wind, Vivienne rose and began walking toward her car. Just before she got to it, she saw Jessie. She was at the far end of the park, wearing her thin raincoat. The wind blew black strands away from Jessie's face as she walked. She was holding a red tartan lead, fixed to a red tartan collar of a white West Highland terrier. Jessie was walking her Westie dog.

Without thinking, without hesitation, Vivienne began to run. She ran across the grass, against the wind as it buffeted her – as if to stop her reaching Jessie. Then Jessie saw her and stood quite still.

Vivienne saw the Westie cock its leg against a steel post, its head to one side: its ears pricked up, two furry points alert to danger.

'What's its name?' Vivienne shook Jessie by the shoulders, 'what is the bloody dog's name?'

'You've been drinking,' Jessie answered in alarm, 'Jock. He's called Jock. What's your problem, Vivienne? Let me go. What the hell do you think you are doing?'

'How long have you had him?' Vivienne shot at her breathlessly, shaking Jessie even harder.

'Vivienne, for goodness sake, calm down. Let me go!'

A grey-haired old man with a walking stick passed by them. His ginger mongrel, out on his walk, playfully greeted Jock. They sniffed each other ecstatically.

'Everything alright, ladies?' The man croaked. 'Don't often see punch ups on my walk. Makes quite a change.' He stopped, questioningly, waiting for a reply.

'Yes,' Vivienne eased her grip on Jessie. 'We're alright. Thank you.'

The man walked on, glancing back every few yards. 'Something to tell the wife, though. She enjoys a bit of gossip.' He carried on walking.

'Vivienne,' said Jessie without anger. 'I've had Jock for years.'

'Why? Why a Westie?'

Jessie's eyes opened up like something had just dawned on her. 'Well, I'll tell you. I was given one...as a present. Years and years ago. I fell in love with the breed.'

No, that was not enough. That won't do, Jessie. 'And what was this present from someone called? Eh? What was he called?' The bitter wind chilled them. Their hair blew about their faces, their cheeks became cold.

'Fraser,' Jessie said quietly. 'He was called Fraser. He was ten years old when he died. They have weak livers you know, Westies. Satisfied?'

Vivienne's arms hung loose, her strength running out. 'Guy gave you Fraser when he went to live in Cyprus? But Natalie was just a child then.'

With nervous eyes, Jessie met Vivienne's, full on. 'Yes, Natalie was just a child then. Look, Vivienne, I don't know what else you want me to say...and I'm getting really cold. I'm freezing.' She pulled the thin raincoat to her.

Looking down at the little terrier, Vivienne thought how much he looked like Fraser: same coal black eyes, little black snout and curly grey-white fur on stocky legs.

How could he? How could Guy have given Fraser to Jessie? Why

hadn't he asked her to have him? She'd have looked after him – gladly
– and loved him. Why had he chosen Jessie? What did she mean to
him? He never told her he had done that. Did Natalie know?

'Natalie?' Vivienne thrust the question down the phone, 'why did
your father give your Westie, Fraser, to Jessie?' Vivienne had finally
caught up with Natalie on her mobile phone.

'What are you babbling on about now, Vivienne? Look, I've got
a cold coming on and its bloody freezing. I'm in a shop doorway
in Putney High Street and I've already had that Matthias ring me
today, practically forcing me to agree to seeing you, pestering me so
I couldn't say no. I don't know, Vivienne, he was probably seeing her
at the time, or something. To he honest, you wittering on about dogs
is about all I can take.'

'But, your mother had just died. Amanda had only just died...'
Vivienne persisted.

'Look, Vivienne. You know my father. For fuck's sake, I was only
a kid then. I didn't keep a record of all his slappers! I'm going to ring
off now. Like I say, I've agreed to see your precious Matthias. I'm off
to get some paracetamol, my head aches.' Natalie rang off.

Well, at least she'd agreed about Matthias – did Natalie realise
Vivienne would be there, too? Anyway, Vivienne's thankful for her
saying yes, at least. Natalie would just have to put up with her being
there. If it was a *fait accompli*, well then, too bloody bad.

Next, Vivienne rang David. He had become used to taking his
mobile with him everywhere, as well. She told him she was going
to be out all day. Sonia would fix something for his lunch. Vivienne
rang off quickly before David could protest or ask questions.

For once, Vivienne found a parking place fairly easily. Through
the approaching winter-grey St Peter Port streets, she hurried
purposefully. Arriving at the terraced town house, she thumped at
the faded blue front door. Its brass letterbox could do with a polish, it
was pitted black. Soon she heard footsteps in the hall. A dog barked
importantly.

'Vivienne!' Jessie tried to push the door shut again, but Vivienne was stronger, pushing it hard until she was in the hallway.

'I haven't come to make trouble, Jessie.' Vivienne breathed evenly, 'But I just have to talk to you. Please, let me?'

Jessie stood aside, indicating for her to come in. 'Perhaps it is time,' she said.

She led Vivienne into a small sitting room. The fire was lit, sending a half circle of heat on the hearth. Jock sniffed Vivienne, checking out she wasn't a burglar, then curled up in his basket, one eye shut – the other firmly on the two of them.

The sitting room had two windows overlooking the back garden: a tiny stone-flagged square. It was completely walled in, with a single tree, almost leafless now, but would look pretty, Vivienne thought, in spring and summer.

In well-worn easy chairs either side of the tiled fireplace, Vivienne questioned her old friend. Jessie wore a lilac jumper with navy slacks, still no stockings but flimsy pumps. Vivienne felt almost indecently robust: overdressed, over made-up.

'Okay. What is it you want to know, Vivienne?' Jessie said wearily. There was a paucity about her – as though life had slivered away at her once voluptuous body. Jessie was left with only the core of who she had been. Somehow, Jessie seemed all eaten up.

'Let's start with Fraser,' and Vivienne didn't stop just because Jessie raised her black-rimmed eyes to the ceiling. 'What is that all about?'

'It was. Well…Guy and I had been…friends, good friends, you know, by the time that Amanda died.'

'How long?'

'Oh, Vivienne. Look, a long time. Guy and I had…we have known each other for a very long time. In fact,' Jessie's pale jaw jutted, lit by the fire's glow as she cast around, seeming to remember dates, times. 'In fact – let's see, not long after he got married to Amanda. Yes, before they went to America, anyway. And then we picked up again, after that.'

'You picked up? Meaning?' Vivienne felt the world judder to a halt. She wasn't really sitting there. She was levitating in one of her nightmares.

'Well, come on, you know what I mean! We saw a lot of each other.' Jessie smiled affectionately, 'Guy used to call me his "Little Miss Wife", instead of his "Little Miss Tress".' Jessie gave a light, coquettish laugh.

Vivienne couldn't smile or laugh. If she was supposed to see some kind of in-joke, it wasn't working. 'So, were you seeing him, as his 'Little Miss Wife' when I...when I... went into the sea, that Christmas?'

'Oh yes,' Jessie said calmly. 'But I'm not trying to score points, Vivienne. You wanted the facts? Yes, we had spent the afternoon together on that day. We exchanged Christmas presents. We do that every year – make our own little Christmas.'

'Your own little Christmas? Every year?' Vivienne repeated, enraged, 'while I tried to drown myself?'

'Oh come on, Vivienne. You are so...'

'Melodramatic? Yes, that's what Guy calls me – not his mistress, not his fucking "Miss Wife" Nothing.' This was all getting too much. Vivienne felt the firelight stifling her. 'And, times like at my exhibition, my art exhibition at the Manor House?'

'Yes. Yes, I knew he was back in Guernsey. Your exhibition was a good... a good neutral place for us to meet. We were able to make some dates. Then we met up later, at my flat.'

'Did you know about me? That Guy was seeing me?'

'Yes. He spoke about you.'

'Spoke about me? What did he say about me?' Vivienne wrung her hands together. She was going to self-destruct at any moment.

'That...you were in love with him. That you had a big thing about him and that he felt sorry for you. But he was fond of you. We were... both a bit sorry for you, really.'

Jock began to scratch himself, sending white hairs flurrying onto the mat. Jessie added a log to the fire, poking it so that sparks flew.

'Sorry for me?' Exposed bruises spread purple all over her but Vivienne still could not desist. 'He felt sorry for me? And when I shared his studio? You telephoned him?'

'Mmm? His studio in Hauteville? Sometimes, yes.'

'And when Amanda was in hospital?'

'Yes. Well, then we had several nights and days together. Almost as man and wife! It was so good.' Jessie stared meditatively at the red coal fire, a light reflecting in her eyes.

'Did Amanda know about you? Did she know about me? Vivienne's eyes burned.

Jessie continued telling Vivienne answers to her questions with no visible emotion. 'Yes, Amanda knew about both of us. She didn't like me! But she understood you. She was…'

'Sorry for me?' Vivienne took a tissue from her bag and blew her nose.

'Sort of, yes. She wasn't sorry for me, though! Amanda found out Guy was helping me to pay my bills – that he was looking after me.'

Vivienne's head fired hot now, as if it was growing – ballooning beyond comprehension. She asked for a glass of water.

'Not some wine?' asked Jessie.

'No. No, I need some water….please.'

Jessie returned from her small kitchen and handed Vivienne a glass. 'I can't drink, now, Vivienne. I'm a recovering alcoholic. And I did drugs. I've had a lot of treatment. A lot of help.' She turned her head toward the fire again.

Vivienne stared at this fragile, white-faced woman: her profile looked beaten. Yet, she had kept Guy so close to her. It didn't seem possible.

'I can't believe I never saw any of this,' Vivienne said, sipping the water like it tasted poisonous.

'Well,' Jessie said gently, 'you were drinking quite a lot yourself, weren't you Vivienne? We don't always see things clearly, when we've drunk too much. And, well I did…I did try to tell you – to warn you. Don't you remember? When we worked together in the newspaper office? In the Coal Hole bar. You were pining for Guy then. Guy and I were writing and phoning each other. Yes, I'd been over to the States – to America twice – actually, to see him.'

'You went to America? And – oh my god, don't tell me – Cyprus?

You didn't go to Cyprus?' What the hell, bring it on, Vivienne thought: a great flood of devastation welled up. What else had sodding Guy Beaufort kept from her? Up his bloody sleeve?

'Yes I did, as it goes. I went there for – well, getting on six months. But Guy was drinking heavily then. It wasn't good for me. It's why we don't live together now. We get on best under different roofs.'

'And Catherine?'

'Catherine hated me! Hates me still, probably. She found out that we had had sex, well – you know – before yes and even on Natalie and Joseph's wedding day. Oh, we were so naughty!' Jessie shook her head. 'Then Catherine knew Guy and I were serious about each other, you see. Yes, that was the day – Natalie's wedding day – that Catherine decided to leave Guy.' Jessie ignored a ringing telephone.

'Guy?' Vivienne asked, numbly.

'Perhaps. More than likely.' Jessie made a smile of endearment, 'he checks up on me, to see if I need anything.'

They really were like an old married couple. Vivienne could scarcely conceive of Guy in this role. It was absurd. It didn't fit in. This was all back to front, inside out and wrong way round.

There was an anxious catch in her voice as Vivienne asked, 'And did – does – Catherine know about me?'

'Now that... no. I don't think so,' Jessie replied slowly. 'She was always too wound up about me and Guy, he says anyway, to think there might be anyone else.'

'Fine! So that's left Guy to pick me up and put me down, whenever he felt fit? I'm sorry, Jessie. But I have had just about enough of this. It is totally unbelievable to me. I can't think you have done all this, behind my back, and for so long. It's quite incredible!' Shaking head to foot, her palms damp, Vivienne got up from the cosy chair.

'Well, you don't own him, Vivienne. That's what Guy always said to me. You want to own him.'

'And I suppose you don't?' Vivienne spat bitterly.

'No. I don't. I love him for what he is – for who he is – and he's the same with me. Get real, Vivienne. Isn't that what you came here for – to get real?'

CHAPTER THIRTY

It was quite incomprehensible: Guy and Jessie? Mister and Mistress? Vivienne's blood surged in confusion and hurt, twisting round so she could barely see. She stormed round to Guy's flat. She banged on his door until he answered it.

'I've just come from Jessie's,' she fumed at him.

'I know. She rang me.' Guy, dressed in black, with an open can of lager in hand, looked gratifyingly drained. He let Vivienne in as the door swung open under the force of her body.

'What the fucking hell have you been playing at, Guy? All these years! You bastard. You utter shit. You have played with me – with my feelings just to suit yourself!'

'Don't be so melodramatic,' Guy said coolly, 'and don't shout at me. I'm not David.'

'Oh, shut up! Why Jessie?' She fired.

'Well, because when we were young,' Guy said slowly, 'she, Jessie, she was just sensational, you know? In bed. She did things I'd only known a French woman do – in Paris it was. Yes, Jessie is the only woman I'd have left Amanda for.'

Vivienne slapped him, hard on his face. Her own hand stung. Bruising her knuckles on the tin, she punched the can of lager out of his hand. It bounced against the wall, spraying beery liquid onto the dusty skirting board.

'So. Amanda knew. Catherine knew. Polly and God only knows who else knew about Jessie?'

Guy raised his dark arched brows. 'I…we,' he sighed, looking watchful, 'I didn't want you to be hurt.'

'We? We? What absolute crap! I've been deceived for half my life. I think I'm going mad.' Rage seized Vivienne's fast fleeing reason. 'Don't you know what I've been through over you? I nearly killed myself, you sod. On that day, the day you'd been playing housey housey having Jessie off, your little Miss Wife giving each other Christmas presents! You louse!'

Vivienne picked up the glass vase with its dying white lilies and threw it at Guy. He ducked, so the whole lot smashed against the wall.

'Now, look here, Viv.' Guy went to the fridge for another lager and tried to put it in her hand. She plonked it down defiantly, unopened, on the table. 'Look, you knew I wasn't committed to you. Right from the start. You knew I was going to marry Amanda.'

'You told me,' Vivienne said, her breath forced level, 'that you didn't do love. That all women wanted to hear was 'I love you.' You made me think I shouldn't expect love from you, only sex. You did, you said that.'

'Oh, no,' Guy said fixing a firm gaze on her, 'wait a minute, Viv. You wanted me to be in love with you. But I was already in love.'

'With Jessie?' said Vivienne incredulously, as a steel shaft shot through her. 'You have played a very clever game, haven't you Guy? Played a long and clever game.' She cried, rigid with dismay.

'Come on, Viv! What about you?' said Guy.

She couldn't believe how measured he was, how calculating.

'You have always had that snug little life, haven't you? With David to go back to, haven't you? We both played games, Viv. We both played games. It wasn't real life, though, was it? Jessie is real life. Me and Jessie – we're real life.'

Through a stupefied haze of near incomprehension, Vivienne heard Guy continue remorselessly. 'Listen, Viv, when Amanda died, I didn't know where to turn. Jessie – well, she saved my sanity. She was there for me: looked after Natalie, shopped, did practical things. Then, when our son was born...'

'Your son?' Vivienne's mouth dropped open.

'Adam. Adam's mine.'

'Adam's yours?'

Guy moved toward her, his face concerned. 'Look, this must all be – awful for you, Viv. You look shocked, you look ill. Look, for

Christ's sake, you don't need me. Not like Jessie always has.'

'I did need you.' Vivienne released a restrained sob, 'I did need you. How can you say that?' She snatched the offered tissue and covered her wet eyes, trying to hide her grief.

'You needed me for sex. That's all.'

'That wasn't all,' sobs flowed into her words, 'I was mad about you. I do love you. I've done nothing but think about you. Oh, Guy! Don't hurt me like this. I can't bear it!' Wracked with misery, her body shuddered uncontrollably.

Guy carried on, telling her he had feared for her, how he knew how depressed she got – how she drank too much: that she was too volatile. 'I never promised you love, or fidelity, Vivvy, because I could never offer you that. Not like you wanted it.'

'You could have shown me some mercy. You could have told me so that I understood.' Wiping her eyes, utterly stricken, Vivienne looked at Guy.

Guy took a deep breath, 'I couldn't stop you being in love with me, could I? Just as I can't help being in love with Jessie.'

'That's the cruellest thing I have ever heard you say. That is a cruel, cruel thing to say to me,' Vivienne sat on the couch, wringing her skirt with her hands. 'And, all along, you had a child, a baby. You fathered a baby that I knew nothing about?'

Guy nodded, sitting down next to her. 'Yes,' he said wearily, 'we didn't know what to do. You remember what it was like in those days? Having a baby out of wedlock? And Jessie was already divorced. She was already a pariah: had a stigma plastered on her. It wasn't easy for her.'

Through the fire of facts, hurtling toward her like shrapnel, Vivienne asked him, 'But you practised birth control, didn't you? At Portelet – at Portelet, I put a condom on you.' She swallowed a painful stone.

'It came off. I felt it coming off. Must have been all those waves?' He smiled weakly, 'I was worried. But, obviously all was well?' His eyes searched for her answer.

'No,' she said numbly, 'it wasn't. I had an abortion. I terminated our child.' In Vivienne's exhaustion, it came out almost carelessly.

'What? Viv? Why in Christ's name didn't you tell me you were pregnant? Vivvy, why ever didn't you say? I could have helped...' he reached for her hand.

Guy's touch still comforted her. She let him take it. 'I thought you were going to have a brilliant future – that you mustn't have me dragging you back. You were going places with your art. You were in that jet set. The Chelsea crowd. I didn't want to be your burden. I wanted you to love me for myself.'

'So,' he made his half-smile, 'I'm not the only one to have a secret, then?' But Vivienne made no response.

Her mouth felt contorted and stiff, 'Yes, but your secret, one of your secrets, is alive, isn't he? Your child is alive. Ours is dead.' Bereft, her head dropped forward as she held it in her hands. 'She's dead.'

'It was a little girl? How did you know that?' Guy held her now as she quivered. 'Vivvy? There were no scans then, no pregnancy tests. Not in the sixties. When Amanda had her miscarriage, we didn't know what...'

'Look,' Vivienne shifted her position from him. 'I can't go on with all this. Only, I knew that it was a girl.' Hah! Now the mocking woman doctor roared revenge – hateful scorn – right in Vivienne's face. Hah! Got you! 'I got depressed. I tried to commit suicide because of you, Guy. I caught a disease – thrush – that was Jessie, I suppose,' Vivienne allowed a wry grin, 'and I thought it was Amanda!' 'It's passed on, Vivienne, woman to woman', of course, her civilised Guernsey doctor had tried to help her. 'You managed to tell me that much, didn't you? That you didn't sleep with Amanda. You managed to tell me that!'

'Yes, Jessie did have thrush, at one time. But you never told me you had caught it. You didn't tell me everything, either, did you?' His dark brown eyes observed her with a kind of guiltless calm.

Astounded, Vivienne met his look, 'You really have been a complete bastard to me, haven't you Guy? A complete bastard.'

'Come off it, Viv. You had what you wanted. Your painting, your marriage, Joseph. I was just a diversion. A bit on the side. We had a really good time – really good. I don't see you were any better than me.'

So, her abortion had been for nothing. Her love for Guy a mere distraction. Vivienne drew herself up, 'Is that what you really think? After all we have had together. Is that what you thought about me? A greedy girl, wanting more than her share?' Vivienne shook Guy off, taking his hands off her, one by one.

As Guy reached out again, saying he was sorry, Vivienne rasped, 'Don't touch me. You may as well have been raping me all these years.' She felt utterly despoiled. He was making their love affair into a gluttonous feast of illicit sex. She could never, ever forgive him.

She told him, 'You just use women, don't you? Me, Amanda, Catherine, Jessie, fucking Rita.'

'Rita?' Guy frowned, 'oh yes! Rita. Sharp little dresser, Rita.' He half closed his eyes then blinked them open. 'But no, no. I don't think I have used any of you. I'm certainly not using Jessie. She's just come out of another detox – rehab at the clinic – I have to treat Jessie with great care. She's done really hard drugs, you know. Has a real problem with them. And we even worry about Adam.' He lit a Rothmans, thoughtfully.

It was as if, Vivienne thought, she wasn't there. Guy smoked his cigarette, thinking of Jessie's well being, no doubt, and his son's. Probably he would be going round to see Jessie, once Vivienne had left. Perhaps they were going shopping later, for their evening meal?

Then it happened. In that stark, lightning moment of realisation: as stealthily as it had insidiously entwined around her for so long – Vivienne's serpent let go. The python, strangling her life with passion for Guy, twisting around her so tightly she had gasped for the oxygen of sanity – died. She felt desire for him uncoil and slither to her feet. As the constricting snake slid powerlessly down, Guy stood before her.

Still smoking, lost in his own thoughts, Vivienne saw, for the first time, an overweight, ageing man with eyes set too close together and ugly, uneven teeth.

Staring at Guy all the while, Vivienne rose silently. Stepping over the shed, sloughed snakeskin, she went to the door and let herself out. She could hear Guy calling out to her, but hurried out into the biting, cold air. Vivienne ran to her car, driving blindly to La Colette.

As the trees lining the drive slipped by, Vivienne thought of Eustace. She had nearly destroyed that good man's respect for her. She had neglected Joseph and David. She had nearly lost her mind and ripped open her own womb, tearing out a defenceless child. She stumbled to her room, fell onto the bed and wept the long and desolate howl of a dying soul.

Jocelyn and Enrico said they were delighted that Vivienne would stay with them for a few days. Jocelyn said she guessed Vivienne wanted some privacy for the meeting with Natalie and Matthias, so she arranged for one of her consulting rooms at her Alternative Clinic to be free for the three of them. Matthias was coming down from Oxford, Natalie from Putney.

Vivienne told Jocelyn how she needed her support just now. Enrico said Vivienne had been injured: she was in distress. Jocelyn just replied, 'That's fine, darling. No problem,' and asked no questions.

Hearing what she had to say about Guy and Jessie, David said that they deserved each other. But he was surprised about Adam. 'That man is an out and out rogue. And not half as clever as he thinks he is.'

David told Vivienne that Catherine reckoned Guy had been incontinently unfaithful throughout both his marriages. 'Amanda must have had one hell of a life with him,' said David. Vivienne agreed with a guilt-filled nod of her head.

'Anyway. My regards to Jocelyn and her toy boy – Rico is it?' David said.

'Enrico. And I don't know about toy boy. Strikes me Enrico is wiser and maturer than any of us,' said Vivienne.

'By the way, Catherine wants me to go over to Cyprus for a few days. I'll go when you see Jocelyn in London, okay? Catherine needs me to check up on some of her tomato plants. She's got a problem with botrytis. Anyway, it'll be a nice break for me. She's paying the air fare.'

'Yes?' Vivienne hesitated, feeling, she knew, an underserved pang of jealousy. 'Well have a nice time.' Quite frankly, she wouldn't trust any man – anyone – ever again. 'And I hope Catherine doesn't need – isn't too in need of you? Are you staying long?'

David merely smiled. 'Catherine says not. She is a nice woman isn't she? Anyway, I'm glad you see that bugger Guy for what he is, now. But I don't see I have to drop Catherine. I'm...I'm thinking things through, Vivienne. I like Cyprus, I really do.'

Vivienne kept recalling all the times Guy must have been with Jessie: when he was seeing her as well. Did Jessie know about the hidden field with the stream and the leafy copse? Probably. Perhaps she had discovered it with Guy? Was Vivienne just one of the women Guy had taken there? He must have gone straight to Jessie after the picnic Vivienne had made, as though it hadn't happened. As though Vivienne didn't exist.

She wondered if she was strong enough to face Natalie. Yet, distraught and needing all her reserve, she managed to pack and get herself off to London and Jocelyn's smart Putney home.

Straightaway, Enrico greeted her. 'So? Something's happened?'

'Yes. You have been so right about a lot of things, Enrico. But I don't want to talk about it, yet. I'm having enough trouble with... Natalie. The Natalie business, you understand?'

'Perfectly, my dear woman. I see a lot of distress in your eyes, Vivvyon, but other things also? A lot going on in there, yes? But I know the outcome. Be not afraid. Your Matthias, your Bacchus, he will bring Apollo back into your life.'

Jocelyn breezed in with aperitifs. They would go to a restaurant in the High Street. Vivienne was tired so they'd do central London later, if they could manage it – if Vivienne wanted to.

'You look well,' Vivienne said, as Jocelyn sat, legs crossed, in a striped designer trouser suit, hair shining, still with her good figure.

Sipping from a long-stemmed glass Jocelyn said bluntly, 'You don't, Vivienne. Enrico, what is the matter with her?'

His dark lashed eyes watched Vivienne. Enrico, dressed casually, entirely at ease with himself, said 'Leave her alone, Jocelyn. She's in a time of great sorrow. And she has to face Natalie yet,' he paused, 'well, at least Matthias will be there.'

Vivienne felt withdrawn and dry. Her heavy eyes showed they hadn't slept properly.

'Guy?' Enrico tested, with great tenderness.

Their London sitting room had high ceilings and a feature, original, cast iron fireplace. They had chosen clear, modern colours – mustard yellow and indigo blue. Under the lamp with its buttermilk shade, Vivienne sat almost motionless.

'Guy. Yes. It's awful, Jocelyn, Enrico. Too much to think about.' Vivienne blinked cried-out eyes.

'Well, don't talk about it now,' Jocelyn agreed with Enrico. 'And save any tears, Vivienne, for someone who deserves it. Guy Beaufort does not deserve your tears. We'll go somewhere nice tomorrow, darling. You can tell us what you want to do then. Only if you want to. We're here for you.'

'Right!' Enrico confirmed decisively. 'Now. Let's go eat.'

The room at Jocelyn's clinic was decorated in white and spring green. Jocelyn had lit a host of scented candles. The scent of gardenia, cardamom and myrrh drifted all around. Dark green fronded palms were tubbed in blue ceramic pots. Three couches, all in terracotta cloth, were scattered with soft, silk cushions in pale green, primrose yellow and white. On a light pine table, reflected in the gleaming wood floor, Vivienne could smell the tray of fresh coffee Jocelyn had provided.

Soft gold lighting lit the three of them. Matthias, with his dark skin and wavy black hair, had ushered in Natalie. They had met in Jocelyn's reception and told Vivienne they recognised each other from her descriptions. They both came into the room together.

Matthias took off his over-sized coat, hung it on the coat stand and kissed Vivienne. He smelt of citrus and cool, fresh air.

'What's happened?' He said with concern.

'It's alright...' Vivienne waved her hands airily. But Matthias would notice everything: the lines fanning her eyes now; her hair freshly washed and pinned back. Lavender blue eye shadow and pink lipstick attempted to add colour. For the chill London weather Vivienne layered a pink top with mulberry wool long cardigan and skirt. She knew she was no longer slim, nor young. And, she was in pain.

Natalie, her black hair cut to a silky bob, emphasising her wide brown eyes, wore a navy, soft woollen dress with matching knee-length boots. Her pregnancy barely showed although Vivienne reckoned she must be well past twelve weeks – perhaps more?

Brusquely, Natalie kicked off. 'Okay, well, firstly I want to say that I am not going to sit here listening to any advice, especially from you, Vivienne. And if you think I have been dragged here, to this meeting to be told what to do – or by you, Matthias, just because you are some kind of, actually, what exactly are you Matthias – ?' She lit a Rothmans cigarette.

'There is no ashtray,' Matthias said, simply.

'Then will you kindly get me an ashtray?' Natalie shot him a defiant look.

Matthias did as he was bid, his glance telling Vivienne he saw no good coming from antagonising Natalie at this stage. He went out of the room, returning with a white saucer, shutting the pale green door silently but firmly behind him.

'All Reception could find. Seeing as no-one is supposed to smoke,' said Matthias quietly. 'And if you set fire to the building, I will take full responsibility.' He smiled at Natalie with studied neutrality. 'And, I am an Oxford graduate. I majored in the Classics and I am now researching a PhD in Philosophy and Greek mythology.' Matthias continued to smile at Natalie, baring white, even teeth. 'But I don't bite.'

'Great. Because I do,' Natalie snapped back, ostentatiously taking quick puffs in rapid succession on her cigarette. She tapped ash noisily into the saucer.

Feeling distracted, Vivienne poured them all hot coffee.

'Thanks Baby,' Matthias accepted the cup.

'What?' Natalie sneered, puffing smoke out in a jet stream. 'Baby? What the hell is that all about?' She gave a short, contemptuous laugh.

'Nothing to concern you, Natalie,' Matthias said soothingly. 'Now. Vivienne. I believe you have something to say to us – to Natalie?'

'I told you…' Natalie began, curtly.

Vivienne interrupted her. 'Yes, I do want to say something, Natalie. It's not just to you. But I think you may need to hear it.'

'Need? Here you go again! Need? I don't need…'

'Be quiet,' Matthias said, stern, now. 'Vivienne has something to tell us. Kindly allow her to, Natalie. None of this is easy for us. But it is far too important to ignore what Vivienne wants to say. Vivienne, come, you tell us.'

'It's just…just,' Vivienne faced them both. They were two educated young people, full of ideas and energy – Natalie with her problem to get rid of. Yes, this was it. Vivienne was going to have to tell them her story now.

'Go on, Vivienne. We are listening,' urged Matthias, placing his hands on his knees.

'What I am going to tell you, well…I've never told a living soul. Only one or two people even knew I had an abortion, but…'

'Oh God! You had an abortion, oh no. Well, I might have known. So that's what all this is about?' Natalie made to leave.

But Matthias pushed her down, hard, by the shoulders. 'No you don't! Now you stay. And you be quiet!'

Startled, Natalie obeyed him, abruptly sitting down again.

'But,' Vivienne continued, 'I have never told anyone exactly what happened.' She clutched at her skirt.

'What happened?' Matthias asked gently. 'Just tell us what happened, Vivienne.' His eyes glowed with encouragement.

Yes, yes. Vivienne could tell Matthias. She began her story.

'I…I was seventeen. I was frightened,' she said, heavily. 'When I got pregnant I thought…well, it wasn't really happening. I used to go into my bedroom, cross off the days on my calendar and just watch the weeks go by. One day I knew I was expecting – then the next I would pretend it had gone away. I thought, if I told him, I would lose Guy.'

Natalie and Matthias sat in complete silence. Their two pairs of eyes never left her as they listened intently.

'I made the…the arrangements with Jocelyn. I felt deranged. Like I was out of my mind.' Slowly, Vivienne let her head lay back on the terracotta couch, tendrils of hair escaping from her clips. She closed her moist eyes.

'I lay on this hard, narrow bed with a circle of light in my eyes and I could feel the baby coming out. I was in terrible pain and didn't know either of the faces around me. There was a nurse. Then there was a doctor: a woman doctor on night duty.

'I was hooked up, tethered, on to plastic sacks of blood. I could see them. But it was all…foreign to me. I couldn't understand what was happening. The doctor delivered the baby. I felt the baby slide out between my legs. I felt the placenta coming out. I heard the baby cry. She was alive…she just cried out, once.' Sobbing, Vivienne let hot tears roll down her face, unabated.

'Go on,' Matthias urged, 'go on, Vivienne. Don't stop, darling.'

Swallowing back, hard, Vivienne's voice is strained and small. 'And I then I heard the doctor…the doctor, telling the nurse that this is a twenty-one, maybe twenty-two week botched termination. Then she came to me and put the little naked girl in my arms. The nurse had wiped the baby's face clean of blood and mucus.'

Vivienne shivered, weeping, 'The baby was warm and red-veined in my arms. She was perfectly formed. She had a perfect little face,' Vivienne faltered, glancing at Matthias, beseeching him to help her.

Matthias rose, stole across the room and sat by her, taking her hand. 'Go on Vivienne. You are being very brave.'

Natalie, biting her bottom lip hadn't turned her head away. She stared at Vivienne, transfixed.

'The doctor just stood there, with her hands on her hips. She was tall and high-waisted, with round glasses. When the nurse came to take the baby from me, the doctor stopped her.

'No,' she said, 'let her see what she has done – to a living being, a human being. Her daughter. And I am going to have to let her die, even though she might have been viable. But now she could not be saved.' Then she sent the nurse out of the room.

'The doctor left me, lying there, holding the baby for what seemed like hours. I lay on the hospital bed, hard as a wooden board. I looked down at the baby. She had delicate little fingernails: just like seashells. She had wispy black hair, like Guy's, sticking out all funny and wet. Then, as I tried to hold her close to me, she opened her eyes. They were glistening dark brown, no bigger than a little bird's. She looked straight at me, with one clear look. She was like a tiny, featherless fledgling fallen out of its nest.' Tears coursed down Vivienne's cheek. She could feel the weight of Matthias' arm around her and leant on him.

Natalie had put one hand over her mouth. The other was clenched in her lap.

'Then...then,' Vivienne drew in a deep breath, 'just as I touched her tiny cheek with my finger, she stopped breathing. She died. She had been warm in my arms. But her eyes flickered and closed. Her heart didn't beat any more. Her head, on its fragile little neck, fell to one side. I thought I had held her wrongly – that I had broken her neck. I screamed out for help.

'I could do nothing for her. I had killed her. The woman doctor, watching me all the time, left me with the baby purposely, in my arms until she became stiff and cold as a small statue on a child's grave.

'Only then did the doctor come and take the baby from me, roughly, forcing her out of my arms, ripping her away from me. She berated me: saying why had I left it so long, when she had a chance of life? Telling me that this wasn't why she went into medicine – to do butchery. Afterward the nurse put the tiny little girl into a metal kidney dish, covering her still body with a white cloth.

'And that was the last I saw of her, being wheeled out on a trolley: a helpless little dead baby, covered with a shroud.'

Vivienne wept out loud in lament. She wept for herself and for her lost baby. Tears spilled over her eyes as she broke down, losing years of profound sorrow in a great fountain of mourning.

As she did so, she re-lived the childbirth again, crying out in tormented release. Great floods of tears filled the room until she thought she might drown in them – choke on them – wishing she could.

Silently, Matthias held her, sitting next to her in her grief, the young man with his arm around an older woman. There wasn't a sound in the room save for Vivienne rocking to and fro, in Matthias' strong embrace. Vivienne couldn't see. Blinded – stricken with inconsolable remorse she lay, crumpled, on the pastel cushions. Matthias let her be, stroking her hair, all spiralled out of its golden clips.

Natalie sat without a word. Her hands were crossed now, on her lap. She looked down at the spotless floor. If she was moved, then it was inwardly for she gave nothing away. Save Vivienne caught the sigh of an almost imperceptible suppression of Natalie's breath.

At length, as her sobs abated Matthias said, just above a whisper, 'Everything was against you: the sixties, girls in your position. She would been illegitimate. Abortion was illegal…'

'I was seventeen, Matthias,' Vivienne's cracked voice was muffled by the dampened cushion her head lay on. 'Old enough to know better,' she blew her nose on a handkerchief, screwing it into a wet ball with her fists.

'No that's not true. If you had known better, you'd have done it. Nothing else was on offer. It there had been something– well then, you would have taken it, wouldn't you?'

'I could have had her adopted,' Vivienne snuffled miserably.

'Now you know your father would have thrown you out? I think he would have done that – whatever you had decided, kept the child or put it up for adoption, whatever. Your mother couldn't cope. She was in no position to offer you guidance or support – none whatsoever. There had been Oscar…neither of your parents came to terms with their own loss, let alone yours. Where would you have gone? Anyway, you were in a state emotionally. You didn't know anything about pregnancy, let alone sensible, grown up ideas like adoption. It's the cool of hindsight: thinking you could have done differently.'

'Oh, I don't know anymore, Matthias.' Vivienne turned round to face him. She wiped her reddened eyes, using her hands to smear away the wetness shining on each side of her bewildered face.

'You wanted to protect Guy, and you did,' said Matthias. 'You have, for many years. You protected him at the expense of your own peace of mind. Now, defend yourself, Vivienne. Nobody else was doing that for you, were they? Nobody. Your father didn't protect his daughter – not from real life. Time to defend yourself, Vivienne. Now is the time.'

Clumsily, Vivienne pulled herself upright and sat up straighter, with staggered effort. She felt like a skewed rag doll with a body sagged in pitiful exhaustion.

But Matthias beamed at her, smiling with those white, even teeth. 'Well done,' he said.

Natalie had stopped smoking. Still saying nothing, expressionless, the heels of her navy leather boots tapping on the wooden floorboards, she walked over to Vivienne. She took her hand, lightly, in her own.

For a second, Natalie's brown eyes met Vivienne's. Fleetingly, just for a second, Vivienne recognised honest sympathy.

Then Natalie went to the door. She stopped, turned around and looked at Vivienne momentarily, then at Matthias. Then she left.

CHAPTER THIRTY-ONE

Vivienne left a message on Natalie's Answerphone: her mobile seemed to have been permanently switched off. Vivienne invited Natalie – along with Matthias, Jocelyn and Enrico – to a West End show, with dinner afterwards, but Natalie hadn't replied. Vivienne didn't know what to think. After all, Guy was Natalie's father. Maybe she had found the whole thing – Vivienne's story, too distressing? After all, Vivienne still felt very shaken herself.

Every one of them wept throughout the entire musical: Victor Hugo's *Les Miserables*. Enrico had done some research on Guernsey, as Vivienne had suggested. He reminded them that Hugo had dedicated his book *Toilers of the Sea* to the people of Guernsey. because they had shown him such kindness when he was politically exiled on the island – did they know that?

'Yes!' All replied, laughing, and in one accord.

'And did you know that Hugo wrote *Les Miserable*s when he was in exile, in Guernsey?

'Yes!' They cried in chorus, still laughing.

'Just checking,' Enrico grinned.

Matthias found them a Greek restaurant in Soho. Over their meal, fortified by her wine, Vivienne told them everything about Guy and Jessie and Adam. No one showed surprise.

'Yes,' Enrico tucked into his *souvlaki*, 'Guy is a man who has ducked and dived all his life. He is a weaver of fantasy.'

'You don't think I was the fantasist?' Vivienne probed him. Certainly, events of the last few weeks now seemed almost unreal – positively surreal, to her.

Matthias answered for Enrico. 'Obsession with someone – yes I think fantasy is believing things about that person that don't actually exist. You were in love with a man you made him out to be – wanted him to be, Vivienne. Mind you, he played along with it, didn't he? Enjoyed it.' Matthias passed bread and an olive oil dip around the table. 'You very much needed Guy to be perfect. Your dream man. And he knew that.'

'Perhaps he wasn't real at all – he was a myth.' Vivienne contemplated, suffused with an unfamiliar ease: a slow unwinding of relief. Her friends' faces were unusually clear to her. The restaurant, particularly, had a more than usual warm ambience. She smiled, 'I... desired the man I wanted him to be, didn't I? The man I needed him to be?'

Three heads nodded, sympathetically.

'You know,' Vivienne held her glass, swirling the red wine, 'When I went to his homes, his and Amanda's. I didn't...I didn't, well register their life together. Didn't see the dirty socks: the dishes in the sink, the washing up, the shampoo for dandruff. I was, sort of, denying they had a life together, wasn't I?'

Vivienne was grateful that neither Jocelyn nor Enrico ever said, 'I told you so.' They were so happy together, thought Vivienne. So completely involved with each other. The London couple soon left so that Matthias and Vivienne could have some time together, 'to talk!'

Before they went, Jocelyn and Enrico told Vivienne they had noticed she seemed much less stressed – did she know she had even told a couple of jokes? Vivienne realised Jocelyn probably guessed the subject of the meeting that had taken place in her Alternative Clinic, but Jocelyn didn't probe any further. Though Vivienne noticed how Jocelyn had thrown some very 'Thanks' looks Matthias' way.

'Your snake is dead,' Enrico grinned at Vivienne, then at a beaming Jocelyn. 'Now you can heal.' He kissed Vivienne soundly.

Jocelyn and Enrico took a taxi home, immediately kissing each other, cuddling on the back seat. They waved to Vivienne and Matthias from the back window as they went happily home: all the way to Putney.

Vivienne took Matthias' arm to find a rowdy pub. Installing themselves in a small, just big enough for two, red-seated booth with flocked red walls, Matthias cuddled Vivienne. She didn't need to tell him how she felt. They ordered large brandies.

'Thanks for rescuing me, my sweet Bacchus,' Vivienne said softly. The dim gold lights shone on Matthias' face and hair. She felt safe and warm, as though they were in a glowing arbour. 'Although, I realise now that you are my Apollo – my god of reason, after all. Bacchus lied. He didn't rescue Ariadne at all. Bet he was dead drunk just when she needed him, dying like that in childbirth. Poor Ariadne.'

'Your Apollo, yes, you're right. I'd much rather be your Apollo! And you showed a lot of courage, Baby. Little Ariadne, what an ordeal you suffered. You so young – all alone. That woman doctor must have had deep problems herself, you know. And your father – well he has his own devils to deal with, doesn't he?'

'Yes, yes he does. Thanks, Matthias. I just hope Natalie doesn't put herself through the same thing.' Vivienne said, thoughtfully, 'what I told you both must have been an awful revelation, especially for her. After all, it was Guy's child: her father's child I – lost. Still, she is very determined. And things are so different now, aren't they? It's all made so much easier. Natalie can so easily abort her 'foetus' – as she calls it. I have no control over what she decides. Nobody does.' Thinking about it, Vivienne shuddered, shaking her shoulders to throw off any more unwanted burden.

'Well, there is a lot more advice given now – far more help,' Matthias sipped his brandy. 'Nineties laws are more enlightened. You've had a rough time lately, Vivienne.' He squeezed her waist fondly. 'But you are a strong, talented lady. Don't let yourself get so low again. Promise? Remember: defend.'

Matthias had a gorgeous smile, Vivienne thought. And such comforting hands. 'I don't know what I would have done without you.' She kissed him lightly on his smooth, dark cheek, smelling his citrus scent, feeling the cool freshness of his skin. But still she dwelled: was the era they lived in now any more enlightened? Women, it seemed to Vivienne, were still left all the really difficult choices. All of the time.

Matthias responded by kissing her hand. 'Now. Would you mind Vivienne, would it bother you, I seem to have lost them – Natalie's telephone number? And her address? She intrigues me.'

'You're pretty beguiling yourself, Matthias. Sure, that's okay. No, I don't mind a bit.' It had occurred to her that Matthias, the clever young Oxford philosopher and Natalie, a modern, young art lecturer might go well together. Yes, Vivienne had thought that, more than once.

Trying not to sound prying, or particularly interested, Vivienne asked David how his trip to Cyprus had gone. How was Catherine?

David smiled: an enigma with clear blue eyes. 'Fine. Catherine's business – it's progressing steadily. I've sorted out the diseased tomato plants. She's started selling her surplus crops – actually, she's made a small market garden. And she sells some of her plants and she's thinking of adding, possibly, garden tools – that kind of thing. And they are going to completely refurbish the Taverna this winter: modernise it but keep to traditional food. Catherine's a bright lady. A good business woman,' he said admiringly as he shot Vivienne a contented glance.

'Did you miss me?' Vivienne asked, carefully.

'Of course,' David replied, too swiftly.

They sat in their conservatory with Christmas nearly upon them. The early bulbs of daffodils were already pushing tips of green shoots through La Colette's rich earth.

Tentatively, Vivienne said, 'I once called you my man of all seasons, David, do you remember?'

'But I wasn't, was I? Not really one hell of a fellow, after all.' David looked at Vivienne candidly. His fair hair had faded to silver; his hands were tanned and gnarled.

'You do your best, David. None of us gets a perfect script.'

'See – I thought, most of all, you needed security, Vivienne. But I did know you were clever – spirited, and everything. But my mother, I never should have...' he trailed off.

'It doesn't matter, David. It doesn't matter now.'

They watched a blackbird, hopping on spindly legs, bouncing around the garden. A hoar frost began to melt back into the earth.

An early spring promised in the plump budding points of sycamore trees. The blackbird, having found its breakfast, flew off, singing triumphantly to the sky.

An excited Polly was the very first to report to Vivienne that her Kim and Joseph were 'An item!' They had met at the College of Further Education. Joseph had been walking around the kitchens, measuring for a proposed new extension when he had spotted Kim and gone up to her. They had got talking and it had all gone from there.

'They are an item kiddo!' Polly said, with her face lit with delight, 'Which, in these days, I take to mean practically engaged!'

Lately, Joseph had begun asking David how to work the land: grow vegetables and salad things at La Colette. He and Kim thought they might start a venture together: he growing fresh, organic fruit and vegetables, Kim starting up her own catering business, 'You know, Dad, using our own home produce?'

As he and Vivienne walked, Joseph said, 'And daisies are truer than passion flowers. It will be better, so.' Isn't that right, Ma? Remember the poem you have always kept in the hall? Roland Leighton's?' They continued their walk around La Colette's fields.

'Course I do, Joseph. And he was right, wasn't he?' Their boots were muddy as they reach the edge of a field, hedged with golden gorse and bare blackthorn. The purple sloes were long gone.

'I see what you mean about respect, now. I do feel that about Kim. I think grandfather Eustace would have liked her. He'd be glad I want to grow on his land, don't you think?'

'Joseph, he would be proud of you. It was important for Eustace, definitely – handing on from generation to generation. And – oh, just look at the sea today, Joseph! Reflecting the sky and full of sparkling light. The air is so fresh. Oh I love winter.' She turned to Joseph. 'Do you know, Eustace told me that if you start as friends in a marriage then you end as friends? He had no truck with thunderbolts, did Eustace. No *coup de foudre*.' Vivienne and Joseph laughed easily, together.

'And Kim makes a mean onion marmalade, Ma. Just like grandma Jean's!'

'There you are then. Obviously your soulmate!' Feeling spots of

rain beginning to fall in single wet drops, Vivienne recalled Granmarie:
'I thought you were more like me, Vivienne. I had hoped you were
more like me.' She lifted up her head, seeing clouds, aching to rain,
drifting over the rapidly greying expanse of sky: over the meadows
toward the sea. Yes, Granmarie would be pleased with her today, too.
Maybe she was, finally, and after all, getting there.

'You look well,' David said one day.

People had begun saying that to her lately. But Vivienne still
would not answer Guy's telephone calls or messages. She gave the
flowers he sent to Sonia. Trouble was, even now, she didn't trust
herself. Guy had always been able to make her change her mind. She
feared his presence, wondering if she could be strong enough – ever
be strong enough – to reject him? The python was dead. But Vivienne
still feared its resurrection.

A surge of creative mental energy steered her firmly into her
studio. Vivienne needed to paint. She had begun thinking again about
another exhibition. Yet she still had not heard a single word from
Natalie.

Natalie had probably had the termination done and didn't dare
tell Vivienne. Vivienne could not even begin to contemplate it. Fear
gripped her heart whenever she looked at the calendar: whenever the
telephone rang.

Sonia was trying for a family, but it wasn't happening. How cruel
life could be: how arbitrary nature was. One woman can so easily
conceive – but not want the child – another can be so desperate, yet
be denied motherhood.

In her studio, with its winter light, Vivienne sketched on a canvas.
Overnight there had been a light flurry of snow. She wanted to catch
the ice-blue shadows under the hedgerows: the crisp, white icing on
the blackened branches. She thought of Monet's *The Magpie* – how
cleverly he used blues, grey and mauve – yellow, even to convey the
white of snow. How skilled he... Her mobile phone, on a small table
near her easel, rang with a bouncing insistence Vivienne never could
ignore.

'Hello? Hello, Vivienne? It's Natalie.'

Vivienne's mouth dried. The mobile shook under her grip. She could not speak.

'Vivienne?'

'Yes,' she replied, almost inaudibly, with a dry, cracked voice.

'Vivienne. You are going to be a grandmother.'

'What? Oh, Natalie! Natalie! You? – I – you?'

'Yes,' Natalie laughed, 'all of those!'

'You...?'

'No. I didn't have it done. I cancelled the – appointment.'

Standing by the window, leaning heavily against its frame, Vivienne wept. Natalie kept quiet. Then Vivienne tried to recover herself, wresting her breath to steady it. She swallowed deeply. Her free hand flew over her own womb.

'Vivienne? Listen, this doesn't mean I'm going back to Joseph,' Natalie said, firmly.

'No. No, of course not. I understand that. Of course not. But... thank you, Natalie, thank you.' Vivienne started crying again.

'Yes, well, look, don't start all that again! Will you tell Joe and David? Maybe you might like to give my grandmother Muriel Le Croix a ring? I think she might like it to come from you.'

'You do? Of course, Natalie, darling. I'll tell everyone, everyone!' Then Vivienne hesitated slightly, but Natalie beat her to it.

'I'll phone Dad. I'll tell Guy. But I wanted you to be the first to know.'

'I can't tell you what this means to me,' Vivienne stammered out, breathing great deep gasps of air.

'Oh, I think I probably know, Vivienne. I'm glad you are happy about it. Listen, I've got to go now. Oh, and by the way, your friend Matthias? Well, we've got on really well. In fact, hope you approve – I'm moving in with him, in Oxford. I don't really want to bring up a child – well, not in London.'

Vivienne raced to tell Joseph and David all of Natalie's news. She rang Polly and Jocelyn, almost choking with relieved excitement, jumping up and down so much sparkly clips flew out of her hair.

Jocelyn and Enrico said they were very glad and they were especially pleased, they said, about Matthias and Natalie.

'A match,' said Enrico sagely, 'a true and lasting love match.'

It was a year and more later and springtime. Vivienne travelled up to Oxford to collect her baby granddaughter: Maddie. Well, her full name was Amanda Vivienne Muriel, which was, even Natalie laughingly agreed, 'A bit of a mouthful!'

Natalie and Matthias were going to have a break, in Crete. Vivienne was to take Maddie back to Guernsey to see her grandfather, David: great-grandparents Edward Normandie and Muriel Le Croix – and, of course, Maddie's father, Joseph.

He would, Joseph said, probably always love Natalie, but that Kim gave him peace of mind. He was able to see Maddie often enough and Matthias was very loving toward his daughter.

Vivienne had spoken to Guy. He wanted, he said, to tell her how pleased he was about Maddie. He knew Vivienne was going up to Oxford. Could he travel with her?

'No!' Vivienne had said, instantly. 'Absolutely not. No, I want some time with Maddie alone Guy.' She had put down the phone.

Guy had sounded disappointed, saying he genuinely wanted to see Vivienne – both Vivienne and the baby. Afterward, Vivienne wavered: it was not displeasing that Guy was doing all the pursuing. So, she would have to think about it, she told him.

Oxford was magical. Vivienne always enjoyed Matthias showing her round the colleges: gleaming pink in an unusually warm sun for the season. She was glad for him and Natalie. Oxford so suited them both.

After they'd said their goodbyes, Vivienne got the train down to London. She took the baby girl in her stroller, to see the National Gallery. Negotiating the steps from Trafalgar Square, Vivienne pushed the chubby baby, safe in her rugs. They went from spacious gallery to spacious gallery, each protected by a uniformed guard.

Vivienne sat on the bench in front of Titian's *Bacchus and Ariadne*. She held the little girl in her arms.

'You see, Maddie,' Vivienne nestled close to the baby's soft face, 'Renaissance means rebirth.'

Maddie wriggled and sucked a thumb.

'Ariadne loved Theseus. But he lied to her and abandoned her. Then, lo and behold! Bacchus came to rescue her! And, taking her crown of stars – for Ariadne was a princess – threw it to the heavens, where it became a constellation. "Come! Join the gods, Ariadne!" said Bacchus.'

Vivienne could feel the baby close to her, feel her warm little body: smelling of baby powder and milk. Maddie's hair, curly black, stuck out all angles. Her eyes shone a lively brown.

'Mortals love to feast and drink and make love, Maddie. It's very human: to enjoy life.'

Still holding the baby safely in her arms, Vivienne took her to see the painting more closely. As she did so, the security guard observed her curiously with a benign expression.

'Ariadne fell in love at first sight, with a madness in her heart. Bacchus gave her the sky. But,' she whispered in the baby's small ear, 'he fell asleep, just when she needed him. He's only legend. Only a myth.'

Placing the baby securely back in her buggy, Vivienne buckled the restraining straps. 'Titian tells us of ancient myths. He shows us enchanted islands of love, Maddie, where our troubled minds can go. There is a refuge for us. But it takes an act of faith to believe in the gods. There is a covenant – that is life. There is a promise – that is love. There is…' nothing was going to stop her now, Vivienne had waited long enough.

'There is a hidden web of love that links us all, Maddie. Socrates says there is a pattern in the heavens, a sacred order, which humans have lost. We must learn to find it. Our gods must help us'.

Turning the buggy away now, Vivienne walked steadily across the room. The guard, smiling, gave her a smart salute. Vivienne smiled back at him. She wheeled the baby out of the gallery. Vivienne knew where she was going now.

Out into the spring day, Trafalgar Square looked spectacular.

Pigeons flew in great flurries – their flapping wings audible above the traffic. The leafy plane trees grew defiantly.

Vivienne trundled the buggy down the National Gallery steps. Just as she reached the last one, she saw Guy, standing on the pavement, at the foot of the stone stairway.

'Hi, Vivvy. Natalie told me you'd be here.' He bent down and kissed the baby girl. 'Been to see *Bacchus and Ariadne*?' He smiled his half-smile. He looked weary, like a big, sad bear, in his black overcoat.

The London sun shone warmly on Vivienne's hair, piled into a chignon. Her eyes felt clear. Her long, grey coat softly skimmed her full hips. At her neck, Vivienne had wound a red velour scarf, patterned gold, emerald green and cobalt blue. Renaissance colours: to celebrate taking Maddie to see Titian.

'The baby is beautiful, isn't she?' said Guy. 'She looks a lot like Natalie – but I can see you in her. You know, Viv, you are still a very…no, don't go. Don't go away, Vivvy. Look, come and have a coffee? I wish we…?'

To her horror, Guy began to weep like a little child – right there in London's spring sunshine.

'Haven't we said all that we have got to say, Guy? You made your choices.' Yet still Vivienne felt pity for him.

'Remember when we came here, Vivvy, to see Titian? All those years ago?' Guy said softly, 'little Vivvy with the blazing blue eyes and her beloved art?'

'All my life I needed art, to make any sense of the – of all the mess I got into. God! The pain you have caused me, Guy.' She looked directly at him. 'It's been my way of coping.'

Guy seemed to cast around for words then said, 'I do love you, Vivvy. In my own way.'

In a heartbeat she saw him young again. Vivienne saw Portelet, 'do I need rescuing, Vivvy? Is it the other way around?'

Guy reached out his hand to touch her.

'No. Oh no, please, not that Guy. Don't start all that.' Vivienne hastily withdrew from him and moved away from him. She was fearful – no, Guy mustn't touch her.

'Vivvy, please,' said Guy, his face suppliant.

The baby looked up at them both, beginning to get fractious. She threw her small plastic toy onto the pavement. Guy bent down and picked it up, giving it back, gently, to her. She grabbed it with glee.

In that second Vivienne saw Guy's great beauty again and wanted to, almost did, reach out to stroke his arm and comfort him.

Then Guy said, 'Jessie isn't well. Adam is giving us a hard time. I don't know what to do, Vivvy. I need you.' Guy looked wretched. He stubbed out a cigarette butt with the sole of his shoe.

'I'd better go,' Vivienne said, shaking her head. 'I've got to get us to Victoria Station for the Gatwick Express. I don't want to be rushing about last thing, not with Maddie.'

'Well let me get you a taxi, I'll come with you,' Guy implored. 'Maddie's my grandchild as well.'

'Yes,' replied Vivienne. 'We managed to share one child together, didn't we? But...but. You go back to Guernsey. Look after Jessie and Adam. They need you, Guy.'

'And I need you! Guy said tearfully. 'Vivvy, I need you!'

'But I don't need you, Guy,' Doesn't she? Didn't she just make herself say that? 'I don't need your approval or your love.' Suddenly – this time – she knew that she did mean it. 'I don't need you, Guy. Not any more.'

Not able to stand any more of it, Vivienne left Guy. If she had turned back she would have seen him watching them walk out of his sight. But Vivienne didn't look back.

She ran along the crowded pavement, paved with timeless Guernsey blue, sparkling like stars. She would take Maddie to the Institute of Contemporary Arts: to the ICA, to an exhibition full of new ideas, new concepts. She had lied to Guy. They weren't going straight to Victoria Station.

Warm in her padded buggy, Maddie played with her toy. Vivienne steered them forward, hurrying through the crowds, her bright scarf flying. She stopped briefly, taking out their air tickets to check what time they needed to be at the airport. Vivienne had a little girl to take home, safely back to Guernsey.

THE END

*Books also by
Yvonne Ozanne are
'Love Apple Island' and
'Love Apples Too'*

'*In these profound, insightful essays,
Yvonne Ozanne immortalizes a world
that is on the cusp of being lost forever.
Hailing from Irish as well as Guernsey
stock, Yvonne is an islander gifted by
that 'otherness' that hallmarks the
best writers. She writes with great
humanity, making particulars universal
and of interest to the discerning reader
anywhere.*'

*Edward Chaney,
Southampton Solent University*

*Edward holds the rights to
EBENEZER LE PAGE,
by G.B.Edwards*

Love Apple Island

… a life on the island of Guernsey

Foreword by Roy Dotrice

This is a colourful and moving account of the beautiful island of Guernsey and her people: ordinary islanders. Neither English nor French, self-governed and fiercely independent, these are the stories of individuals from a fast disappearing, gentle nobility who lived through the post-war years of enemy Occupation in the Fifties and Sixties. Love Apple is an old name given to the tomato since it was considered to be an aphrodisiac. The tomato growing business and Guernsey families, with their strong sense of identity, thrived. Yet resourceful islanders, unafraid of the modern world, faced new challenges as they always had and always will.

Yvonne Ozanne, née Bréhaut, was born in England in 1942 during World War II. She lived in the Vale parish of Guernsey until her marriage to Tony Ozanne when they moved to the higher parishes of Forest and St Pierre du Bois. Yvonne first worked for the Guernsey Press newspaper as a typist. She gained an Open University Honours Degree in Art History and in 2001 became a writer then a contributor to the Guernsey Press. Yvonne lectures on the Italian Renaissance, enjoys oil painting and exploring every one of the very beautiful Channel Islands.

Love Apple
Island

... a life on the island
of Guernsey

Yvonne Ozanne
Foreword by Roy Dotrice

ISBN 978-1-903341-45-2

Price £7.95

www.yvonneozanne.com

LOVE APPLES TOO
... A life in the Bailiwick of Guernsey

This is a moving account of Guernsey, her beautiful Bailiwick islands and their people: ordinary islanders. Neither English nor French, self-governed and fiercely independent, these are the stories of a fast disappearing gentle nobility who lived through the post-war years of enemy occupation. *Love Apple* is a name given to the tomato, considered to be an aphrodisiac. Guernsey, Alderney, Sark and Herm families with their strong sense of identity have thrived. These resourceful islanders face the modern world and new challenges as they always have and always will.

'Yvonne Ozanne is one of Guernsey's national treasures. Her books and articles have enriched all our lives. She has a rare talent that can bring to life the islands' past, painting a written portrait of the social and cultural changes that have shaped Guernsey and her Bailiwick over her own and her parents' lifetime and beyond. This is another beautiful portrait of the memories we all cherish.'

Dave Jones, States of Guernsey Minister

'In spite, or because, of its size, Guernsey upholds a remarkable layering of memories and experiences of its resilient citizens. Trust Yvonne Ozanne to lay them out with such sensuous, uplifting and evocative, often even bubbly, discourse. This book is a wonderful and powerful testimony to a lived 'sense of place', elicited through the perspicacious eye of both a careful and carefree, island authoress.'

Godfrey Baldacchino, Canada Research Chair (Island Studies),
University of Prince Edward Island, Canada